PRAISE FOR WOMAN IN BATTLE DRESS

"*Woman in Battle Dress* by Antonio Benítez-Rojo, which has been beautifully translated from the Spanish by Jessica Ernst Powell, is the extraordinary account of an extraordinary person. Benítez-Rojo blows great gusts of fascinating fictional wind onto the all but forgotten embers of the actual Henriette Faber, and this blazing tale of her adventures as a military surgeon and a husband and about a hundred other fascinating things is both something we want and need to hear."—Laird Hunt, author of *Neverhome*

"A fascinating novel, in a brilliant translation, about the unique fate of Henrietta Faber who played a gender-bending role in the history of Cuba."—Suzanne Jill Levine, noted translator and author of *Manuel Puig and the Spider Woman: His Life and Fictions*

"A picaresque novel starring an adventurous heroine, who caroms from country to country around the expanding Napoleonic empire, hooking up with a dazzling array of men (and women) as she goes. A wild ride!"—Carmen Boullosa, author of *Texas: The Great Theft*

"Very few novels dare to explore the historical representation of women to the extent that *Woman in Battle Dress* does, with impeccable veracity and bravado. The idea that a woman must pretend to be a man in order to become a physician, and is then punished by being forced back into a woman's identity, only to escape to New Orleans as a fictional character, works as a Stendhal novel in reverse. Napoleonic France and the colonial Caribbean are chartered by men; New Orleans is extraterritorial, ready for a new saga. A true Doña Quijota, Henriette Faber takes on these roles to gain her freedom in a novel, the only modern space larger than life."—Julio Ortega, Professor at Brown University, author of *Transatlantic Translations*

"As detailed as any work of history and as action filled as any swashbuckler, *Woman in Battle Dress* is not only Antonio Benítez Rojo's last and most ambitious book, but also his masterpiece. In this graceful English translation of Henriette Faber's autobiography—more than fiction, less than fact—American readers will have access to one of the most engaging novels to come out of Latin America in recent years."—Gustavo Pérez-Firmat, Columbia University

"Reviving the Renaissance and Baroque figure of the virago, in Spanish Golden Age theater the *mujer varonil*, Antonio Benítez Rojo creates a fascinating woman protagonist who dresses and acts like a man, mostly as a qualified medical doctor, while participating in major historical events in Europe and the Caribbean. The reader's attention is captivated by the suspense generated by the fear that her true sex will be discovered, and entertained by her wiles in trying to prevent it. *Woman in Battle Dress* is a rich and engaging historical novel."—Roberto González Echevarría, Sterilng Professor of Hispanic and Comparitve Literature, Yale University, author of *Modern Latin American Literature: A Very Short Introduction*

WOMAN
IN BATTLE
DRESS

Antonio Benítez-Rojo

Translated by Jessica Ernst Powell

City Lights Books | San Francisco

First published as *Mujer en traje de batalla* by Alfaguara in 2001

Cover art: *The Hour Between Wolf and Dog* (detail), oil painting by Marc Chagall, 1943

Library of Congress Cataloging-in-Publication Data
Benítez Rojo, Antonio, 1931-2005.
  [Mujer en traje de batalla. English]
 Woman in battle dress / Antonio Benítez Rojo ; translated by Jessica Ernst Powell.
    pages cm
 ISBN 978-0-87286-676-8 (alk. paper)
 ISBN 978-0-87286-685-0 (ebook)
 1. Faber, Henriette, 1791-1856—Fiction. 2. Women physicians—Fiction. I. Powell, Jessica Ernst. II. Title.

 PQ7390.B42M8513 2015
 863'.64—dc23

                            2015013717

City Lights Books are published at the City Lights Bookstore
261 Columbus Avenue, San Francisco, CA 94133
www.citylights.com

*To María Cristina Benítez and Hilda Otaño Benítez,
always courageous*

"The prejudice that had closed women off from any opportunity to practice the professions and trades traditionally reserved for men dramatized the life of a bold and enterprising lady who, dressed as a man and graduated as a surgeon, served as a soldier in Europe without her secret being discovered, only to have it revealed in Cuba in 1823."

LEVÍ MARRERO, *Cuba: Economy and Society*

"Don't bother me with History as theater. What matters here is poetic illusion. . . . "

ALEJO CARPENTIER, *Baroque Concerto*

"Everything will have to be reconstructed, invented all over again."

JOSÉ LEZAMA LIMA, *American Expression*

"The truth is, doctor, that I no longer know if it happened to me or to my little friend or if I made it up. Although I'm sure that I didn't make it up. And yet, there are times when I think that I am, in reality, my little friend."

GUILLERMO CABRERA INFANTE, *Three Trapped Tigers*

ABOARD THE SCHOONER
THE COLLECTOR

AND SO, IN THREE DAYS you'll disembark in New Orleans. Four, at the most, if the wind fails. As hard as you try to take heart, you can see no reason that you should be any better received there than you were in Cuba. What they know of you in New Orleans is nothing but secondhand gossip spread by travelers from Havana; rumors repeated by sailors and merchants who, hoping to amaze their listeners, turn every drizzle into a downpour, every chicken's death into a horrifying murder. God only knows what abominations they are telling about you there! If there's one thing you're sure of, it's that the dock will be full of gawkers hurling insults. Some will even spit at you. There'll be the usual hailstorm of eggs and rotten vegetables. There will even be those who'll try to pinch your backside or claw at your face. Master and slave, lawyer, barber, shoemaker and tailor, each and every one of them will heap their own guilt and resentments onto you. The saddest part of all is that there are bound to be some good women among the crowd, women who'll condemn you without even knowing why. Their minds constricted by ignorance and prejudice, they'll see you only as an indecent foreigner, a degenerate; never a friend. How well you know their accusatory cries. They have dogged you from one end of Cuba to the other, from Santiago all the way to Havana. The only difference is that this time they'll humiliate you in English, and even in French, your own mother tongue. What you fear most, what you've begun to obsess over, is that moment when you'll step off the boat—your first steps onto the dock, exposed to all those stares, those hungry eyes fixed upon you, wishing to strip you bare. Today, more than ever before, you understand the cruel shame suffered by so many women who, on their way to the bonfire, the guillotine, the hangman's noose, or the executioner's axe, were paraded through an excited crowd, lathered up by the promise of a spectacle. It's true that,

11

in your case, there's never been talk of a death sentence, but you've been insulted so repeatedly that the thought of being subjected to public ridicule all over again has come to feel intolerable. Despite all that you saw during the war—the battlefields of Austria, Russia, and Spain, among others, you've never managed to get used to the insensitivity of human beings, especially those in so-called "polite" society. And of course, the satirical bards of New Orleans will have their verses at the ready. Eager to show off their wit, they impatiently await your arrival. Later, they'll publish their rhymed couplets in the newspaper, attaching to them names like Sophocles and Euripides. Poor devils, they don't even know that, had you lived in those classical times, your glories and miseries might have provided the worthy inspiration for some famous dramatic poet. But no, now that you think back on your reading, you realize that you don't fit as a character in a Greek tragedy; Electra, Ariadne, and Clytemnestra have nothing whatsoever to do with you. Only a woman of your times could understand you completely, perhaps a Madame de Staël, Swiss-born like you, with a free spirit to match your own. But the baroness has been dead nine or ten years by now and you can think of no one else who might defend you with her pen—that is to say, to do you justice for posterity's sake. If only you had half the talent of that Mexican nun whose works you read in prison, what immortal verses you would compose, what sage letters you would write! What other woman knows what you know of men, what other woman knows their bodies and souls as well as you! And what's more, who could possibly define a woman's place better than you, you who have proven yourself within the most exclusive of men's worlds? But God did not grant you the gifts of a poet and you will never be the one to elegantly describe the ups and downs of your life. Face it, Henriette; your fate is sealed. You have nothing left to hope for. Even if you manage to go down in history, it will be as a libertine, in the best of cases, an infamous impostor. Judges, scribes, witnesses, registries, briefs, signatures, seals—all of the instruments of jurisprudence have allied themselves against you; they have omitted any favorable depositions and exaggerated those that malign you. They have judged you hastily, with single-minded determination, as though you were an abhorrent social error that must be rectified immediately and never allowed to recur. Your past has been meticulously dissected, disputed, and criticized, you've been reviled as a negative example, too dangerous in a world held in thrall to outmoded ideas from fifty years ago. And so, your truth— all that you have left—will remain buried alongside your bones in some Louisiana cemetery. And it will all begin again three days from now, perhaps four. Imagining yourself humiliated all over again by the throngs, seeing yourself disembark with your head shaved practically bald, wearing the threadbare habit you inherited from a nun, dead of yellow fever, you know that you can't take it anymore. You have reached your limit. In Santiago de Cuba, when they threatened to parade you along the main thoroughfare, dressed in a shift and mounted atop a donkey, you considered killing yourself right there in your cell. What a pity that you didn't go through with it, Henriette. What a pity. And now, when all of your efforts and good deeds have proven worthless, when your entire body aches from so many restless nights, you wonder why you ever asked the ship's captain for a pen and paper. What you write at this very moment may well prove to be your final letter, your final act. Yes, a letter to yourself. And perhaps of farewell.

☙

You take up the pen after reading what you wrote last night. How fickle emotions are! All it took was to be allowed on deck to take in the beautiful morning and to exchange a few pleasantries with Captain Plumet to transform your emotional state, though physically you're still slow and aching. And really, how vain you are, my friend! Did you actually think that those "glories and miseries" that you so boasted of yesterday—with the rhetorical style of a provincial lawyer, no less—would merit the attentions of a famous writer? Were she still alive, Madame de Staël would not have even bothered to listen to your story. You're no Joan of Arc, after all! Only women of high moral principles should become the subject of literature. The perfect heroine should act selflessly, unaware of the personal consequences of her actions. If her behavior is praiseworthy, it is so precisely because it cannot be bought or led off course. These are the women's names that deserve to be etched in stone, certainly not yours. I'll grant that you've never been lacking in presence of mind or in perseverance, but, as painful as it may be to admit, you must recognize that if you have defied the law for many years, you did it first out of compassion, then led by ambition, and finally, for love. It's not that you've stopped believing that both the courts and the public have judged you maliciously, but you must confess that it was your excessive self-confidence, or better, your vanity, that landed you in prison. This time you gambled and lost, and that's all there is to it.

And now you've begun to wonder what the mayor of Havana has written in your convict's passport. Your future in New Orleans depends, in good measure, upon what it says. Fortunately, he didn't seem ill-disposed toward you last year when he visited the women's hospital. You may also count on support from Bishop Espada, who has proved himself sympathetic. In any case, it's likely that you'll find out what it says tonight, since the cheerful and gallant Captain Plumet—something about him reminds you of your uncle—has invited us to dinner, and it is he who safeguards all of our documents. You speak in the plural because on deck you met two other deportees: a mulatta suspected of witchcraft and a melancholy whore of about your age, both from New Orleans. Although you were unaware of their presence on board the ship, they were certainly aware of yours. The respect they have for you is strange. To judge from their words, you have become rather famous among women of illrepute. You could even say that they envy your celebrity. Imagine! But now you must overcome the febrile exhaustion that has come over you and try to fix yourself up to look at least passably presentable; your two admirers have outfitted you with clothes, makeup, shoes, even a wig. How many years has it been since you last dressed as an elegant woman?

(Three hours later.) Undeniably, Captain Plumet is the spitting image of your Uncle Charles: the same prominent jaw line, the curved nose, the suntanned face, the sparkling blue eyes, and that desperate, roaring laugh that he adopted in his last days. Perhaps this is why, yesterday, you got up the nerve to ask him for writing materials. In any case, my friend, you have little to be happy about. Your passport reads: "Enriqueta Faber Cavent. Born in Lausanne, Switzerland, 1791. Subject of the French Crown. She has served four years of reclusion and service in the Women's Hospital of Havana. She has committed the following crimes: perjury, falsification of documents, bribery, incitation of violence, illegally practicing medicine, imposture (pretending to be of the masculine sex), rape of a minor, and grave assaults against the institution of marriage. She has been forbidden to reside in Cuba or in any other territory under the Spanish Crown. She is hereby remanded to the authorities in New Orleans."

You had it right yesterday: your fate is sealed. And more than sealed, signed by the mayor and approved by both the governor and the captain general. Even so, some hope remains. Plumet showed you a sealed letter in which, according to him, the bishop asks the Mother Superior of the Sisters of Charity in New Orleans to take responsibility for you. Does this mean that you'll have to live in a convent and go on wearing a nun's habit? What do they want from you? How long must you wait for your freedom? Plumet had shrugged his shoulders; he knows nothing. He would like to do something to help you, but his hands are tied. Years ago, when he commanded one of Jean Laffite's ships, he would have hidden you in an empty barrel and that would have been that. But everything's changed since the war. The port authorities are ever more persnickety and even the slightest irregularity can cost a captain his license. He told you this in a rush, as if hoping to forestall any further conversation on the topic, while urgently ushering you out of his quarters so as to be left alone with Madeleine and Marie, since as far as womanizing goes, well, that's another thing he has in common with your uncle. In any case, you may at least be grateful for his good intentions and an excellent dinner.

⚮

How peculiar that here, in the middle of the ocean, aboard this aging schooner transporting goods as ordinary as leather, tobacco, and mahogany, your old dream about Robert should have returned. There was a time when the dream recurred two or three times every year. Later, as if the names Enrique and Henri had erased Henriette's past, it returned less and less frequently until finally disappearing from your nights altogether. In any event, the dream came back to you exactly as before. Although now that you think about it, there is one important difference: within the dream you were aware that you were dreaming the same dream you had dreamt before. So much so that, seeing yourself once again in that strange and desolate room, you tried to leave so as not to feel the sadness of Robert's arrival.

But, no matter how you tried, you were scarcely able to move your limbs, and then suddenly, there he was, his frame filling the dark recess of the doorway, awaiting your cry of surprise so that he could shyly enter the room. As always, he is dressed in his exquisite Hussar's uniform—Hungarian *culottes* made of blue cloth, red Dolman with gold fringe, bearskin hat topped with a long feather, tall calfskin boots, and, draped over his left shoulder, the splendidly embroidered fur cloak. His curved saber hangs from his wrist, tied on by a silk cord. His other hand holds the reins of Patriote, his favorite mount, the saddle covered with a leopard skin given to him by Field Marshal Lannes. Suddenly Patriote startles; his eyes bulge with fear. Robert tries to calm him, but the horse struggles to go back outside and Robert lets him go with a gesture of resignation. From the moment you saw him, you realized that he'd grown taller since the last time you had the dream. He also seemed thinner, although perhaps not, perhaps you had merely misjudged after seeing him so tall alongside Patriote, who, for some reason, was the same size as always. Now Robert examines the room's bare walls. His gaze moves slowly over the dimly lit corners, the beams of the ceiling, the grand silver candelabra, filigreed in dust and cobwebs, which stands on the mantelpiece above the empty fireplace. There are no candles in this candelabra. The hazy glow that floats in the room does not come from any visible source of light. Although Robert has seen you—or better, has moved his inexpressive gaze over you—he has not noticed you; to him, you must be like a sort of reflection or a transparent presence. Knowing that now you can walk, you decide to get up from the bed. A sense of infinite compassion impels you toward him. Robert has grown so large that, although you stand on tiptoe, your lips barely brush against the cross of the Legion of Honor that he wears on his chest. "Ah, it's you. Doesn't it seem that spring is awfully late to arrive here in Foix?" Upon hearing his words, you realize that he doesn't yet know that he is dead. You wonder if you should tell him, but decide against it. Whatever his condition, he does not appear to be in pain. Confused by this situation, you manage only to lead him by the hand toward the bed. Curiously, his hand is not cold. You notice that he has recently shaved and that his tremendous mustache has been newly waxed. Robert allows himself to be undressed like a child—you always marvel at seeing him naked. After untying the saber from his wrist and removing his cap, you take your time unbuttoning his clothing. At last you lay him down across the bed, loosen the braids against both sides of his face, and pull off his shiny black boots and tight-fitting *culottes*. His body is intact. There is not even a trace of his old scars. A faint opalescent glow emanates from his long and conspicuous penis, resting flaccidly against his left thigh. "Ah, it's you. Doesn't it seem that spring is awfully late to arrive here in Foix?" End of the dream.

The sun was just rising when you came up on deck. You were dressed as a woman and wearing Madeleine's wig. This is how you'll disembark tomorrow in New Orleans. To avoid thinking about Robert and the dream, which always unsettles you, you distract yourself by watching the bustle of the sailors. What a complex thing, a ship! Even Plumet's small and aging schooner, with its wooden hull, rigging and sails, seems an indecipherable puzzle. You assume that each and every one of the ship's innumerable parts has a specific name, something like the drugs in a pharmacopeia. That large, deep sail could be called laudanum, and the triangle of sailcloth that they raise at the prow could be eucalyptus, beneficial for respiratory ailments. This is how Madeline found you, immersed in your little game. Marie, the mulatta, was in her berth, suffering from seasickness. Madeline is a dispirited sort. She is also younger than she appears. Hard living has withered her face and set its expression in a deep scowl. She moves like a sleepwalker. Were you to choose one word to describe her it would be this: exhausted. You can imagine her used up breasts, her anus worn to shreds from the arduous work of making a living off her body. As she tells it, both she and Marie traveled to Havana with the Théâtre d'Orleans opera company. Madeline doesn't sing, but the manager needed an obsequious woman with loose morals and a passing knowledge of Spanish to hand out programs to passersby. Marie doesn't sing either; she joined the troupe as a hairdresser. Why did they decide to stay in Cuba? For the same reason you did, Henriette: to make money.

A cabin boy, the very same one who tried to enter your cabin last night and whom you dispatched with a slap across the face, interrupted your conversation. "Captain Plumet has invited you both to have breakfast with him," said the boy, scarcely looking at you. When you made as if to follow him, Madeleine took you by the arm; she had something to discuss with you. Her proposition, delivered quickly and nervously, rendered you speechless with surprise. You knew, of course, that she despised her line of work and held a very poor opinion of herself, but it had never even crossed your mind that donning the habit of the Sisters of Charity would seem so marvelous to her. Madeline, simply put, wanted to be you, wanted to trade the whorehouse for the convent. "But in order to exchange passports we would need Captain Plumet's help," you told her. "It is already guaranteed," replied Madeline. "I bought it at a very good price last night. Truth be told, it's not a problem for him at all. They put him in charge of transporting three women, and three women will disembark at the dock." "And Marie?" you asked. "She's like a sister to me," Madeline smiled. "She'll shave my head to look just like yours."

And so, my friend, you shall arrive in New Orleans with a new name, Madeline Dampierre, and the good nuns at the convent will receive a false Henriette Faber. Damned if this isn't a true comedy of errors! Well, you wish them both the best of luck. Naturally, Plumet's complicity came at a price, which turned out to be exactly the one you had expected. How simple it is to manipulate certain types of men!

Hours later, your head fuzzy and aching from so much wine, you went up on deck to take in some fresh air. The moon was full. When you leaned out over the gunwale to feel the ocean spray, you saw a line of dolphins following behind the boat. Their polished backs, bathed in moonlight, looked like enormous silver coins rolling edgewise among the waves. Surface. . . . Submerge. . . . Surface. . . . Submerge. What else is life but a continual cycle of abundance and scarcity? One way or another, you'll sort things out when you get to New Orleans. Nothing could be worse than that retreat from Moscow in which nine of every ten who marched alongside you had died. And now you think again of your dream about Robert. Could it be some kind of sign? Oh, my beautiful and distant Hussar, what times we had together! How I missed you, how I wept for you! Rest in peace in my dreams. You will always be with me. For better or for worse, I owe to your death much of what I have been, what I am today, and what I forever will be.

ROBERT

1

THERE WAS ONCE A SWEET and lost time when the days passed
so slowly that each one seemed to contain all four of the seasons.
Now that old age has abbreviated my sleep and I tend to awake before dawn, when the street looks like a long black cat stretched out
beneath my window, it is not unusual for me to attempt to conjure
up the contours of one of those days. At times I try to reproduce
the landscape of some extraordinary event, imagining it on a grand
scale in which I appear inlaid like a blade of grass. At others, I trace
the details of a beloved face, a beloved body—lately they've been
Robert's—in order to place them, first still, then in motion, within
one of the intimate scenes guarded in my memory: the first waltz at a
gala ball, a furtive caress in a box seat at the opera, or simply Robert
and me, stretched out on one of his precious animal skins, drinking
wine by the fire and talking about nothing in particular. I can spend
hours bewitched by these tender reveries, until, still wrapped up
in my daydream, I hear the Irish servant boy leaving the breakfast
tray and the *New York Herald* outside my door. Soon after, Milly,
my dedicated secretary and traveling companion, appears, with a
steaming cup of tea, a slice of rye bread, and an ounce of light rum,
forcing me to leave behind that splendid autumn in Vienna, 1805,
full of golden leaves and military triumphs, or the sudden kiss that
caused us to slip upon the icy cobblestones of a street in Warsaw,
leaving us splayed on the ground next to a spur-stone, laughing like
idiots until the cold against our backsides obliged us to rise, only to
slip all over again. Today, this very morning, I saw him once more
on the staircase of our lodging-house in Berlin, his new leopard skin
slung over his shoulder, mounting the stairs with his back hunched

and his head lowered as though bearing the weight of an actual flesh-and-blood animal, all just to make me laugh, to set the jubilant and celebratory tone occasioned by his promotion to captain. Once again I heard him say, between bites of sausage and swallows of schnapps, that after the next battle Lannes would have to give him a tiger skin, and, who knew, maybe a lion's or even an elephant's, and then we'd made love again, taking our time, my tongue traversing the trail of scars that mapped his body, taking in the inexplicable smell of his skin, like moss and fresh bread.

Are these silly vignettes just an old lady's attempt at solace? Perhaps. But it would be so much worse to await the gray light of dawn counting sheep or the days I might yet have left on this earth. What's more, how could I write about my life without first reconstructing it, using the dubious glue of memory to piece together the innumerable fragments of my past, scattered like the pieces of a Chinese vase thrown from a bell tower to the street below? In any case, at my age one no longer worries about seeming ridiculous, especially not here in New York where I have come to seek the clamor and tumult found only in the world's greatest cities. Nowhere else but here, surrounded by masses of immigrants, by energy and hunger, trains, exotic music and violence, could I have rediscovered my youth, a youth spent on the battlefields of Europe. No other city on Earth is so like that which was Napoleon's Grande Armée, army of armies, legion of nations. It was just a few weeks ago that, riding in a coach through squalid neighborhoods and outdoor kitchens, I smelled the stench of injured flesh mingled with the scent of borscht, and it was as though I were right back in the field hospitals in Dvina, Dnieper, Niemen. . . . This city fits me like a ring on a finger. I knew it from the very first day. It's here—where one must live in the moment, run always at a gallop, and both love and hate with a soldier's passion—that I will speak of the horrors wrought by war: blackened rubble, vast, anonymous graves, widows and orphans, cripples and blind men, but also mutilations of the soul. And yet, like certain parts of this roiling city, life on the battlefront has its beautiful side, its own poetry. At times it can be a joyous retreat where the hours stretch out like a clean sheet and one may lie down and rest and dream and sing and laugh, forgetting all about the hiss of shrapnel and the clamor of death. It is this small corner of refuge, a place that belonged to Robert and me, that I wish to speak of now.

How is it possible that I can no longer name the waltz that we, strangers just a moment earlier, danced together, beginning to know one another through the measured glide of our feet and the gentle pressure of our gloved fingers? How could I have forgotten the melody that accompanied my growing fascination with that Hussar lieutenant with the face of a Mameluke who, with no more introduction than a brief nod, had taken me by the arm, led me away from the sofa of timid debutants where Uncle Charles had left me, and planted me, rigid and blushing, among the other couples waiting for the music to begin? At this very moment, as I write by the frozen glass of my windowpane, I try yet again to tease the notes of that waltz from my memory. But, as always, I see myself dancing with Robert encased in the most pitiful silence, twirling like a music box ballerina to the one-two-three, one-two-three rhythm, surrounded by dizzying tulles and epaulets, the great ballroom of the Boulogne Prefecture decorated in full military pomp, with tri-color wall hangings, bronze eagles, regimental flags, drums, crossed swords, the vibrant green of the laurel crowns anticipating the glories of the new campaign. And me, fourteen years old, suddenly enraptured, melting at his strange elegance, at that mix of lofty arrogance and animal grace that I had seen only in engravings of classical marble statues.

I can, however, remember the music of *Fidelio*, the voices ascending upward toward the opera boxes while Robert, standing behind my seat, sank his fingers into my coiffure and caressed the nape of my neck. (And it's not that I remember the music because the libretto of that particular opera in some way influenced my decision to pass as a man. The time when, imitating the brave Leonore, I would dress as a young man, was still a long way off. In that Viennese autumn, the rue de Vaugirard, medical school, and the name Enrique Fuenmayor were still far in the future. Back then I was simply Henriette, a girl drunk with love, who gave herself over to be sipped slowly, like a glass of Tokay wine, her sweetness savored until the very last drop had been licked from the rim. If I remember entire passages of that prophetic opera it must be for the same reason that I remember that desolate Russian tune, as monotonous as the steppes, that the Uhlan sergeant with bandaged eyes had hummed while Nadezhda's hand, tucked inside my cloak, made my nipples swell in a frigid Smolensk hospital. But why I am thinking of Nadezhda here?) Leaving aside the matter of the irretrievable waltz,

23

I have certainly not forgotten the events leading up to that night; events that had to occur in their proper order, like the stages of a long journey, so that I could arrive at last in Robert's arms.

First was the interminable luncheon at which Doctor Larrey had set out to enlist Uncle Charles and some of his colleagues into service with the Imperial Guard. Seated across from Aunt Margot—as out of town guests, and relatives of Uncle Charles', we had been invited to join the table—I watched with alarm as she devoured, with the dexterity of a sword-swallower, a steaming bowl of bouillabaisse, half a capon, an enormous plate of stewed wild boar, a salad and a raspberry tart. At five o'clock in the evening, while I was trying to decide which of my soirée gowns to wear, Uncle Charles appeared at my room at the guesthouse, his arms held open in a gesture of helplessness, to inform me that we would not be attending the ball after all because Aunt Margot was ill. Uncle Charles seemed quite concerned, which was unusual for him.

"It's probably just indigestion, but she is complaining of a sharp pain high in her stomach, and I've decided to bleed her. She's a bit warm and looks rather flushed to me."

"I could help," I offered, alarmed. But Uncle Charles flatly refused, taking it for granted that the sight of so much blood would upset me. He would make do with Françoise or one of the servants from the guesthouse, someone who could hold the basin for him. He told me there was no cause for alarm since the Cavents almost always died of heart maladies. He was merely taking precautions. He would keep me informed.

A short while later, when my tears had begun to dry—tears shed, in all sincerity, for Aunt Margot, but also from the disappointment of missing what was to be my first gala ball—Uncle Charles returned, quite content.

"My sister is feeling much better. She refused to let me bleed her. The indigestion has taken its proper course and the pain has vanished. I'm certain it was only gas. I did warn her. She shouldn't eat so much. One of these days she's going to give us a real scare." Françoise, Aunt Margot's maidservant, poked her red head through the half-opened door.

"Henriette, your Aunt wishes to see you. And you as well, Doctor Cavent."

Much to my surprise, Aunt Margot was out of bed, holding a

candle up to peer at her tongue in the mirror of the armoire. Upon seeing us enter, she straightened her ample dressing gown and turned around.

"My tongue doesn't look nearly as bad as you said," she said to Uncle Charles. "Doctors always exaggerate. Just imagine, he wanted to bleed me!"

"You should be in bed."

"I feel perfectly fine. Nothing hurts anymore. And anyway, I've moved my bowels again. You may see for yourself, if you wish," she said, waving her arm vaguely in the direction of the folding screen that obscured one corner of the room. "Well, Henriette, don't just stand there like a statue. It's getting late, my dear. Don't you think it's high time you got dressed for the ball? If you arrive too late there'll be no one left to ask you to dance. As it is, you're quite tall for your age, which intimidates the young officers. And you, Uncle Charles, you should be quite finished inspecting the fruits of my intestines. Follow Henriette out, and go change your uniform. You've got a sauce stain on your sleeve. Or is it shit?" she said, laughing. "You should take a cue from Doctor Larrey, who is always dressed to the nines."

"So . . . you're really feeling all better?" I asked her, taking the candle so that Françoise could help her into bed.

"We should stay, Margot," said Uncle Charles. "We'll have dinner together here in your room. That way at least I can be sure that you only have a bit of broth."

"Don't be a hypocrite, Charles. You're dying to capture some pretty little heart before marching off to war with that Emperor of yours. I've already told you, I feel perfectly fine. And anyway, I have Françoise, who fusses over me as though I were made of whipped cream. She's reading me my favorite novel. Oh, what a rascal, that Valmont! Ah, those were the days!" she sighed. "Enough! To the dance! It's getting late."

And so the night had begun. While Uncle Charles went to the hospital to put on his dress uniform, I kissed Aunt Margot goodbye and went to my room to get dressed. In a flurry, I threw open the armoire door and pulled out the first gown that I saw. I did my hair the best I could, powdered my nose, dashed on a few drops of perfume, covered my shoulders with a shawl, put my fan in my purse and went downstairs to wait for Uncle Charles. I had no inkling that, with the same ease with which a child paints a square, a door, two windows and a smoking chimney, my life was about to open up into a new space, into that place of refuge that I would share with Robert.

By the second waltz I had already sunk irremediably into those Levantine eyes. I was astonished that he stayed by my side, that he hadn't returned me to the green silk sofa where he'd found me. Drenched in sweat, we took turns fanning ourselves, waiting for the military band to start up again and give us an excuse to draw our bodies near once more. Two or three times I glanced about for Uncle Charles, but, grateful for his promotion to Surgeon General, he had reserved his full attention for Doctor Larrey. I was soon holding my second glass of champagne. Then, Robert grazed my lips with the back of his hand and I lost count. Three? Four? Then he said the name of a certain Madame Polidor, recently arrived from Saint-Domingue, and I found myself looking at a fascinating woman with a languid smile and bronzed shoulders. I noted that she spoke familiarly with Robert and it occurred to me that perhaps she had once been his lover, although she was quite a bit older than him. After complaining of the heat and asking us if we weren't tired of dancing, she invited us to her house to listen to gypsy music.

"I came with my Uncle, Doctor Cavent. We should be leaving soon," I said quickly, determined not to shirk my duties as a niece.

But everything happened in such an effortless way that, a short while later, while the musicians played an old-fashioned minuet and Robert was leading me to a chair, it was Uncle Charles himself who, arm in arm with Madame Polidor, said that it was only ten o'clock and we should accept the invitation and enjoy some gypsy songs and violin music, of which he was quite fond.

"In that case, it would be best if Robert went with you," she said, looking at me with amusement. "My house is not easy to find at night. I am so pleased that you'll come. I've invited only a small group," she added, and, raising her hand to her temple, she turned toward my uncle. "Please forgive my rudeness, Doctor Cavent. The atrocities I witnessed in Saint-Domingue have left me with no manners whatsoever. Allow me to introduce Lieutenant Robert Renaud, a good friend to whom I owe a great deal. Among other things, he has helped me organize my modest salon."

"Charles-Henri Cavent, Surgeon General with the Imperial

Guard, at your service," said my uncle. "Do you serve with Field Marshall Lannes, by any chance?"

"Yes, in the 9th Hussar regiment, stationed at Etaples. I am in Boulogne as an official adjunct to the General Staff."

"Ah, I do believe I've heard tell of you," said Uncle Charles, winking one of his sparkling blue eyes. "Yes. Very good, very good. We'll give a sound drubbing to the Austrian. We'll take Vienna, you'll see. I'd be delighted if you'd accompany us this evening."

Suddenly I knew that I was set on a new course. All the old things were already behind me: the little town of Foix with its three towers, Aunt Margot's château on the banks of the Ariège, the works of La Fontaine and Madame de La Fayette, games with the gardener's daughters, village festivals, embroidery, picnics in the forest glade where I would talk to the fairies, happy trips with Aunt Margot to Toulouse and Carcassonne, studying the classics, piano and geography, taking riding lessons. . . . Upon climbing into the coach, dizzy from the wine, I had the distinct impression that all of that was becoming a distant memory, turning rapidly into the remote past as if a magic wind had transported me to the other side of the earth. Now, all that was left to do was follow the adventure wherever it might lead me.

⁊

Madame Polidor's house was outside the rampart wall, adjacent to a road lined with artillery batteries and field tents that curved along the coast. I don't know why I had imagined that it would be a castle. It turned out to be a partially ruined tower, no longer of any military use (as Uncle Charles observed), surrounded by piles of rubble. Since the coaches could not make it to the door, it was necessary to walk in the dark among bivouacking soldiers and enormous cannons pointed out to sea. My disenchantment only grew upon seeing the guests' lack of decorum; some were singing, while others laughed and shouted to one another in greeting. I felt like a fish out of water. I asked myself what I, so timid and quiet, was doing there among such freewheeling sorts. Robert walked in silence. He held me by the arm in an impersonal way, as though still testing his will to seduce me. Suddenly, an insistent, feminine voice called out to him. It came from someone who had been walking behind us. I held my breath. I feared he would leave my side. But he didn't even turn around and, taking advantage of the fact that Uncle Charles had moved a few steps ahead of us, I showed my gratitude for his gesture by resting my head, briefly, on his shoulder. The poor impression I'd formed of the place disappeared the moment I entered the tower. Now, at this very minute, lost in nostalgia as I recall the exotic look of Madame Polidor's sitting-room, I suspect that it is the very same room that, years ago, used to appear over and over in my dreams: the bare stone walls, the huge silver candelabra on the mantelpiece, the thick beams supporting the ceiling and, of course, Robert. The only difference was that, in my recurrent dream, there was an enormous bed (a memory, perhaps, from my childhood in Lausanne, when my parents were still alive?) and possibly a mirror. In any case, in my dream there hadn't been the Egyptian rug or the heaps of red and black pillows that, piled up here and there, served as chairs, and even as divans for the guests; or the small tables, scarcely a hand's length high, upon which accumulated bottles of wine, glasses and, here and there, a candlestick; or the white silk wall hangings, painted with strange hieroglyphs that contrasted with the worn and blackened stone walls; or the massive trunk upon which rested a Spanish guitar and church censer, burning an aromatic resin. Above all, in my dream, there was no Claudette, the girl with honey-colored skin, dressed as a Turk, who, as soon as we entered, whispered her name and began collecting the furs, shakos, and twenty-franc pieces—the obligatory donation for the gypsies—that the gentlemen held out to her. (I have just remembered that in my dream I was always wearing her Moorish slippers.) Then we arranged ourselves in easy groups of two and three around the tables. There were, perhaps, a dozen of us, fifteen at the most, including Madame Polidor and the enchanting Claudette.

Seated between Uncle Charles and Robert, who began politely filling our glasses, I discovered that I had been mistaken in my impression that the guests were people of low social standing. Sprawled comfortably upon the cushions were five women, all of them covered in jewels and dressed in that summer's latest fashion, styles inspired by the Empress herself. The rest of the guests were officers, mostly Hussars. Their uniforms, with their great furs, were the only ones I knew how to identify. Madame Polidor reclined in

Romanesque fashion, supporting herself on one elbow, her head resting in the palm of her hand. I decided that her irresistible beauty resided in the shape of her lips, voluptuously full, and ever so slightly down-turned at the corners, suggesting just a hint of weariness. (Oh, Maryse, my dear Maryse! Though it's true that, back then, you were still Madame Polidor to me, in remembering you now, in detailing your mouth, I find it difficult to relegate you to a minor character in the scene, nothing more than an extra in this comic opera that I'm composing, and yet, this is how it must be until your moment arrives and you step onto center stage. We shall proceed then, for the time being, with the name Madame Polidor.) Next to her was a man with a gray mustache and a patrician air about him who, upon entering the tower, had exchanged greetings with my uncle. "Colonel Marnot, a friend from the Egyptian campaign. Were he not serving with the Guard he'd be a General by now," Uncle Charles had whispered to me. And suddenly, from above and to my right came the sound of violins and tambourines.

I had seen gypsies in Toulouse, but those had been Spanish gypsies who had crossed the Pyrenees with the Saltimbanques from Aragon and Catalonia. These, now making their way downstairs, were dressed completely differently, especially the men, who wore long hair, wide shirts, leather doublets and colorful scarves tied around their necks. Since I hadn't noticed a staircase behind the wall hangings, their sudden arrival surprised me so much that, for a while, I didn't even notice the music they were playing. "I'll wager they're Transylvanian airs," said my uncle, revealing himself somewhat a connoisseur of those plaintive ballads, a bit too slow for my taste, that melded with the dusky light of the room, evoking a remote and inconsolable sadness.

"Are you familiar with the history of the gypsies, monsieur?" I asked Robert brightly.

"Not with their history, no. But I do know about their lives. Much of what we understand today about horses, their dispositions, quirks, illnesses, good and bad crossbreedings, we learned from them," he said in a didactic tone, smiling.

"I assume, then, that there are gypsies among the Hussars," I said, naively.

"Heaven forbid! Gypsies are thieves. Although one must admit that they are also good musicians and coppersmiths."

29

"The Hussars are elite troops," Uncle Charles put in, raising his glass to Robert and offering a toast to his health.

While I was formulating an apology, Uncle Charles looked at his watch, stood up a tad unsteadily, and told me it was time to go. "'Tis a pity, but it's past midnight already," he added, shrugging his shoulders in his customary gesture of resignation. And destiny is a tricky thing, for had Madame Polidor not appeared at that very moment and insisted that we stay because the best of the music was yet to come, my relationship with Robert would never had been more than a mere flirtation, at most, one of those fleeting war-time romances fueled by letters filled with plagiarized verses and covered with little drawings of hearts and bordered in flowers, tepid epistolary idylls whose tender words of endearment, burdened by repetition, culminate only in boredom. It did not take much to convince Uncle Charles, who sank back into the cushions, accompanied, this time, by Madame Polidor. "We'll leave in fifteen minutes. All right with you?" he whispered, turning toward me. And what was I to say? I responded with silence.

Meanwhile, Robert, who had stopped wooing me ever since we left the dance, decided to renew his advance, and I, terrified and unsure what to do, felt his left hand slip between the cushion and my dress. I was about to push him away, but my resolve faltered: the waltzes, the champagne, his eyes, his imperiousness, and yes, his well-rehearsed lines: "Henriette, what does it feel like to be a perfect being, to have everything: beauty, grace, youth, wit? Tell me, what does it feel like to fly above it all, up there with the angels?" Such words, though they seem completely ridiculous to me today, transported me to the heavens that night.

Our hostess had not lied when she'd said that the musical evening had not yet reached its finest moment. Firmly anchored in place by Robert's hand, which had felt its way to my clothed privates, I joined the others in applauding the raucous gypsy woman who, accompanied by an allegro moment of a tune in a major key, had descended the stairs in a flurry of twirling skirts and bare feet. My eyes hooded with pleasure—no hand other than my own had ever touched me in that way—I allowed myself to be swept away by the woman's deep, husky voice, to be transported by her hands on her hips and her brazen expression that, a mere hour earlier, would have caused me to blush. As I followed her unabashed movements with my eyes, my gaze met with Colonel Marnot's. His eyes appeared to burn with indignation, with a deep reproach. Though Robert had allowed his fur to slide down his arm, half-hiding it from view, I knew that the Colonel had discovered our secret game, and my pleasure disappeared instantaneously. Blushing and trembling with shame, I stood up so abruptly that the woman interrupted her song. Everything seemed to be spinning: the wall hangings, my shadow, the gypsies; it all wheeled about me, as though I were dancing a frenetic waltz. I closed my eyes. I felt my legs go weak and I let myself go.

I was scarcely aware that it was Robert who carried me back to the coach. When I came to, we were entering the city again, and Uncle Charles was waving a bottle of ammonia from his medicine kit under my nose.

"You must have had too much to drink," he affirmed, after taking my pulse. "Don't worry, I won't say a word to your Aunt. As far as I'm concerned, you only drank one glass of wine."

When we arrived at the guesthouse, we saw immediately that something was wrong: Françoise met us with a long wail and ran toward us, her head in her hands. It seemed that Aunt Margot was having chest pain and could scarcely speak. She had sent Françoise for a priest.

We ran to her room. Uncle Charles bled her immediately, assisted by Pierre, the postilion. While the basin filled with blood, I knelt next to her bed and took her hand. I could see that she was suffocating and I tried to cool her with my fan. But nothing seemed to help. Her strong constitution allowed her to hold out until Françoise returned with the priest. As soon as she had received the Last Rights she fell into a sweat-soaked trance. At dawn, her irregular breathing ceased completely.

2

JUST HALF AN HOUR AGO, while Milly and I were turning the plants toward the light and picking dead leaves from their stems, the memory of Aunt Margot felt so vivid that I was compelled to sit down and write about her, and also about my family.

I must begin by saying that I have almost no memory of my parents. Whenever I try to evoke them, their faces appear blurry and incomplete, like fragments of worn daguerreotypes that someone's left under my pillow. Mama sitting before a mirror, her back to me, combing her long, copper-colored hair, or a faint smile in her blue eyes as she let me take a sip from her cup of hot chocolate. My father's vigorous hand, pointing out my first rainbow, or tying, too tightly, the laces on my little white booties. Neither do I remember Lausanne, nor the house in which I was born. Sometimes, in the deepest recesses of my memory and at the end of a long hallway, I think I can see a dog; at others, hanging from an invisible wall, as though floating in the nothingness, a bird in a cage and a cuckoo clock, that, come to think of it, could have been the same thing; perhaps a full-length mirror and a big bed with two giant white pillows, and yes, also my tiny chamber pot. All told, nothing too terribly precious.

My years in Foix passed happily among my Aunt's conservative ideas and the clandestine revolutionary rumors spread by the servants at the château. Despite my Aunt's best efforts to educate me in accordance with her values—instruction in piano, voice, dance, sewing, Italian and Spanish, flower arrangement, and etiquette were entrusted to a long-nosed woman named Madame Montiel; grammar, Latin, Greek, mathematics, logic, geography, and didactic lectures were dutifully imparted by abbé Lachouque; riding lessons and fencing were the province of the good Captain Laguerre—my contact with the gardener's clever daughters, with whom I carried out make-believe decapitations next to a dead tree that we called The Guillotine, Pierre's Jacobean diatribes that he delivered, undaunted by my curiosity, to the other servants in the kitchen while my Aunt napped, and my intense conversations with Françoise, a secret admirer of Rousseau and of the *Philosophes*, had marked me with a vague sense of anti-monarchical patriotism that, though I never dared to express it, had grown within me as spontaneously and disorderly as a flowering vine, ideals that I continue to hold to this day with the same lack of political discipline. In any case, my childhood and adolescence belong to Aunt Margot, as does the sum total of my filial love. In truth, I couldn't have asked for a better mother. And if, at the time of her death, I did not share some of her convictions, I nevertheless owe to her example my only three virtues: perseverance, physical stamina, and the capacity to make decisions in difficult moments. Of all of my belongings, the one I value most is a tiny portrait of her that I wear, to this day, on a chain around my neck. It has been no easy task to keep it all these years. On three separate occasions I have lost the gold chains that it hung upon: the first was in 1812, during the terrible retreat from Moscow to the Niemen; then in Spain, when I fell prisoner in the Battle of Vitoria; and finally, in jail in Santiago de Cuba, when I was stripped of everything of value I'd had with me. I have just opened the stubborn little door of the locket to say hello to Aunt Margot, an Aunt Margot at age nineteen, a newlywed, surprisingly thin, but already wearing her customarily resolute expression, a portrait painted by one of those miniaturists who found fame in the Court of Versailles.

The Cavents, enterprising people from the Languedoc, had sought refuge in Geneva, fleeing religious persecution. There they had prospered as manufacturers of knives and scissors. My maternal grandfather, Antoine-Marie Cavent, had embraced the Roman Catholic faith—a creed loathed in the city—in order to marry the heiress to a great textile empire. From this union were born, in consecutive years, my mother, baptized Suzanne, Aunt Louise, Aunt Margot, and Uncle Charles. Widowed and suffering from an ailing heart, my grandfather ended up bankrupt due to competition from British manufacturers. All that remained of his considerable fortune was the house in which he lived. Since the profitable marriages he had expected for his daughters were no longer possible, he married them off the best he could, to men of various professions: Paul Faber, my father, the owner of a modest printing press in Lausanne; Guillaume Curchet, of Geneva, an employee of a bank owned by the Necker brothers, proved worthy of Aunt Margot, and a certain Brunet, a lawyer in Lausanne, obtained a "yes" from Aunt Louise, the eldest and most beautiful of the three sisters. Each of these marriages was born purely of love, since none of my grandfather's daughters had any dowry to offer other than a solid conservative education. As for Uncle Charles, my grandfather dissuaded him from following his true inclination toward a military career, convincing him, instead, to go to Paris to study medicine.

With his daughters' domestic situations arranged, my grandfather sold his house, complete with all of the furniture inside it. The following day he went to see his son-in-law, Curchet, in his office at the bank, and deposited all of the money in an account to be managed by Curchet himself. From that sum, Uncle Charles was to receive a modest allowance for thirty-six months, provided that he continue with his medical studies; the remainder would go toward a dowry for the first marriageable granddaughter, or, in the case that there were no granddaughters, it would be given to the first grandson when he came of age. After making these farsighted provisions, he went to the best hotel in Geneva, ordered a Pantagruelian dinner, and died that same night, in his sleep, from his second heart attack.

A few weeks later, Curchet and Aunt Margot's social life took an unexpected turn. Upon being named Finance Minister in France, Jacques Necker asked his brother Louis to send him two or three trusted employees from his bank in Geneva, requesting Curchet in particular, as he was his wife's cousin. From one day to the next, the young couple found themselves living in a house in Paris. Owing to Curchet's loyalty and intelligence, very soon they were living a life of ease. From then on, Curchet's destiny would advance in tandem with Necker's, whose turbulent career in politics and finance is well known. In any case, following his protector's second term as Finance Minister, whose unpopular dismissal sparked the storming of the Bastille, Curchet withdrew from public life and consolidated all of the wealth he had amassed though his lucrative speculations. He intended to return to Geneva, but Aunt Margot, fearing political excesses, categorically refused. Geneva was nearly as tumultuous as Paris, and she was of the opinion that it was not conducive to a comfortable, carefree life. Her ancestral instinct drew her to the Languedoc. They settled first in Toulouse, but, during an excursion to Ariège, Aunt Margot was captivated by an old château that was for sale on the outskirts of Foix, on the banks of the river. Curchet, who indulged her in everything, bought it for her without a second thought, heedless of the cost. Further, in the following years, he dedicated himself to renovating it and beautifying the gardens. He also acquired three neighboring farms and two vineyards, joining them to the estate. (It would become our habit to call the château and estate "Foix," although the actual village was downstream and, except for its proximity, had nothing whatsoever to do with the property.) Meanwhile, Uncle Charles, having graduated from medical school, joined the cause of the Republic, inspired by his friend Larrey, whom he had met at the School of Anatomy at the University. After the medical schools, considered "institutions of privilege," had been shut down, Uncle Charles served for a few months as a surgeon in the Hôtel Dieu. His military vocation revived by the war, he joined the Army of the Rhine, distinguishing himself in the Battle of Wissembourg, in which he was wounded in one arm. He went on to pursue a distinguished career as a military surgeon—almost always alongside Larrey—that would take him to Spain, Italy, and Egypt.

Aunt Margot was not pleased with Uncle Charles' political conversion, although she did approve of his defending France's borders. While she had always detested the Jacobins, whom she called "those regicidal charlatans," she was obstinately disdainful of the non-Latin world, and of England and Austria in particular. To her way of thinking, Marie Antoinette, of whom she held a very poor opinion, was to blame for the blood-drenched anarchy that had befallen France. She never would become accustomed to being called *citoyenne*, nor to the new names for the calendar months that the National Convention had adopted. Had she lived long enough, it's possible that she would have come to tolerate—though certainly not to support—Napoleon's government after his reconciliation with the Church and the victory at Austerlitz.

As Aunt Margot told it, no serious disagreements ever arose between her and her husband. With all hope lost for a parliamentary monarchy, which Curchet considered the only viable solution for France, he disengaged from politics and dedicated himself to protecting his lands from local threats, which ranged from outright confiscation to the reduction of his property lines. The fortunate fact that he had never defended the monarchists, his generous donations of grain "for the people's bread," as well as his flexible attitude and the tricolor cockade he wore everyday in his hat, were sufficient to hold the community counsel members' radicalism in check. Around the time of Robespierre and Saint-Just's executions, his health began to decline. The southern climate never had agreed with him, and, as Aunt Margot told it, "the poor man never stopped coughing." It was then that my Aunt received a devastating letter from her sister Louise: my parents had died, burned to death in the fire that had consumed our house in Lausanne, and her husband was opposed to me—a nearly silent girl, with an ugly burn on my left foot—living with them any longer. Aunt Margot, infuriated by Brunet's insensitivity and by Aunt Louise's weakness, arranged to travel to Lausanne immediately. Thinking that perhaps his lungs would benefit from some time in a cooler climate, she assented to Curchet's wish to accompany her on the trip.

Many times I heard Aunt Margot recount the details of that calamitous journey across France, full of mired coach-wheels, broken axles, and bolting horses. Worse still, she and Curchet, suspected of being aristocrats on the run, had very nearly been thrown in jail on two separate occasions. Unfortunately, the privations of the journey would prove fatal for Curchet. Upon their arrival in Lausanne, the dear man began coughing up blood, and died in the hospital a few days later, Aunt Margot holding fast to his hand. After the funeral, my aunt returned with me to Foix. According to her, it was there that I learned to laugh and began to show interest in the world again. She never spoke to Louise again, nor did she respond to her letters. Seven years later, upon receiving word that her sister had died of a heart attack, I heard her sobbing softly behind her closed bedroom door.

❧

Dejected and hollow-eyed, dressed in mourning and seated in the dining room of the guesthouse in front of a bowl of porridge, I reread, for the tenth time, the wax-sealed card that an orderly had delivered to the innkeeper, on which Robert had written, in a clear hand, the letters tall and straight like little soldiers at attention: "I have been informed of Madame Curchet's death. I must leave shortly and greatly regret that I will not be able to express my condolences in person."

Once again I asked myself what I was doing there, waiting passively while Uncle Charles decided my fate, while he weighed whether I was to return to Foix with Pierre and Françoise or else be allowed to follow him to the front, as did many daughters, wives and even lovers of high-ranking officials. Why did I not put on my black hat, follow my own heart's desire, and march straight down the three blocks that separated me from Robert's barracks, speak his name to the guard at the gate, wait until I saw him coming toward me, and say: "I came to thank you for your note, Monsieur Renaud," or better: "This is my address. I would very much like to hear from you again"? But what address was I to give him, when I didn't even know where I was going to be?

Suddenly, I felt a hand on my shoulder. It was Uncle Charles. "Henriette, my dear child. I have reached a decision," he said, sitting down next to me. "It pains me not to be able to grant your request, but it would be foolish for me to allow you to stay with me. As was your Aunt's wish, I am your guardian now, and I must see to your safety and financial well-being, although the latter doesn't much concern me. Your dowry is in a bank in Toulouse, and Monsieur Lebrun, the executor of your Aunt's estate, will see to the administration of the Foix lands, which will be yours when the time comes. What truly concerns me is the thought of your coming with me to the war. Life in the rearguard is not easy. We're in a different place every day. Everything is provisional. One rarely finds decent lodging. You are not accustomed to suffering hardship and, further, one must always think of the worst. Suppose something were to happen to me."

I begged, I cried, I pleaded, I said everything I could think of to convince him not to send me back to Foix. And it wasn't only because of Robert, because I longed to see him, to touch him again. In truth, I was then at a passive age, an age of daydreams and elaborate fantasies in which my body was more inclined to imagination than to action. I did it for my own sake as well. It terrified me to think of myself all alone in that enormous empty house, hearing Aunt Margot's unforgettable laugh echoing through the rooms, her beautiful contralto voice calling me down to breakfast. I feared I might look out the window and see her sturdy figure dismounting from her horse with surprising agility, or raising a bow and letting fly an arrow that would find its precise mark in the red center of the target, or that I might behold her coming out of the river some oppressive summer afternoon, her shirt glued to her skin, her powerful thighs advancing with each step, her voluminous belly, the wide rosettes of her breasts, her prematurely gray hair dripping about her face like a garland.

"Oh, Uncle Charles, I could never, never ever, live there all alone!" I implored him, this time on my knees, taking his hand and bathing it in tears. "Don't you understand that you are the only family I have left? That you are that only person in the whole world who cares about me? I would die of loneliness and grief. I'm begging you, Uncle. You'll see, I won't be any trouble to you. I promise!"

What good-hearted man could refuse such arguments?

After laying a wreath of flowers on Aunt Margot's grave, we left Boulogne immediately. The marching orders received by the bulk of the army coincided with a sudden summer thunderstorm that frayed my nerves and put Uncle Charles in a foul mood. The city's streets seethed with soldiers and horses, and our carriage, laden with trunks and bundles of clothing, seemed to irritate everyone, infuriating the musicians in a military band on one corner, and blocking the passage of some transport wagons carrying provisions across a bridge. I couldn't understand the angry impatience of those men who shook their fists and glared at us with fire in their eyes each time our carriage interrupted their forward progress.

"They are fed-up with waiting. Fed-up with everything," grumbled Uncle Charles. "It's been two years since we received the order to invade England, and we still haven't crossed the canal. And now the Emperor has changed his plans. If he hadn't, you'd be on your way to Foix right now, even if you'd cried your eyes dry. I would never have taken you to England. The truth is that neither you nor your Aunt should ever have left Foix," he muttered, looking at the empty seat where Aunt Margot had always sat. "It's true that I needed money, but she could have sent it to me through her lawyer. And as for my promotion, she barely had the chance to celebrate it." I realized that Uncle Charles wasn't really talking to me, but rather, to himself. "It was that stupid engraving that made her want to come. I'm sure of it. The first thing she asked me when we arrived was if they had finished constructing the tunnel." (My Uncle was referring to a popular illustration showing the Grand Armée invading England by sea, by air, in a flotilla of hot-air balloons, and by land, through a tunnel that ran underneath the canal.) "She didn't want to miss that absurd spectacle, dreamed up by some infernal artist just to dupe romantics like her. And then that shameless way she was eating, and of course you see what happened. . . . " On and on he went, talking aloud to himself, trying to unburden his guilty conscience. I understood completely, because I felt guilty too. It tormented him to think that while he was wooing Madame Polidor to the strains of gypsy violins, Aunt Margot's heart was slowly ceasing, never to start up again.

⚭

What can I say of that inexorable march that would take us to Strasbourg by summer's end? To begin with, Uncle Charles had to return to his traveling hospital and I almost never saw him anymore—in accordance with the new regulations, the only women authorized to travel with the troops were the sutlers and washerwomen. In those four weeks I never once slept in a bed, and considered myself lucky to find a straw pallet in some barn or another to sleep on, in public, fully clothed and surrounded by strangers. Usually though, I spent the night in Aunt Margot's carriage, Françoise and I making do on the seats, and Pierre on the roof, in the open air, wedged among our luggage. On the occasional afternoon, if we came to a river—we crossed the Oise, the Mosa, the Mosela—we would clean the crust of sweat and dust that covered us and wash our laundry in the muddy water, though no matter how we scrubbed our sheets and blouses they always came out a dingy earth color that was impossible to remove. The peasants rarely sold us anything other than bread, cheese, and fodder for the horses, and even these items came at extremely high prices. Fortunately, we were positioned between the carriage of a grenadier colonel's wife and that of the jovial Italian family of a fortifications engineer, assigned to the General Staff of the Imperial Guard—it was from

40

those women that I learned that the section of the column we were traveling in was especially for officials with the Imperial Guard. Sometimes, to distract ourselves, we would visit one another and gossip happily over the false rumors that were circulating. It was said that, upon invading Bavaria, the Austrians serving under General Mack had discovered that the inhabitants, in a show of collective disgust, would not speak to them or answer their questions; we were assured that Villenueve had toppled an English squadron in Spanish waters and that, due to some murky event in Poland, a serious problem had erupted between the Russians and the Poles. Also, while we took turns reading chapters aloud from *Paul et Virginie*, or *Delphine*, we would share the few sweets we still had left: a delicious chocolate *confit*, half-melted from the heat, a lump of sugar, a licorice candy, the very rare cup of tea, a piece of biscuit soaked in wine. It was not easy to find fresh water and milk, and as a result we all suffered from stomach ailments, especially Françoise and Silvana, Signora Grimaldi's younger sister.

From time to time my uncle would appear and offer a glum report, lowering his head to speak with me through the carriage window without dismounting his horse: "Our wagons are overflowing with febrile soldiers. If things go on like this, six to eight thousand men will arrive ill at the Danube." He'd leave us a few bites of beef or ham for supper, then set off again for his wagons, which were traveling half a league ahead of us. I don't know exactly where our carriage was positioned within the column. We must not have been too far to the rear though, because once, when our carriage paused on the crest of a hill, I climbed up to Pierre's coachbox and looked behind us. A veritable army of women extended as far as I could see; they traveled by coach, carriage, wagon, cart, horse, mule, donkey and their own two feet. Many of them left the road to take care of their personal necessities, and their colorful dresses and hats dotted the recently harvested, straw-colored countryside, like flowers in full summer bloom.

One night, while we roasted a miraculous chicken that Pierre had bought at a nearby farmstead, Uncle Charles arrived, glowing with contentment. He had come from Strasbourg, where the troops were setting up camp on the outskirts of the city. They would wait there until the Emperor arrived from Saint-Cloud to resume the march. There were to be two days of tributes and festivities. Thanks to Doctor Larrey's generosity, he had been able to secure lodging in a local clockmaker's home.

"I'll sleep in the workshop and you'll take the upstairs bedroom. The carriage won't make it," he said, gesturing at the overcrowded road. "You'll go on my horse. I'll come for you at dawn. Right now, I'm off to say hello to a friend." As he was leaving, he added: "What coincidences do occur in this life! Can you guess with whom you'll be sharing the room? No less than Madame Polidor! I assume you won't object. She's a refined and intelligent woman and you can trust her. I'm told she was a famous opera singer."

Naturally, coincidence had nothing to do with it. As I was soon to discover, during his nocturnal rides to and from our carriage, Charles had come across Madame Polidor's coach, and an intimate friendship had sprung up between them.

⚘

The clockmaker—an old man named Simon Lévi who welcomed me in a high-pitched, singsong voice—had a modest house that seemed, to me, more sumptuous than a palace. After devouring an enormous salad with hard-boiled eggs and vegetables, I washed myself from head to toe with soap and hot water, put on a clean shift—with the inevitable earth-colored tinge—and collapsed on the bed. I was so exhausted that, no matter how I tossed and turned, trying to find a comfortable position, I couldn't manage to fall asleep. Suddenly, a strange song, barely audible over the street noise below, curled its way up the spiral staircase that connected the workshop to the upper floor. I couldn't understand the words, but I recognized the clockmaker's inimitable voice. I imagined that he sang as he repaired the mechanism of one of the many clocks that I had seen downstairs. I pictured him bent over, with the magnifying lens affixed to his forehead, his black silk cap half-covering his white hair, his voice issuing through his whiskers like an irrepressible flock of swallows. Mesmerized by the song, I fell, little by little, into a dream in which Aunt Margot and I were floating high above the towers of Strasbourg, surrounded by flotillas of hot-air balloons, angels with enormous feathered wings, and flying carriages.

I awoke the next day, startled by the sound of cannon-fire and the ringing of bells. "Napoleon has entered the city," said a voice from the floor, just next to the bed. It was Madame Polidor, stretched out on a pallet, completely naked, a bundle of clothing under her head as a pillow. "When I came in last night, you were sleeping so deliciously that I didn't want to wake you," she added with a smile, speaking to me familiarly, as though we were already dear friends. "But now we should get dressed and fix ourselves up as quickly as possible. Your uncle is coming for us this evening, but first, I want to confirm the whereabouts of some friends, Robert among them. I know that he's in Strasbourg."

Any shred of reservation that I'd had about her disappeared instantaneously. Her personality was enchanting, lively and warm, and a powerful aura emanated from her still beautiful body, disarming the rigid mores that usually defended my timidity. It didn't seem to concern her one bit to be naked in front of me. Sitting up in bed, I watched her open her valise, take out an iron and a blue muslin dress. I had never seen anyone move her arms and hands with such natural elegance. While she lit the coals in the brazier, I asked her if she knew Robert well.

"I met him last year. I appreciate him a great deal. He's a gentleman, which is hard to come by these days. A man who protects his honor."

"Does he have a lover?" I dared to ask her.

"What Hussar doesn't? Her name is Corinne. They were living together when Claudette and I arrived at the encampment in Boulogne. I visited them once. A modest, two-room flat near the cavalry's barracks. Things must not be easy for them, though. They have very different tastes," she said, spreading the dress out across the bed.

"If I'd known . . . " I murmured, utterly crestfallen.

"Darling, single men almost always have a lover or an affectionate friend they like to sleep with. If you're worried about Corinne, I'll tell you that you are younger and more beautiful than she is. And anyway, things must not be going well between them recently. Remember that he went alone to the dance in Boulogne. But above all, remember that you are here and she, as far as I know, has not accompanied him. Not all women are willing to follow their men to war."

I was silent a moment, savoring Maryse's last words: "Follow their men to war." It was the use of the possessive *their* that had struck me; I had never heard it used for a woman about a man, only the inverse. I started laughing, at the thought that Robert could be *my* man.

"What are you laughing at?" Maryse asked, surprised. "A minute ago, you seemed on the verge of tears."

"Don't pay me any mind. I'm a silly girl."

All it had taken for me to feel as happy as I had a month before was a good bath, twenty hours of sleep, the news that Robert was alone in the city, and the conviction that I had followed *my* man to war. Thinking about the calendar, it occurred to me that my birthday might have already passed.

"What's today's date?" I asked Maryse (it's become impossible for me to go on calling her Madame Polidor).

"The fourth of *Vendémiaire*," she replied, flicking water on the iron to see if it was sufficiently hot.

"Yesterday was my birthday. Aunt Margot had promised me a grand ball at her château. Who would have thought that I'd spend it asleep?"

"We shall celebrate it today. The entire city's a party."

"You're forgetting that I'm in mourning," I said, indicating my tattered black dress.

"And what of it? I'm not going to take you to a dance, but I'd wager that it would make your aunt happy to see you enjoying yourself after being cooped up in that carriage for four weeks. You know," she said, gesturing in irritation, "it leaves a bad taste in my mouth to have left Claudette behind. But someone had to drive the carriage. Poor girl. By the way," she added, "how old are you now? Seventeen, eighteen?"

"Do I really look that old," I said, flattered that she'd thought me nearly a woman. "I turned fifteen."

Maryse lifted the iron and stared at me. The corners of her lips, slightly downturned, descended even further, and her face became that mask usually used to depict Tragedy. Her eyes filled with tears and a drop rolled down her cheek.

"What's the matter?"

"Nothing, nothing. I burned my finger," she said, her voice breaking, and raising her index finger to her mouth. "Hand me your dress," she added. "I'll iron it while you do your hair. We should hurry."

While I got ready, I asked myself what painful memory had clouded her mood. But the time had not yet come for me to know the reason for her tears that afternoon.

In any event, I'll never forget the expression on Robert's face when, an hour later, we ran into each other in front of a café along the canal. Serious and indecisive, he looked at me over the rim of his mug of beer as if he couldn't quite place the girl dressed in the too shabby black dress—the journey had robbed me of the better part of my hips as well—smiling stupidly in the doorway. It was only when he saw Maryse that he was able to react, which he did so clumsily that, in standing up, he toppled his chair and soaked his uniform in beer.

It was a perfect evening. The dinner in the packed hotel dining room. Maryse and Uncle Charles, arm in arm, walking ahead of us along the brightly lit streets. The cathedral's spire, laden with torches, reaching up to the heavens like a pointed flame. And Robert, ever didactic, pointing out the place where, it was said, Rouget de Lisle had composed *La Marseillaise*. Later, while we strolled along the canal, we began to share some of the details of our lives. I told him about my grandfather, about the fire that killed my parents, and about being adopted by Aunt Margot. I spoke of Foix, of the beauty of the Garonne River and the valleys of Ariège, of the majesty of the Pyrenees. Robert, obviously, said nothing to me of Corinne. He focused entirely on recounting the motivating forces behind a duel he had fought, six months prior, with a certain Captain Varga. "He accused me, publically, of cheating at cards. What else could I have done, Henriette, but rebuff him? A man must guard his honor as a gentleman, don't you think? And it's not that I'm a great fan of duels, or of cards, for that matter. They are things that happen, things one simply falls into, despite oneself." In any case, Varga had been obliged to withdraw from the fight due to a wounded shoulder, and the matter had been satisfactorily resolved between the respective seconds. Did I approve of his behavior?

"Of course, monsieur. You behavior was . . . Homeric," I said, smitten, imagining him brandishing a sword, the walls of Troy in the background. Then he charmed me with a description of his fur collection, of how he carried them, rolled into bundles, everywhere he went.

"One day we'll invade Russia, Henriette. If you'll allow me, I'll bring you a souvenir. What would you prefer, a cap made of ermine or of sable? And if one day we were to make it all the way to the jungles of Africa! Just imagine it! Panthers, leopards, tigers, lions . . . all at your feet, Henriette. Even rhinoceros horns and elephant tusks," he added, laughing at his own mania for exotic animals. Hearing our laughter, Uncle Charles and Maryse turned around. I could see by their smiles that they approved of our budding relationship, and I was filled with joy.

At the strike of ten, Napoleon appeared in one of the windows of the city's palace. It was the first time I'd ever seen him. He wore a sash across his chest. It was difficult to make out his facial features in the light from the candelabra held aloft by one of his attendants, but, by the way he gestured with his hat, he seemed in good spirits. I was amazed at his popularity; the moment the crowds of soldiers and civilians walking by the palace recognized him, a collective cry of *"Vive l'Empereur"* went up. *"Vive l'Empereur!"* shouted Robert, with the most sincere enthusiasm. *"Vive l'Empereur!"* I cried, caught up in the moment, though more out of imitation than conviction. The crowd began to envelop us and we were suddenly pushed toward the palace gates. The cries were deafening, and continued on long after the darling of France had withdrawn from the window. Separated from Uncle Charles and Maryse, we stayed right where we were, not speaking, surrounded by the clamor and the multitudes. At that moment, I felt his hand against my derrière. But when I saw his arms reaching to encircle my waist, I realized that it wasn't his hand pressing against me. Faint with pleasure, I half-turned my head and allowed myself to be kissed luxuriously.

Thinking back on that night, I realize that it wasn't only to Robert that I opened my body. In truth, my virginity—like that of so many thousands of French, Austrian, and Russian women—was one of the first casualties of that campaign; mild casualties, I must admit, and even desirable, in many cases, but casualties nonetheless, as recorded in the private registers of virgins who, across the villages and cities of my era, carried the voices of priests and nuns, fathers and mothers about in their consciences. And in the same way that nature regulates the times of estrus in animals, the survival instinct that drives the human species generates carnal desire during wartime. A deficit of so many thousands of deaths, countered by a credit of so many thousands of births. These are God's calculations, and I was but a number in that simple equation.

I should explain myself better. The last thing I want is to diminish Robert's importance in these pages. I am not saying that it was the war that made me love him. I think I would have fallen in love with him in times of peace or under any other circumstance. Nonetheless, I will say that if we had met before the war, I would not, that night in Strasbourg, have followed him docilely to the door of his barracks, nor would I have sat astride his horse, high in the saddle, nor allowed myself to be thrown, like a sack of potatoes, on a pile of foul-smelling hay, nor would I have allowed him to deflower me, dressed in mourning, in the open air, in the middle of the night on the outskirts of the city. And it's not that I regret having done it. Quite the contrary. It was the culminating moment of an unforgettable day, my first day as a fifteen-year-old, my first taste of love. I only mean that, because I'd already begun to live a bit like a soldier during that journey to Strasbourg, I had felt the imminence of battle. Truth be told, I made love not only with Robert that night, but also with the war.

When we returned to the clockmaker's house, Uncle Charles and Maryse were still out looking for us. Our moment of passion had occurred so quickly that the streets were still full of people and ablaze with light, and even dear old Simon Lévi was still up, leaning in the doorway of his workshop, talking with a neighbor, a woman holding a sleeping gray cat in her arms. After the requisite introductions, Robert took my arm and led me a few steps away from them.

"I am very sorry about what happened, Henriette. I must have lost my head," he said in a low voice, arranging his face into an expression appropriate to the circumstances. He looked ridiculous, like a bad stage actor. To top it off, the drooping tips of his mustache, mussed by my kisses, lent him a pitiful air.

"Me too," I said, to say something. In truth, the only thing that I wanted at that moment was for him to take his leave. I felt terribly confused, in a sort of limbo, suspended from reality. I was also exhausted and sore. All I wanted was to go up to my room, undress, and confirm that the sticky wetness I felt between my thighs was blood. "Good night, monsieur," I said, turning to go.

"I return to my regiment tomorrow. Please, let me hear from

you. Remember: 5th Battalion, Gazan Division, 9th Hussar Regiment. We must see each other again," I heard him say, hastily.

The clockmaker had put fresh water in the washbasin. Just as I was squatting down to wash myself, Maryse appeared, ascending the spiral staircase, holding a candlestick aloft to light her step. "Well, well, the missing girl," she said happily. "Your uncle and I have been all over Strasbourg looking for you. Thank God we decided to come by here again. The clockmaker told us that you'd arrived just a few minutes ago and. . . . What happened to you?" she asked, concerned, seeing the pinkish water running down my legs.

"It's nothing. . . . You know. . . . Women's concerns," I stuttered, trying to cover myself with my hands. "Please, leave me for just a moment."

But as she was leaving, Maryse spotted my dress, thrown over the back of a chair. One by one, she plucked up half a dozen straws of hay that had gotten caught in the cloth. "I see," she said, perplexed. "I see," she said again, this time with a sigh, crumbling the straw between her fingers, letting the golden dust fall through her hands. "Your uncle is waiting for me downstairs," she said, not looking at me. "I'll be out for a while. Sleep well. We'll talk tomorrow." And, lifting the hem of her dress, she disappeared down the dark mouth of the staircase.

⚘

I awoke late the next morning. The sun was hitting me full in the face, making me blink. I heard the clamor of horses and carriages from the street below, and I guessed that the troops were already leaving the city. Maryse, already dressed, was reading a book in the chair where I'd left my incriminating clothing. I closed my eyes again, pretending to still be asleep. More than ashamed, I felt completely incapable of withstanding reprimands and laments. "What time is it?" I asked at last.

"Late," Maryse replied, without raising her eyes from her book. "It just struck eleven. While I finish this chapter, read the letter over there, by the washbasin."

"Is it from Robert?" I asked, leaping out of bed.

"Is there someone else you've not told me about?" she teased from behind her book.

"But it's addressed to my uncle," I said, reading Uncle Charles' name.

"You have his permission to read it. Robert left it here at dawn, before going off with his regiment. Read it. Its subject matter concerns you."

I have received some good news in my lifetime, but as hard as I search through my memories, I cannot find a single letter that has brought me such happiness as that one, despite its brevity.

"Robert is asking for my hand!" I cried. "He wants to marry me! Can you believe it? Isn't it a miracle?" I said, jumping up and down. Mad with joy, I fell on the bed to read the letter again.

"A miracle? Why? Who better than you could he possibly marry? You're young. You're tall and pretty. You have it all. And if that weren't enough, you have properties and money. Your uncle told me. You kept it quite a secret, you little imp. Don't think one comes across many young women like you out here on the road."

Listening to Maryse talk, a bit too spontaneously, it seemed to me, I began to suspect that she had played an active role in the matter at hand.

"You spoke with him, didn't you?"

Maryse looked down at her book without answering.

"You spoke with him last night. Why would you do that?" I reproached her.

"Very well, yes," she said, closing the book.

"You begged him to marry me. No," I said, correcting myself, "you waved my dowry in front of his nose. That was it. Am I right? Why did you play matchmaker behind my back? I would have so much preferred for him to want to marry me of his own accord," I said, incensed, and buried my face in the pillow.

"Robert is my friend," I heard her say, coolly. "We met under what were very painful circumstances for me. I owe him a great deal. I went to look for him at the café and we spoke as friends. That is all."

Surprised by what I was hearing, I rolled over on the bed to look at her.

"You owe him a great deal?" I said, incredulous. "He's told me nothing."

"Last year, when I arrived in Boulogne, he was of great service to me," she continued. "One day I will tell you all about it. But not today."

"Then—"

"When I say that he is my friend, I mean only that: *my friend*," she interrupted. "Yes, we talked for a while. Not long. He had to be ready to leave at dawn. I merely advised him that, if he had ever considered getting married, he shouldn't miss the opportunity that you so beautifully embody. Of course we spoke of money. Dowries and inheritances are not State secrets. And don't think that I had only his well-being in mind, my friend. After your adventure last night, which I do not judge, your life is no longer the same. Yesterday it was Robert, later it could be another dashing officer, and then another and another, and so on. And along that chain of sabers and mustaches, the risk of finding yourself enmeshed in duels, in gambling, in coarse dealings, in betrayals and humiliations. What can I tell you? I know what I'm saying. It's something that, unfortunately, I know all too well. The society in which you've chosen to become a woman is the army, my dear. And, I must add, the army in time of war. You'll see when the battles begin, when they start to count the dead and wounded, the heroes and cowards. Right now, we're all rational beings. But just wait until the smell of gunpowder hits. Then you'll see. People change. They live in the moment. You must see for yourself to understand."

Maryse stood up abruptly and, turning her back to me, leaned against the windowsill. Her words had stunned me. Little by little, I began to feel afraid. I turned over on the bed again and pressed my face into the pillow. I closed my eyes and wished I had stayed in Foix. My uncle had been right. I had no business living this kind of life: discomfort, little privacy, constantly moving from one place to the next. Battles. Death. Blood. I began to cry. I could feel the hot dampness of my tears on the pillowcase. And it would be so easy to return. All I had to do was wait for Pierre and Françoise to come with the carriage. They wouldn't be long now. But in thinking of the carriage, of the leagues that separated me from the Ariège, I understood that life was not a clock whose hands could be moved backwards with the nudge of a finger. Foix would never again be what it had once been. The carriage had rolled across many days and many roads. Along the way I had lost Aunt Margot and my girlhood; I had also found Uncle Charles, Maryse, and Robert. For better or for worse, time had marched on, and it was now no longer possible to return, if, by return, I meant a reencounter with my bucolic early life. There was nothing to be done. At the end of the day, I had people here. In Foix, I had no one. Resigned to moving forward, I raised my head, wiped my tears away with the back of my hand, and asked Maryse: "What does Uncle Charles think of all of this? Do you think he'll give his consent?"

"Robert has a good reputation," she replied, turning toward me. I could see by her tender expression that she had guessed at my feelings instantly. "He fought in a duel. I don't know if you knew. A personal matter with a Captain of the Cazadores regiment, a sinister man, a duelist of ill-repute who relished humiliating any woman unfortunate enough to be within his reach. But in Robert, he met his match."

"So he fought over a woman. Was it Corinne?" I asked, curious.

"No," Maryse replied, sharply. "Or, perhaps. . . . I don't know," she wavered. "If you ask him, he'll tell you it was for a different reason. As I've said, your suitor is a gentleman. In any case, the duel was much talked about in the encampment at Boulogne. These sorts of things matter a great deal in an army, my dear."

"Well, so much the better. I suppose that Uncle Charles won't object to our getting married," I said, relieved, though I had the distinct impression that Maryse knew much more about that duel than she cared to say.

"He will not oppose it. Before returning to his ambulances, he told me that it was for you to decide if you wanted to marry or not, that he would defer to your wishes. The truth is, quite apart from the positive opinion he has of Robert, I think that your uncle is none too comfortable having you under his guardianship. It's not that he's said as much to me. But if he has chosen not to have a family of his own, it must be to avoid responsibilities other than those occasioned by his military service. But come now, my friend," she said, changing her tone of voice in an attempt to direct my attention to the day's affairs. "Napoleon is already on the march. I can't imagine how you could have slept through all this noise. I expect our carriages will be arriving shortly. It's been two days since I've seen Claudette and I'm worried about her. If you only knew how fragile she is."

"I'd like to go with you. One carriage would be sufficient for us. Pierre and Françoise would be thrilled to return to Foix. It would also be much more economical for us. Maintaining two horses is much different than four. Don't you think? We could share expenses."

"Never relinquish a carriage, my dear. That's a piece of advice I'll offer you. A carriage means freedom of movement. Suppose you wanted to return to your château. How would you get there? And anyway, my carriage is full to overflowing. So full, in fact, that Claudette and I generally ride in the coach-box. I'm traveling with everything you saw in my tower in Boulogne. I take my little world of illusions with me. My scenery. In the tower, I used it as a backdrop for the gypsies; next week, or the week after, I'll use it to present an Italian tenor or a string quartet, or even Claudette, who performs the Dance of Salomé like no other. I'll have you know that I play guitar and piano quite passably and that I can sing a Mozart aria as readily as a Creole melody from the islands. I made my living this way in Paris and in Saint-Domingue, my pet. And that's what I plan to do here as well. I'll open my salon wherever Napoleon takes it. My audience, at twenty francs a seat, is now the Grand Armée."

"And Uncle Charles? I'm certain he's interested in you."

Maryse came over to the bed and sat down next to me. Looking me in the eye, she said: "Oh, Henriette, you have much to learn about your uncle. He's happy in his profession, but I can't imagine him working in some provincial hospital, much less in an office on the main thoroughfare, his name engraved on a bronze plaque. His true vocation is the war. War intoxicates certain men, my darling. You'll soon see what I mean. Letting blood from a businessman in his underclothes is simply not the same as amputating an arm or stitching up a saber-wound on the battlefield. He was born to do these things in the same way that I was born for the life I lead. To each his own. Don't fool yourself. Charles and I will never be anything, or, I should say, anything serious. It's just not in our nature. We are both too independent. You must accept us both for who we are: Charles with his ailing soldiers, me with my traveling salon, and you with Robert. That way we'll all be just fine."

"I understand," I sighed. Changing the conversation, I added: "As I said, I would very much have liked to travel with you. I would have learned so much from you. I'm just a foolish girl. I don't even know how to find Robert."

"Oh, don't worry, my pet," Maryse replied, getting up from the bed and returning to the window. "I'll wait for your carriage to arrive.

I'll go in front and you'll follow me. If you really think about it, we *will* be traveling together. We'll visit one another. But, chop chop! It's getting late and we still need to eat something. God only knows when we'll have the good fortune to sit at a proper table again!"

"Where is my dress?" I asked her, looking around the room. "I left it on that chair last night. Did you put it in my trunk?"

"Who's ever heard of a fiancée dressed in black?" she said, and, with a languid gesture, indicated a dress with a daring décolletage hanging in the armoire. "It will be a touch short on you, and a bit loose, but I've scarcely worn it. In the next city, we'll go shopping."

"Which city will that be?" I asked,

"Whichever one strikes Napoleon's fancy, my dear."

3

THE URGENT NEED TO SEE Robert, to feel myself in his arms and to hear him say that he loved me; to fall asleep at his side in a big bed with white pillows and feel the heat of his body on my skin; to walk, arm in arm, along a tree-lined avenue, the leaves already crisp, glorious in their agony of gold, burgundy, and orange, and to swear my eternal love for him; to sit with him in some café in Ulm, or perhaps Munich or Augsburg, full of tobacco smoke and the sweet smell of fried onions and sausages smothered in mustard, to agree on the date and the place and the church and the time and all the other details of our wedding. ("The sooner the better," counseled Maryse.) Yes, my desire to reunite with Robert grew within me like an endless stairway that seemed to lead to nowhere; the hours passing slowly and torturously as we doggedly followed the wagons laden with munitions and provisions through the streets of Württemberg, of Swabia, knowing that up ahead, somewhere far up ahead, marched the 5th Hussar Battalion, with Robert among them. There was no way to quiet my mind, nothing to distract me. Françoise, for some mysterious reason, was reading *The Genius of Christianity*, her lips moving as though gnawing on the words, her finger tracing the lines so as not to lose her place with the continual jolting of the carriage. If I decided to take advantage of a moment in which our carriages were stopped to visit Maryse and Claudette, I invariably found them going over song lyrics and dramatic dialogues, and I couldn't help but feel like an intruder in their artistic endeavors. I didn't doubt the affection Maryse felt for me, but she and Claudette were bound by links forged in Saint-Domingue, by a tumultuous and private past to which I did not have access, which they shared in the simple exchange of a glance, or a slight smile of understanding. And so it went all the way to the Danube, with me writing desperate letters to Robert whenever we stopped, copying the same paragraphs over and over again, watching the ink supply dwindle while still receiving no news, or at least any worth mentioning, beyond the laconic "all's well" that circulated daily among the 5th Battalion, all the way from the Chief of Staff down to the last supply wagon. Just at the break of dawn one gray morning, we heard a distant thundering from the east. Half-asleep, I stuck my head through the carriage window and asked Pierre if a storm was coming. "It's the war, mademoiselle!" he shouted from the coach-box. "We've arrived at the war!"

The following day we discovered that the battle had been fought in a place called Wertingen, on the south bank of the Danube. We passed a long line of Austrian prisoners, their white uniforms earth-stained and bloodied. They were being led by a contingent of Mounted Chasseurs who drove them forward, shouting at them as though they were oxen, and threatening the stragglers with their curved sabers. I jumped out of the carriage and planted myself in the middle of the road: The Hussars of the 9th Regiment? No, they had not participated in the battle. Robert Renaud? He is with General Treilhard. No, he's with Field Marshal Lannes, as an aide-de-camp. No, I saw him yesterday in General Gazan's convoy. Don't worry, I'll be sure he receives your letter. Consider it done, *citoyenne*, I'll give him your message as soon as we return from Stuttgart. I'll do what I can, *citoyenne*, I promise you. . . .

After that first victory, the nervous unease I'd been experiencing transformed into an ardent patriotism—a feeling that grew, from one day to the next, from a simple fluttering to a veritable fervor. I longed for more battles, more victories, and, above all, to see Robert marching triumphantly through the streets of a conquered city. While I'm sure my zeal had something to do with the enthusiasm of youth, I wasn't the only one infected with what Maryse called "Napoleonic fever." Françoise, who, a week earlier, had declared Europe to be drowning irrevocably in a bottomless pit of blood, and who dreamed of one day living serenely among the savages of America, stopped reading Chateaubriand and began praying with me for the triumph of France, of Napoleon and of all the heroic soldiers in *our* Grand Armée. Pierre, for his part, appeared to have forgotten his republican ideals and began to wear, night and day, a Cuirassier's helmet that he'd found under a tree, greeting everyone he met along the road with an adamant: "*Vive l'Empereur!*" Even Maryse and Claudette, until that moment nonchalant, brimmed with joy at the printed proclamation, crumpled and smudged though it was by the time it reached us, that announced the Austrian debacle at Ulm. Mack's army, in fewer than three weeks, had melted like butter: of one hundred thousand men, twenty-five thousand had died, forty thousand had fallen prisoner and multitudes of cannons and flags had been captured. The proclamation concluded with the revelation of Napoleon's next objective: to take Vienna.

That evening, we uncorked two bottles from our wine stores. Then, under a boundless October moon, Maryse joined her guitar with the jubilant violin and traverse flute issuing from nearby carriages, and, in time to Claudette's beats of the tambourine, she sang and danced well into the night.

ༀ

After the victory at Ulm, we stopped fearing that an officer of the *Intendance* might requisition our horses. Mack's surrender had re-provisioned the Grand Armée with hundreds of excellent mounts; so many, in fact, that some animals—though certainly not those that had belonged to the Austrians—were sold among the women and Jews following behind the troops. Other, more exhausted horses, were sacrificed in order to provide fresh meat to the regimental field kitchens. Pooling some of our money, Maryse and I bought an enormous horse with an indifferent expression and flayed hindquarters that had served with the Cuirassiers. He was thin and his ulcers reeked, but Pierre had insisted on the convenience of having a mount that would allow him to be in better contact with the farmers and merchants traveling behind us, and we deemed his judgment a reasonable one. We named him Jeudi, for the day of the week we'd acquired him, and we tied the lead on his halter to the rear of my carriage. By the third or fourth day, I worked up the courage to ride him. I put the bit on him myself and moved the reins from one side to the other so that he could become accustomed to my hand. Then, with the help of Pierre, who had also loaned me his boots and a pair of breeches, I leaped up into the saddle and took him out onto the road. Immediately, I knew we had not wasted our money. Jeudi had been well trained and obeyed, with little resistance, the pressure of the reins and spurs. Even if his walk was a bit ponderous and his trot too pronounced for my weight, it turned out that my legs were long enough to squeeze him tightly about the flanks. I was soon awash in the joy of riding and I remembered the afternoons in Foix when I'd gone riding with Aunt Margot—both of us mounted astraddle, as men do—along the edge of the forest until we met up with the road to Toulouse, where we would turn and race at a dead-level gallop all the way back to the château. (How grateful I am for the six years of riding lessons she paid for! The old cripple Laguerre, a former Captain who had lost an arm at Valmy and who lived, much beloved, in the village, used to tell me almost daily: "A horse, at the proper moment, can be worth more than a castle, mademoiselle. I will stop accepting payment from your Aunt when I see you gallop all the way to the forest ranger's cabin without using your hands, jump over the hedge and ford the river with the water up to your neck." That old centaur was the best teacher I could ever have asked for. When had Laguerre died? Why had I not asked after him when I returned to Foix? Oh, the things one leaves undone!) As I rode happily across the expansive plain, alongside the slow-moving train of carts and wagons, a feeling of independence swelled within me, a self-confidence that I'd never known before. For the first time ever, I felt in charge of my own life. I felt like a woman. As I dismounted, a resolution sank into my brain with the decisiveness of a nail: I would go to see Robert.

"You're mad," Maryse said, when I told her of my intention.

"Yes," I replied, laughing. "Mad with love. I want to see my man, I want to hug him and kiss him and speak to him of our wedding and tell him that I love him more than anything else in the world. I must see him, Maryse."

"Don't be a fool, Henriette. I wouldn't be able to go with you. Even if we were to buy another horse, I wouldn't know how to ride it. I'm a city girl, my dear. However," she added, suspecting that my decision was irrevocable, "there is Pierre. Pierre could go with you. Claudette or Françoise could drive your carriage and—"

"I appreciate your good intentions, but no. I feel I must go alone. After all, Robert is my business."

"You don't know what you're saying. Do you imagine that you can just trot calmly by an entire army division without anything happening to you? You'd do well to think of yourself as a jar of honey and of Lannes' troops as flies. Here, in the rearguard, things aren't so bad. But there, out in front of the provisions wagons, where the bugles sound at dawn, you'll be under the dominion of war. It's not by accident that the regulations prohibit women from visiting the troops."

"I've thought of all that. I'll pin up my hair and put on Pierre's Cuirassier's helmet. I'm sure he still has his white doublet among his things, as well as his blue dress livery. Françoise is an excellent seamstress and I know she could work miracles with all of that. What's more, I'll travel across the plain, bordering the road. From a distance, they'll take me for a Cuirassier."

"A Cuirassier! And where, may I ask, are your mustache, your saber and your cuirass? Did you forget them in Strasbourg, or at the encampment at Boulogne? Don't you see that, sooner or later, you'll have to travel on the road and mix in with the soldiers? For the love of God, Henriette, you're not a child anymore!"

Claudette and Françoise, who had been listening to us while roasting a rabbit under a solitary oak tree, came over to join in the conversation. Neither of them approved of my little adventure, particularly Françoise who, because of a few ill-fated affairs in Tarbes, where she was from, now kept her distance from men. But over the course of dinner, once they saw that I was not going to budge, they gave up trying to talk me out of it and fell silent.

"The fact is, you'll never pass as a Cuirassier," said Maryse, chewing pensively on a rabbit foot.

"I'm as tall as a man," I protested.

"It's not only height that makes a man, my sweet. Oh, how well I know that to be true! A man is many things," said Maryse.

"You could be an aide-de-camp, they are usually quite young," ventured Claudette timidly.

"No, no," interrupted Maryse. "Even the most inexperienced soldier knows what the different uniforms look like. Henriette would be noticed immediately. Some will think she's an Austrian spy; others, that she's a prostitute. It would not end well for her. We must think of a different disguise. Something improbable. The more improbable the better, in fact: a priest's frock, a Jew's topcoat, a Bavarian vest. The mustache won't be a problem. I have them in all colors and sizes in my costume trunk. I even have beards for a

Turk or a king. In Boulogne, we had the opportunity to perform parts from various operas, among them, *The Caliph of Bagdad* and *Richard the Lionheart*, both highly praised, I might add. I even managed to convince your beloved Robert," she added, flashing me a coquettish smile, "to perform an inspired rendition of a passage from Grétry's *Blue Beard*."

"With or without a beard, in a cassock or a topcoat, she won't fool anyone," asserted Françoise, shaking her head in disapproval. "What would your Aunt think of all this!"

"If Aunt Margot were here in my place, she wouldn't hesitate for even a second. In fact, she'd probably be in Robert's arms at this very moment," I replied blithely.

"Well, that's enough arguing," said Maryse. "May it be as God wills it. We'll just keep thinking."

In the end, it was Claudette who came up with the solution.

"We do have a Caliph's outfit," she murmured. "Wide-legged red pants, a green vest and a turban. Henriette could pass as a Mameluke. Their uniforms are very irregular. We also have a curved dagger and a scimitar."

"I've never once seen a Mameluke on these roads," said Françoise. "And anyway, I've heard that they have dark skin."

"Claudette is right," said Maryse, her eyes flashing with excitement. "The Mamelukes serve under General Savary, in the Imperial Guard. It might be assumed that you were delivering an important message. The matter of skin color is nothing; I have makeup for every possible race of humanity. The only problem I can foresee is that Mamelukes, when they open their mouths, invariably mangle our beautiful language."

"I know quite a bit of Spanish. I can imitate the Spanish accent," I said, enjoying myself. "I am a Mameluke with General Savarrry," I added, garbling the words and hollowing out my voice.

"That could work if you invert the genders of nouns and only use verbs in the infinitive. *Merde*, if Molière could only hear me!" concluded Maryse.

☙

And there I was, trotting along the left-hand side of the road, my skin tinted a chestnut brown and dressed up as a Caliph, although

I must have looked more like a Turkish clown, since every soldier I passed, without exception, pointed and burst out laughing at the sight of me: "Have a good day, Lieutenant Mohammed! Mecca is behind you, cretin! Ugh, it reeks of of camel! Has the carnival arrived?" they shouted. But the fact was, pressing ahead through the mockery and the laughter, I was getting closer and closer to Robert, and leaving the rest behind: the carts laden with barrels of flour, rice, peas and lentils, jugs of oil, strings of garlic, casks of wine and cognac and huge rocks of salt, as well as the contingent of walking meat—old cattle slavering at the mouth, lame and poorly patched-up horses. By midmorning I had already counted fifty wagons piled high with animal fodder, uniforms, saddles, harnesses and even drums. By noon, thanks to Jeudi's long stride, I had come to the ambulances, and to the wounded, calm and as silent as blindfolded marionettes waiting for someone to pull on their strings (and if Robert were among them?). Then I passed the wagons filled with powder kegs and munitions, the cannons pulled along by four horses—the howitzers by six—and the lines of artillerymen on foot, whose gray uniforms I had already learned to recognize. Then I left behind the endless companies of musketeers, many of them barefoot and in rags, some clenching empty pipes between their teeth, others talking amongst themselves, but most of them quite serious, surely thinking of all they were missing—a bed, a meal of roasted meat, the kiss of a loved-one. And thus marched the 5th Battalion on the road to Linz, across the plains and cropped, straw-colored fields, through a sudden cool breeze that foretold of rain, a wind out of the west that sent shakos and balls of snarled hay tumbling.

"Where are you going, Mameluke?" demanded a Dragoon lieutenant who, flanked by half a dozen men, had blocked my way.

"9th Hussars!" I cried, pulling up on the reins and forcing poor Jeudi, who was already past the point of exhaustion, to rear up on his hind legs.

"They are over there," said the lieutenant, looking at me curiously and extending his arm toward a distant cavalry troop whose colors were blurred in the whirls of dust and the strange violet light of that afternoon. "Your horse is on the verge of collapse," he added, noting Jeudi's ragged breathing and lathered muzzle. "But this is not a Mameluke's horse."

"Cuirassier horse. My horse break hoof," I said firmly.

61

"From whom is your message?" he asked, with a suspicious air.

"General Savary. Imperial Guard."

The lieutenant nodded assent. Before turning his horse, he advised me to dismount and to go by foot along the road. "You needn't hurry. We'll be stopping shortly, as soon as the sun sets . . . or the rain begins," he added, peering at the thick clouds in the western sky.

Accepting his advice, I crossed my leg over the fleece that covered Jeudi's saddle and jumped to the ground. After ten hours of riding, my muscles ached atrociously. I took a few steps and promptly realized that the pain in my waist and upper thighs would make it nearly impossible for me to walk. Suddenly, as though he'd only been waiting for me to climb off his back, the noble Jeudi folded his front legs, gave a muffled snort, and fell on his side, hooves in the air, smacking the ground with a dull and fatal thud. I knew immediately that there was nothing to be done. That old horse had fought his final battle. This time, he hadn't charged against an enemy battalion, but rather, against time, my time, my desire to reach Robert as soon as possible. And he had lost. Unable to stand, he'd be slaughtered at dawn and served to the musketeers I'd seen marching a few hours back. Yes, I thought, horrified, Jeudi will be disemboweled, quartered, and eaten, just like so many other useless horses. I could not bear to think of it further. I merely untied the saddlebag containing my jewels and papers, and abandoned the rest of my luggage. With an abrupt gesture, I turned away from Jeudi, and began walking toward the road, by now scarcely visible. My legs were stiff, as though made of wood. On top of everything, it started to rain, first a few fat, scattered drops that pelted my ridiculous turban like hailstones, but quickly becoming a torrential downpour.

I have no idea how far I walked. In my memory, I see myself— as sometimes happens in dreams—wandering through the rain and the night like a lost little girl, crying out in anguish and desolation, my voice gone hoarse from screaming Robert's name.

෴

This morning, as I always do after drinking my ounce of rum cured with garlic cloves—a Cuban remedy, highly recommended for rheumatism and as a strengthening tonic for the body—I began to revise the pages I wrote yesterday and crossed out, in red ink, many unnecessary adjectives, a defect characteristic of my writing, as is my illegible handwriting—a doctor's script that is difficult, even for Milly, to transcribe cleanly. I also discarded an episode that, no matter how hard I tried, I could not manage to narrate in a natural way, perhaps because, in it, I spoke of how I had finally reunited with Robert on that harrowing night. In any case, my conscience is clear; I have spared from posterity those "sublime and poignant lines"—as my Milly, ever the romantic, called them—in which I described our reunion, how safe I felt under his cloak, the tender words and professions of love that we whispered in each other's ears beneath the drumming of the rain, how, from then on, Robert called me, affectionately, "my little Turk." To complete my narrative of the episode, I'll mention that, days later, I entered Vienna hidden in a wagon belonging to Ma Valoin, sutler of the 9th Hussar battalion, a voluminous and good-natured woman, without whose complicity I would never have been able to remain by my lover's side.

Vienna surrendered on the 11th of November. The Grande Armée's triumphal march lasted two full days and nights, though I, myself, was witness only to the cavalry passing by. Although the Austrian Court had fled to Budapest, the vast majority of Viennese citizens did not appear to fear our troops, so much so, in fact, that thousands of them lined up, on both sides of the road, to watch, openmouthed and somewhat shamelessly, as the incomparable military machine that had conquered them paraded by. Upon seeing the Mamelukes pass by, I asked myself how on earth anyone had mistaken me for one of those exotic-faced Moors with jet-black eyes. It also amazed me, dressed now in Ma Valoin's drapey clothing, with a red handkerchief knotted about my head, that people were unable to see through my latest disguise. ("The habit makes the nun, my dear," Maryse would say, years later. "If you dress in mourning, you'll be a widow or an orphan; if you dress as an old woman, you'll look ten years older than you are; if you don an ermine cloak and a golden crown, you'll be a queen.") In any event, after spending an entire morning watching thousands of Grenadiers, Dragoons, Chasseurs, Cuirassiers, Carabineers, Gendarmes, Lancers, and Hussars file past, I had the thrill of seeing Robert parade by in his dress uniform, his saber unsheathed, his white glove holding the reins of his mount Patriote as delicately as if he were carrying a cup of tea. We were married that same week.

My honeymoon lasted for three nights—during the day Robert worked inspecting the city's arsenal, whose stores of weapons and gunpowder had been captured intact. I could narrate those nights one by one, during which Robert went about successively filling all the portals of my body with love, erasing the rushed and mediocre experience in Strasbourg. How shall I explain those long hours dedicated to my apprenticeship in the erotic arts? Though "apprenticeship" isn't the right word, since what I mean has to do with that false passivity of the novice who, though appearing to give herself over like a living statue, does so with all of her senses in a heightened state of alert; sight, touch, smell, sound, taste, all of them presaging pleasure, anticipating it by means of a damp and secret memory, an ancient memory that goes beyond instinct and that springs fluidly forth from the great goddesses, the immortal women, Hera, Leto, Demeter, Aphrodite. How can I describe those hours during which my body signed the sexual contract once and for all, the contract of all contracts, origin of all origins, the indelible writing of the fingers and the nipples, of the tongue and the clitoris, of the unyielding junctions and the intimate liquors? What words could I use to recreate, with my pen, the fatigue that comes from continual pleasure, that fainting from desire at the end of the night, when starlight and candlelight burn out to make way for a clear dawn of sweat-soaked sheets, tousled hair, and swollen eyelids, when sleep, sudden and heavy, drapes over the temples like an iron crown, vanquishing the body, exhausted, fingernail-raked, bitten, sucked, bruised; a body that soon wakes, yawning and stretching sleep-numbed arms to bolster itself with a breakfast of wine and cold meats and pleasantries until a deliberate kiss ignites desire all over again?

"I can't anymore, Robert. I can't," I'd told him. "If I don't get up this very minute, I'll die between these sheets. I need to come up for air. And anyway, I must see to the matter of my dowry."

And a short time later, bathed, my hair done up, bejeweled and attired like a Viennese lady—I'd spent the last of my money on two new dresses, a cape and a hat—I watched as Robert braided his hair down the sides of his face and waxed his mustache in front of the mirror, an operation he carried out with great seriousness in spite of my teasing. Satisfied with our appearances, we said goodbye to

Frau Wittek, the widow who'd provided us with a room on the second story of her house on Bäkerstrasse, and stepped out into a lustrous morning in which the sun set the colors of the fallen leaves ablaze with light and shone cleanly on the monumental façades of Vienna—St. Stephen's Cathedral, the Hofburg Palace. . . . Oh, my beloved Robert, how proud I felt on your arm as we wandered the streets in search of the banker that the kind priest at St. Michael's had recommended to us. How surprised I'd been by your command of German: *Guten Morgen, gnädige Frau. Wir suchen Herrn Kesslers Bureau.* Once we'd found the house, we crossed the vestibule and entered a busy office in which several men with black bankers' sleeves affixed to their shirts were pouring over account ledgers and piles of papers. "Herr Kessler?" Robert inquired, and an elderly man, hunched and very pale, with hairy, agile hands, stopped moving the balls on an abacus and stood up.

Herr Kessler spent half an hour carefully examining our papers, scrutinizing mine in particular. Finally, he cleared he throat and addressed Robert in a guttural and disjointed French: "Everything appears to be in order, isn't that so? Were it not for the war. . . . Ah, the war. . . . I would be able to advance you a larger amount. Surely you understand. . . . The collection fees, no? Excessive, Monsieur Renaud, excessive. Just imagine, a bill of exchange to be cashed in Toulouse. We are in Vienna. . . . Such an ill-fated war, don't you think? Well, we shall be able to do something for you. Not much, to be sure, in these times. . . . There is hardly any money left at our disposal. And gold, well, gold is scarce, monsieur. The Emperor has taken it with him to Hungary. Of course, I realize . . . you are a newlywed. . . . The madame has a dowry. . . . Quite a large amount, I should be able to advance something to you . . . " And on and on he went, talking without pause as he consulted a mysterious ledger that he had taken from his desk drawer, and knocked the balls on the abacus together, moving them from here to there with vertiginous speed.

"And?" said Robert impatiently.

"I can give you, tomorrow, at the same time . . . four hundred Guldens."

"We need five hundred," bartered Robert.

In the end, the amount was fixed at four hundred twenty-five Guldens. Since Robert was to rejoin his regiment the following day, early, as always—Lannes had not stopped over in Vienna and was already on the march in the direction of Olmütz—Herr Kessler agreed to bring the money to me at the flat on Bäkerstrasse, initiating a business relationship between us that would be revived some months later.

With nothing better to do until six that evening when the opera would begin, we headed toward the Prater, an enormous park on the outskirts of the city that we'd been told was nothing short of miraculous. (You, reading me now, if you can travel through time—and I say this with more hope than irony—do not fail to visit the Prater of my youth. There you will find gorgeous paths lined with chestnut trees, shops, cafés, taverns, restaurants where you'll eat fried chicken and drink Pilsner beer and Hoffner wine. Seated at a table facing the Danube, you'll admire the tall willow trees that line its banks and the groups of deer, gentle as sheep, that graze upon the grass. If you like horses, as I do, you could ride on an excellent course without fear of crashing into anyone, or step up to an arena at which you'll be dazzled by daring equestrian exercises. Or, you might simply pass the time watching the children wave to their parents as they spin about on a carousel, mounted on brightly-colored plaster steeds. If you're a lover of music and dance, follow the main avenue until you come to the Augarten, where you'll find dance and concert halls and where the air is filled with waltzes and marches and songs and the sweet murmurings of lovers.) After a lunch of sausages and beer, we returned to the city.

Despite the normalcy with which the Viennese had carried on with their daily lives, at sunset they began to return to their houses. Few people remained in the streets, and, upon arriving at the theater, we saw that the foyer was nearly empty. There were scarcely any women, and the men, for the most part, were officials with the Grand Armée. Given the low attendance, we had no trouble securing a pair of box seats. As the orchestra was tuning their instruments, a hushed murmur ran through the theater; a dignitary with gray hair and a deliberate mien had just occupied the Imperial box. "It's Talleyrand, the Grand Chamberlain of the Empire," whispered Robert, rising from his seat to stand behind me, his bearskin hat resting, in a soldierly manner, between his forearm and right shoulder. At a sudden burst of applause, I turned my gaze to the orchestra pit. In walked the conductor, a small, bespectacled, dark-haired man who acknowledged the applause with a brusque nod of his head, then sat down perfunctorily on the bench in front of the pianoforte. I looked at the program. He was the composer of *Fidelio*, the opera being premiered that evening. The music was quite good but what really fascinated me—possibly because Robert had sunk his fingers into my hair and was caressing the nape of my neck—was to see how the resolute Leonore, having donned men's clothing in order to rescue her husband, went about seducing the jailor's daughter, arousing in her an ardent passion that resonated within me. Motioning to Robert to bend his head near mine, I whispered in his ear: "You see, I'm not the only one who dresses as a man to get what she wants." Robert smiled and said nothing. That night, the last we'd spend together on Bäkerstrasse, we made love until dawn. When we said our goodbyes and I begged him to be careful, he began a sentence, but left it unfinished, as if he had decided that saying it would have hurt me too much: "Any hussar who hasn't died . . . " Then he kissed me once more and, looking me in the eyes, murmured: "I'll be careful, my little Turk."

؆

All my efforts to locate Maryse and Françoise in Vienna had failed. And not only that; I had reason to believe that I might not see them again for a long time. It was rumored that days ago, near Linz, a pack of marauders had attacked the women and merchants following the army. True or not, the fact was that all camp followers had been detained in Linz, making it impossible for them to continue on to Vienna. The detention order had come down from the General Staff, and had been published in the *Wiener Zeitung*, now directed by an Austrian in the service of the French. Robert himself had translated the curt text for me on the morning of our wedding. As it was rumored in the cafés, the order was an attempt to mitigate the burden on the Viennese, who would already be overwhelmed with the necessity of feeding and housing the twenty thousand men that Napoleon would leave behind to secure the city. "Don't worry," Robert had said, seeing my anxiety rise. "You know Maryse. She'll find a way to get to Vienna and find out where I'm stationed. If she arrives after I've finished my assignment, I'll leave her a note in the arsenal." But a week had gone by and there was still no word from her.

Fortunately, the same was not true of my uncle, who appeared at Frau Wittek's door two days after Robert left. Always thinking ahead, Doctor Larrey had determined that, while the bulk of the medical service would follow the Imperial Guard on their march to Moravia, Uncle Charles would remain in Vienna to organize large-scale convalescent hospitals. When I told him of my adventures as a Mameluke and of how I'd found Robert in the middle of that stormy night, Uncle Charles rose from the armchair and took me in his arms as affectionately as if I were his own daughter. "You have no idea how happy it makes me that things have gone well for you. Your aunt must be helping you from heaven. I owe you a wedding gift. You know, army life is not easy for any woman, but it's especially difficult for unmarried women. Anyway, have you heard from Maryse?" he asked in an off-handed manner, returning to his chair.

"I'm sure she's in Linz. Françoise too. If I could get my hands on a safe-conduct pass that would allow me to come and go freely, I'd rent a carriage and go in search of them," I said, hoping that he would help me attain such a permit.

Frau Wittek appeared in the doorway and gestured for us to come to the table. Refusing to sit with us, probably for patriotic reasons, she served us the wine that Robert had bought, white bread and the best of what she had left in her cupboard. She was a good woman who, torn between loyalty to her country and her habit of treating her guests with generosity, couldn't make up her mind how to behave with me, the wife of an invader.

After helping himself to a thick slice of ham, my uncle raised his glass and said: "A toast to those not with us tonight."

"Yes," I said, raising my glass as well, "and may their absence be brief." Swallowing my first mouthful, I added: "You have no idea how much I miss Maryse."

"Maryse, yes, of course. I miss her too. We are good friends. It's just that now is not the best moment to travel to Linz," said my uncle, and, turning to address Frau Wittek, who was setting a delicious-looking apple tart on the table, he said, still smiling: "Your mother was a whore and your food smells like shit."

Frau Wittek, whose knowledge of French was limited to two words—the *bon jour* with which I greeted her each morning—smiled back, and served him an enormous helping of apple tart.

"Well, one can never be too sure. There are many spies," Uncle

Charles said, by means of apology. "The fact is, somewhere in Moravia we will fight a great battle against Kutuzov's Russian troops, who are coming down from the East with Czar Alexander, and against what remains of the Austrian Army. Only Napoleon knows exactly where it will take place. Larrey told me this before leaving. It will be a decisive battle. Just imagine it; a battle of three emperors."

And, as it happened, this was precisely what Austerlitz would come to be called: the battle of the three emperors. At first it was nothing more than a rumor, dismissed by most of the Viennese; then, as the details of the great French victory came out in the newspapers, many said it was pure Bonapartist propaganda; days later, when the prisoners and the wounded began to arrive in the city by the thousands, there were some who still insisted that those ragged men were Russian deserters, forced to take part in some great ruse. But—as Aunt Margot always said when faced with an undeniable truth—one cannot cover the sun with a finger, especially not the sun of Austerlitz, the sun that illuminated, as no other, Napoleon's military career.

4

I HAVE SEEN THE SOLDIERS of many nations in my lifetime. I've seen them dressed in black, green, gray, white, yellow, blue, and red; I've seen them in shakos, fur caps, plumed helmets, and turbans; I've seen them on the battlefield, in taverns, in hospitals, in parades, in concert halls and in theaters; I've seen them in times of war and in times of peace, in triumph and in defeat. And so, I can attest to the fact that none of them could ever compare to the allure of the French Hussars of 1805. Of course, their resplendent uniforms had something to do with it. But there was something else, a rare magnetism that radiated from within them and that united them despite their different ages and features. The night I met Robert, I couldn't put a finger on what made him so irresistibly attractive. Nor could I in Vienna. It wasn't until after the peace at Austerlitz that I figured it out, when his regiment was stationed in Bavaria and I spent a good deal of time with several of his friends. It's that the Hussars under Napoleon lived to die, and it was the enchantment of death that defined them, that fleeting splendor of twilight, the rose unfurled, the autumn leaf. "Any Hussar who hasn't died by the age of thirty is a coward," General Lasalle, the most respected among the Hussars, would always say. And that terrible sentence had become popular in the Grand Armée; it was the sentence Robert had left unfinished that morning in Vienna.

The ten months of peace that we enjoyed were more than enough time for me to realize that Lasalle's words would be prophetic for Robert. The first sign occurred in Passau, where he was recovering in the hospital from a severe saber wound. We were strolling peacefully through the hospital's garden, surrounded by thrushes and tulips, when the postman arrived, carrying a bundle of letters and several small wooden boxes. "They're crosses," said Robert, letting go of me. "Crosses of the Legion of Honor." And, leaning on his cane, he limped eagerly over to the bench where the postman had sat down to remove the medals from his haversack. Somewhat perplexed by the brusqueness of his behavior, I hung back on the path. From that vantage, I saw him gesticulating and scolding the man for taking so long to lay the boxes out upon the bench. I saw him pick one up, open it nervously and hold the medallion in front of his nose as though it were a glass of fine wine. I heard him exclaim, exhilarated: "My cross, my cross has arrived at last!" And, turning to look at me, he cried: "Look, my little Turk, my cross! When they kill me, they'll bury me with it!"

But the thing that most convinced me was listening to him read the *Moniteur*, the French newspaper that arrived consistently, although somewhat delayed, in the cafés in Munich. Surrounded by Hussars, the table covered with mugs of beer, I listened to Robert read every article, every official communication aloud, in search of some indication that the war they all yearned for would soon begin. "It will come, soon, it will come, there's no reason to worry, we'll soon have another go at the Russians, at old Kutuzov, at Bagration, and at the Prussians too, that herd of perverts, if you'll forgive me, *citoyenne*, they'll be the first, followed by the Saxons, that accursed breed, just you wait, Robert, just you wait, Michel, just you wait, Jean-Louis, just you wait, Constant, and those cowards have the gall to call themselves the Hussars of Death. *Merde, we* are the true Hussars of death!" Hours went by like this, pining for the war, their sabers ever sharp, the barrels of their pistols clean, their horses healthy and well trained. Oh, the horses! Early on, I discovered that Robert had a good deal of the centaur about him, that he and Patriote were a unified and effective war machine, deployed daily, parting only at sunset: Patriote to the barracks' stables, Robert to the cafés, where I would find him speaking excitedly, smoking his pipe, his mustache dripping with beer, singing the praises of the saber over the lance, of the light horse over the Percheron draft.

Apart from Robert, none of those Hussars were married. None of them shared their wine or their dinners with the whores who'd come along from Metz and Strasbourg, or with the German girls they dabbled with. They were a brotherhood of single men, a type of chivalric society with Napoleon as Grand Master, all of them young and tall and beautiful and conceited and doomed. I never knew why they tolerated my presence. Perhaps because of their collective admiration for Robert, or because they saw me riding in *culottes* and hunting jacket, or because I had learned to hold my liquor almost as well as them and because whenever anyone would finish speaking I would say things like: "That's right, monsieur," "I do agree," "well said," and the like. Probably, although I don't like to think of it, they also accepted me because they knew that Robert's money came from my dowry—now fully cashed, thanks to the ministrations of Herr Kessler and my lawyer in Toulouse—and that, of my own accord, I was the owner of valuable lands and a château in the Languedoc. Rare was the week that Robert didn't put on a grand five- or six-course banquet, or an evening of musicians and singers, or lost a hundred francs on the gambling table, or surprised me with a piece of diamond jewelry. We bought a large house and I finally had my enormous bed with white pillows and my cuckoo clock; he, a stuffed crocodile and a rhinoceros horn—old fantasies for each of us. The rooms quickly filled with furs and animal heads, rugs, drapes, flower vases, tapestries—one depicted a courtly tableau and the other, the head of a deer—tailors, dressmakers, fencing instructors and incompetent painters who did portraits of us together, and separately, and even on horseback. We didn't have a cook because Robert wasn't accustomed to home-cooked food and preferred to allow the hostelry to take care of meals. For a maid, we had Ma Valoin, who, seeing her clientele diminish in this time of peace, had decided to shutter her wine and cognac wagon, and accept the irresistible salary that Robert had offered her. Another presence in the house was Bernard, an orderly who spent his working hours shining boots, ironing uniforms, and pilfering coins from our pockets. One might say that I was foolish to allow such squandering of our money, or even that I was weak. One might also believe that I was too timid or insecure. But, though it's true that when I first met Robert I was all of those things, the march from Boulogne to Vienna, the death of Aunt Margot, my friendship with Maryse, my relationship with Uncle Charles, the dangers of war, the company of the Hussars and the discovery of physical pleasure had changed me into a different person altogether. If I never suggested to Robert that he limit his spending, that he should think of the future and of the children we might have, it was because it would have been utterly useless. What's more, I didn't do it because I, too, had learned to squeeze every drop out of the moment, because I knew that come the next war, or the war after that, death would separate us.

We made love almost every night; we did it in the big white bed or on one of his furs; we did it limitlessly, without forethought, whenever the mood struck us, sometimes tattooing each other in scratches and bite marks, at others, trembling with tenderness. After midnight, our fountains gone dry, floating, we would find each other again, through words, professing our love and saying that everything was just right and how lucky we were to be together and that when the war ended we would move to Foix and go hunting and give grand banquets and dances and watch many children grow up and grow sweetly old together among horseback rides and pastoral violins. Sometime we fought. We fought over silly things and he would shout at me and I'd hurl shoes, bottles, and elaborate Hussar insults at him. But soon we'd make up, each of us taking the blame for having started the quarrel. On Sundays we'd stroll through the city and have lunch at the hostelry or at a café. In the afternoons we'd entertain ourselves playing cards or chess, although we played other games too; that we were God and could create the world anew, for example, beginning with a second Earthly Paradise—which we would describe in exhaustive detail on the embossed *Intendance* paper—full of everything except forbidden fruits, talking serpents, and trees of the knowledge of good and evil. Other times we played the difficult-to-attain-treasure game, searching the house for an imaginary prize, guided by a crack in the parquet floor, the gaze of the Florentine lady in the painting that hung in the vestibule, the slant of a nail, or a sudden ray of sunlight filtering through a slit in the window, finally reaching a hand under a piece of furniture to pull out a stray stocking, a button from his fur cape or a dusty plum, finds we would celebrate with great merriment and Rhine wine, pretending that life was an eternal lark, as if, in some way, we already knew that it was to be our last summer together.

∞

And in the middle of the summer Corinne arrived, with her beautiful eyes and her shabby shoes. I can still see her in the doorway, a cheap traveling case in her hand, asking resolutely after her brother Robert. Stunned, with no idea what to say, I stepped aside to allow her in.

"Robert is away for Field Exercises. Four days. He'll return on Saturday," I said, motioning for her to sit on the davenport.

I knew for certain that she was Robert's old lover. Surely she had presented herself as his sister in order to avoid any uncomfortable explanations; perhaps, in her place, I would have done the same. I don't know why but, seeing her seated rigidly on the edge of the sofa, looking obliquely at the tapestries, it occurred to me that she'd had a baby by Robert and had now come seeking money. But as she spoke, I realized with growing alarm that she seemed not to be lying, that Corinne was revealing herself to be, quite plausibly, Robert's sister, and not just that, but his Jewish sister because, to begin with—as difficult as it was for me to believe—Robert's name wasn't Robert, but Yossel Dorfman, although she'd always called him Yossi. They had been born in Haguenau, near Strasbourg, first him and then her, as she was a year his junior.

"My father, like his father before him, was a shoemaker, a poor man, though not uneducated," she said, after drinking a glass of wine, hurriedly, in the same way she was telling her unlikely story. "Yossi and I left home years ago, although not together. Times had changed and it was the young people's moment. It was not uncommon for Jewish boys of Yossi's age to buy a birth certificate with a Christian name and go off in search of a better destiny, a patriotic destiny. Wars claim lives, madame, but they also offer opportunities. My experience was also fairly common. I went to Italy with a man, Jean Blanchard, a quartermaster who obliged me to be baptized before he'd give me his name. He wasn't a bad person. He died in a dark alley, stabbed to death. I never found out why. In any case, with what little I had, I went to Paris. There I found work as a seamstress in a uniform factory. Do you know how many stitches there are in a Hussar's dress uniform, madame?"

"Many, I'm sure," I said, perplexed, asking myself what this woman, who'd fallen on my home like a mortar shell, could possibly want from me.

"Many, no, madame. So many. Thousands upon thousands. You have no idea how long it takes to sew an entire uniform. I made sleeves. How many sleeves must I have made! Thousands and thousands. As for Yossi, I can tell you that he always dreamed of becoming a cavalry soldier. When he was twelve years old, when he was still a shoemaker's apprentice, he ran away from home to go to work as a stable boy at the guardhouse in Strasbourg. From there he went to war under a different name and has not been home since. He doesn't even write. And it's not that Yossi is a bad son, madame. Surely you'll understand that being Jewish is quite a disadvantage," she said, pausing, as if to give me time to take in her turbid tale which, for some reason, although I told myself it couldn't be true, was slowly turning my insides to ice. How could I ever accept Robert's deceit, his hypocrisy?

"Of course Yossi will have told you all of this. And it's not just religion that makes us different; it's also our customs, our traditions. My father, for example, used to throw my letters into the fire without reading them, and if my mother heard anything from me it was because I wrote to her at a friend's address. Even today, mute and paralyzed though he is, I can read the rage in my father's eyes at my presence. Our tradition is strict. Don't misunderstand me, madame, but I know Yossi much better than you do. You should forgive him his . . . how shall I put it? His eccentricities. It's not easy to pull the past up by the roots, the name of one's father and grandfather, the rituals of the faith one was born into. It's not easy, madame. You must know of the poverty, of the filth of our neighborhoods, and, more than anything else, of the hatred and the scorn that we inspire; that's the worst part. Jews are conscripted into the army, but only as cannon fodder. You'll not find a single Jewish name among the Hussars. That's why I didn't hesitate to go to Boulogne and pass myself off as his lover."

"But what do you mean, madame? Please, explain yourself!" I said, standing up and backing toward the wall.

"Well, just think of it. The troops had been deployed for so long, for more than two years, and Yossi would have called attention to himself had he not had a woman in all that time. After all, he was a Hussar, a man of honor and reputation. But is it possible that you didn't know that we lived together in Boulogne?" she said, seeing my expression of disbelief. "Well, if you don't believe me, just ask his friend, Madame Polidor. She visited us on occasion. An enchanting woman. Yossi fought a duel for her. Don't worry, madame, it was not a romantic entanglement. Her lover, an officer with a foreign-sounding last name, hit her in public and Yossi cuffed him.

'A lovely gesture that will add to my reputation,' he told me when he returned home. Reputation. That's the most important thing to Yossi, madame. To have a good reputation. To be respected in his regiment. To be loved by women such as yourself."

Crying with indignation and shame, I let myself sink down the wall to the floor. Crouched in the corner, I covered my face with my hands. Just when I thought I'd hit the bottom of that well of humiliation, along came the biggest insult of all: "But what camp follower in Boulogne could be trusted? They're all whores, madame. If Yossi didn't sleep with them, they would say he was impotent; if he did, they would tell everyone that he's circumcised, a Jew. I served as his cover, until he met you."

But if what that woman said were true, Robert had remained celibate for more than two years, an unimaginable situation knowing, as I did, the blazing urgency of his desire. Who, then, had been his lover, if not his very own sister?

Corinne's voice broke: "My God, madame, you don't think that Yossi and I—!"

"What is the purpose of your visit?" I asked, incensed, wiping my eyes with the hem of my dress. "Tell me what you want. I have things to do."

"The purpose of my visit? I need money, something that you and Yossi have plenty of. You see, my father, as I've said, has suffered an attack of paralysis and mama has nothing. I wrote to Yossi at the barracks, as I always do. I had already written to him at the Passau hospital to tell him that I had returned home to Haguenau, but he's stopped responding to my letters and we have run out of time. We are penniless, madame. Plain and simple. I had to sell our grandfather's watch, the only thing of his we had left, to pay for this visit. If only Yossi had been at the barracks. . . . "

"How am I to know that you aren't lying?" I interrupted her, defiant.

"Look at my face, madame. Look at it carefully and tell me that you don't see him. Don't you recognize your Robert's eyes, his lips? They are our mother's."

"Enough! You shall have your money!" I said, standing up suddenly. I had recently received the rent from my tenant at Foix through my lawyer, Monsieur Lebrun. I ran to the bedroom and emptied the desk drawer of money into a pillowcase.

"Here. This is all I can give you," I said, holding out the bundle. She grabbed it from my hands and looked inside.

"It's a lot," she said with an ironic smile. "Enough to buy Yossi's entire past—no? But what am I saying? I meant the honorable Hussar Lieutenant Jean-Baptiste-Robert Renaud. Neither you nor your husband will ever see my face again. Take care, madame," she added sarcastically, and abruptly turned her back to me.

How I missed Maryse in the days that followed! But Maryse was traveling through the Grand Armée encampments in Germany with a wagon and three carriages—one of them mine—putting on shows with the help of Pierre and Françoise, who, as I learned from her letters, had become actors. Though, in truth, the fact that I weathered that spiritual storm alone had its benefits; it allowed me to discover a part of myself I'd never known existed, a shameful part, I must admit. Because not only did I reproach Robert for his inexcusable deception; I also reproached him for being a Jew.

During those days I barely ate, and drank nothing but water. I locked myself in the bedroom, a prisoner to my own mind. Standing in front of the mirror in my nightshirt, my hair uncombed, I confronted a hypothetical Robert, practicing my harangue, throwing his betrayal in his face, demanding that he go back to the barracks and leave me alone until Maryse came back with my servants and my carriages. But in the end, I threw myself on the bed with choking sobs, knowing that I wasn't going to break with him, that I didn't have the strength to leave him. And it was my love for him that hurt the most, my unjustifiable love for that traitorous and opportunistic Hussar who only wanted me for my money, my love that, come what may, he would never deserve. But in a small corner of my pain I soon found a handhold, something to grab onto, an excuse that I held up in front of my own eyes that would allow me to stay with him: the war with Prussia was imminent. Robert would die and the least I could do was to bury him with his cross. It was the certainty that he was going to die that, for an instant, dissuaded me from leaving him, that made me swing, like a pendulum, from one conviction to another, trapped between rupture and reconciliation. If only he weren't a Jew. Did Maryse and Uncle Charles know? And if someone were to find out? And if Corinne continued to blackmail me and the day came when I could no longer pay her? And even if that didn't happen, why assume that she and Robert hadn't been lovers, hadn't rolled about like pigs in the muddy filth of incest? How was it possible that I had fallen in love with an incestuous Jew? How would I feel entering a dancehall on his arm, people whispering behind our backs? And once again, the pendulum would swing back the other way. What did it really mean that he was Jewish? What was written on his face or in his character that would damn him? Because eyes like his were common among the Marseillaise, the Spanish and the Italians, not to mention the Corsicans and the Creoles from the islands, and even Josephine and Napoleon himself. And really, what proof did I have that he and Corinne had been lovers, why not believe that he'd had a secret lover in Boulogne, some married woman with whom he couldn't be seen in public? And in any case, aside from their reputation as leeches, I had to admit that I knew absolutely nothing about those men in black overcoats who had followed us from the Rhine all the way to the Danube, buying silver, clothing, shoes, and stolen objects at one tenth of their value, then turning around and selling them at a profit. But silly me—I remembered with relief—what of the clockmaker in Strasbourg? He could not possibly have been kinder to me. Maryse and I had slept in his bedroom, his distant songs sweetening our dreams. And wasn't I in favor of equality for all in the eyes of the law, had I not always defended this principle against Aunt Margot's contrary opinion? In short, what harm had the Jews ever done to me? There didn't seem to be any in Foix, or if there had been, I'd never noticed. I had to admit that, for me, they were little more than a vague entity that came into being who knew when: a scattered biblical tribe that didn't believe that Jesus was the Son of God; a passionate and miserly people who attended temples called synagogues in which rabbis officiated and who circumcised their male babies. ("Circumcision," a word I'd discovered in Aunt Margot's dictionary—my secret source of knowledge—along with "penis," "foreskin," "testicles," and "semen," words that aroused me just to read them, and made me want to masturbate. How was I to know that Robert was one of them, I, who'd only ever seen the gardener urinating from a distance?) Ultimately, I had no reason to reproach Robert for having been born Jewish—he wasn't stingy, wasn't a money-lender, and didn't practice Judaism—but even so, he was circumcised, and that thought alone was enough to torment me.

Joyful shouts from the other side of the door shook me from the exhausting seesawing of my emotions: Robert had returned. That night we made love, as was to be expected after an absence, my gaze seeking out his penis, trying to guess what it had originally looked like, wondering what other men's penises, untouched by the rabbi's knife, might be like. But, as the days passed that pernicious curiosity waned. Almost without realizing it, the moment arrived when the only thing I faulted him for was his deception, his lack of honesty. And for that, I had not forgiven him.

I chose to remain silent. What would I have accomplished had I thrown his lies in his face? But even if it's true that I never told him about Corinne's visit, it's equally true that my reserve, joined now with his, drew new parameters around my love, a less luminous configuration, still beautiful, but mediated by the compromises of guilt and blame. Soon my relationship with Robert ceased to be the absolute surrender that it had been in the days before Corinne. My orgasms, which before had always opened the doors to heaven, were now limited, even mediocre. Yes, my love had lost not only passion but also innocence, freshness, and the game of playing God now seemed stupid to me; I preferred to match him, hand to hand, on the green cloth of the game table. The get-togethers with the other Hussars began to bore me with their predictability, and instead of going down to meet him in the café I would wait for him at home, playing the piano or lying on the sofa reading what Madame de Staël had to say about literature, or an enormous tome of Shakespeare in translation.

Robert, for his part, threw himself into winning me back, without knowing that nothing could ever restore things to the place where they had shined the brightest, to that place of illusion. He did everything within his power: gifts, kind gestures, professions of love. Like a child who needs to be the center of attention, he did extravagant things like shaving his head and trying to make me jealous by flirting with the magistrate's daughter. When he'd tried everything, he got drunk and told me the truth, told me he was Jewish and that his last name was Dorfman and that he'd been born to a shoemaker in Haguenau.

"I already knew that you were a Jew," I said, hoping to wound him, to make him pay for the suffering he'd caused me. "I've known since that night in Strasbourg. There are some things that can't be hidden."

Oh, human nature!

But oddly, in belittling his confession, in seeing him defeated and drunk—in his last months he never stopped drinking—a feeling of compassion moved me to thank him for his belated honesty with a caress to the cheek and a: "I'm glad you told me." I led him by the hand to the bed and began to undress him tenderly, as if he were a child. Afterwards, he fell asleep, and I remained there, pressed up against him.

The reinitiation of the war did us good. As soon as Field Marshal Lannes arrived from Paris, I went to see him in his office. As Robert was on duty, guarding the barracks, I was perfectly content waiting in the foyer until nearly midnight. Lannes received me without interrupting his work. He had a pleasant face and a beautiful mouth. Through Robert, I knew that he was thirty-six years old and that Napoleon considered him his friend.

"Yes, *citoyenne*?" he said, seeing me enter, almost without lifting his eyes from the enormous map spread across his desk. Standing before him, I spoke quickly, and got straight to the point: I wanted to accompany my husband to the war because I knew that he was going to die. I had followed him from Boulogne to Vienna and did not fear long marches.

"And how did you manage to enter Vienna?" he asked, placing the point of his compass on the map.

"First I dressed as a Mameluke and then as a sutler," I replied.

"I see. Congratulations, *citoyenne*. You are a good patriot and you love Renaud well," he said and, turning to one of his assistants, he ordered: "Tell Huet to name this woman as second sutler to the 9th Hussars."

❧

Saalfeld, Jena, Auerstedt. . . . It took only two weeks in October to sweep away the Prussian army. Since Ma Valoin's wagon traveled at the rear of the regiment, the only time I saw Robert was when he turned up wounded. He came on foot, his fur soaked in blood. A musket ball had opened a furrow in his neck and he was walking with his head exposed and rigid. The surgeon had insisted that he go to the wagons for the wounded but he'd refused, explaining: "Do you imagine, my little Turk, that I would ever pass up an opportunity to sleep with you?" Ma Valoin made space for us and, curling up in her sheepskins, she spent the night between the wagon's wheels. We didn't sleep; he couldn't. Excited from the battle, he told me how the Prussian cavalry had been decimated, how a Hussar named Guindet, an old friend of his, had killed Prince Louis Ferdinand with his saber.

"But this is only the beginning. You'll see. A great battle is coming. We'll take Berlin, just as we took Vienna," he said, enthusiastically.

As I listened to him talk in the darkness, hoping in vain that he'd offer me a kind word, or even take an interest in me, I decided once and for all that Robert was not made for times of peace. As much as he loved me, he would always love the war more. In the end, Corinne had been right: Wars claimed lives, but for people like Robert, they represented the means to achieving a personal destiny, and this was something that neither I, nor anyone else, could ever offer him. At the break of dawn, he drank his glass of cognac while I changed the bandage on his wound. Then he put on his clean uniform, gave a gold coin to Ma Valoin, and kissed me on the forehead. "Off I go, my little Turk. It's time to reap some Prussian hay."

A short time later, Berlin already occupied, we celebrated his promotion to captain. He was ecstatic: Lannes had given him a leopard skin to drape over his saddle. We were happy again for a few days, but it was a provisional happiness, one we had to feed continuously—usually by trying to make one another laugh—like a bird that required constant care to ensure that it would keep singing. We no longer spoke of the things we would do together after the war was over. In December, in a shabby guesthouse in Warsaw on the eve of a somber winter campaign, Robert, already very drunk, suddenly stopped laughing. On the way back to the hotel, he had slipped on a sheet of ice covering the street, pulling me down with him as he fell. Later, in our room, with a melancholy smile that I'd never seen before, he stood up and staggered toward the window, broke one of the frosty windowpanes with his fist and hurled his glass of vodka to the street.

"You could have thrown it into the fire," I said, from the bearskin rug where we'd been stretched out.

"No, my little Turk. If I'd done that, you would never have remembered this moment. We only remember the exceptional things, the strange things."

"And why do you want me to remember this moment? The

room smells bad, the soup is cold and I've had too much to drink. So have you, don't you think?"

Robert, leaning against the wall so as not to fall over, raised his cut hand to his face and began to lick the wound with all the gusto of a stray dog. He looked pathetic.

"It's not only this moment, my little Turk. It's all of them, it's everything," he stammered. "I mean, you and me . . . every moment. It's hard to explain. Don't pay me any mind."

Then he zigzagged his way back to me and collapsed at my side, his left arm encircling my waist. (Odd, how inconsistent our memories are. Once again, I've tried to remember the music of our first waltz, to no avail. And yet I can still feel the weight of his motionless arm on that night, smell his vodka-and-tobacco-laced breath on my cheek, and hear the ceaseless wails of a small child in the next room.) It took me a very long time to fall asleep. When I awoke, he had already left.

After the terrible battle at Pultusk, widowed and weeping in desolation, I stared at length at his uniforms, his pipes, his things on the dressing table. I had decided not to take any of his things with me. What purpose would it serve? Everything would remain there, just as he had left it in that frigid room in Warsaw. As I was leaving, my eyes came to rest on the piece of newspaper covering the hole in the windowpane, and suddenly I understood what he'd been trying to say that night. It wasn't just that moment that I should remember, but all of the moments I had lived with him. Breaking the window, hurling the vodka glass and licking his wound marked out the sequence of a metaphor for our marriage; a compact poem that alluded to the space where, bewitched at first glance by his persuasive charm, I'd been drawn into a kind of emotional duel whose feints, retreats, attacks and blows I would carry in my memory like indelible scars. Taking his death as a given, he had shaped me as if I were one of those miniature oriental temples that, patiently carved out of a piece of marble, represent the entire life of the artisan. Even his final words, terrible and sad, which he'd uttered in the hospital, throwing up blood, had been to that purpose: "Ah, it's you. Doesn't it seem that spring is awfully late to arrive here in Foix?"

Yes, it's true that there is reason to think that Robert married me for money. There is also reason to think that it was Robert himself who sent Corinne to test the strength of my love. But the threads of life are not tied together with reason. He saw something in me that impelled him to choose me as his great work, his grand project; so that his memory would live on in the world of my dreams, so that he might reign supreme in the limbo of my memory, my nostalgia, in the place where loneliness is less perishable. And I'm grateful to him for it.

Did he achieve his goal from beyond the grave? Yes and no. The deep chord of his presence still vibrates within me. How could it fail to be so, when it was he who launched me into the world? But it vibrates alongside other, no less sonorous chords, which come together to form something like an arpeggio. Did he truly love me? I believe he did. He loved me as much as he was capable of loving, as much as a man who no longer belongs entirely to this world can love. A man who had risen above his lineage and religion in order to become someone, in order to conquer me and his cross of honor and his posthumous rank as squadron leader; in order to prove to himself that he was no less than the best of them. Robert made me a woman so that I would never forget him, so that I'd become his funeral urn, his great pyramid. He loved himself through me. His love—there really is no other way to see it—was as selfish as the pharaohs. "But, my little Turk, is there any love in this world that isn't selfish?" he's just whispered in my ear. Robert, my Hussar of death.

MARYSE

5

AT THE BEGINNING OF SPRING, after an uncomfortable journey across Prussia and Saxony, I stopped in Munich to put my affairs in order. I stayed in a guesthouse on the banks of the Isar and hired an agent to take charge of the sale of the house where Robert and I had lived. I insisted that I didn't care if I lost money in the sale; I needed to leave as soon as possible. I spent the eighteen days that I ended up staying in the city wandering through its streets and plazas, pointedly taking my time so as to fix in my memory the red bricks of the cathedral, its unfinished towers, the black statue of the great Ludwig, and, waving from the pillar of the nave, the Turkish flag captured in Belgrade; the baroque façade of the Theatinerkirche, where I liked to go from time to time to look at the Venetian paintings; the old doors on Neuhauser Strasse, the Marienplatz, with its column honoring the Virgin Mary, patron saint of the kingdom, and, facing the plaza, the squat building of the café, *our* café, the Hussars' table, Robert reading the *Moniteur*. . . . It was a means of saying goodbye.

I was planning to meet up with Maryse in Stuttgart. I would spend a few days with her, then travel to Paris to visit Uncle Charles, who'd recently been put in charge of improving medical instruction in the city, and from there, continue on to Toulouse, where I would stay until my tenant's rental contract was up and I could move into the château. Foix had suddenly become not only the tiny kingdom of my childhood and adolescence, full of tranquil days and pleasant horseback rides, but also something like a place of retreat, a silent monastery surrounded by forests where I could mend my heart in solitude. Robert's death had left me empty of emotion. I ate and drank without appetite and my sleep was broken and exhausting.

More often than not, I awoke with a headache and the taste of ashes in my mouth. Although I wasn't terribly hopeful, I had the idea of asking Maryse to come with me, together with her Théâtre Nomade—I'd learned from her letters that this was the name of her traveling show that, in little more than two years, had become a retinue of carriages, wagons, wheeled cages, and mules that transported more than forty people, "and that's without counting, dear Henriette, the many *animaux savants*, dancing bears and dogs, a mathematical horse and a pair of ubiquitous doves that appear and disappear at the sound of the words *hocus pocus*. . . ."

I scarcely remember the journey to Stuttgart. I know only that when we saw one another, Maryse and I fell into each other's arms in a commotion of hugs and tears. Oh, how we wept! We cried all together, Maryse, Claudette, Françoise, and I. We cried at the guardhouse, in the street, at a table at the guesthouse, and finally, in my room. Our eyes swollen and our noses red, we listened as each of us told what we had to tell, which turned out to be a great many things. The most surprising news was the romantic relationship that had developed between Claudette and Françoise. "It happened without us even realizing it," said Françoise, matter-of-factly.

"In Linz," added Claudette timidly.

Perplexed, I turned to Maryse for an explanation, but she merely smiled and shrugged her shoulders.

"And Pierre?" I asked, to hide my displeasure.

"He's in charge of transportation for the troupe," replied Maryse. "A very complicated undertaking. It's not just a matter of leading our entourage, that's nothing for him. It's that there's always one problem or another, a wheel to be replaced, too much cargo, a fire in the gypsies' wagon, a lame mule, a leaky carriage roof, anyway, why bore you with the details, my sweet? He's always busy. At this very moment he's combing the streets in search of Tom, one of Frau Müller's dancing dogs. I do hope he finds him; he's the lead dog, and the show starts in three hours."

That first night, overcoming my exhaustion from the journey, I allowed Maryse to take me to the theater, a humble and poorly lighted space. In any event, at the six-thirty curtain, not a single seat was vacant, despite the fact that this was their third performance in Stuttgart. Maryse's appearance onstage was greeted with hearty applause. She wore a Venetian mask that resembled a cat's face, and she was enveloped in a provocative white silk wrap that accentuated the sinuous movements of her body. I had never seen Maryse on stage before. I was amazed at her grace, her naturalness, the feline cadence of her undulating shoulders as she presented the evening's program. Suddenly, there was a great boom and she disappeared in a scarlet cloud of smoke, replaced by the four Pinelli Brothers, acrobats whose skills were far superior to those I'd seen in Toulouse with Aunt Margot. They were followed immediately by the discordant strains of an off-key French horn, announcing "The Pursuit of the Unicorn," a charade in which Pierrot, Harlequin, Pantalone, and Punchinello, mounted on broomsticks topped with horse's heads, ran higgledy-piggledy about the stage, chasing a strapping, horned Columbine who is, at last, and as expected, mounted by Harlequin amid much kicking and bucking and waggling of hindquarters. Then came the gypsies with their bears, Pythagoras the horse, a group of fearless tightrope walkers, and Frau Müller's dogs that, dressed as little ladies and gentlemen, danced a minuet and exited the stage, leaping through a ring of fire. The end of the first act belonged to Doctor Faustus Nefastus, whose black brocade cape sparkled with comets, stars, and moons embroidered in silver thread. His tricks were unparalleled, and I imagined that he must be one of the better-paid members of the troupe. For his final act—which I can't resist describing—he locked Harlequin in a square box so that only his head stuck out, then covered his head with a red silk handkerchief that he pulled from between his fingers. Accompanied by a sudden drum roll, he sawed off the head, lifted the kerchiefed bundle from the box, and walked across the stage, gravely showing it to the audience. A clarinet sounded the tremolos of a Turkish tune and Claudette, dressed as Salomé, unfolded herself from inside the box, rhythmically beating a tambourine upon which the magician placed the red bundle—the presumed head of John the Baptist on the infamous platter. Then the pealing of the clarinet became frenetic and Claudette, changing the voluptuous modulations of her dance, began to describe quick circles across the stage, holding the tambourine aloft, first in her hands, and then atop her head. She came to a stop at last and the magician, covering her with his cape, intoned a spell that I would come to memorize from hearing it so often: *Hocus pocus tontus talontus vade celerite jubeo.* A tremendous thundering reverberated throughout the theater and, as the smoke cleared, a fully intact Harlequin appeared, straightening, in pantomime, his wayward head. Ignoring the hailstorm of applause, Faustus Nefastus—his real name was Piet Vaalser—repeated the same spell, and the four sides of the box fell to the floor, revealing a smiling Claudette, the silk handkerchief in one hand and the tambourine in the other.

After intermission, Pierrot, Harlequin, and Columbine, dressed in tight-fitting leotards, performed exquisite tragicomical pantomimes to the strains of a solitary and sublime violin. This was followed by two impassioned Shakespearian soliloquies translated into German, and two lively Mozart quartets, featuring Maryse herself. The evening ended with a circular, Roman-style march, in which horses, wagons, consuls, magistrates, and soldiers paraded repeatedly in front of an allegorically painted backdrop, inciting such a monumental reaction from the audience that the deafening beat of the drums was accompanied, to the very last, by applause and the incessant cries of "Bravo! Bravo!"

❧

Captivated by the success of the Théâtre Nomade and its members' lighthearted and carefree way of life, I felt my own life turning, day-by-day, away from nostalgia and toward unpredictability. My appetite returned, my sleep improved, and I realized that my vitality was returning. Halfway to Karlsruhe I decided to cancel my trip to Toulouse and I asked Maryse if I could stay with the troupe until my tenant's lease was up in Foix.

"But dear heart, this business is as much yours as it is mine. Didn't we start it together in Strasbourg with our two carriages?"

"Oh, no, Maryse! I couldn't!" I said, moved by her generosity, and I slid over to sit by her side and hug her.

"Don't be misled; we only manage to cover costs. The theaters keep the lion's share of the money from our ticket sales. But when it comes to business, I've always tried to be a serious person," she said, pulling away from me and giving me an affectionate shove toward the carriage window. "Come on, let's talk seriously. To start with, I'll tell you that it's only by dint of a miracle that our little variety show even survives. Perhaps you, coming in from outside, can explain our success better that I can. I would not be lying were

I to tell you that, for the most part, the show has created itself, as though it's had a life of its own, independent of my desires and precautions. And it's been that way from the very beginning. Musicians, actors, singers, gypsies, acrobats, well, everyone you've met, has joined up with the troupe purely by chance, without my having lifted a finger. Here's how it happened: two years ago, when our carriages were detained indefinitely in Linz, I happened to see a concert hall still displaying a week-old program. I knocked on the door, intending to ask to rent it for a few nights, but the owners, like many Austrians, had fled to Hungary before our troops occupied the city. The caretaker who opened the door was terrified and allowed me to enter without argument. The place was small, as was fitting for Linz, but struck me as absolutely marvelous. There was a German pianoforte, a harp, and cabinets filled with printed scores and unused sheet music. Ignoring the presence of the caretaker, we installed ourselves in the theater. As we knew that the city's newspaper was already dedicated to military use, we spent two days writing out the details of one of the programs we'd performed in Boulogne. While Claudette and I rehearsed, I sent Pierre and Françoise to pass out the announcements in the cafés. What can I tell you? The theater was filled to capacity, and not just that night, but all the others as well. The pianoforte was well tuned and my voice as clear as ever, although the one who stole our soldiers' hearts was Claudette, who performed the Salomé and sang and danced *merengues* and *calendas* from Saint-Domingue."

"She stole Françoise's heart as well," I said archly.

"It's true. Although it surprises me less than it does you. I don't know anything about Françoise's past, but Claudette has more than enough reasons to distrust men. In any case, the Théâtre Nomade was born there in Linz. Surely you'll remember the huge number of women who'd been traveling with the 5th Battalion. It's true that there were all types among them, but some of them, like Claudette and me, were theater people. And not just theater people, but theater people whose resources had all but vanished, and who needed to earn a living. A young Jewish boy who was marching to Strasbourg with his father also joined us. Guess who he is? None other than Maurice Larose, our clarinetist, the jewel of our little orchestra. Of course the day arrived when we were finally allowed to move on toward Vienna. But I'm superstitious, my dear. I don't know if

I've told you that before. I prefer not to travel east if I can get away with traveling in any other direction. If you think about it, for us French, everything bad has always come at us from the east. It's something my father used to say. And so, after buying a wagon and a new carriage, we set off for Salzburg, where we found the Pinelli Brothers and the Venetian Mimes. And there, I had to make a decision. My show had always been limited, more or less, to what now makes up the second act. And we'd gotten along reasonably well like that. But Rocco, the eldest of the Pinelli Brothers, convinced me that I'd do much better if I joined forces with his people and made room in the show for some circus acts, *danseuses de corde*, magicians, contortionists, *animaux savants*. 'This way we'll have something for everyone,' he told me. And he was right. Later, in Mannheim, Frau Müller joined us with her dogs, as well as the gypsies and their bears, and in the market in Frankfurt, I found Professor Kosti with Pythagoras and also Piet, who'd just returned from touring in London, with Joseph Grimaldi, no less, and who, like me, was traveling across the Rhineland. And so it's been. With the exception of giants, midgets, bearded women, hermaphrodites and other *phénomènes* that serve no purpose other than showcasing their physical oddities, I'm willing to accept anyone and anything in the realm of circus arts. And I'll tell you another thing: if we continue to attract such experienced performers, I don't see any reason that we couldn't work in France, although not just yet; the public's expectations are much higher there. But one day we shall cross that border. I've thought it all out: Strasbourg, Metz, Nancy. Little by little, we'll be moving toward Paris. My city. Ten years, Henriette. It's been ten years since I left Paris."

"You'll be back soon enough now. But what you've told me is simply amazing," I said, in awe at the apparent ease with which she had organized such a complicated show. "Although I believe it's more than just coincidence at work. I'd say it was your destiny. Of course you'll return to Paris. You were born under a lucky star. That's the main thing. I've heard that Napoleon, before promoting anyone to the rank of general, asks first if he was born under a lucky star. My star, on the other hand, well you know . . . Aunt Margot, then Robert."

"Oh, Henriette, how little you know about my life," she sighed.

But I did know at least a little. And I don't mean her unfortunate relationship with Varga and the matter of the duel, things I never let on that I knew about. But one night in Vienna, in that moment of intimacy one slips into after making love, I asked Robert what he knew about Maryse's life in Saint-Domingue. Whether because he always shied away from talking about other people, or because he actually knew little about Maryse's past, he told me only that she and Claudette, after suffering many hardships, had left Saint-Domingue just before General Rochambeau's surrender. "But let's speak of happy things," he'd said. "The stories about Saint-Domingue are too frightening. What do you think about throwing a banquet in honor of Constant's birthday?"

"Forgive me," I said to Maryse, ashamed. "I spoke without thinking. I know from Robert that you were very unlucky in Saint-Domingue."

"Unlucky? I've suffered a great deal. First I lost my daughter's father," she said in a low voice. "Then I lost my daughter," she added, turning her face toward the carriage window.

"Oh, Maryse!"

"It's all right, Henriette, it's all right," she said after a moment, trying to smile beneath her tears. "But promise me something. Promise me that you will never speak to me of these things. I don't know what came over me. I shouldn't have told you."

But those painful memories had already surfaced, and, like blind birds, they flew about between us, unable to return to hiding or to take flight. I drew her close. I hugged her until she understood that it would be better to give in to it and tell me everything. And so, beginning that very day, she surrendered up her story to me little by little, like the chapters in a *feuilleton*.

❧

Shortly before the turbulent days of the storming of the Bastille—an appropriate date from which to begin many stories of my time—Maryse was a young and talented singer, increasingly well-received on the stages of Paris. She was in love with a married man, a wealthy mulatto from Saint-Domingue by the name of Jean-Charles Portelance, who had traveled to Paris to lobby in support of the rights of citizenship for people of color in the colonies, a category to which he himself also belonged. To this

93

end, he was active in the *Société des Amis des Noirs*, an organiza-
tion prominent in those years, whose members included notable
men such as Mirabeau, Necker, Sieyés, and La Fayette. One day,
Maryse discovered that she was pregnant. It was something that
neither she nor Portelance had wanted, but they both adjusted to
their new reality, if not with enthusiasm, then with calm resignation. And so, their daughter, who they named Justine, was born.
After the first few months, and after a great deal of consideration,
Maryse decided to live alone with her daughter and the wet nurse,
since she believed it would be morally unhealthy for the girl to be
raised in an illegitimate household. At first, Portelance did not approve of this separation, but, little by little, he grew accustomed to
the arrangement and, like Maryse, came to believe that it was for
the best, given their situation.

Despite the sincere love that bound the couple, their relationship was far from happy. This was not because Portelance's marital
status presented an emotional obstacle—his marriage was the result
of an arrangement between families, and Madame Portelance, having already performed her marital duty in giving birth to a son,
lived an independent life in Boston—but rather because their professional interests did not coincide and they scarcely found time to
see one another. In addition to being an ardent idealist, Portelance
was an intense and dedicated man who only had eyes for his political projects; when he wasn't in his office writing an editorial for the
Mercure, he was editing a pamphlet against the *Club Massiac;* when
he wasn't attending an *Amis des Noirs* meeting, he was at a secret
meeting with an English abolitionist. Maryse was no different. Her
career was on the ascent and, even during the lulls when she wasn't
part of the cast of a given opera, her days were full of other activities, from watching Justine play in the Jardin de Luxembourg,
to taking voice lessons, from performing in a play or a concert, to
visiting her dressmaker's atelier for a fitting. Moreover, knowing
that she was greatly admired, she enjoyed attending the theater and
making appearances in musicians' and artists' salons, activities that
held no allure for Portelance.

As time went on, and the revolution took an anti-Christian
turn, their political opinions began to divide them as well. Maryse
thought it an act of barbarism that the Notre Dame Cathedral
should be co-opted in the name of Reason: "For the love of God,

Portelance! Where will this end? Now we're supposed to worship at the feet of the great Goddess Reason? What a disgrace!" she would lament. But more than anything, she was growing to detest the guillotine, and not only because the number of victims was constantly increasing, but also because she was convinced that the spectacle of public executions was irreparably corrupting people's emotions.

"We're becoming animals. How can you support this bloodbath?" She would demand.

To which Portelance would reply: "The road to hell is paved with good intentions. We're at war and in the midst of a revolution, my love. Think of the guillotine as a necessary evil. It's true that they're taking extreme measures, but they're also creating justice. Scarcely two years ago, despite my wealth and my education, I had no rights whatsoever. And today I do."

And as their arguments went on with neither of them budging an inch, Maryse would feign a headache and leave Portelance's house in a sour mood. Other times it was he who, taking his hat and cane, would brush Maryse's lips with his own and take his leave, suddenly remembering that he had a dinner that evening with an influential member of the Convention. And it's not that Portelance wasn't repulsed by the continual rolling of heads, it was just that, a politician to the end, he believed that if the Convention were to abolish slavery once and for all—which had become his most cherished dream—it would do so impelled by its most radical faction. When the day finally arrived for that longed-for decree to be made public, Maryse, brimming with joy and immediate plans, ran to Portelance's house to celebrate the occasion.

"You must be so pleased, my love. No one knows better than I how much time and effort you've dedicated to the toppling of that horrible institution. A toast to your success," she said, raising the glass Portelance had just filled.

"A toast to the fraternity of races," he said, raising his own glass. "It doesn't seem possible. Can you imagine it? No more slaves. The French plantations will be worked by free people. The black man will be master of his own body again. Oh, if only ships could sail as swiftly as lightning! While we're here celebrating the triumph of social justice, weeks will go by before those poor souls in the colonies will receive the good news."

"Don't spoil this happy moment with your impatience, my dear.

The news will arrive in due course. Tonight we should think of us," she said, setting her glass aside to caress Portelance's hand. "After all, our moment of happiness has also arrived. You've finished your work and your affairs are in good order: your son is in school in Boston, your brother is in Philadelphia, managing your ever-increasing fortune, your wife leaves you alone, and I love you madly. The time has come for you to enjoy what you have, Portelance! In fact, just a few minutes ago, I was thinking that it wouldn't be such a bad idea to leave Paris for a while."

"Leave Paris? Good heavens, I'd have wagered that you wouldn't leave Paris for all the gold in the world!" exclaimed Portelance. "And your career? Your friends?"

"Things have changed, my love," said Maryse, deciding to reveal her most recent preoccupations. "Perhaps you aren't aware that theater folks are falling out of favor with the Convention, or at least with Robespierre. Not even Talma the Great is exempt from suspicion. It's rumored that he's going to be denounced as a conspirator. It's not exactly that I'm afraid, but you know well the opinion I hold of the Jacobins and you also know how I am. Sometimes I express my ideas a touch liberally and . . . who knows what could happen? But above all, I'm thinking of Justine."

"Come now, Maryse. If you were under suspicion, someone would have let me know. I can assure you that you're not in any danger, my love," said Portelance in a soothing tone. "And yet, it's true what you say: my work here is done. There can be no doubt about that."

"Do you mean that you wouldn't object to leaving Paris?"

"No, I would not object. In fact, I'd planned to tell you this evening that, eventually, I'd be going on a trip. I had been putting off telling you because I'd never imagined that you'd be of a mind to accompany me. Paris has always been your home."

"Oh, my love, how happy you make me!" said Maryse, standing suddenly and moving to Portelance's lap. "Do you know where I'd like to go? To Spain. According to Monsieur de Olavide, it's quite easy to cross the border. There are theaters there . . . Madrid, Barcelona, Seville. How happy we'll be! We'll live apart from politics, isn't that so? Promise me? And we'll live together, like a family. Now that Justine has been asking me questions about her father, I see that my decision to keep her from you was a mistake. She'll come to understand. . . . Tomorrow I'll introduce you to Don Pablo de Olav-ide, a celebrated political exile. He'll tell you all about Spain."

"But, my dear, what would I do in Spain?" he said, smiling. "It wasn't Spain I was thinking of."

"Where, then?" asked Maryse, intrigued.

"To Saint-Domingue, of course."

"But you yourself have told me that there are violent uprisings going on there, that the colony has been invaded by foreign troops," protested Maryse.

"Precisely. They have named Chambon to implement the aboli-tion of slavery decree. Any anarchy will disappear once they have the news. The black insurgents will unite with the French. The Eng-lish will have no choice but to evacuate their forces. As for the Span-ish, they'll be relegated to their part of the island."

Maryse disentangled herself from Portelance's embrace, stood up, and, looking at him disconsolately, said: "And you'll be going with Chambon, is that it?"

"Not exactly. I'm waiting to receive a large sum of money from my brother. We shall depart in a few weeks." Portelance removed a *habano* from a case on the table, held a straw to the candle flame, used it to light the cigar, and watched the smoke rise. Finally, he said: "I won't hide anything from you. I've been charged with a se-cret mission. I am to observe what happens in the country until the Convention sends a group of officials with legal powers."

"I see. Back to blood and politics," lamented Maryse. "As if nothing else existed in the world. Oh, Portelance, I'd had such hope!"

"I'm sorry to upset you, my love," he said, trying in vain to draw her near. Without getting up, he watched her fix her hair and take her overcoat from the coat rack. "Don't be silly, stay a bit lon-ger. We should talk."

"I'm all in a muddle, Portelance. I need to think," said Maryse before closing the door.

That very night, on her way home, Maryse decided to break with her lover. She would go to Spain with Justine. It was a sudden decision, made from one moment to the next, without deliberation. When the carriage stopped at her street she told the driver to take her to Talma's house. She knew she'd find Olavide there, fond as he was of rubbing elbows with musicians and theater types. She would ask him to write letters of introduction on her behalf to his friends in Madrid and Seville. But when she arrived at Talma's house, Maryse saw two guards at front of the door. Fearing the worst, she instructed the driver to take her to Gervaise Duclos' house, her closest friend and frequent castmate. When she arrived, a man dressed in a footman's livery, whom she'd never seen before, said to her in a mocking tone: "The *citoyenne* Duclos was arrested this afternoon." Guessing that he was actually a police officer, Maryse, enraged, shouted in his face: "This is what happens nowadays to decent people! I assume others of my friends have met with the same fate."

The man, looking her lasciviously up and down, replied: "Correct, *citoyenne* Polidor, and if you weren't caught in the raid as well it was only out of consideration for your *mulâtre*. You be careful now, and don't go looking for trouble."

Curled into a ball on the seat of her carriage, Maryse wept out of helplessness and rage. For the first time ever, she felt like a stranger in her own city. She felt an urgent need to hear a kind voice, feel the warmth of a caress. Crying convulsively, declaring her love amid sobs, she surprised Portelance in his nightshirt, who, as he held her tight, had absolutely no idea just how close he'd come to losing her.

❦

When Portelance and Maryse arrived in Brest, they learned that the port authorities had prohibited all passengers bound overseas from boarding the ship. It was a preventative measure: the previous night, a special messenger dispatched by the Convention had delivered news of the events of the 9th of Thermidor, namely, that Robespierre and Saint-Just had been sentenced to death. On the way back to Paris, Portelance was stopped and interrogated about his mission and his relationship with the Committee of Public Safety, and, in particular, with Robespierre. His response was clear and direct: "For many years my sole objective has been to restore human dignity to the people of color of Saint-Domingue. If that constitutes a crime, then I am guilty." As there were only suspicions, but no serious accusations lodged against him, he was assured that the interrogation had been merely a formality and that he should not be concerned. "Calmly return home. You'll be contacted soon," he was told.

But months passed, and no one sought out his services. It was true that the new Government, in altering the radical course that the Revolution had been following, now faced problems far more serious and immediate than the chaotic war in the Antilles—prices were going up, currency was being devalued, people were hungry and rebelling and the Jacobins were perpetually plotting—but it was no less true that, in the new political circles, Portelance was generally mistrusted.

However, the moment finally arrived for Saint-Domingue to return to the stage. In the wake of a series of decisive victories, the Republican armies had occupied Belgium, the United Provinces, and the German territories to the west of the Rhine. From this position of power, France had negotiated a deal with Spain: France would return the occupied territories on the other side of the Pyrenees in exchange for Spain's ceding the colony of Santo Domingo, which bordered Saint-Domingue.

"A wise move by the Directorate. Now the entire island is Saint-Domingue. This means that colonial issues have regained importance," said Portelance, showing the newspaper to Maryse. "If only the Directorate would consult with me. Who better than I to recommend a political course of action there?"

"My darling. I want you to know, above all, that I am perfectly happy with you and am ready and willing to follow you wherever you choose to go. But I'm concerned about your health. You don't eat well, you sleep poorly and you spend your days waiting for them to contact you. I have promised not to interfere in your affairs, but there's a limit to everything. I'm afraid for you, Portelance. If you continue like this, you're going to go mad. You must do something to escape this situation."

"Such as renounce my principles and go to live in Spain? Isn't that right?" he said bitterly.

"It wouldn't be all bad, but it would make you unhappy," said Maryse, without losing her composure. "What I propose has everything to do with precisely that: your principles. You have waited more than patiently and you now run the risk of being forgotten. Why don't you write a letter detailing what should be done in Saint-Domingue and send it to Barras or to any other member of the Directorate? Or better yet, why not request an interview?"

"Maryse, Maryse, how little you know me! I have already

written three proposals and the answer is always the same: 'We are grateful to *citoyen* Portelance for his *Discourse on Fomenting Peace and Industry in the Colony of Saint-Domingue*, which we have forwarded to the corresponding office of the Minister of the Navy and Colonies.' And I have asked to see each one of the members of the Directorate not once, but twice. The truth is . . ."

"Then why do you continue to torture yourself?" interrupted Maryse. "If they don't want to listen to you, it's their loss."

"No, it's Saint-Domingue's loss. France's loss. I must keep trying, especially now that the entire island is French."

"What are you going to do? You can't go on like this."

"I'm thinking of writing a book. That way I could express my political and economic ideas as fully as they require. But above all, I'll write about Toussaint Louverture, the only man capable of pacifying and reconstructing Saint-Domingue. A black man, an ex-slave, who has proved himself an excellent military man and a capable administrator. The territories under his control are peaceful, orderly and industrious. What's more, he's the only one who truly understands the futility of racial wars. He knows that the only way to reestablish the island's production of coffee and sugar is through cooperation among whites, blacks, and mulatos. I have this all from a reliable source. My brother Claude represents his business interests in Philadelphia. If our plantations were once the wealthiest in the world, there is absolutely no reason that they shouldn't be again, especially now that slave labor is a thing of the past. But power must be in Louverture's hands. He and he alone should be the next Captain General and Governor of the island. And when I say 'the island,' I am no longer referring to a colony, but rather to an overseas province with sufficient autonomy to govern itself and trade freely. If it fails to follow this course," concluded Portelance, "France will lose Saint-Domingue."

Maryse, moved by Portelance's unshakeable perseverance, offered to help in any way possible: "I'll stop taking voice lessons and cancel my commitments. Just tell me how I can be of use to you."

They worked tirelessly for four solid months. While Portelance wrote, Maryse went to the library and copied the documents and articles he requested. But they were also in love like never before, united, for the first time, by a common purpose. When the book was finished, Portelance took it to the printer, paying twice the established rate so that it would be published immediately—the Directorate had yet to name the new Commissioners who would take charge of Saint-Domingue, and Portelance hoped that his ideas, once in print, would spur them to bring him on as an advisor.

When the book was published, Portelance followed Maryse's advice and invited a group of friends, politicians, and journalists to a grand dinner. Only a very few accepted, all of them Jacobins. At that moment, he realized that his dealings with Robespierre, limited though they had been to issues concerning Saint-Domingue, had been misinterpreted. "They take me for a Jacobin, plain and simple, a spy for Robespierre," he told Maryse bitterly. "Now I know the reason they have marginalized me. No one will read my book. All our work has been in vain."

A few weeks later, the newspapers published the names that would comprise the Commission to Saint-Domingue: Sonthonax and Roume, on the civil side; Rochambeau, on the military. There were also members of lower rank. Upon reading the name Julian Raymond, his old ally from back in the days of the *Amis des Noirs*, Portelance commented sarcastically: "At least they named a mulatto."

"Listen, love," said Maryse, bound and determined. "What's stopping us from boarding the same ship as the Commission and traveling to Saint-Domingue of our own accord? Don't you own property there?"

"It would be pointless. I have no official title to back me. If I meddle in their politics, they'll turn against me. No, my love, now is not the moment to travel. But mark my words," he added, smiling, "that day will come."

And, in time, the day did come: through his brother, Portelance would receive the incredible news that Louverture had learned of his book and wanted him at his side without further delay.

6

AFTER OUR SHOW CLOSED IN the city of Karlsruhe, our traveling theater headed south. It felt rather odd to find myself, once again, in Aunt Margot's sturdy carriage, dressed in mourning, with Pierre in the coach-box while Françoise, seated to my left, read a volume of plays by Beaumarchais, moving her lips and tracing the printed lines with her finger. Had it not been for Maryse and Claudette, who were also traveling with us, one would have thought that time had spun in reverse back to the sweltering days of that long journey from Boulogne to the Danube, a journey that held such meaning for me, one that I now mythologized, imagining, for some mysterious reason, that it was destined to repeat itself over and over again, like variations on a theme, each one initiating a new cycle or phase of my life. What would the journey bring me this time around?

"Don't you find that certain moments seem to repeat themselves?" I asked Maryse.

"Yes, especially the bad ones," she replied, still in a foul mood. The previous night, as we slept in a roadside inn, the gypsies had stolen Maryse's excellent carriage horses from the stable, hitched them to their wagon, and disappeared, leaving an old mule and a sick bear by way of compensation. I had never seen my friend so irate; she swore like a soldier and unfairly accused the innkeeper of having been an accomplice to the theft. Nothing would calm her down, not even my offer of money to buy new horses.

"What bothers me the most, goddammit, is that I've always defended the gypsies!" she shouted, furiously kicking hay about the stable. Finally, realizing that it was growing late, she informed the innkeeper that he'd pay dearly were anything to happen to her carriage, and then she'd climbed into mine, followed by Claudette.

At last we arrived at Baden-Baden, where we'd been invited for a few days' work in the municipal theater. In those days, the city was nothing like what it is today—to judge from what I read in the newspapers. Not only was it a gathering place for European aristocracy, it was where the French nobility, fleeing the Revolution, had emigrated. Sitting in a box seat with Françoise, I watched as the theater filled up with those pathetic courtiers who, in order to demonstrate their allegiance with the Monarchist cause, dressed in the old style, delicately taking their snuff and behaving with the same affectation as if they were attending a palace soirée. I would later find out that their numbers were dwindling. Feeling themselves at risk under the new Confederation of the Rhine—Baden had become a grand duchy under French protection—many sought refuge in Austria, Russia, England, and even America. But traveling was expensive, and while there were those bankers and dandies who had managed to escape with their fortunes intact and who could permit themselves the luxury of settling wherever they saw fit, others, less fortunate, had resorted to gambling in the hope of, one day, imitating them. The result was that Baden-Baden, best known for the virtues of its thermal springs, had, in a very few years, become a city full of gamblers, and was now attracting people from all over, including Italy, Switzerland, and the Rhineland.

After the show, we went out into the hallway that led to the staircase. The crowd was so dense we could hardly move. Fanning myself was useless; I could feel the sweat dripping down my body. It seemed like no one was leaving the building and, when I complained of this out loud, a woman with a tall coiffure turned around and informed me that the majority of the people were headed to the game rooms. At last we made it to the first floor, where Maryse, Claudette, and a few of the Italians were waiting for us at the entrance to the restaurant. After waiting more than half an hour we finally managed to secure a table. The food was well prepared despite the huge number of diners, but I couldn't help but notice how high the prices were. Andrea Morini, who played the role of Harlequin, suggested that we visit one of the game rooms. But at the thought of being suffocated once again by the crowd, I declined.

"Perhaps tomorrow," said Maryse, agreeing with me. "My

head hurts and I need to rest. Those damned gypsies have ruined my whole day."

When I awoke and saw the sun lighting up the room, I decided I was finished with dressing in mourning. The unusual heat of that June cried out for cool, white clothes, and further, I realized that black was no longer an accurate reflection of my state of mind.

I began to regret the decision the moment I went down to breakfast. Andrea and Piet stared at me with such insistence that I flushed bright red. It was clear that, to them, I had ceased to be a bereaved widow. As I ate breakfast, surrounded by their flirtatious attentions, I realized that I needed to come up with a defensive strategy before any unpleasantness arose. My feet were already being sought under the table, and I did not wish to allow things to go any further. But what might be the most effective way to discourage my two sudden admirers? And it wasn't that I was entirely indifferent to them. They were both intelligent and attractive, each in his own way. It was just that, after Robert's death, no man seemed to warrant my affections. My desire still belonged to him, to the point that I sometimes awoke with the pillow pressed between my legs and an urgent need to feel him inside me. When this happened, I would close my eyes and, straddling the pillow, evoke his body, his voice, his kisses, his caresses, trying to recover one of our nights in Vienna or Munich or Berlin.

After the show that evening, I went with Maryse and Professor Kosti to the theater manager's office to collect our money. Professor Kosti, whose real name was Erich Kraft, had volunteered as the troupe's bookkeeper. He was from Berlin, tall, and middle-aged, with pale eyes which, magnified by the thick lenses of his glasses, intimidated anyone who didn't know him well. In his youth he had been fruitlessly obsessed with demonstrating some geometric property or another of parallel lines. Frustrated in his aspirations, he had instead succeeded in training a horse in such a way that it appeared to know arithmetic. His most popular act had two parts to it: in the first, he would ask the audience for two numbers of up to six digits each, which he would then multiply and divide by each other on the spot, without the aid of paper and pencil, coming up with the answers minutes before anyone in the audience could calculate them; in the second, one of the tightrope walkers would appear on stage dressed as an Amazon, leading Pythagoras by the bridle. The horse would then be asked to solve any mathematical problem—including square and cubic roots—so long as the answer was not longer than a single digit. Once he had arrived at the number, Kosti would move to the horse's ear, translate into horse language the operation to be carried out, and Pythagoras would give the answer by elegantly raising and lowering his right hoof.

After she'd received the money owed us for the two nights of performances and distributed it among the members of the company, Maryse collected five francs from each of us so that Kosti could play roulette—after studying the game, the mathematician believed he had hit upon a winning system. Roulette was still a novel game in those days, having been brought to Baden-Baden by exiled aristocrats. The advantage it held over *rouge et noir*, a card game that had also been introduced by the French, was that, in addition to being faster, more players could participate at once, making it more like a raffle or a lottery. The roulette room was so packed with players that we had a difficult time even getting through the door. Since the Germany of those days included dozens of states, and the largest of them minted their own money, the game room cashier used the new franc as the base currency of exchange. So as to avoid confusion, one didn't play with real money but with tokens made of bone, with a different color corresponding to each player.

Aside from the rounds of faro that I had played with Robert, the only purpose of which had been to prove that I could beat him, I had never been interested in gambling. Raised in accordance with Aunt Margot's customs, I had always preferred outdoor pastimes. Nevertheless, I tingled with impatience and excitement in anticipation of watching my friends play. Would Kosti's system work? Could studying the diagram on the roulette wheel for a few hours really be sufficient to uncover the secret to the game? Could it be true that the probability that the marble would fall on a given number was predetermined by a law of mathematics? If that were so, I thought, the future would be predictable and those who understood numbers would take the place of astrologers and fortunetellers. Suddenly, my memory took a kind of leap and I remembered a forgotten episode: as a child, in Toulouse, a Spanish gypsy had read in my palm that I would marry three times, none of them in France. "*Les jeux sont faits, rien ne va plus,*" she'd said in a mechanical voice. I looked over Maryse's shoulder toward the roulette table: the ball jumped from one number to the next until at last coming to rest. "Nine, red," announced the croupier. Maryse could not repress a cry of joy: she had won seven hundred francs.

Standing behind my friends—only those playing were permitted to sit—I watched them play for a while. Kosti's system did not appear to be such a miraculous thing. Though he did win more than he lost, his winnings did not amount to more than a hundred francs. As for Maryse, who played independently from the mathematician, she had not managed to hit upon a winning number again. Tired of losing, she dropped the few tokens she had left in her bag and turned to me. "I feel like something sweet. Care to join me?" she asked.

In the restaurant, we joked a bit about how seriously Kosti took his mathematical system, and moved on quickly to the subject of my life. Maryse had noticed Piet and Andrea's flirtations and she was curious which one of the two I preferred.

"Neither," I replied. "Robert is still very present for me."

"Yes, it takes time," she said thoughtfully, and took a long sip of champagne.

"I feel useless in your theater, Maryse," I said to change the subject, although, in truth, it was something that had begun to worry me. "Pierre is in charge of transportation, Françoise handles the costumes. Even the animals do their part."

"But my dear, you accompany us and share everything with us. But, if you'd like to be on stage, well, let's see. . . . You have a lovely voice. I could give you a few lessons, and in no time you could be a mezzo-soprano in a quartet."

"You only say that because you've never heard me sing. Although I like music, I'm the least musical person in the world. The only thing I do well is ride horses."

"I'm not so sure of that, my dear. I've heard tell that any horse you ride ends up dead," she said, teasing me. "A toast to the soul of the good Jeudi," she added, raising her glass.

"A toast," I said, raising mine.

"We should get back. Kosti must be on the verge of breaking the bank by now."

When we entered the roulette room, very few players were left, and even Kosti had retired for the evening. "He must have lost all of the troupe's money," commented Maryse. But when we asked the croupier if the gentleman in the glasses had lost a great deal, he replied: "Quite to the contrary, Madame Polidor. Professor Kosti won over a thousand francs."

Maryse and I looked at each other and started to giggle like a pair of idiots. "In that case," said Maryse, emptying her bag onto the table, "I'll put everything on number nine."

"Pardon me, madame, but the nine came up twice in a row not ten minutes ago." The speaker was not one of the players we'd left at the game table when we'd gone to the restaurant; of this I was certain. He was a man in his late forties, tall and good-looking, possibly Spanish, to judge by his accent. He was dressed in black, and a majestic pear-shaped gray pearl hung from his left earlobe. His salt-and-pepper hair, tied back with a red silk ribbon, was nearly as long as mine.

Maryse, without apparent surprise, held the gaze of her exotic interlocutor. Then, turning back to the croupier, she said: "Everything on the nine."

"In that case, allow me to join you," said the man in black, nodding his head slightly, and, addressing the croupier, he indicated the nine square on the roulette table and said: "A thousand francs on madame's number." I noticed that, like Uncle Charles, he wore no rings on his fingers.

"Monsieur?" asked the croupier, obviously thinking he'd heard him wrong. Then the man in black removed his pearl earring and rolled it across the table.

After hesitating a moment, the croupier gestured to a man who appeared to be the manager of the game room. The man approached, examined the pearl and, without a word, placed it on the number nine. Then he took the marble from the croupier's fingers and, with a practiced motion, spun the roulette wheel in one direction with one hand and sent the ball rolling in the opposite direction with the other. For a moment I thought the ball was going to stay on the nine, but the wheel was still spinning and it jumped onto other numbers.

"Twelve, black," announced the croupier.

"Well, madame, it could be worse," said my friend's admirer from the other side of the table.

"So it could, monsieur," said Maryse. "But I think you should not have played your beautiful pearl on my number. I don't tend to have good luck."

"Luck does not exist, madame. What is meant to be, will be."

"Who knows? Something to consider." She took her bag from the table and said to me: "It's late. We should go."

"Good night, madame," he said, looking at her intensely and ignoring me entirely. "Perhaps we shall see each other again."

"If it's meant to be, so it shall be."

❧

Arm in arm with Portelance, Maryse stepped onto the dock in Jacmel and stood there, amazed. Everything she saw seemed so unreal that she felt as though it were one of those monumental stage sets that one used to see years before in the Palais Royal Theater, which, in an effort to capture the ambiance of the Southern Islands, included everything from giant fanciful figureheads to thatched-roofed huts. All along the narrow road that passed in front of the dock moved ox carts and teams of picturesquely adorned donkeys, people on horseback wearing huge straw hats, soldiers and national guardsmen. Vigorous-looking black men came and went, some bare-chested, carrying large baskets, bundles of goat skins, cages filled with chickens and demijohns of rum. Black women, dressed in lightweight cotton and colorful turbans, could be glimpsed among the crowds, balancing baskets of fruit or vegetables on their heads, one hand on their hips, which they swung back and forth as they walked in a careless manner that Maryse determined to imitate as soon as she could find a mirror. Further ahead, at the top of a road paved with rounded stones, the plaza opened out, a fountain with bronze griffins at its center, encircled by rows of little stands in which old women rested on their haunches, selling their wares laid out on tables: fruit, flowers, herbs, pottery, brilliantly colored swaths of cloth, red and yellow silk handkerchiefs, fish, seafood, barrels of salted fish; there were mountains of oranges, pineapples, watermelons, coconuts, great plumed cabbages, white cheeses, bunches of bananas, onions and limes scattered among stalks of sugarcane and hairy-looking tubers that she'd never seen before. Everyone was bartering, gesticulating, laughing and gossiping loudly in the harmonious *créole* of the colonies.

Maryse looked at her daughter, already almost ten years old,

109

walking wonder-struck between her and Portelance. "Do you like it?" she asked her. Justine, who was rendered speechless, nodded happily.

"And you?" Portelance asked her. Maryse breathed in the dense tropical air, raised her hand to her heart, and said: "It's the same as it was with you: love at first sight."

From Jacmel they traveled on a small schooner to Cap-Français. There, they settled in to the grand, Norman-style stone house that Portelance's father had built. The city, sacked and burned a few years back, was being reconstructed with astonishing speed. Here a new tile roof was going in, over there a façade was being restored or a wall torn down. An army of carpenters and bricklayers worked from sun up to sun down, their Creole songs carrying through the streets on the morning breezes. To Maryse, all that activity seemed like a good omen. At sunset, leaning her elbows on the balcony railing, taking in all the colors of twilight, she liked to think that she, Justine, and Portelance were a kind of prophetic family, in an Old Testament kind of way; a family that, founded on the diversity of races, answered the call of a new era. It was as though the world had become young again in order to welcome them in a sort of celebration.

Inspired by this moment of epiphany, Maryse decided to offer voice and acting lessons with the objective of reinstating the arts in the city. The house soon filled up with students and, after many months of work, she managed to organize a miniscule theater company that performed selected scenes from Racine, Molière, and Beaumarchais. Dazzled by the abundance of talented musicians, she succeeded, with Portelance's help, in convincing the Government to provide modest funding for an extraordinary musical group that could play, with equal skill, a Rameau overture or a syncopated Creole quadrille. And so, while Portelance assisted the Louverture government in any way he could, while the planters returned from exile and production and commerce improved from day to day, Maryse found herself ever happier in Cap-Français, thanking God for the good health they all enjoyed, and watching Justine grow into a beautiful and vivacious young woman with the slender curves of an amphora and the toasted-almond eyes that she'd inherited from her father.

One morning, sitting before the remains of a glorious breakfast of tropical fruit, Maryse noticed that Portelance was staring fixedly out to sea.

"Your coffee's going to get cold, my love."

"Yes, you're right," he said, and downed it in one gulp.

"You're preoccupied. Has something happened?"

"Something that had to happen," sighed Portelance and, laying his finger atop the broken red seal on a letter lying next to his plate, he added: "From my brother Claude, with news from France. The Directorate no longer exists. A general has taken over control, General Bonaparte. A *coup d'état*. He has proclaimed himself First Consul."

"Consul? A Roman title? How ridiculous . . . so *nouveau riche*!" exclaimed Maryse, as Portelance lit a cigar. "But wait! Bonaparte is married to a Creole from Martinique. This is good, my love. Surely he'll take an interest in Saint-Domingue."

"That's precisely what worries me."

"But everything's going well here. There's peace and order and greater prosperity by the day. I don't see what harm Bonaparte can do to us. To the contrary, I think he'll take Louverture's Government as an example of how to reform colonial politics, don't you agree? At least that's what logic would suggest."

"Politics is not logic, Maryse. Politics is politics," said Portelance, tapping an inch of ash onto his plate.

"I know what politics is. It's here that I've come to understand it. Politics is nothing; it's like the smoke from your cigar. What matters are the men behind the politics. Louverture is a good man, a virtuous man, therefore his politics must necessarily be good and just."

"You say that because you're on his side. But just ask the enemies he's defeated; ask Rigaud, for example. Even more, ask those who conspire from within his own ranks. I've seen him order the execution of a hundred men who had won many battles for him. And I don't criticize him for it either; it's how politics works."

"But, my dear, doesn't God punish the wicked with damnation? Why must you complicate matters when everything may be reduced to a conflict between good and evil? There are heroes and there are villains, just like in the great operas and tragedies, and that is that."

"My love, the world is not a stage and life is not an opera. Yes, there are heroes and villains, but consider that there are villains who become heroes and heroes who end up as villains. And this occurs because all of us have both a hero and a villain within us, and we ourselves don't know when we might behave as one or the other."

"You'll never convince me that a villain hides inside you, my love. But, very well, I think I understand you. You think that Bonaparte, the hero of Italy, has revealed dangerous ambitions in staging a *coup d'état*. In other words, he may have switched from the category of hero to that of villain. Am I right?"

"It's what I fear. But the truth is, what worries me the most is that Louverture has asked me to work on a constitution. I must warn you that this is a secret project, and it must stay that way, between you and me."

"Say no more, Portelance," Maryse said, her brow furrowed. "You know that I've never told anyone the things you tell me. Go on. . . ."

"A few months ago, when the government of France was weak, such a constitution would have enjoyed much better prospects than it does now, with Bonaparte in power. Further, I know very well what kind of constitution Louverture wants; I myself have contributed greatly to his ideas. You know them well: they're in my book."

"But, my dear, those are your principles. It's a fact that what you were able to see before anyone else has indeed occurred. That should fill you with satisfaction."

"Except that the autonomy that Louverture wants for Saint-Domingue is more radical than I think prudent: practically speaking, it's independence. Furthermore, Louverture intends to remain in power as Commander in Chief and Governor for Life. No matter how hard I think about it, I still cannot see which is the best political path to follow. It is, of course, easy to say that dictatorships are abhorrent, that they set a bad precedent, but, what chance does Saint-Domingue have to move forward under any government other than Louverture's? And so, what course am I to recommend? And finally, of course, is the question of how Bonaparte, a general with autocratic ambitions, would respond to an ex-slave, a black man who, ten years ago, didn't know how to read or write and who believed in voodoo spirits, proposing himself as the constitutional dictator of France's wealthiest colony. Do you suppose he'd tolerate him? I seriously doubt it. What's more, Bonaparte has the support of all those who've gotten rich off the war industry, hundreds of contractors and businessmen who also harbor visions of grandeur.

It wouldn't surprise me if he were to revoke the abolition of slavery and attempt a return to how things were before."

"But, my love, even if he did revoke it, who could force so many people who've tasted liberty back into servitude?"

"He could try, Maryse, he could try. Didn't he invade Egypt with thirty thousand men?"

Maryse remained quiet for several minutes. She knew that Portelance had confided all of this to her because he needed to be able to discuss the situation with someone he could trust. And yet she couldn't find the words to continue the conversation. But there he sat, the love of her life, waiting for her, pretending to study the way the breeze dissipated the column of smoke from his cigar.

"Portelance," she said at last, "do not take on Louverture's burden, much less Bonaparte's. May each of them act in accordance with his own conscience and interests. It will be as God wills it. You are only an advisor and, as such, your duty does not extend beyond suggesting to Louverture the constitutional project you deem most viable for Saint-Domingue. That is, open your heart to him, and tell him of your concerns. He knows better than anyone that anything you say is guided by the best of intentions."

"We shall see, we shall see," repeated Portelance, dropping the cigar in his coffee cup. "Now let's speak of another matter, something that affects you and me, and even Justine," he said gravely.

"My goodness, Portelance!" exclaimed Maryse, alarmed.

"The letter I received was not written by Claude, but rather by his wife, Sophie; Claude has suffered an embolism that has left him paralyzed on the right side of his body.

"Oh, my dear, I'm so sorry!"

"He is very weak and has asked me to travel to Philadelphia. We have never divided up our inheritance. Fearing the worst, he's decided that it is time to do so. He wants to prepare his will and the situation is complicated. First, there are his wife and children; we also have two older sisters who emigrated to Cuba, and, of course, Madame Portelance and my son Jean-Charles. And then there are you, Justine, and me. In addition to the lands, houses and plantations that we have here, Claude has invested a great deal of money in various North American companies, and my sisters, both widows with children, have bought sugar mills in Cuba. In any case, it's not an easy matter to sort out; we need to decide how to divide everything up among ourselves and our beneficiaries. My sisters will travel to Philadelphia with their account books and their lawyers, and I should go as well."

"And if you should have difficulty returning?" protested Maryse. "How vexing this is, Portelance, when you and I are so happy! How could you think that your absence wouldn't affect me? Don't you know that every day I spend without you causes me to suffer? And Justine, who adores you as though you were her guardian angel, have you even considered her?"

"I'd assumed that you and Justine would go with me," said Portelance, surprised.

"Go with you? But what would Justine and I do there, with your wife and son? Claude knows about me, but what about your sisters in Cuba, and their children, Justine's cousins? We would not be welcome, Portelance. We'd be undesirable presences, illegitimate. No, no," Maryse said emphatically. "This is something that concerns you alone. As for me, I do not need you to include me in your will. I was poor when I met you and so I shall be again, if I survive you. By God's grace, I can make a living from my profession. Honestly, I don't see any reason for the trip," she reproached him. "What are you going to say there that you couldn't put in a letter?"

"Maryse, listen to me. I have a son there, I have a brother whom I love and who could die at any moment. It's been years since I've seen them. And anyway, even if you want nothing from me, there is Justine to consider. Don't you see that, by law, she should have every right as my son Jean-Charles?"

"Do what you think best, Portelance. Let's not speak of this further. Justine and I will stay here."

"Maryse, please," he said, hurt. "Don't you see that I'm doing all of this for your well-being, and hers?"

"Enough, Portelance. It's fine. End of discussion. I am aware of your reasons," and, softening her voice, she added: "Don't worry. I'll be happy here. I have my theater, my lessons and recitals, my new friends. I have things to do here. And I'll be well entertained. Ma Kumina, an ex-slave, is teaching me the basics of voodoo. I have a million things to do, my love."

That night they talked at length. Portelance realized, for the first time, how important marriage was to Maryse—something that, to him, was a mere juridical formality—and he promised to speak with Madame Portelance about the possibility of a divorce under French law. As for the issue of the constitutional project, he would let Louverture know that this trip was imperative. In three or four months, he'd be back.

After putting his papers in order and contracting with an agent of a North American enterprise for the sale of his coffee harvest, Portelance left for Philadelphia on the same boat that had brought the letter from his brother. He did not fear for Maryse and Justine's safety. Not a corner of the island was outside of Louverture's firm control. In addition, France was at war and Bonaparte would find himself, at least for the time being, too busy to think about Saint-Domingue.

As the ship disappeared into the horizon, Maryse felt a sudden chill. A bolt of lightning, silent and blinding, caused her to close her eyes and a gust of humid air struck her in the face. Once she'd recovered, she opened her eyes and looked around: the palm trees along the quay were still and the people who'd gone to say goodbye to the travelers were leaving the dock, talking easily amongst themselves. Then she suspected that the vision had been meant for her alone, and she had a premonition that she would never see Portelance again. Biting her lips so that Justine would not see them trembling, she began walking hurriedly in the direction of the church.

Eight days later, the ship carrying Portelance would sink, with all hands and passengers, in the middle of a furious winter storm.

7

WHO TODAY EVEN REMEMBERS THE Confederation of the Rhine, that interminable list of tiny states—kingdoms, duchies, grand duchies, principalities and free cities—concocted by an ambitious Napoleon only to evaporate in the wake of his defeat at the Battle of Leipzig? But back in the days when Maryse and I traveled those German cities, the Confederation had just come into being and was a topic of much discussion. Many approved of it. They believed that the alliance with France would shake the dust off the provincialism and bureaucratic torpor of the federated states and have a modernizing effect on public administration, education, and social life. Others, looking toward the future, saw the Confederation as the first step toward a united and powerful Germany, a Germany independent of the influences of Austria and France, destined to play a historic role in Central Europe. But it was not all Franco-German harmony. Here and there, groups of radical patriots criticized the order imposed by Napoleon, an order that required unconditional—and in this they did not exaggerate—political and military support. These Germans, proud of their traditions and inflamed by nationalistic ideas, despised the presence of our soldiers in their cities, considering them unwanted foreigners whom they were obliged to feed and clothe. They looked askance, without distinction—and in this they were mistaken—at everything that came from France, from books and newspapers and social customs, to the arts and fashion. I say this not because the politics of that time interest me in particular, but rather to help you better understand the causes of the tragic episode that would put an end to our time in Germany.

But all that was yet to come. For the time being, we were happily heading north. We were bound for the city of Kassel, having been invited to perform there by an agent of the court of Jérôme Bonaparte, King of Westphalia. We were giddy with excitement because, should the King be pleased with our show, we might secure the possibility of working in France. As we traveled along we sang, memorized lines and rehearsed new numbers in the barns and stables along the way—we had decided that works by Shakespeare and Mozart quartets might not be to a Bonaparte's liking. We had great hope for our new finale, a kind of operatic ballet that, accompanied by volleys of cannon-fire and the unfurling of flags, would represent the recent triumph of the Battle of Friedland. Françoise, taking on the role of head costume designer, supervised Frau Müller, Claudette, Columbine, the contortionist, the sopranos and the five tightrope walkers who, working industriously on a wagon bench, mended old uniforms we'd bought from a junk peddler. Pierre, for his part, had employed Kosti's substantial roulette winnings—our stay in Baden-Baden had stretched out over one lucky week—to replace the horses stolen by the gypsies, to pay a backdrop artist to paint a convincing battle scene, and to secure an abundant provision of cheeses and cured meats, as well as three dozen rusty rifles, two drums, a bugle, various sabers and an old Prussian cannon, smelted in the foundries of Frederick the Great, all of which had been abandoned in the fields and collected by the locals.

But the changes went further than those made to our variety show. Maryse, whose romantic encounters had not, since Portelance's death, been anything more than simple dalliances, was looking with growing fascination at her dashing admirer from Baden-Baden, allowing him to meet up with us along the road and to court her openly. It appeared to be love at first sight: "That man *is* tremendously attractive," she'd told me as we were leaving the game room that night, and she had not been soliciting my opinion. The emphasis she'd placed on her words, that emphatic *is,* had leant her pronouncement a tone of irrefutable truth (to wit: the shortest distance between two points *is* a straight line). They had eaten breakfast together in the guesthouse the next morning and, while Pierre conducted his business on the outskirts of town, she had suggested, with the buoyancy of an adolescent, that we go on an excursion to a castle set into a nearby mountainside. With some of us riding in the wagons and some on horseback, we arrived at the foothills of the mountain. The path was so steep that it was necessary to go up by donkey. This seemed like an uncomfortable extravagance to the majority of the troupe, most of whom opted to return to town and join Kosti at the roulette table. Those of us remaining at the foot of the mountain were more than sufficient to rent the few available donkeys. Maryse and her admirer, my two suitors and I, were joined by Columbine—whose real name I don't remember—and one of the Pinelli brothers. Cross-eyed Vincenzo, who portrayed the white-faced Pierrot, was left without a mount, and bid us farewell in sad pantomime.

The castle was in ruins. Its walls, blackened over the centuries and covered here and there by vines and wildflowers, seemed to grow out of the rock itself. We entered through the crumbling doorway, me ceding my position next to Maryse to that bronze-faced traveler, who had stepped in and claimed it as if it had always belonged to him. (I knew very little about him, as Maryse kept him quite to herself. His name was Julián Robledo, a well-to-do Spaniard from the Americas. He would accompany us as far as Kassel, which was on his way, and from there continue on to Prussia.) After climbing a narrow stone stairway, we arrived at the rampart walls. From there we entered a side tower and climbed up to the top. A magnificent panorama opened up before our eyes: the rise of the Black Forest, the meandering Rhine River, the rooftops of small villages on one side of its banks, the distant buildings of Strasbourg on the other, the cathedral's spire towering over them all. I turned toward Maryse to make a comment about Strasbourg, but neither she nor her paramour were there. We searched everywhere for them, but they didn't turn up until much later when, our outing finished, we waited for them by the donkeys. Maryse returned, excited and flushed, and, to distract us from the fact of her disappearance, began immediately talking about deep dungeons and dark narrow passageways they'd nearly gotten lost in.

I'd be lying if I said that I wasn't upset by this turn of events. In that moment, I realized that I was in danger of losing her, that, should a romantic involvement come between us, I'd no longer be her traveling companion, her closest attachment, the confidential book in which she'd begun to write the story of her life. Today—certainly not back then—I understand that what I was asking of Maryse was much more than her friendship. I also yearned for a more complex form of love, a mother's love, and a sister's. My jealousy sprang from the fear that I'd no longer be the focus of her affection, her understanding smile, her protective embrace; from the fear of abandonment, the fear of a solitude which, admittedly, I had thought to seek out in Foix only a few months earlier, but now wholeheartedly rejected. There was something else: as she told me of her past, I had begun to construct a future for her in which I would always be present. I had turned her into one of those resigned female characters in a Madame de La Fayette novel who, on the verge of being consumed by passionate love, instead finds salvation in filial love. Who better than I to replace her dead daughter? Hadn't I reminded her of Justine that day in Strasbourg, when, upon learning my age, she'd shed a tear?

Nevertheless, I decided not to meddle in her love affair and to allow time to take its course. After all, Robledo would be leaving once we arrived in Kassel. And yes, I would accept Andrea and Piet's advances, more than anything to prove to Maryse that I could get along without her company.

℘

We passed through Mannheim en route to Kassel, and were offered the opportunity to stop and perform there; after some consideration, however, we decided to postpone it until a later date.

"One does not keep a king waiting, my dear, even if he's a Bonaparte. Don't you agree?" noted Maryse. I should say that, even though Maryse traveled with Robledo, took her meals and went out in the evenings with him, she always sought me out when anything relating to the troupe arose. Despite my general chagrin, it flattered me that she should consider me an equal partner in the Théâtre Nomade. On those occasions she would speak to me with the same naturalness as always, except that she never mentioned Robledo.

After arriving in the kingdom of Westphalia, an unpleasant incident occurred, one that I may have, at least in part, unwittingly caused. In an attempt to keep Andrea and Piet interested in me, I not only encouraged them to continue to court me, but I also permitted them certain liberties such as allowing them to accompany me in my carriage. My flirtation had reached the point where I would invite them to join me individually, and on alternate days, so that the one would never know what had happened with the other. The truth was, nothing was happening, or almost nothing, a few controlled kisses here, an insignificant caress there. In any event, Andrea had been with me one sweltering afternoon in Fulda, and I'd been slightly more tolerant of his advances than usual. That same night, when I entered my room at the guesthouse, I found him dressed in his Harlequin costume. His back was to me and he was wrapped in a cape that revealed only his legs, sheathed in black and red diamond patterned tights. He must have come in through the window and, for some reason, he had blown out the candles that I'd left burning before going down to dinner. I was too surprised to speak. I just stood there in the middle of the room, a candlestick in my hand. When I was finally able to demand that he go back to wherever he'd come from, Andrea turned around. He was wearing his big-nosed mask and was using both hands to support an enormous jutting phallus, as thick as my arm. Frightened, I backed toward the door, but when he saw that I intended to leave the room, he began to tug on his penis as though trying to pull it off, and let out a long and doleful moan. Bewildered, unable to move, I watched by the faint light of the candle as he detached that grotesque appendage from his body and deposited it on my bed, affectionately tucking it in as though it were a child. Then, without a word, he performed a bizarre bow and, laying his hand upon the windowsill, jumped nimbly into the night.

Terrorized, I ran from my room and knocked at Maryse's door. When she didn't answer, I went downstairs to the dining room where I was met with such a surprise that I sat down on the bottom step. Andrea, dressed in his regular clothes and smoking a cigar, was playing cards with Pierre, Maryse, and Robledo.

"Has something happened, my darling?" asked Maryse from the table. When I didn't respond, she added: "If you've seen a ghost, don't be too concerned. According to the innkeeper, it's a benign spirit, a wayward soul who appears in the hallways from time to time."

"A spirit of flesh and bone," I said, standing up. "I would appreciate it if you'd come to my room with me. I want to show you something." Everyone stopped playing and came over, intending to come up with me. "Thank you, but I only need Maryse," I insisted.

When we entered the room, all of the candles were lit and there was nothing on the bed.

"I don't doubt you, my love," Maryse said, after I'd told her of the incident. "The only thing I can say is that your visitor was not Andrea. He'd been with us a good fifteen minutes when you came downstairs. Someone must have gone into his things and taken the Harlequin costume. As for the phallus, I can assure you that I've never seen such a thing in the troupe. I think it must be a cudgel or a piece of painted wood, maybe the leg off a piece of furniture, something that could be made in half an hour."

"Yes, but who could it have been?"

"Who knows? There are more than forty of us."

"Well, there are about twenty men. It was one of them."

"And how do you know that it wasn't a woman? You never did hear whoever it was speak."

"But the phallus?" I said, unconvinced. "Only a man would think up such a thing."

"How little you know women, my dear. I'd say it was someone who desires you, man or woman. Someone who dreams of you desperately, who wants to possess you but is too afraid to be identified. It's not that strange really. Here, everyone thinks of you as a *grand dame*, a rich widow from the Languedoc. God only knows what things Pierre and Françoise have told them. But even if they've exaggerated, the fact is there's a huge difference between your economic situation and that of the rest of us." Seeing me about to protest, since the truth was that I felt at a disadvantage to the most modest saltimbanco, Maryse added: "Like it or not, it's the reality, my dear. I'm certain that many see you as inaccessible, as far as romantic relations go."

"That's certainly not the case with Andrea or Piet. For heaven's sake, Maryse, the last thing I needed was for you to make me feel excluded from the entire troupe!" I protested.

"That's not what I mean," she said gently, without losing her composure. "Everyone loves and respects you because you are a good girl and you treat everyone the same. But it's one thing to eat dinner with you and quite another to share your bed. As for Andrea and Piet, I'm sure they don't take more liberties with you than those you allow. And now that you mention it, you should know that it's assumed among the troupe that you're involved with both of them at the same time, something which gains you little favor. Perhaps that's another reason your admirer doesn't dare to express his or her love directly. Your admirer may think that if you've already got two lovers you couldn't possibly need a third. But my point is that whomever this person is who so desires you has not let you know because they feel intimidated by you in some way. If you really think about it, this whole business with the phallus is nothing but a pathetic ode to the impossibility of making love to you."

"All right. Point taken," I said, hoping to get back to the topic that was really of the most interest to me. "But who do you think my desperate inamorato—or inamorat-*a*, which I seriously doubt—might be? Seeing as Andrea is innocent, I'm leaning toward Piet."

"No," she said categorically. "His muscles are not trained for stunts such as jumping out of windows. For the same reason I rule out the six musicians, Frau Müller and Kosti; the singers as well. Nor could it have been Columbine, who's too big to fit into Harlequin's tights. So, we're left with six actors, three mimes, the four Pinelli brothers, five tightrope walkers, three jugglers, and the pair of contortionists. Count how many that is."

"Twenty-three," I said, adding them up on my fingers.

"Okay then. The Gizots are married and seem happy. Two of the tightrope walkers, Michou and Nicole, are self-declared lesbians and live in affectionate wedlock. One juggler and three of the actors are homosexual and, as I'm sure you've noticed, they work it out perfectly well among themselves."

"That leaves fifteen," I said, discouraged.

"Fifteen, my love. A very high number. As you can see, we can't accuse anyone. At least for the time being. Perhaps, down the road, the circle of suspects will tighten. But for the moment, I think it best to keep this between you and me. Things could get complicated if the police were to intervene. We'd be forced to stay here until they'd finished their investigation, and probably in vain, to boot."

"Yes, I think that's best," I sighed. "Please, I wouldn't want you to tell anyone about this."

"I won't. You know what? I'll sleep with you tonight. You'll feel calmer that way. Tell me what side of the bed the phallus was on. I'll sleep there," she said, laughing. "How big did you say it was?"

We undressed down to our nightshirts, blew out all of the candles except one, and lay down to talk. Maryse, as always, was brimming with ideas and projects. She dreamt of returning to Paris, a city she missed more and more every day.

"If we're well-received in Kassel, Jérôme Bonaparte's recommendation could open the doors to the circus on the Rue de Temple. We could have multiple equestrians in our show and you could be in charge of directing them. What do you think? Equestrian acts are always crowd pleasers. Ideally, we could get enough money together to build a circus. Just imagine if we had our own circus in Paris! We would no longer be the Théâtre Nomade. What would we call ourselves? What do you think of The Grand Faber-Polidor Circus? No, no. Not original enough. Let's see. . . . The Grand Olympic Circus. But what am I saying! We would call it The Imperial Circus! Napoleon and his court would love it, don't you think?"

"Do you have a sense of how much it would cost to build a circus?" I asked, thinking I could sell some of my lands in Foix. I thought Maryse's plan was wonderful, and I could already see myself, in the middle of the arena, dressed as a Hussar, directing the choreography of a half-dozen horses and riders to the thunderous applause of the audience.

"I see where you are going with this, my love. But my answer is no. I must look out for your economic security and I would never allow you to invest your money in a circus. Let others take care of that. For the time being, enjoy life, which is what I'm trying to do myself. You've already got more admirers than you know what to do with, although you really should decide on one of them."

"I've been so foolish, Maryse," I said, turning toward her side of the bed. "As I told you in Baden-Baden, I'm not interested in any man. The thing with Andrea and Piet is nothing. Pure flirtation."

"Of course, my sweet. I've never thought otherwise. When one is flirting one feels . . . how shall I say this? Important? Don't you think?"

"I've been a fool," I repeated.

"Enough of that, my dear. Life must be lived to the fullest. And anyway, I know that you've been lonely lately."

"More than lonely. Abandoned," I reproached her.

"Come on, Henriette, it's been barely three weeks. Don't you think I have the right to be happy for a few weeks?"

"And what if you go away with Robledo? He's a wealthy man, and he's not wearing a wedding ring."

"He's a widower. He says he's crazy for me. I know I'm but a shadow of what I once was, but it must be true because he's asked me to marry him."

"You see!" I cried bitterly, and I sat up in bed and looked her in the face. "I thought you wanted to lead an independent life. At least that's what you told me, once upon a time. Do you remember?"

"But I'll never marry him," Maryse went on, unflappable. "I'll admit I'm head over heels in love with him, something I thought would never happen again. He's enchanting, Henriette. He has it all. Even his vanity is enchanting, it's like a child's. But," she shook her head, "Robledo is not the man for me. Oh, if only Portelance had never existed! Although perhaps not even then. I detest the source of his fortune. Do you know what it is? A vast sugarcane plantation on the island of Cuba."

"But you told me that Portelance had plantations," I said, surprised.

"It's true, but when he took them over, slavery had already been abolished in Saint-Domingue. Robledo's plantation, on the other hand, is worked by slaves. He's master of hundreds of slaves. Don't you see? Hundreds of slaves who, if I were to marry him, would work, inevitably, for me. That is something I could not bear. And not just because of Portelance. Also because of my own convictions."

"Have you discussed all of this with him?" I asked, curious to know the most intimate details of their relationship.

"Yes, at length. He says he understands me. He swears that he, too, abhors slavery, but he's not well disposed toward selling his sugar mill. For him, sugar is much more than a commercial venture or a way to get rich; for him, it's destiny. He says that without sugar, his island has no future. Even his travels have been motivated by sugar. If you only knew all of the exotic places he's visited: China, Guinea, Tahiti. . . . Do you know what he's going to do in Prussia?"

"Yes, he told me, the one time I've spoken with him. He's interested in the cultivation of beets."

"Actually in beet sugar, a new product. He wants to know how much it costs to make and what it sells for on the market. Just imagine, traveling to Berlin with that as your sole purpose. Afterwards, he'll go to London. A dangerous adventure; the blockade against the British is fiercer than ever. I don't know what he's going to do there, but I've no doubt it has something to do with sugar. It's his obsession." Maryse stopped talking and closed her eyes. I thought she wanted to go to sleep and I lay quietly next to her. Suddenly, she said: "If you really think about it, maybe all men are like that, maybe they're all obsessive. I've never met one who wasn't—I once had a lover who was obsessed with duels, of all things. It's a shame: they miss out on so much in life. Robledo could very well sell his plantation, marry me, and live a very good life. We'd have a circus in Paris and our show would be full of acts from China, whose operas, from what he's told me, are extraordinary. We'd have dancers from Java and India, elephants, tigers and lions . . . and monkeys, which are very funny. And Transylvanian gypsies. Don't you agree? It wouldn't be so bad, right? And Red Skins from Canada and some act or another from Japan. Do you know anything about Japan? I know very little, but I love those silk kimonos. But now that I think about it, we'd really only be in Paris three or four months out of the year. The rest of the time we'd spend traveling with our show. Imagine it, my darling, instead of traveling these boring German streets like we're doing now, full of dour people and monstrous phalluses, we'd traverse all the world's oceans. And you with us, my love. You with us always, as a family. And when you find the prince of your dreams, you'll convince him to join up with us as well. What do you think? Oh, I could give Robledo so much!"

"But isn't there any way for the two of you to work it out? Tomorrow we arrive in Kassel. Everything just ends tomorrow?" I asked, to bring her back to reality.

"He'll stay two or three days in Kassel. He's to be received by King Jérôme. Then he'll go." Quickly she added: "He says he'll find me when he returns from London, though I doubt it. It's much harder to skirt the blockade leaving England than entering."

"Who knows? Maybe he'll return and change his mind," I said, hoping for exactly the opposite.

Maryse, breaking the thread of our conversation, asked me: "Do you have anything to drink in your luggage?"

"A few bottles of German white wine. I've been terrified to drink alone since Robert died. I always end up crying. Would you like a glass?"

"Have you ever tried rum?" she asked me, sitting up on the edge of the bed. When I shook my head she quickly started getting dressed. "I'll bring a bottle from my room. It's a little bit like cognac, but less full-bodied and with a lighter spirit," she said, as though describing a person.

I realized that Robledo was most certainly waiting for her and that I should let her go. I walked her to the door and threw the latch, then began looking through my traveling case in search of my silver goblets, a corkscrew, and a bottle of Moselle wine, in case I didn't care for the rum. When I'd laid everything out on the table, Maryse knocked at the door. I opened it partway, and she stuck her head in.

"Put on a robe, my love. You have a visitor."

I was greatly displeased to see that she'd brought Robledo with her and I started to motion to her with my finger that he should leave. But when she pushed open the door, I had no other option but to scurry about looking for my robe.

After the requisite introductions, I saw that Robledo was quite amused by the situation. As always, he was dressed in black, although the pearl he wore that night was oval-shaped and ivory-white.

"Well, my dear. I've brought my friend along because he's just told me that he knows who your harlequinesque visitor was."

"I though we'd agreed that you weren't going to tell anyone about that," I said, feigning a smile.

"I have never betrayed a secret," said Robledo, holding his hand to his heart in a somewhat mocking way, as if to indicate that he'd kept secrets of much greater importance than mine. "In any event, madame, I believe I know who the intruder was."

"None of this 'madame' business," Maryse corrected him. "We'll have no formalities here. Tonight she is Henriette and you're Robledo, and that's that. But, come now, we should sit and there's only one chair. Robledo, please move the table over by the bed."

Once we'd settled in, Robledo lit another candle and Maryse pulled a bottle of rum from her bag. When I tasted the liquor, I couldn't help but think of Robert. How he would have loved it! It was strong but excellent. No schnapps could ever compare.

"Well," said Maryse, looking at her lover. "Don't keep Henriette waiting."

"Vincenzo," said Robledo, after downing half a glass of rum. "It was Vincenzo."

"That cross-eyed old man?" I said, surprised. "How do you know?"

"When he saw your terrified face when you came downstairs,"

interrupted Maryse, "Robledo assumed that someone had gone into your room and he remembered that he'd seen Vincenzo in the garden looking up at your window."

"There's something else, Henriette," said Robledo. "Do you remember when we went to visit the ruins of that castle in Baden-Baden? Vincenzo just missed out on the last donkey and bid us farewell with a pantomime worthy of the best Pierrot."

"Yes, I remember when he told us goodbye."

"Not us, Henriette. I noticed that he looked only at you. Since then, during these days that Maryse has allowed me to accompany her, I've observed that he never stops looking at you. You've just never noticed him."

"How disgusting!" I said, repulsed, thinking that I'd have preferred for the phallus to have been exhibited by someone else—Piet, or one of the Pinellis, certainly not by that sad, ungainly, runty, gray-haired man who always seemed to be looking skyward.

"Face it, my dear, you're his fantasy," said Maryse, filling our glasses with more rum. "The things he must imagine doing with you!"

"I don't even want to think about it," I said, draining my glass. "I don't want to see him again, Maryse. I assume you'll fire him."

"As you wish, my dear. Although it will be quite difficult to replace him with another mime of the same quality. And that doesn't take into account the fact that they've all worked together for years. But, anyway, you'll have the final word."

"Have some compassion, Henriette. Think of all the unrequited desire of those less fortunate than us, the beautiful people," said Robledo without the least hint of modesty, including himself in a broad hand gesture that, after passing across Maryse's face and mine, came to rest on the pearl in his left earlobe. "Think of how terrible it must be to be despised because one is cross-eyed or hunchbacked or lame or simply ugly."

"Or a slave," Maryse added, admonishing Robledo with a knowing look.

"Or a slave," repeated Robledo, not returning her glance.

"Well, we can resolve the matter of Vincenzo tomorrow," said Maryse, taking her lover's hand so as to soften the reproach. "Now, Robledo, tell Henriette how you came by all of those magnificent pearls in Tahiti. And then about the operas and the customs of the Chinese. . . ."

"As you wish, my sweet."

And so the night flew by, Robledo telling us of his adventures traveling the world: his affairs with the women in Tahiti, the run-ins with the law he'd had in Guangzhou and how he'd managed to spend a night inside a harem in Senegal. His unbridled vanity was at first surprising, though somehow not off-putting, and later caused me to reflect that it was perhaps preferable for one to show it off in a natural way, as he did, rather than to flaunt it archly as the Hussars did, or to hide it behind false modesty. And so, to humor Maryse, and with the innocent pride of a child, he untied the ribbon that held back his majestic hair so that I could admire it. "Even Absalom would have envied it," I said to flatter him, and I nudged Maryse's leg under the table to indicate that I'd joined in her little game, since it was clear that she'd brought him to my room so that I could share in her conflict: on the one hand, her love for that beautiful and gallant prince of the Indies, a love that I feared now more than ever; on the other, a profound abhorrence of the institutions that he represented. At daybreak, when, taking his leave, he took me about the waist and kissed my cheeks, when I felt the firmness of his grip and experienced up close the warm magnetism that emanated from his body, I realized that Robledo was something like the Tree of Knowledge, that any daughter of Eve who had tasted of his fruit would be his forever. "I understand," I whispered to Maryse as we kissed goodbye at the door.

"I knew you would," she murmured in my ear.

❧

Immediately after Portelance's death was confirmed, Maryse decided to take the next boat back to France. She had no money and she still had some good friends left in Paris. But one morning Monsieur Delacour, Portelance's diligent lawyer, knocked at the door to notify her that his client had left her, in usufruct, all of his properties in Saint-Domingue. "If you'll allow me to explain, madame," the lawyer had told her, "said properties do not belong to you. They are subject to the Portelance family estate, the records of which are kept in Philadelphia. Now then, given the complexity of said estate, I'd venture to say that you could collect the rent from said properties for at least one year, a conservative estimate, madame."

This provision led Maryse to change her immediate plans. Now the most sensible thing to do would be to remain in Cap-Français. In the event that Justine were not recognized as Portelance's heir, Maryse would at least have had the chance to save enough money to settle in Paris.

Two years went by, and not a single day passed that Maryse didn't miss Portelance. Though it was not her way to display her grief publically, as many widows feel obliged to do, she felt an inexpressible private nostalgia for all the little things that, with repetition, had shaped their life together—Portelance's general indifference to food, the smell of cologne and tobacco in his clothes, the innocent way he'd made love, his fixation on politics, and so many other things that she'd responded to with predictable words and attitudes, everything repeating itself daily as though it were a performance of a dramatic dialogue. To offset this nostalgia, Maryse would take her breakfast on the balcony and, while Justine slept late into the morning, she would talk with Portelance in her head, imagining him seated in front of her, reading his correspondence between distracted sips of coffee. Sometimes she spoke of her musicians or actors, other times, of how well Monsieur Delacour was managing the plantations or of the new constitution that Louverture had sent to Bonaparte or of how General Christophe, now governor of the city, had completed the reconstruction projects. This morning ritual completed, she would fix her hair, get dressed, and throw herself into her work.

Sometimes while watching the sunset with her daughter, she would remember as though it were yesterday, that morning when she'd disembarked onto the bustling dock in Jacmel, and had been instantly captivated by the island. The years seemed to have flown by. It was only when she noticed the small cone shapes that Justine's budding breasts now made in her dress that she registered the passage of time. The lawyer Delacour kept her up to date on the goings on in Philadelphia: Claude had died, and the subsequent changes to the various heirs' legal situations were enough to instigate furious rounds of litigation among his widow, his sisters, and Madame Portelance, to the effect that they had not yet reached an agreement vis-à-vis the inheritance of the estate.

"This should come as no surprise, madame," he'd said. "In every family there is one member who serves as the axis. When this person is gone, the mechanism breaks down and the remaining members are sent flying in all directions. I have known of cases in which the execution of a will has lasted an entire lifetime."

"Do you think that the current situation will continue?" Maryse asked the lawyer.

"Indefinitely, Madame Polidor."

"In that case, I'd like to spend some money in Port-au-Prince. I'll start an arts program similar to the one we have here. Doesn't that seem like a good idea? Little by little we'll refine the tastes of the planters and the merchants, maître Delacour."

"You may do what you wish with your money, madame," replied Delacour respectfully, "but permit me to tell you that Achille Despaigne wants to sell La Gloire, his old sugar plantation in Morne Rouge. The machinery and all of the buildings were destroyed in the rebellions of '95, but the land is among the very best in the Northern Province. It's a good opportunity. I know that Monsieur Despaigne plans to go to the United States and is prepared to sell at a low price."

"Even so, I'm certain I wouldn't be able to pay what he's asking. But you say that Monsieur Despaigne plans to leave the country?" Maryse asked, surprised.

"I just spoke with him this very morning."

"His daughter, Claudette, hasn't said anything to me about it. Well, I hope he takes his time, we're rehearsing *Le Calife de Bagdad* and she's one of the principals," said Maryse, with a touch of dismay. "As for buying Monsieur Despaigne's land, as I've already told you, I couldn't afford it."

"Perhaps, madame. I was thinking that . . ." Delacour hesitated. "I was thinking that if you and I were to join forces . . . a partnership, I mean to say . . . we could buy La Gloire. The prospects for sugar are much better than they are for coffee. And General Louverture has pulled off a true miracle. His Government is recognized on the entire island and the future looks auspicious. On another note, La Gloire would not be subject to the Portelance estate. It would be yours and mine."

"But maître Delacour, I've no head for business," Maryse said, starting to laugh.

"You have a daughter, madame," Delacour insisted.

"You make a good point," conceded Maryse. "But I can't make

this decision right now. I need two or three days to think. Who knows, perhaps you're right. I would like to leave something solid to Justine."

But Maryse would never reach a decision. The following day, after a night rent by disquieting noises, the sails of a dozen ships and numerous military transports appeared beyond the bay. It was the armada of General Leclerc, Napoleon's brother-in-law. It was the expedition Portelance had so feared: an army of twenty thousand men whose orders were to sweep away Louverture's black power, take over political and military control of the island, and reinstate slavery.

8

AFTER LIVING WITH THE TROUPE for a few months I had learned that there was no such thing as a perfect performance. As those who work in theaters and circuses, and even street-performers, well know, it doesn't matter how many times the troupe rehearses an opera or a play or a symphony or an acrobatic act, mistakes always occur. Of course, most mistakes go unnoticed by the audience—an entrance a bit late, or early, a forgotten line, a note slightly off key, an unplanned movement, an accidental stumble, and so on. In reality, only those who know the work inside and out ever take note of these imperfections. This is why, on that Saturday, the night of our debut in Kassel, I was probably the only spectator who noticed the secret struggle the Pinelli brothers were waging with their act.

"My back's hurting a bit," Rocco Pinelli had said to me that morning in passing, not making much of it, and clearly assuming he'd be fine in no time.

"Take care of yourself, Rocco. Without your back, the Tower of Pisa would come down," I'd replied, alluding to a number in which the stalwart Italian held up his three brothers, each one standing on the shoulders of the other, forming first an upright tower, then leaning, inch by inch, in a gravity-defying imitation of the famous monument. It was a very popular number that, after eight years of work, generally came off cleanly and elegantly. But that night there was a pinch of pain in Rocco's smile and his legs trembled more than usual. Having held the lean for a few seconds, the brothers jumped down one by one and, instead of moving on to the next number, in which they reconstructed the tower with acrobatic leaps off the trampoline, they began to perform somersaults around the stage while Rocco, his face waxen, disappeared into the wings, the audience unaware that anything was amiss.

"Poor Rocco," I said to Robledo, applauding as the jugglers took the stage, "I doubt he'll be able to work tomorrow." I told him how much pain Rocco must have endured.

"I carry a truly extraordinary Chinese unguent with me everywhere I go," said Robledo, patting the pockets of his black frock coat. "It takes away any type of pain, from headaches to muscle cramps. You'll see how quickly he'll be good as new."

The jugglers' act and Kosti and Pythagoras' mathematical number went off beautifully. The out-of-tune blare of French horns announced "The Pursuit of the Unicorn," and I watched with satisfaction as Andrea and Vincenzo—Robledo had been correct, his cross-eyes had found me and didn't stop staring at me, in their unique way—shone as never before; Columbine, not to be outdone, exaggerated her comical leaps and facial expressions, and was immediately imitated by Pantalone and Punchinello. I looked up at the royal box and saw that King Jérôme and his august wife, Catalina de Württemberg, were both at great pains not to burst out laughing. I was pleased to see that they were enjoying themselves; as Maryse had said, a recommendation from Jérôme Bonaparte would open the doors to the theaters of France and—who knew?— maybe even to a circus on the Rue de Templar. What would they be like, Notre Dame, Les Tuileries, the Louvre, Les Invalides, the University, the Seine, all of those buildings, plazas, gardens, and streets that Maryse had told me about with such genuine nostalgia? I imagined Uncle Charles' surprise upon receiving my note, inviting him to our first performance. Where would it be, in what circus, in what theater? Would we have our equestrians by then? And now the rotund Frau Müller and her dogs were taking the stage, the latter decked out in tiny knickers, jackets, tutus, and wigs, and the orchestra, the grand Kassel orchestra that had joined forces with our own musicians for the performance, had begun to play the customary minuet while Frau Müller raised and lowered her ridiculous little boxwood baton, giving terse instructions to her disciples, when all of a sudden I realized that the act was going to end badly: Tom, the English Terrier who was the lead dog, could barely stand upright on his hind legs and kept falling down on all fours, creating great confusion among the rest of the dancing canines and setting off a murmur of disapproval from the audience. The act's finale was catastrophic: Tom's leap through the ring of fire fell short and, when his head clipped the bottom of the ring, it knocked it off its stand and sent it rolling toward the curtain at the same moment that the dog dropped like a stone, one of its hind legs jerking spasmodically. Suddenly, a terrible scream issued from the front rows. A burst of flame leapt up from the bottom of the curtain, began to climb, and threatened to catch the entire theater on fire. Fortunately, Andrea, who had been watching the act from the wings, pulled off his Harlequin cloak and managed to stifle the flames with passes of his cape, matador-like, with no consequence other than a blackish cloud of smoke and the stench of burned cloth. Everything happened so quickly that no one even had time to leave their seats. King Jérôme got to his feet and began to applaud Andrea's efforts, a gesture instantly imitated by everyone present. Frau Müller took advantage of the moment to scoop Tom's lifeless body from the floor and, cradling him tenderly in her arms, she ran offstage, between the charred curtains, sobbing. We learned later that the loyal animal must have died mid-leap.

Suddenly, the musicians launched into a tarantella, and the five French tightrope walkers popped up merrily from the box seats on either side of the stage. Tied to the boxes were two parallel wires, like subtle bridges, suspended about fifteen feet above the orchestra pit. The accident happened almost immediately, when Michou, after successfully undressing atop one of the wires, tossed her corset to Nicole, who was standing on one foot on the other wire with a parasol in her hand.

"The stupidest thing I've ever done," Michou would say half an hour later, still in her underclothes in the ladies' dressing room, while Robledo smeared her swollen ankle with his Chinese pomade. "I was a bit nervous what with the fire and Tom's death," she added.

"It's probably just bad luck," Maryse said, putting on her make-up in front of the mirror. "Every time I play the part of Eurydice something bad happens. I'm cutting *Orpheus* out of our repertoire."

And the truth is, it had been the most unlikely of accidents. If anyone had been in danger of losing her balance and falling off the wire it had been Nicole, who had to catch in one hand, and even with toe of her shoe, the articles of clothing that Michou was tossing at her.

"It's not for nothing that the first thing one learns in our profession is how to fall like a cat, always on our feet," said Nicole. In any case, the only irreparable loss was sustained by the Kassel orchestra's first chair violinist, upon whose instrument Michou had fallen, smashing it against the musician's shoulder. As for the rest of the show, order appeared to have been restored in the theater and we soon heard the applause and standing ovations that always crowned Piet, Andrea, and Claudette's act.

After Maryse shooed us out of the dressing room, Robledo and I took advantage of the intermission to drink a glass of champagne. I was curious to know if he would be willing to let go of his plantation and I didn't beat about the bush.

"If you hope to marry Maryse, you should know that she will never consent to live off the fruits of slave labor," I said point-blank.

"Yes, that does appear to be the case," he said, not paying much attention to my words, trying to distance himself from them as though he were tired of shuffling them around in his mind. I watched him take a silver owl from his pocket, unscrew its head, and pour a generous part of its golden contents into his cup. The sweet and stimulating aroma of rum wafted to my nose.

"I've christened this mixture *Ron Elegante*. I recommend it quite highly," he said, extending his arm. "Two parts rum, one part champagne. The bubbles complement the rum rather well; they lend it a certain elegance, a certain distinction. On the other hand, the rum gives the champagne a bit of vigor; it gives it weight and a slight edge; it transforms it from a fencing foil to a cavalry saber. Wouldn't you like to try it?"

His remarks reminded me of the way the Hussars had of talking and, for a moment, I felt as though I were back in Munich with Robert and his friends. But no, the *Criollo* was not bewitched by death. Quite the contrary. His charm emanated from a terrestrial, equatorial energy, linked to the lush forests and enormous waterfalls depicted in artistic renderings of the New World.

"No, thank you," I replied, rejecting his offer. "It's not that I don't like rum, but I prefer to drink it straight, like cognac. I never would have thought that sugarcane could render a liqueur of such high quality."

"It can also be mixed with tea or coffee, although in Cuba almost no one drinks tea. Oh, if you only knew how much I miss Cuban coffee! Thick and strong . . . rum complements it quite well. Not a lot, let's say half and half, although for you I'd recommend one part rum and two parts coffee. Give it a try tomorrow, before breakfast."

"Very well, I shall," I smiled. "Do you make rum on your plantation?"

"Some. Rum that's been aged only a year—we call it *aguardiente*. You wouldn't like it. It's too strong and harsh on the palate. The rum you've tried, the same as I have here, has been aged six years. It's not Cuban rum, it's from the British Antilles and was made in the English way. But soon we'll be producing a similar rum ourselves. It's the wood, and time to age, that gives it its flavor. White cedar, not found in Cuba. We'll have to import it from England or the United States."

"I've heard that there are many plantations on the outskirts of Havana," I said, trying to steer the conversation back to the topic of slavery.

"Yes, when the wind comes out of the south, which is where most of the sugar mills have been built, some people say that the air smells like molasses. And it will be getting more fragrant by the day," said Robledo, enthusiastically. "The mills are multiplying like chickens. If you could only see it! The valleys are full of plantations and smoking chimneys. It's a sight to behold, I assure you. Thanks to sugar, my island will grow to be as rich as England; it will be the Albion of the Americas, as my friend Arango likes to say. We already have different varieties of cane from Tahiti and China that are quite productive, and soon the milling machinery will be powered in a new way, by steam. That's why I'm going to England. We'll double our sugar production in no time."

"I suppose you'll need more slaves then. Poor Maryse, it seems she's destined to remain single," I said, feigning a little smile, and immediately, I regretted having spoken in such poor taste.

"Not necessarily," said Robledo, turning serious. "I think that, in the future, there will be no more importing of Africans. We'll bring in white workers. Catholics, Irish, Sicilians, Canarians. Slavery will gradually disappear."

"How far in the future?" I asked him in Spanish, so that my words would carry more weight.

"Well, in the future. . . . I didn't know that you spoke my language," he said, surprised.

"How many years, ten, twenty, thirty?" I continued in Spanish.

"For the love of God, Henriette, stop nagging me!" he exclaimed, waving his hand as though surrounded by wasps. "I love Maryse, if that's what you want to know. I've loved her since I first saw her that night in the game room in Baden-Baden. I'd give up the last hair on my head to have her always by my side. But the price she puts on her love is very high. Very high, Henriette," he repeated, soberly. "Without slaves there is no sugar, and without sugar there is no Cuba. At least that is the current situation. You must believe me when I say this."

"I do believe you, Robledo. I understand." And, remembering his words in Baden-Baden, I added: "What is meant to be, will be."

As Robledo led me through the crowd to our box, I thought it was very unlikely that a man of his age would throw not only his fortune at a woman's feet, but also the powerful conviction he held about sugar, a conviction that had the flavor of religious zeal to it, a Word that he was compelled to follow.

The curtain went up and Harlequin, Pierrot, and Columbine appeared on stage, each engaged in a different activity: Harlequin pretended to fly a kite while Columbine picnicked upon a blanket and Pierrot, seated on a basket, read the newspaper at high-speed, keeping his painted white face still and moving the paper comically from right to left. It was an excellent pantomime, quite elaborate, in which a pretend storm would blow up and Pierrot, after losing his newspaper to the wind, would find Harlequin foisting the string to his kite upon him. He'd be hoisted into the air by the kite, while down below, Harlequin and Columbine would be rolling amorously about in the blanket. I don't know if it was because I was already on the alert, but from the very beginning of the act it seemed to me that Vincenzo's white face was fixated on me rather than on the newspaper. I truly began to worry when the clown, while moving the paper from one side to the other, also began, little by little, to stick out his tongue, an incredibly long and red-tinted tongue, something he'd never done before and which, despite my disgust, the audience appeared to accept in good humor. The orchestra began the song that accompanied the imaginary storm, the notes ascending in a long chromatic phrase, the kettle drums resounding like thunder while Punchinello, hidden in the wings, pulled the line attached to the newspaper, yanking out it of Pierrot's hands. Andrea, swerving about the stage as though pulled along by the kite, at last reached Vincenzo and tried to hand him the kite string. Except that Vincenzo, instead of taking it, reached into the picnic basket and pulled out a parcel that appeared to contain a sausage; it was the phallus, the same thick and knobby phallus that he'd displayed for me in the guesthouse in Fulda. Holding it between his legs, Vincenzo showed it proudly to the audience and began to thrust his pelvis with vulgar abandon. Andrea, furious, lunged toward him, but it was too late: the stagehand had already given Punchinello the signal and Vincenzo, suspended by the harness he wore underneath his white smock, began to ascend, swinging back and forth in the air, all the while staring at me with the phallus clamped between his thighs and his tongue darting in and out of his mouth like a lascivious angel. I covered my face with both hands, feeling them tremble against my cheeks.

"I'm going to set that indecent scoundrel straight once and for all," I heard Robledo say, between cries of outrage and the sound of chairs being knocked to the floor. The din seemed to go on forever. I don't know if I was crying from rage or shame, for myself or for Maryse, her hopes shattered like a trampled mirror. When I finally decided to look around, all of the boxes were deserted and, below, in the main auditorium, amid toppled chairs and dozens of irate patrons, a squadron of *gendarmes* was leading Vincenzo away, his nose and mouth bloodied and his wayward eyes turned to me, a victorious smile on his parted lips. The stage was deserted except for Maryse and Robledo, motionless as statues, Maryse still wrapped in Eurydice's funeral shroud, and Robledo holding her in a protective embrace.

❧

Upon hearing the news of Leclerc's landing in l'Acul and seeing for himself the multiple Ships-of-the-Line jockeying for position to enter the bay at Cap-Français, Christophe decided to evacuate its residents and set the city ablaze. At dawn, while his soldiers coursed through the streets, banging on doors with their rifle butts and shouting the order to evacuate, he felt certain that the city would soon be deserted. The men were led in an orderly fashion to the Plaine du Nord, where they were to set up camp in the hopes of obstructing Leclerc's enclosing march and, in doing so, buy a few additional hours for Christophe's troops to make their retreat over the mountains. The women, escorted by a select detachment of mounted Dragoons, were herded to the nearest mountaintop, the place where Christophe had deemed they would be in the least danger. By nine in the morning, he was perplexed to see the streets still teeming with carriages and people fleeing on horseback and on foot despite his carefully laid out plan. The stragglers were mainly affluent whites and mulattos who had found it difficult to decide which of their belongings should be saved from the flames. Like lines of ants transporting precious grains of sugar, they carried with them all manner of trunks, baskets, and bundles, and even the odd piece of furniture invested with practical or sentimental value. Perhaps with the aim of speeding along the evacuation—he wanted desperately to find Louverture so they could begin to organize their resistance campaign—Christophe gave the order to set Cap-Français ablaze, and he himself set a torch to his own house. A strong breeze caused the flames to jump from rooftop to rooftop, and from yard to yard, spreading the fire with devastating speed, escalating the terror of those who had not yet escaped.

Maryse and Justine, their arms locked together, found themselves suddenly separated from their servants and belongings, and there was nothing they could do but allow themselves to be swept along by the terrified tide of women, pushed toward the hills that served as the city's natural rampart. Here and there, amid the sounds of barking dogs and whinnying horses, came the cries of mothers, daughters, sisters and friends calling out to one another in desperation. Almost without realizing it, Maryse left the Place Montarcher behind and, as in a murky dream, crossed the Rue Espagnole and the cemetery. She would, nevertheless, remember with perfect clarity the brilliance of the sun reflecting off the golden epaulets of three Dragoons—one of whom was her worst acting student—who, like dark angels signaling some biblical expulsion, pointed, with military rigidity and flashing swords, in the direction of the mountain top. She would remember the difficult climb through the bushes and scrub brush and, most especially, the court clerk Monsieur Dinard's daughter's hopeless wave as they passed alongside each other, the clerk using his straw hat to fan his wife's purple, bloated face. She would remember stopping to rest against an acacia, and leaning, short of breath, against its slanting trunk as Justine kept climbing, telling her mother as she passed: "Let's go higher, mama. We'll be able to see the fire better from the top." She would remember staying there, leaning against the acacia, with Justine's green muslin dress disappearing into the foliage, and turning her gaze toward the city, now a pyre, dense smoke rising from the rooftops, from the Quay all the way to La Fosette, and looking at the women all around her, some crouched in the tenuous shade of a bush, others standing on the mountainside; dozens and dozens of women watching in silence as Cap-Français burned. Finally, she would remember asking herself how it was possible that the city in which she'd enjoyed and suffered so much, the city that had been enthusiastically reconstructed, street by street, Portelance's city, Justine's city, *her* city, could be disappearing into embers and ashes before her very eyes. And that would be her last memory of that sad day, for she wouldn't recall the thunderous blast of gun powder, nor the avalanche of rocks unleashed by the explosion, nor Justine's scream as she tumbled down the mountain to her death.

℀

In the early morning, from my window in the hotel in Kassel, I saw Robledo bid farewell to Maryse. I assumed that the real goodbye had occurred in the room they had shared, since now Robledo merely kissed her hand and gestured affectionately with his hat before stepping into his coach. There were still two hours before the troupe meeting that Maryse and I, as directors of the Théâtre Nomade, had called in the hotel dining room. King Jérôme wanted nothing more to do with us and we needed to head toward Mannheim as quickly as possible so as not to lose the only job we still had for certain. Naturally, the most important topic of the meeting would be the reorganization of the company. Without Tom, Frau Müller's act would be discarded; without Michou, whose dislocated ankle would prevent her from working for several weeks, the tightrope act had little to offer. And, of course, there was the matter of finding replacements for Vincenzo and Rocco; the former had been jailed and the latter had thrown out a vertebra and planned to return home to his village until he'd recovered. But these were only the problems that Maryse and I were aware of, and there were sure to be others. To start with, something strange had happened among the troupe since Saturday

141

night's disastrous performance, something that not even Maryse could explain. It was as though some spell had bewitched every one of the performers, turning them reserved and taciturn. Even Andrea and Piet, who'd always been so flirtatious, avoided my attentions, withdrawing into some dark corner of their personalities to which I was not granted access. Someone knocked at my door. It was Kosti. It was enough to see him in the long gray frock coat and yellowing wig that he always wore during his act for me to understand that he had something very important to tell me.

"I have come, Madame Renaud, to smooth some rough edges," he said in a cryptic whisper, without even bidding me good morning, and before I had even finished asking him in.

"Sit down, Herr Kraft, sit down," I said, indicating a chair.

"Thank you, madame. Ehem . . . well . . . as I was saying . . . to smooth some rough edges."

"What rough edges would those be, Herr Kraft? You and I have always understood one another. I can't think of anything that has tested our friendship," I said, surprised.

"I mean to say, future rough edges. Things that I'll say at the meeting that might upset you. You and Madame Polidor. I'll speak with her as well, of course," he said, taking out his watch and bringing it near to his glasses. His pale eyes seemed larger than ever. "The truth is that I went to her room first, but she was still asleep. When I've finished speaking to you, I'll try her again. I wish to remain in her good graces. Madame Polidor is an admirable woman . . . and generous. What a fine spirit she has! An exceptional woman. And you as well. This is why I have come. In truth, you and I have never spoken much."

"What is it, Herr Kraft?" I said, in order to put an end to his detours. "Allow me to remind you that we don't have all morning to talk."

"Yes, yes. You are quite right. I understand. And in any case, we should have breakfast before the meeting. Isn't that so? Well then, I've come to tell you that I'm leaving the company. There. That's it," he said abruptly. "I'm leaving the company," he repeated, looking down at his shoes.

I didn't know what to say. I felt betrayed and Kosti, whose loyalty to Maryse and the company had never been in doubt, was the last person I'd have expected to be the cause.

"But you know that your act is a pillar of our show," I protested. "And what's more, you'd be leaving us at the very moment we need you most. I don't know if you're aware that Rocco is also leaving us, although, in his case, involuntarily," I hastened to add. "And that Michou. . . ."

"Yes, I know, madame," he interrupted. "I'm aware of all the problems. That's why I'm sorry to tell you that the mimes are also leaving the company. They plan to remain in Kassel. You see," he added, upon seeing my surprise, "theirs is a very unusual situation. Perhaps you don't know this, but Vincenzo is their father and they've decided to stay here until he's completed his three-month sentence."

"You're telling me that Vincenzo is the Venetians' father? Impossible! If that were true, Madame Polidor would have known."

"It is true."

"But what reason could they possibly have had for hiding something of so little consequence?" The truth was, I was asking myself why Andrea had not confided in me something that others already knew.

"You are not familiar with the customs of *saltimbanquis*. For example, acrobats and jugglers must always pretend that they are members of the same family. But in the case of mimes and clowns, at least those who follow in the tradition of the *commedia dell'arte*, it's just the opposite. Even if they *are* family they must appear in the program with different last names. I know this little trick must seem childish, but what can one do? It's what the public expects. The Pinelli Brothers, for example, are not really brothers. One of them is Greek and the rest of them weren't even born in the same part of Italy."

"Who else is leaving us?" I asked, exasperated.

"I think my great rival, Doctor Faustus Nefastus, is also considering desertion."

"Piet Vaalser? But what are you saying, Herr Kraft! Who told you that?"

"It came straight from his own mouth, madame. He might not leave today, but he will soon enough. He has other plans. He wants to start his own circus. A new kind of circus that he saw in Rotterdam. Not a grand circus like those in Paris and London, that have their own buildings, but a more modest and portable circus that the spectators watch standing up. The idea seems to have come from a group of sailors. It has to do with a system of poles, ropes, and canvas that can be easily taken on the road. The pieces of canvas are cut and sewn together so that they form a giant round piece with a hole in the center that allows it to be raised around a ship's mast. I think it's an ingenious and economical system, since you wouldn't have to pay for the use of theaters."

"Madame Polidor would never approve of such a thing," I said, thinking aloud. "She'd never abandon the stage or the great amphitheater of a true circus."

"I agree. Madame Polidor comes out of the grand tradition of French opera, certainly admirable. But Doctor Faustus Nefastus, just like the Pinelli Brothers and the Venetian Mimes, comes from the street."

"But you, Herr Kraft, you're also abandoning us!" I exclaimed, both angry and hurt. His defection seemed unforgivable to me, though less so than Andrea and Piet's secretiveness. "Tell me your reasons. Are you planning to join up with Piet Vaalser and his miserable canvas? Now I understand! The ship's sinking and you don't want to go down with it. Isn't that right? Isn't that why you're leaving?" I said brusquely.

"No, madame. In my case it's the law of numbers, the law of probabilities."

"Oh, so you're leaving us to go back to the roulette tables in Baden-Baden," I reproached him. "What disloyalty! You should have just stayed there."

"No, no. I'm not going back to Baden-Baden, at least not right away. The truth is, seeing as we're so close to Prussia, I'm thinking of going to Berlin, to my city. You'll see. I'll explain myself," he said, standing up. "Allow me to stay like this. I express myself better standing up. I'm going to ask you a few questions and you'll answer them."

"Thank you for putting me on equal footing with your horse," I said sarcastically. "But go right ahead, don't mind me."

"Very well." Kosti cleared his throat. "Would you agree with me that, until last Saturday, the company had been enjoying a long string of successes?" he asked.

"Agreed."

"Quite so, madame." He removed a carefully folded piece of paper from his pocket, opened it, and showed me some lines sketched in ink. "Look here. It's a graph of our earnings. Look at the ascending line. You see it? All right then," he said, putting the paper away. "Now I'll ask you another question. Can you think of anyone who got sick or had an accident before coming to Kassel, including Frau Müller's dogs, Pythagoras and the pack animals?"

"No . . . no one."

"No one. Isn't that right, madame? We have all enjoyed excellent health until last Saturday. And what happened on that night? Tom dies mid-leap, Michou falls inexplicably and Rocco throws out his back. All true, correct? And now, the final question. You'll forgive my impertinence, but it's necessary to the demonstration of my theorem. My question has to do with love and I'll begin by telling you that Frau Müller and I, ehem. . . . How shall I put it? We've been romantically involved for several weeks."

I couldn't help but smile, despite my irritation. Kosti and Frau Müller, in love!

"Congratulations. But if this has something to do with your plan to leave us, I'll tell you that neither Madame Polidor nor I had any intention of asking Frau Müller to go. It's true that Tom's death creates a problem, but we have full confidence that Frau Müller could train a substitute."

"No, no, madame, the situation with Frau Müller has nothing to do with it," Kosti said briskly. "I've already told you. It's the law of probabilities. Love."

"Love? What does love have to do with the law of probabilities?" I asked, annoyed that our conversation seemed to be going nowhere. "Herr Kraft, we've been talking for quite a while and I must remind you that you still need to see Madame Polidor before the meeting."

"I'm almost finished, madame. I'll answer my own questions. You will concur that Eros has visited us recently. Am I right? Frau Müller and me. Don Julián Robledo and . . . ehem. . . . And then, Harlequin . . . Doctor Faustus Nefastus . . . You, if you'll permit me. Even the unfortunate Pierrot, come to think of it."

"None of that concerns you," I said, insulted. What right did that charlatan have to meddle in my private life, and in Maryse's? "Please leave my room. Get out, I said!"

"I'm going, madame, this very minute. But first, listen to what I have to say: one cannot have success, money, health, and love for all one's life. Happiness is also subject to the law of probabilities. The good times are balanced out by the bad. What happened on Saturday was nothing more than the beginning of an unlucky streak for anyone and anything related to the Théâtre Nomade. Success and health, which we had taken for granted, have already begun to fail; soon we'll find ourselves without money and, what is perhaps worse, without love. Notice that the gentleman from Havana has just left. It's a sign. Oh, how I wish this weren't the case!" he sighed. "But think about what I've told you. Mathematics is never wrong. It's true that the *saltimbanquis* know nothing of numbers but, given that their very lives depend on chance, they know instinctively when the winds of fortune have stopped blowing and the winds of woe have begun. If they are constantly moving from one place to another, it's to escape bad luck. And now, that time has come," he concluded resolutely and, bowing his head in a gesture of farewell, he opened the door and left me, my mouth hanging open in bewilderment. Bewilderment? No, it would be more accurate to say disillusionment. But even disillusionment seems too weak a word. Two metaphors come to mind: A little girl goes out to play on the beach and spends hours constructing a tall monastery out of damp sand, complete with spiral staircase, cloisters, stairways, vaulted arches, bell-tower and steeple; or maybe she takes a deck of cards and begins to build a walled city, something like a majestic network of hollowed stones, with moats, rampart, bulwark, towers and drawbridge; a giant and unexpected wave comes and submerges the monastery, leaving nothing but a bubbling mound of sand in its wake; grandmother opens the kitchen window and lets in a gust of wind, really nothing more than an evening breeze or gentle zephyr that, though it but curls subtly about the kitchen, bursts into the dining room with devastating force, leaving a heap of motley rubble on the table.

It may be said that my metaphors are ridiculous, if not in outright poor literary taste, but after Kosti's visit I felt like both of those little girls.

By noon, after the meeting, all that remained of the Théâtre Nomade were the ruins left behind by the waves and winds of chance in the ill-fated city of Kassel.

§

In the days that followed the destruction of Cap-Français, multitudes of grief-stricken survivors could be seen wandering among the blackened ruins. Only the stone houses had survived the fire, although their roofs, floors, and furniture had burned like coals in a furnace. All of the important buildings—the Government House, the cathedral, the hospitals, the arsenal, the courthouse, the warehouses along the harbor—had been rendered useless, and the military engineers had to construct a provisional palace for the Leclerc family, as the general was traveling with his wife Pauline and their son Dermide. With nowhere else to go, the evacuated residents had returned to what remained of their homes. At night, they slept beneath the meager shelter of strung-up rags; during the day, or at least during the part of the day when the heat wasn't too oppressive, they combed the streets looking for vanished relatives, or labored to remove the charred remains of their homes, looking for anything of value. Everything was scarce in Cap-Français: water, food, sheets, clothing, medicine. The only things in abundance were misery and pain.

Refusing to accept that Justine was dead until she actually saw the girl's body, Maryse had given all of the gold she had to a sapper corporal and four of his men to use their tools to remove the mounds of earth, rocks, and vegetation that the avalanche had deposited at the foot of the mountain. When they found her remains, Maryse had the men carry Justine's body to the highest spot in the cemetery, where she buried her. She spent the night by her daughter's grave, crying and reflecting. At daybreak, seeing the sun rise to her right like a radiant eye impervious to any and all calamity, she felt terribly alone, like the victim of a shipwreck whose raft drifts aimlessly between empty horizons with nothing to offer. She missed Portelance more than ever. She ached to have him by her side, to hear his voice, his words of solace. Portelance would know what to do, how to go on living without Justine. But, above all, Portelance would share in that indescribable rending of the spirit she felt in the face of her loss. Was it really worthwhile to go on living, to drag her life along those streets of solitude and heartbreak?

When she arrived at the smoking walls of her house, she found Claudette in what had been the garden, sitting on a bundle of clothing and clutching a heavy silver ladle in her hand.

"I've come to beg your charity, madame," said the girl, standing up and handing Maryse the ladle as though it were a flower. "My father has fled. The house has fallen down and I don't have anyone I can trust," she added, so ashamed of her helplessness that she scarcely raised her head.

"Your house is here," replied Maryse, moved. "Or, I should say, what's left of it." And she was surprised to learn that she was still capable of smiling.

After just a few days, spurred by the necessity of supporting one another amid such profound scarcity, Maryse and Claudette's destinies had already become irrevocably intertwined.

∞

Though Maryse had known Claudette for more than two years, they had never been particularly close. It wasn't that Maryse hadn't tried to gain her friendship, but Claudette, despite what one might think upon seeing her dance so provocatively, her undulating body scantily wrapped in tulle, was extremely shy and reserved off-stage. The other members of Maryse's artists' group, generally an extroverted lot, were always surprised that Claudette never joined their dinners, teas, parties, or any social gathering for that matter, nor would she accept flowers or sweets from her many admirers. If one of these dared to come to call at her house, the mute maidservant who always accompanied her would open the door and show them a piece of cardboard that read: "Mademoiselle Despaigne is busy." On one occasion, during those moments of rest that break up the monotony of rehearsals, Maryse had surprised her at the window in the back of the theater, leaning her elbows on the windowsill and intently watching the brood of hens that the doorman kept in a pen in the yard. "Do you like chickens?" Maryse had asked her, simply to initiate a conversation. "I hate them, madame," she'd replied, and had immediately withdrawn from the window, excusing herself to go drink a glass of fresh lemonade. This brief encounter set Maryse to thinking. The harsh frankness with which Claudette had responded to her question seemed strange to her, since her timidity usually prevented her from making definitive statements on any topic, even the most trivial. Maryse decided that Claudette was more complicated than she had originally suspected but, as always, she had "a million

148

things to do," a phrase she repeated often, and she stopped thinking about the dancer in order to attend to other matters.

The truth was Claudette had good reasons to behave the way she did, reasons that Maryse would only learn after taking her in after the fire: The girl had been raped by her own father since she was six years old. The only son of a colonel from the Northern Province, Achille Despaigne had had the good fortune to inherit La Gloire, a magnificent sugar plantation near Morne Rouge that he had happily spent the better part of his life running. In the days before the Revolution, when coffee, sugar, and slavery had turned Saint-Domingue into the jewel in the Crown, he would only be seen in Cap-Français on the days slave auctions were held, since he never entrusted the purchase of this particular merchandise to any of his employees. On these occasions it was common for some planter from Limbé or Limonade to ask his advice; it was widely accepted that, when it came to newly arrived slaves, no one knew more than Achille Despaigne. And in truth, this was not an unfounded assumption in the least. Since the afternoon on which his father had locked him in the coal-shed with two Fula slave-women, what had been mere adolescent curiosity toward the Africans became a true obsession. From that day forward, Despaigne would observe his slaves' lives with the passion of the most dedicated naturalist. So much so, that his decision to live at La Gloire and take direct charge of the thousands of tasks required on a plantation of that size, was, in large part, dictated by the opportunity it would provide him to follow, up close, the lives of his three hundred and twenty slaves—men and women, old folks and children. In possession of a grade-school education, courtesy of the private tutor and vast technical library his father had brought over from Paris, Despaigne had continued his education on his own. Methodical by nature, he set about reading, one after the other in order of publication, all the books that had anything to do with sugar and slavery, from the entertaining volumes of the *Nouveau voyage aux isles de l'Amérique*, to the Marquis de Cassaux's brief study in which he describes his conversation with the inventor of a steam engine capable of powering sugar mills. But La Gloire's remarkable productivity, its incredible yield per hectare, was not due entirely to Despaigne's expertise, but rather to that of a certain Lacouture whom Despaigne had employed for many years to put his innovative ideas into practice. With everything on the technical side taken care of, Despaigne moved into a more advanced stage in his study of the slave. The first thing he did was begin a journal for each and every one of them in which he noted, as a sort of title, each slave's name, purchase price, African country of origin, sex, probable birth date, shade of skin color, height and weight, and any unusual detail found on their body. These headings were followed by daily entries that made note of the quantity and quality of work completed, errors committed, punishments, sexual conduct, superstitious practices, moods, illnesses, remedies administered, death, if it came to that, and any other interesting pieces of information that he and his *surveillants* might observe. At the end of the year his accountant would aggregate the entries and transfer them to master books that Despaigne would then painstakingly analyze. His mania reached the point that he considered constructing a circular tower, something like a lighthouse, from which he would be able to keep watch over the movements of his slaves with the aid of a maritime telescope. Five years after the start of his research, Despaigne could tell at a glance if a new arrival was Ibo, Mandinga, Zape, Fula, Congolese, Mina or Angolan and so on, as well as each one's age, aptitudes and defects, filling in any gaps in the lists the slave traders typically kept. He was not always correct, of course, but his opinion carried far and away the most weight of all of the planters. Two years later, at which point he could call by name every one of the children whose job it was to collect the cane that fell from the wagons, he initiated a general redistribution of La Gloire's entire workforce, moving each person into the post to which he or she was best suited. In this way, washerwomen and cooks who were given to talk too much were moved into the fields to cut cane, or field hands who demonstrated a capacity for concentration were sent to work in the sugar mills or at the sugar kettles. Around this time he also fired the chaplain, who'd always been an annoyance, and turned the little chapel into a bodega stocked with handkerchiefs, beads, trinkets, jerked beef, salted cod, bacon, paper cones of muscovado sugar, and other trifles that his slaves could purchase with little wooden tokens carved with Despaigne's initials, tiny prizes he used to encourage those who had worked hardest during the week. At the same time, he eliminated punishment. He simply sold any slave who didn't obey. Let others whip his back to shreds without taking into account that after dragging him half-dead to the infirmary, he'd spend entire weeks there, unable to work. Also, by way of incentive, he brought in materials for drum making—mostly wood and goat hides—since he'd confirmed that a slave was more productive when allowed to dance from time to time. If some *grand blanc* from the Northern Province had happened to visit La Gloire on the magical date of solstice or equinox, he would have thought that Despaigne had gone mad: they would have found him with a cane and a bicorn hat worn at a rakish angle, proudly presiding over a ritual performance of an ancestral Yambala dance accompanied by Rada drums. On a holiday, such as Despaigne's or the King's birthday, he could be found distributing half a liter of rum per head and applauding the dancers as they performed the "handkerchief *calenda*" or pounded out the daring drumbeats of the *mandoucouman*. Very secretly, with no explanation whatsoever to the foreman, he began a campaign to better the bloodline of "his people." He selected the tallest and most strapping of the men, whom he called his *grenadiers*, to impregnate the women with the broadest hips. He gave preferential treatment to the resulting progeny, from better diets to obligatory attendance at a type of gymnasium where, while they developed their muscles, they were also taught to speak correct basic French, without irregular verbs or the past perfect or the subjunctive, and how to carry themselves with respect, decency, and an economy of movement. He called them his "children," although he didn't give them his name. And so, by the time he turned fifty, the world of La Gloire was ordered precisely to his liking, and Despaigne decided that it was time to settle down and live with only one woman. It never crossed his mind to marry the daughter or sister of another planter, as had been the custom of the first clans to dominate Saint-Domingue. In the first place, Despaigne had never been interested in white women, whom he dismissed as lazy, vain, and meddlesome. On top of this, he'd never had confidence in the institution of marriage—French law had not yet established the practice of divorce—and in any event, he had no need for a dowry, given that his income from La Gloire was more than he would ever need. "Has the Creator ever made a better Paradise or Heaven?' he would ask himself. After pouring over the journals and master books he decided to take home a dignified, well-groomed mulatta named Mercedes, an excellent cook he'd acquired from the Spanish part of the island. Very soon she would give birth to a honey-colored little girl whom he would name Claudette and inscribe as his legitimate daughter in the civil registry of Morne Rouge. It should be said that this type of union, while not approved of in Cap-Français, was quite common among the *grand blancs* of the interior. A less frequent, though not exceptional arrangement was when a planter, or "colonist," as they were called in old Saint-Domingue, would sleep with both his favorite slave woman as well as any daughters he had with her. This was the custom Despaigne adopted as soon as Claudette grew taller than his hip. Of course, La Gloire had always been closed to any type of visitor, from the curious traveler, to the owner of the neighboring plantation. Suspecting that the unique form of governance that he employed in "his village" would be met with disapproval from the bishop or Captain General, he had ordered anyone caught trespassing the boundary lines of his realm to be escorted out with musket-shot. As might be imagined, he was fiercely criticized in Cap-Français: for most, he was an insufferable eccentric, while for others he was an anti-social element or a Voltairian *philosophe* or a disciple of Cagliostro or a vicious recluse. The truth was, no one knew for certain what went on in the mysterious limbo world of La Gloire. The *surveillants* who got loose-tongued in the taverns would tell such far-fetched tales of the goings-on there that almost no one took them seriously, thinking that Despaigne must surely be feeding them their lines, purely for the pleasure of shocking them. Around the time of the beginning of the Revolution, Mercedes' body—though certainly not Claudette's, which he'd began to abuse around this time—ceased to interest him. The same thing happened with respect to his responsibilities on the plantation. Perhaps because he couldn't fathom how he could elevate La Gloire to a status higher than perfection, he began to feel bored by the monotony of his day-to-day obligations. His world became tedious, empty of purpose. It was not that he regretted the years of effort he'd put into studying the chaotic nature of the black race. Lying awake at night, he felt great pride in the fact that his patient watchfulness had turned his slaves into "a people," with modest aspirations, to be sure, but who were nevertheless disciplined and hard-working and who, while preserving some of their primitive customs, were capable of keeping La Gloire functioning like a stopwatch perfectly synchronized with the sugar production calendar: harvest time, machinery repair time, cultivation time. And he had done this alone, without the help of ferocious dogs, pillories, or whips, or even priests with their promises of eternal happiness in the divine hereafter. Without a doubt, his had been a categorical triumph. Nevertheless, he felt his triumphs were behind him, like the celebrated labors of Hercules, and he had no further victories to look forward to. He very much wanted a son to carry on his lineage, but Mercedes had only given him Claudette. Had he been a different man he'd have brought half a dozen slave women into his bed, and surely one of them would have borne him a son. But he wasn't a different man; he was Achille Despaigne, and such behavior would have violated the order that he had established with such high hopes in La Gloire, an order that began and ended with him. Of course, there was Claudette. After all, according to his reading of Genesis, humanity had been born of primogenial incest. Except that Claudette was still an unripe fruit. But wasn't it better for her, and, in the final analysis, for everyone, to initiate her early into incest, for her to find it natural to be alongside her father, naked and erect? He tried, without success, to convince Mercedes of the logic behind his arguments. Saddened by having to take extreme measures, he went to see her in the kitchen and told her: "Either comply with me or I'll sell you. Choose! I'll have my way in either case." Although it didn't prove necessary to dispatch with Mercedes, the new situation wasn't enough to alleviate his boredom. He scarcely paged through the journals and master books anymore, and ceased to supervise the work of his *surveillantes*. Since production did not decline, he assumed that the manager, accountant, sugar technician, and the rest of the salaried workers were continuing to run things in good order. This brought him a great sense of peace: he had given La Gloire an autonomous existence, his hand had set the gears and other mechanisms in motion and, like a grandfather clock, it now ran of its own accord. And so, it didn't surprise him that, when the time came, only four of his slaves left to join Bouckman's rebellion. One afternoon, bored, he tried to kill some time in his father's technical library, which he hadn't visited since he'd contracted the services of the masterful Lacouture who, incidentally, had become a famous author of treatises. Though he discovered that the humidity, mold, dust, and worms had finished off the books, he also found, jumbled and covered in a thick patina inside a mahogany chest, the silver spoons that his mother had once collected. As wonderstruck as a child by his discovery, his obsessive character drove him to pursue the spoon-collecting enterprise further. Now rescued from the chest and polished to a resplendent shine, he lined the spoons up on the shelves where the books had rotted away. It was not uncommon to find him there, past midnight, handling the spoons, classifying them by size, noting the names of their previous owners on little labels which he then tied with thin string about their slight waists. Soon he would come to own seven thousand spoons, almost all of them acquired from his agent in Brest. Many of the most recently arrived batch had belonged to *émigré* nobility, beheaded or simply impoverished; others had belonged to the bourgeoisie of the Third Estate who, gathered on that Tennis Court had set off, without realizing it, their bloody match with the monarchy; and still others had belonged to lawyers and doctors whose radical ideas had cost them their lives— as was the case, for example, with a heavy soup ladle that had once graced Marat's table. It would not be an exaggeration to note that some of the caresses that Despaigne lavished upon his spoons were charged with sexual significance. Claudette had seen him nest together two charming teaspoons that had belonged to Marie Antoinette and Madame de Lamballe, respectively, and then force himself relentlessly upon her child's body. In any case, thanks to the weekly sale of some of his spoons, Despaigne would have the means to survive when La Gloire was destroyed in a single night by his own slaves, among them a raging and vengeful Mercedes, before they went to join forces with Louverture. If Despaigne wasn't hacked to death by a machete it was because, upon seeing unfamiliar signs of feathers and bloodied fetters hanging from certain trees at La Gloire, he suspected that something exceptional was about to occur. Without awaiting further confirmation, he took Claudette and left for Cap-Français with the intention of depositing all of his spoons in the fort and asking the garrison chief for a detachment of soldiers. Once there, however, despite his repeated pleas and threats, he was met only with the indifference of military bureaucracy. The following morning, when the news arrived in the city in the form of a dead *surveillante* who'd been lashed to a horse, Despaigne didn't even try to go back to survey the damage. That very same day he rented a house in the city and contracted the services of a mute servant. And it was this very same land, those razed acres of La Gloire, that the lawyer Delacour would try to persuade Maryse to buy. This purchase, of course, would never come to pass, since, upon learning that the burning of Cap-Français was imminent, Despaigne filled four haversacks with the remainder of his prized collection, threw them into a wheelbarrow and headed for the docks where he intended to board the first ship bound for the United States—a journey he'd planned to undertake sooner or later, in any event. Untroubled at the thought of abandoning his daughter, whose apparent lack of fertility had proved greatly disappointing, he bought a lavishly expensive ticket aboard the schooner *Charleston Belle* that, already brimming with terrified passengers, was just about to weigh anchor. In the months before Maryse and Claudette would leave Cap-Français forever, no one heard a single word from or about Achille Despaigne, and no one showed the slightest interest in buying the land that had once been La Gloire.

One afternoon, when Maryse was trying to transform a nightshirt into a dress for Claudette, the girl suddenly revealed the reason behind her on-stage exhibitionism: if she had danced lasciviously on the sets of *Salomé* or *The Caliph of Bagdad*, or waggled her behind more than was strictly necessary while dancing the meringue or the *calenda*, it was because her father, who'd always been aroused at the sight of others desiring her, had required her to do so. "Although after doing it like that so often," the girl added innocently, "at some point my body began to enjoy its own sensuality." When Maryse asked why, even after she'd offered to help her, she had hidden Despaigne's perversity from her, Claudette didn't know how to explain herself clearly. She spoke of fear, of guilt, of weakness of character, of the poor opinion she held of herself, of the powerful force of habit. Finally, after a long hesitation, she replied shyly: "I think it's because he was my father."

9

OUR THREE PERFORMANCES IN MANNHEIM and the sole show we'd managed to book in Frankfurt were disastrous, just as Kosti had predicted they would be, and Maryse and I agreed that it was time to dissolve the company. The news was met with a few tears but, in truth, we all felt relieved to be liberated from pointlessly dragging along the weight of a show that was going from bad to worse. Even Pierre, who, after his turn as director of transportation for the Théâtre Nomade, had gone back to being my coachman, told me philosophically: "Madame, as my father always said, a cobbler should stick to his last. I'll finally be able to sleep in peace."

After we'd sold the last wagons and mules to the owners of a brewery, I tried to convince Maryse to come with me to Foix, but the place where we were conversing at that moment was not the most conducive to serious discussion. We'd gone out shopping and, as we were poking about in the shops, a sudden downpour had held us captive in a furrier's next to a display of a horrible-looking black horse. The shop, full of shoes, boots, valises, and harnesses, smelled like a storeroom for the *Intendance*.

"But tell me, what would we do in Foix?" she asked me, testing the soundness of a huge suitcase with the toe of her shoe.

"So many things. For example, we could. . . ." I let the sentence go unfinished because I'd remembered that Maryse didn't ride horses.

"We could what?" she insisted.

"We could go down to the river and swim from one bank to the other."

"I don't know how to swim."

"We could take a picnic to the woods. There is a lovely clearing surrounded by mushrooms and dandelions. I used to go there to talk with the fairies as a child. And we could host dances at the château. And grand dinners. And of course, go to Toulouse. There's a theater there, and good shops. They sell things from Spain there that you'd love. We could organize a theater group. Something like the one you had in Saint-Domingue," I said, my hopes soaring. "Who knows? Maybe we could even build a circus in Toulouse."

"Don't talk to me about circuses! My talents are music and singing!" she said, laughing, and turned toward a young shopkeeper who, pretending to dust a row of boots, had moved near us so that he could eavesdrop on our conversation. "I'm through with clowns, tightrope walkers, acrobats, and jugglers, with professors and doctors, and animals! Especially mathematical horses and dancing dogs! To hell with each and every one of those *saltimbanquis!*" she shouted, startling the shopkeeper. "Do you hear me? Yes, you there, with the rabbit teeth!"

"And so, what do you say?" I asked, after the shopkeeper had disappeared quickly into the backroom of the store. "Will you come with me? We don't have to head straight for the Languedoc. We'll go to Paris first. It's high time for me to see all of those marvelous palaces and churches that everyone's always telling me about. And anyway, it seems like centuries since I've seen my uncle. What do you say?"

"Oh, your Uncle Charles! A good-hearted man. Don't think that I've forgotten him," she said. "I know that he loves you a great deal. He told me so in Strasbourg. Has it been a while since you've heard from him?"

"I received a letter from him when we arrived in Kassel. He's well. He's in charge of medical instruction in the city's military hospitals. But tell me: are you coming with me or not? Come on, Maryse! Doesn't it pain you to think of separating Claudette and Françoise?"

"We shall see, my love, we shall see," she said thoughtfully. "Paris is quite tempting, although, well, you know, I'd had such aspirations. You do make a good point about Claudette and Françoise."

Looking back on that day at the furrier's in Frankfurt, I realize now just how close Maryse had been to accepting my proposition. So close, in fact, that had chance or fate—I've never been sure which it was—not interrupted our conversation at that exact moment, her life, and my own, not to mention the thousands of lives that would brush up against ours, in one way or another, would have been completely different.

"What is that noise?" Maryse asked, standing up abruptly and moving over toward the door. "Come here, Henriette, look what's coming this way."

I went to the door. The rain had slowed to a drizzle. Looking to the left, I saw a cavalry troop making its way down the street.

They were Hussars. French Hussars. They were wearing the regulation gabardine against the rain. I knew at once by the color of the feathers they wore in their caps that they did not belong to Robert's regiment. They had come a long distance. Their mustaches hung limply on either side of their mouths, the wax long since worn away. They rode with their heads down, so sodden with water and boredom that most of them didn't even look at us as they passed by. It was obvious that their barracks were not in Frankfurt, for, had that been the case, their horses would have sensed their proximity and, instead of plodding along at a walk, the reins slack against their necks, they would have been straining against their riders, starting and snorting, trying to leave formation and trot off toward the stables. The sky was still cloudy and the clop, clop, clop of the horses' hooves through the puddles, splattering mud and dirty water only added to the squadron's forlorn march. Hearing the sound of the cavalcade, the shopkeeper came out of the backroom and drew near to the window. Seeing that it was a French regiment he made a crude hand gesture and returned to his last and leather. His disgust didn't surprise me. I had already begun to notice the disdain our supposed allies, particularly the young people, expressed for all things French.

"What were you thinking about, my love?" asked Maryse, as we retreated back inside, our dresses splattered with raindrops. "You were looking at those young men with such a pained expression on your face."

"I was thinking that Hussars are not made for times of peace."

"Strange. I was thinking nearly the same thing. But something occurred to me. I was thinking . . . I was thinking that perhaps we could do something for them."

"Like what?" I asked, alarmed.

"It was only a thought. Nothing important."

159

"Go on," I demanded.

"It's not that the idea of Paris and Foix doesn't interest me. Quite the contrary. It's just that. . . ." she hesitated.

"What?"

"It's difficult to explain, my sweet. Or it's that I don't think you'll understand me."

"How can you say that, Maryse, after everything we've been through together! How could you even think to say that?"

"You're right," she said gently, to calm me down. "You see, it's actually quite simple. I don't like to feel defeated. Or, to put it another way, I only give up struggling against adversity when I'm certain there's no other option. It's as though life were a challenging opera and the entire world is judging my performance. And I'm not just looking for applause and bouquets of flowers; it's that I believe I should always be at the peak of my abilities, my very best self. Do you know what I sometimes think? I think that when I die and Saint Peter asks me what I've done to deserve entrance into heaven, I'd like to be able to answer him: 'I've always been completely loyal to the small talent that God has given me.' Whether or not he opens the gates is his business. Who knows what the saints think? But at least I'd have given him my reason. Look, it's started raining again, what a nuisance!" she exclaimed.

"It must be a sign from Saint Peter," I said, annoyed. "So, you're not coming to France with me. Isn't that how I'm to interpret your celestial parable?"

"Sit down, Henriette. This storm's going to last awhile," she said, pointing to the chair set up for customers trying on shoes. "Hopefully our Germanophile friend won't throw us out of here. Don't you think he has teeth like a rabbit's? I'll sit on this suitcase, it looks sturdy enough. Now then, seeing the Hussars' sad procession I was reminded of Linz, of how well we did there back when Claudette and I entertained the troops. That's actually how the Théâtre Nomade got started, visiting the barracks in Austria and Germany. After that, everything got complicated. Little by little the *saltimbanquis* arrived and suddenly we were doing performances in German theaters and adding acts in German to our repertoire. A big mistake, my friend, a big mistake. If we had just stuck to our own soldiers then, we wouldn't find ourselves sniveling and demoralized by failure today."

"What is it you have in mind? Though I'll tell you right now I'm asking purely out of curiosity. Tomorrow I'm heading for Paris with Pierre and Françoise."

"There's nothing for it," she sighed. "You know enough about life by now to know what's best for you. I, on the other hand, think I'll stay in Germany a while longer. Before I declare myself defeated I'd like to stage a small show, something very intimate and modest, you know? Something sentimental. Something that will remind those poor Hussars of things like their mothers, their grandparents, their childhoods, games they played with their younger siblings, Christmas cakes, the warmth of the hearth, the feeling of being loved unconditionally. Don't be fooled, there's no homeland better than that one. So, can you guess what I have in mind?" she asked me with a rapturous expression. When she received no response other than my sullen silence, she went on: "The stories that our parents and grandparents told us, my love. That's what I'm thinking of. Our first books, you know, the stories by Perrault and Madame de Beaumont."

"Maryse, my dear, sweet Maryse," I said, almost pityingly. "Do you really think that a Hussar would be moved hearing the story of *Beauty and the Beast* or *Little Red Riding Hood?*"

"Moved? My dear, they'd laugh and cry until they'd soaked their own mustaches. Of course, it all depends on how you tell the story. Just imagine it, the room lit only by candelabras, and me at the piano, singing those stories in the old songs from Provence, Brittany, Normandy, and so on, touching everyone's little corner of France, and Claudette and a few others dancing, or better, their bodies keeping time to the rhythm of the music, their movements echoing the action in the stories, sort of like mimes do. Just imagine it: the lights are dim. No elaborate scenery. Just a little platform stage and a few curtains. Maybe another, smaller platform, to use as a bed or a kitchen or a forest or even a castle. Oh, and some crates here and there. Can't you just see it? I'd do all the sound effects with the piano. When Blue Beard or the Beast come on stage, for example, I'd play bom, bom, bom, brobobom, and for Little Red Riding Hood walking through the forest I'd play. . . ."

"Bim, bim, bim. . . ." I interrupted her. "Very imaginative. But where would you find a French poet to do all the rhyme schemes for your songs?" I added, a touch of triumph in my voice.

"There's no shortage of poets, my dear. But that matter's already resolved. I know those rhymes by heart. Did you think I was talking about a new show? No, no, not at all. I came up with the idea when I was working as a governess in Saint-Domingue. As I said, I have all of the material stored right here in my head. The only things we'd need to buy are some masks."

"When you were a governess in Saint-Domingue? You seem to have forgotten to tell me that part," I said, utterly taken aback.

"I'll tell it to you in a letter, my love. When you arrive in Foix, it will be waiting for you there. Now then, let's talk about something else until the rain lets up. Something practical, let's say . . . let's talk about money. Before you go we need to divide up the money from the sale of the last of the set designs."

"Go to hell, Maryse! Really, go straight to hell!"

"Shhh! Lower you voice. That Germanophile rabbit will take us for a couple of whores."

"Let him take us for whatever he wants. I don't care one bit. But tell me: how long do you plan to go on with your ridiculous bim, bim, bim and bom, bom, bom?"

"Well . . . not long. A few months, I suppose. Long enough for me not to feel defeated," she concluded.

We sat in silence. The last thing we wanted at that moment was to part like that, and both of us were hoping that the other would change her mind. The shopkeeper, no longer hearing our voices, must have thought we'd left and came out from the backroom.

"Go back to your goddamned burrow!" Maryse shouted at him.

"I want to spend Christmas with Uncle Charles," I said after a long pause, thus announcing my defeat. "Do you promise me that we'll be in Paris by the middle of December?"

"I promise. Count on it. But come here, my little black sheep. Were you really thinking of going astray and abandoning me here among the Hussars and patriotic bunny rabbits?" she said, smiling, as she walked over to hug me close.

⚮

Maryse would enter into the employ of Pauline Bonaparte, known at the time as Madame Leclerc, thanks to the intervention of the ever-helpful Delacour. It was not easy for her to move to the palace.

It wasn't because she feared leaving Claudette alone—Dou Dou, one of Maryse's servants, had returned to the house in search of shelter and would stay with the girl. In truth, it was difficult because she associated Leclerc's presence with Justine's death. And then there was the matter of Leclerc himself, whom she considered of dubious honor and uncertain scruples. Yes, it was true that after defeating the black resistance forces he had welcomed their leaders into the French army, even maintaining the ranks of such officers as Christophe, Dessalines, Pétion and so many others who had fought over the years against white hegemony. Nevertheless, he had laid a trap for Louverture, capturing him and shipping him off to France as though he were an exotic animal, serving him up to Bonaparte on a silver platter. And even worse, it was taken for granted that slavery would be reinstated, that everything would go back to the way it was before; in other words, exactly what Portelance had so feared. On the other hand, there were the immediate realities of life. To put it bluntly, Maryse and her young companion did not have food to eat. Portelance's plantations had been destroyed during the first days of the resistance. Had the lands been hers, she could have sold them. But they weren't hers. Her once bountiful wardrobe, jewelry, furniture and other valuable objects had been reduced to rubble; what hadn't been turned to ash or looted by her cook and coachman, she herself had sold to make it through the spring. All she had left, buried under the patio as a means of last resort, was the silver ladle that Claudette had found underneath Despaigne's bed, where he must have inadvertently left it in the rush to flee his plantation. And, in any event, Maryse was saving that for Claudette. Claudette's fragility and her painful past made Maryse feel compelled to protect her, especially because her tiny body and naïve expression made her look younger than she was. And Maryse was also aware that the girl, while not filling the empty space left by Justine's absence, did somehow make it more bearable.

Weeks before, the lawyer Delacour had paid her a visit in order to let her know that, thanks to Lieutenant Michel Simonet, a nephew on his mother's side, he had been named chief of the Property Registry. It was only a mid-level position, but it would be enough to support him and his wife. Almost as an aside, he added that he'd be pleased to recommend her to his young benefactor, whose poetic talents had gained him a place in Madame Leclerc's lively court. He couldn't guarantee her anything, but it was at least something that he could do for her. Maryse had kindly refused the lawyer's offer because, at that point, she still had some things she could sell to the peddlers and junk dealers who hawked their wares out in the streets, turning the general state of misery to their advantage. The day came, however, when the only things she saw in the tin crate that served as her cupboard were a few pieces of sugarcane and a half-kilo of stale bread. That morning, she plucked up her courage and headed to Delacour's office with the intention of taking him up on his generous offer.

The days following Maryse's visit to Delacour passed excruciatingly slowly for Maryse and Claudette. Their situation had been made even more difficult by Dou Dou's meek return; having been thrown out by her lover and with nowhere to sleep, she had decided to go back to her former mistress's house, repenting her foolishness and begging Maryse to take her back without pay. Just as Maryse was considering going out to sing in the cantinas in the hopes of earning a few coins, she received a visit from a clerk with the Civil Registry who announced: "Monsieur Delacour is indisposed. He asked me to deliver this message to you." Not waiting for the man to hand the missive over, Maryse snatched it from him, broke the seal and desperately read its contents: General Leclerc's son's governess had taken ill with fever and Madame Leclerc would be interviewing candidates for said position between the hours of nine and eleven the following morning. Maryse, familiar with Delacour's handsome and precise penmanship, did not fail to notice the great pains that had been taken to compose that hopeful letter. That night, when Maryse stopped at his house to thank Delacour for his intercession, she learned that the lawyer had just died from yellow fever. "A rare case," noted the doctor who opened the door for her. "The fever usually attacks the recently arrived, not those well-seasoned by the tropics such as Monsieur Delacour. And, in any event, it's quite early in the season. This does not bode well, madame. Mark my word. If I were you, I would not go into the house. I fear that Madame Delacour is also infected."

The following day, after sitting for a few minutes in the palace vestibule with the other applicants, an aide-de-camp's aquiline gaze fixed upon her, silently inviting her into the music room. As soon as she saw the familiar shape of the concert piano standing in front of a picture window, she felt a warm wave of confidence roll up from her toes to her head. Shifting her gaze, she saw, in a corner of the room, surrounded by flowers and betel palms, a beautiful, straight-nosed woman, barefoot and dressed in a tunic, lying languidly across a simple sofa. Maryse promised herself that, should she ever have a music room, she would greet her guests in that very same posture, her left elbow resting on the sturdy spiral at the end of the sofa, the palm of her hand holding up her head as if it were a piece of fruit, and a slight, though pleased smile on her lips. "Show me what you can do, madame, if it pleases you," said Pauline cheerfully, gesturing toward the piano. Maryse, her customary sense of ease restored, sat down in front of the keyboard and, without looking at the notes on the score propped on the stand, played from memory the well-known Mozart rondo that was expected of her.

"Bravo, madame! My compliments," said Pauline sincerely. "Now I'd like to hear your voice. Sing whatever you'd like." Maryse opened with an aria by Cherubini and followed it with another by Boieldieu. "Very good. That will be all. I only wanted to confirm what I've been told about you, and I'm quite pleased. Now that I've heard you, I've decided to divide the governess position into two parts. Your only responsibility will be to entertain my son Dermide, or, I should say, to enchant him with your splendid artistry while he plays. He is scarcely four years old, but I want him to become familiar with music as soon as possible. Can you come tonight with your things? There are devastating fevers going around the city and tomorrow we'll be moving to Tortuga Island. One more thing, madame. I'm told that you are caring for a ward in your home. Give her the purse that's on top of the piano. I'm aware that circumstances are difficult these days."

Maryse left the palace as though she were floating inside a soap bubble.

❧

Maryse plucked the last strawberry from the dish, savored it slowly and wiped her fingers on a napkin. "And so, it may not have been my greatest artistic triumph, but it was certainly my most timely," she concluded. We had stopped at a roadside farm stand to snack on wild strawberries and cream. I wiped the dish with my finger and licked off the last of the delicious bittersweet flavor.

"And? You can't stop there," I said. "Is it true what they say about Pauline Bonaparte? Andrea told me that she had three lovers at the same time." Maryse made a gesture with her hand, as if she were about to answer my question, but opted instead to simply shrug her shoulders. After taking a sip of water she said: "We should go, my pet. Claudette and Françoise will have finished by now and if we don't get going they'll be carrying on like a couple of lovebirds. There they are," she murmured, turning her gaze toward a nearby bench. "Just look at them with their bare feet entwined, happy and as in love as ever. They haven't even realized that we're watching them. They're in their own world. Look how they're attracting bees. It's the perfume of love. The perfume of life and of nature. I read somewhere that the true measure of love is sacrifice. What nonsense! Sounds like something for a suicide case. For me, the measure of love is feeling loved in return. The days, weeks, months, and years that I feel myself loved. Look at those two, they've loved each other since our days in Linz. That is their measure of love. I won't deny that there are situations and ambiances that are conducive to being in love. For example, this strange summer that keeps holding on, as though the trees, teasing the calendar, are refusing to undress. People speak of spring, but for me, the season most favorable to love is right now, these magical days of late summer. Days of enchantment, days of fairies. Why not assume that those bees crowning Françoise's hair are actually a swarm of fairies? Oh, Henriette! Where could my Oberon be?"

"Fairies disappeared from my life years ago and your Oberon is exactly where he's supposed to be: in England," I said, putting an abrupt end to her romantic reverie. "As for Françoise's hair, if you look closely, you'll see that it's covering up a pair of donkey ears. I still can't understand her love for another woman, even if it is Claudette."

"Love is always inexplicable. You only talk like this because you're not in love," protested Maryse.

"You're mistaken. I'm still in love with Robert. I dream of him. He comes to me, as tall and handsome as ever."

"No, my dear, if you'll forgive me. You only think that you're in love with him. I thought the same thing about Portelance. But the truth is that it's a trick our hearts play on us to make us think that we'll always love someone, even though that someone no longer exists on this earth. That way we can feel respectful and loyal to their memory, which is all very well, except, of course, it's like living in a dream. But if Sleeping Beauty's prince were to find and kiss you, you'd wake up instantly and marry him."

"And what if Robert already was my prince?"

"Well, then you'll stay asleep dreaming of him until another prince arrives."

"All right then, since you seem to know everything there is to know on the subject of love, tell me: how many princes does one get to have in a lifetime? You know, just on average, as Kosti would say."

Maryse grew thoughtful. She served herself some cool water from the pitcher, took a sip, and said resolutely: "Princes, princes, what we call princes with their white steeds and tall castles and the cliché of 'they lived happily ever after,' of those, I'd say very few. It all depends on how long one lives and on how much love one spends."

"I agree about the number of princes, but you speak of love as though it were money."

"No, my dear. Money comes and goes, it's lost and recuperated, it increases and diminishes; love does not. The love that you give is irretrievable. And not only that: love doesn't regenerate inside a person like anger, sadness or hunger. My prince of the Indies has me reflecting a great deal about love lately. If I told you that I know where love originates, I'd be lying. The only thing I can say is that, wherever it begins, in the brain, the marrow, the heart, the liver, or in the soul, it isn't an inexhaustible well. When it's gone, it's gone. Love is like the water in this pitcher. I can drink it in huge gulps or sip by sip, I can toss it out all at once on the grass, I can use it to splash you on the nose," she said, dipping a finger in her glass and flicking the drops at my downturned face. "I can save it up, or I can just leave it sitting there, unspent, out of greed or an excess of precaution, or perhaps because I've been told that it's poisoned. Take my case, for example. I gave Portelance no less than half of the jar; to the rest, I've given only a few sprinkles, as I did to your nose. . . ."

"And Robledo gets what's left," I interrupted.

"I have given Robledo a small drink. Much less than you think. But if his thirst were truly great, if it were an enormous and authentic thirst, then yes, I'd allow him to drink what was left in the pitcher. Well, one exaggerates. Let's say I'd keep a few little drops in the bottom just in case."

"Very instructive. I'm grateful for the lesson," I said, only slightly in jest. "According to your theory, I've got quite a bit of water left to spend, isn't that right?"

"A half-pitcher, at the very least. Though I think it's rather more."

"A gypsy woman in Toulouse saw three marriages in my palm."

"Well, then, we're in agreement. You still have two-thirds of the jar left," she teased. "Let's get going, my love. We need to make it to Cologne by nightfall." She left a few coins on the table and stood up.

As we were walking toward the carriage I said: "Pardon my curiosity but, if Robledo should decide to come look for you, how will he ever find you if we're forever moving from one place to another?" It was something I'd been wanting to ask her for some time.

"Very easily, my pet. We agreed that, starting in Kassel, I'd leave him a paper trail by means of sentry posts, inns, and guesthouses. This morning, for example, I should have left a note in his name at The Green Hare, telling him that we were bound for Cologne."

"But you didn't!" I said, as though she'd made a fatal mistake. "Look, I've no objection to going back."

"Don't worry, my love. I do this from time to time. It's like playing roulette with destiny. There's nothing to worry about. If his thirst is powerful enough, he'll pick up my trail. My heart tells me that he's a good bloodhound."

And so we traveled along that unending summer, talking about anything and everything and stopping at each barracks to perform, with great success, the tales of Perrault and Madame de Beaumont.

૪

Maryse's account of her life in Saint-Domingue had rolled off her tongue without major difficulties so far. Her natural loquacity faltered on a few occasions and she sometimes jumped about chronologically, leading to omissions and digressions I felt compelled to remedy with questions such as, "And did this happen before or after. . . ?" But on the whole, her story was gradually reconstructing itself in my mind like a novel in installments. One night, however, the thread of the narrative was irrevocably cut. And it's not that the night hadn't begun well enough. After finishing *Beauty and the Beast*, the story with which Maryse always closed the show, the colonel of the regiment had honored us with a pleasant dinner, full of childhood memories and anecdotes of village life. We had eaten so much that, when we arrived back at our rooms, I suggested to Maryse that we sit up talking for a spell before going to bed. We met in her room and, after drinking a bit of rum as a *digestif*, I asked her to take up her story again where she'd left off. And so I learned that a certain Lieutenant Simonet, the nephew of the ill-fated Delacour, had composed the rhymes for *Little Red Riding Hood* that Maryse would sing to entertain little Dermide, accompanied by the strains of a Provençal melody. Then she related how Pauline and her friends, entranced by Maryse's subsequent adaptations of Perrault, had gone so far as to quarrel among themselves as to who would get to play the part of Cinderella or Blue Beard. Then she spoke of the time she'd spent living on Tortuga Island—going into particular detail about a hallucinatory Negro dance in the cemetery under the light of the full moon—and she'd even cracked a small smile when, accosted by my questions, she'd admitted that Simonet had kissed her breasts on the return journey to Cap-Français. And suddenly, as she was beginning to speak of the plague that, like a voodoo curse, had returned with renewed intensity, I noticed a trembling in her voice. It was not the first time that it had happened. I remembered the afternoon she'd told me about the fire and Justine's death. She tried to regain her composure with a large swallow of rum but, instead of brightening , her expression turned somber.

"Do you feel ill?" I asked her. She didn't answer. "Do you want me to open the window?" Then, resting her head against the back of the chair, she closed her eyes and said in a low voice: "Everything that followed was a perfect pile of shit." I said nothing. I remained calm. I knew that a single word from me, an abrupt gesture, would be enough to vanquish that moment of dark confession. Then she began to speak. Her voice no longer trembled, but it came out dull and painfully hoarse, as though she were singing the ballads of The Beast. "Yellow Fever. They also called it the Black Vomit. The doctors didn't know how to cure it. We all lived in terror. Pauline fired me, thinking I was infected. Leclerc died. At first, they made a hospital in the ruins of La Fosette. They fashioned the roof out of sugarcane. Soon there were no doctors left to tend to the sick. People were dying in the streets. Even in the dancehalls and banquet rooms. Hundreds and hundreds of unburied corpses. They threw them into the sea, and they just came back. The stench was horrible. And then the fighting. The fighting, all over again. The city under siege. The voodoo drums. Night and day. Neither side took prisoners. Poor Simonet! And then that pig Rochambeau. *Salaud!* If you only knew the things I've seen! Negroes impaled on cavalry lances. Dogs gnawing on the bones of children. Men vomiting their own shit. They would put cartridges filled with gunpowder up their asses. You don't want to know the things that went on there! And all the while, the whoring . . . everyone naked, dancing right on top of the guts and the shit. Do you understand? Everyone dancing to the music of death, everyone trying to mask their fear with their most secret perversion. Yes, the whoring was the worst part . . . I. . . . But enough of that. Don't make me talk any more. Please leave me be." I left her room then, knowing she was only pretending to be asleep.

The following morning we met in the dining room, as was our habit. Her eyes were swollen and I suspected that she hadn't slept at all. As soon as she saw me heading for the table she said in a firm voice: "Not one word about what happened last night, and especially about Saint-Domingue. My story has come to an end."

Days later, taking advantage of her good mood, inspired by the news that Robledo was on her trail—having finished his business in Prussia he'd abandoned his plans to go to England—I insisted that she finish what I called "the final chapter of your novel." But it was no use. The only thing I could get out of her was that, shortly before the surrender, thanks to the intervention of two American women, she and Claudette had managed to secure Rochambeau's permission to travel.

(Shortly after I arrived in New York, I came across a book in which was published the interesting correspondence between an American woman and Mr. Aaron Burr, dated from the time the latter had been serving as vice president of the United States. The letters had been written from Cap-Français, and they provided details about the Yellow Fever epidemic, Leclerc's death, and, above all, the orgiastic tyranny of Rochambeau, who'd had an affair with the woman's sister. Although none of the letters mentioned Maryse or Claudette, certain clues led me to suspect that my dear friends had escaped Cap-Français on the same boat as those American sisters.)

❧

As Autumn wore on, our little show became well known among the garrisons on the other side of the Rhine. We had not visited all of them but, thanks to the continual communication among them, our notoriety preceded us everywhere we went. In general, we did three performances: two for the soldiers and recruits, and one for the officers, charging more for the latter. The venue varied depending upon the specific characteristics of the garrison. In accordance with regulations limiting those not in the service from entering the barracks, we were generally offered some sort of auxiliary structure such as an unused farmhouse, a granary barn, a stable or a storehouse. As for the pianos, we never had to worry; there was always a perfectly tuned one waiting for us, generally borrowed from one of the city's well-heeled families. Unfortunately, given that the Confederation of the Rhine had to maintain an army of more than sixty thousand men—both French and allied troops—and keep them all housed, armed, fed and well-mounted, our troops "borrowed" things of much greater value than a piano. Many things were scarce, and the blockade against English goods only worsened the situation. Additionally, there were the large sums France required as contributions to the war effort, and the continual requisitioning of horses and cattle. And so, the great hope that had at first accompanied the alliance with Napoleon was rapidly unraveling.

That afternoon in X—I have my reasons for not revealing the name of the city—the Germans' problems were far from my mind. According to a hasty letter from Robledo, left at the sentry post in Cologne, he would rejoin Maryse in two days, at the latest. Although my friend swore that her conditions for accepting his marriage proposal were the same as always, his sudden arrival made me uneasy. But it wouldn't be completely honest if I didn't admit that I also looked forward to seeing him, to his noble air, his good humor, his frank and worldly conversation, even his arrogance. I was thinking about all of this in my room at the guesthouse, lying on the bed, half-asleep from the laudanum that, since my days in Boulogne and at Uncle Charles's recommendation, I always took as a remedy for my irregular and painful periods. Although I had decided not to perform that evening—Maryse would have to do without one of Cinderella and Belle's sisters, and Pierre would have to play Puss in Boots—I hoped to attend the performance, which would take place in an old stable next to the barracks. But, without meaning to, I fell asleep, and so I stayed, until repeated knocks at my door slowly awakened me. When I opened my eyes I saw that there was barely any light coming through the window. In addition to the repeated knocking, someone was shouting my name. It was Robledo.

"Good God, Henriette, I thought something had happened to you!" he exclaimed, and, heedless of the fact that I was in my nightgown, he took me in his arms and peppered me with kisses. "And Maryse? Where is my *chiquita linda*?" he asked immediately. "I've come at a dead gallop from Cologne." After explaining that we had a show that night and that surely Maryse would be putting the finishing touches on our modest set design, he agreed to wait a few minutes so that we could go find her together.

It is not easy for me to relate what happened next, perhaps because, faced with the double blow of the terrible and the unexpected, our minds only manage to preserve fragments of memory. I know that when we left the guesthouse it was growing dark and, arm in arm with Robledo, I could scarcely keep up with his long strides. Then, the sound of an explosion. It's odd that, despite having heard thousands of cannon shots, my ear can still distinguish today that dry thunder that illuminated the street in a quick flash, frightening the horses hitched to a hay wagon. Then, I see myself running behind Robledo, turning a corner and stopping in front of the barracks gate. Two scenes remain burned in my memory. I can describe them in all of their details, as if they were daguerreotypes held right in front of my eyes. The first is the nave of the stable enveloped in a cloud of smoke and a group of soldiers with blackened uniforms coming through the door, some running, others walking like puppets, without their shakos, some covering their ears with their hands. The second occurred a few moments after, and I'm surrounded by the smell of gunpowder and shouts and people and I see Robledo coming toward me, his mouth and eyes terribly open, his hair a crown of flames, with Maryse's smoking body in his arms. Thinking her dead, I fainted.

In X, there was a great deal of talk about the episode. When the investigations were concluded, we were told the same thing that had been published in the newspaper: the explosion had occurred when Claudette had lit a candelabra which, unbeknownst to her, was sitting on top of a powder keg that had been forgotten in a corner of the stable. But the story that Maryse and Françoise told was different. To begin with, Maryse remembered well having inspected the kegs that were in the place, since they had to decide which could be of use for the show and which should be removed to make room for the benches and piano that were to be brought in from the barracks. Before going to have lunch at the café, she'd left an empty keg on either side of the space that was to serve as the stage. As they weren't tall enough for the candelabras to light the stage sufficiently, Pierre had placed some small barrels like those used for cognac, also empty, atop each of the two kegs. Then they had come back with the costumes and masks in order to rehearse the more difficult passages. At seven on the dot, Claudette, already dressed as Little Red Riding Hood, lit the candelabras, the sign that those waiting outside could now enter. A few minutes later, the powder keg exploded right next to Claudette. My dear friend—I can still see her dressed as Salome, springing happily from Piet's box, tambourine in one hand, red handkerchief in the other—was killed instantly. Oh, what sorrow!

From their hospital beds, Maryse and Françoise had told the officials investigating the matter over and over again that someone had put the gunpowder in the kegs while they were having lunch at the café. This opinion was corroborated by Pierre, himself miraculously unscathed: he had left the stable just a second before the explosion to urinate in the alleyway. But—as Robledo would conclude with his habitual frankness—it was not in France's interest to tell the truth to the people of X about what had happened; to say that a conspirator had switched the empty keg for one full of powder would be to concede a victory to those who defended the cause of an independent and unified Germany, especially in light of the fact that, in addition to Claudette, two soldiers had been killed. I should add that other "accidents" occurred that same year, fomenting a general rumor that a secret league was in operation in X and in other cities. But this would all come later, when my friends had already recuperated, thanks to the dedicated attentions of Uncle Charles—for whom Pierre had been sent on the night of the explosion.

Françoise was the first to recover. Pierre, entering through the back door of the stable, had seen her sitting among the burning staves of a powder keg. Grabbing her by the legs, he dragged her outside and, piece by piece, yanked her flaming dress off her body. Robledo, for his part, had run inside the stable and, wending his way through the smoke and the scorched uniforms of fleeing soldiers, had arrived at the heap of smoking wires, keys, and planks that had once been the piano. There was Maryse, collapsed between two smoldering boards. Her burns were extensive and some of them quite deep, particularly along the left side of her body, including part of her face. Robledo's, if less severe, would also forever mar his handsomeness; his long hair, catching fire, had burned the skin on his back and head. Despite great reluctance, Uncle Charles would be forced to cut off one of Robledo's ears, the very one he had always adorned with his pearls. Naturally, burns of this sort are slow to heal and, for many weeks, Uncle Charles and I scarcely left our friends' bedsides. It was there, in that hospital room, that I learned to take a pulse, to recognize the signs of fever and pulmonary congestion, to perform bloodlettings, to clean bedsores, to apply unguents and to dress wounds. As time went on I felt increasingly useful, even necessary—a new sensation that filled me with satisfaction. Uncle Charles, noting that I followed his instructions to the letter, allowed me to perform the various ministrations, only intervening when he saw that I was on the verge of making a mistake. It was there, in fact, witnessing the healing results of our efforts, that I first heard the call of my medical vocation. It was a powerful, unwavering impulse, a thirst as difficult to quench as the yearning for love. And yet, it was an impossible love. Why had the Revolution, which had effected so many changes in society, not won women the right to pursue the study of liberal professions? Why had Marat, himself a doctor, tempered his revolutionary zeal when confronted with the barrier between the sexes? Why had Robespierre decided to unleash the Terror without considering first how much more radical it would have been to vote to authorize women to practice law? Further, why did Napoleon, a genius at the art of war, only allow a few sutlers and washerwomen to join his army, when it seemed so obvious that the efforts of the *Intendance* would have run so much more smoothly in the hands of women? I cast these and all manner of other reproaches to the world at large as I sat up nights at Maryse's bedside, waiting for her to awake so that, after serving her breakfast, we could amuse ourselves imagining a utopian country in which women and men were amiably distributed among the various occupations in accordance with each individual's capabilities and skills.

"Could women say Mass?' Maryse asked.

"If that is their calling, I don't see why not. Mass, confession, baptism . . . they could administer all of the sacraments," I decided.

"Can you imagine how entertaining it would be to hear men recount their sins in all their inglorious detail?" Maryse asked, lifting her hand to her mouth so that it wouldn't hurt her to laugh. And so we passed the time, Maryse improving day by day, and me feeling the desire to become a doctor swell within me.

One morning I confessed my obsessive ambition to her: inspired by Leonore from *Fidelio*, I pictured myself dressed as a man, at the University of Paris, studying the intricate secrets of the muscles, nerves, bones and organs of the human body, the mysteries of blood circulation, digestion, pregnancy, lactation. . . .

"But there's one enormous difference between Leonore and me," I told Maryse. "Once she managed to free her husband, she went back to being a woman like any other. I, on the other hand, must pretend to be a man for as long as I practice medicine."

"Well," said Maryse, broad-minded as ever, "you would have the option of living a double life: doctor by day and woman by night, which doesn't sound all bad, actually. It would be as if you were an actor permanently on stage. But, my darling, I advise you to think carefully about the consequences of leading such a life. There's the matter of love, for example. It would be extremely difficult to find a man willing to accept such an arrangement. And there's the matter of children. Suppose you got pregnant? What would you do then?"

At the beginning of March, when Maryse had finally stopped limping and Uncle Charles' period of leave had come to an end, the day came for us to say goodbye. It wasn't as painful as I'd anticipated. Claudette's death—a devastating loss for Maryse and Françoise—and the interminable weeks of work, uncertainty, and suffering in the hospital had strengthened my resolve. I'll never forget the night when Uncle Charles, noting that the bloodletting he'd performed had not succeeded in calming Maryse's delirium, had made his customary gesture of impotence and had looked me sadly in the eyes, telling me wordlessly that there was nothing more to be done. Nevertheless, by dawn we were hugging and crying with relief that Maryse appeared to have pulled through the crisis of pulmonary edema. Nor will I forget the afternoon when Robledo, by then his wounds nearly scarred over, stood in front of a mirror to put on the long-haired wig he'd sent his footman to procure, then gone to Maryse—who'd just begun to speak through her bandages—and asked her, strutting about happily: "What do you think? Who'd ever know that I have a lopped-off ear?" It occurred to him the second the words were out of his mouth that it would not be so easy to mask Maryse's scars, and he'd added: "But do you really think I'm going to go around wearing a wig like an old fop? It's only a joke, my *chiquita linda*. I was only hoping to hear you laugh."

The lessons I learned during those months! Looking back at my life with Robert, a period I'd seen as the pinnacle of human experiences, I could suddenly see how it had been stitched together by narcissism. In truth, for me, the world had been reduced to asking myself if he loved me or if I loved him, as though plucking the petals off a daisy. In those days, my worries did not extend to my fellow man or woman; much less did they encompass the idea of solidarity, the authentic suffering and rejoicing because of and in the service of others.

"Oh, Henriette, I'm going to miss you so!" Maryse had said the night before her departure.

"What can I possibly say at this moment?" I'd replied, my face streaked with tears. "You have been my sister, my friend, my companion through life's adventures. If you only knew how much I've learned from you!"

"From me? Very little, Henriette, very little, to be sure. 'One doesn't learn from others' mistakes,' as the saying goes. And anyway, what have I been able to teach you, except perhaps how to play a convincing Puss in Boots? Really, my love, you didn't need anything from me. And you couldn't exactly say that I've been a shining example of committing to one's principles. As you see, I'll marry Robledo even though he hasn't made a decision about his slaves. And let it be clear that it's not because I'm ugly now," she said, stroking the patch of parchment-like skin that had grown over her burn.

"Don't worry about that. If there's one thing I'm certain of, it's the love Robledo feels for you," I said, wiping away tears. "But you'll be amused to know that what you call lack of commitment is, for me, your greatest virtue. It's all too easy to simply say yes or no to something in the name of unyielding principles. That's how my dear Aunt Margot was, and she refused to ever have anything further to do with her sister Louise after she'd been too cowardly to adopt me in the face of her husband's opposition. And it wasn't that Aunt Margot didn't love her sister—oh, how she wept when she died!—it's that, for her, affection should never triumph over principles. Naturally, I do not fault Aunt Margot for any of it. She was a true mother to me and I still wear her portrait here, over my heart," I said, looking down at my locket. "But I'm not blind. What she called her principles were really nothing more than the rules my grandfather had instilled in her, the standards of a certain class and era. To give an example from your own life, consider that your love for Portelance jumped the barriers of your social, political, and even religious convictions; that out of compassion for Claudette you consented to playing the clown for Leclerc's little boy. No, Maryse, your character is far from weak. The truth of the matter is that you know how to put things in their proper place. As you once told me, no matter how difficult a situation life hands you, always try to put on your best performance. Do you remember? You'll be surprised to know that I'm very happy that you're going to Cuba. Not for me, but for you, and that you *did* teach me."

"Come on now, my love, that's enough. My cheeks are redder now than they were from the fire. But tell me: do you still want to be a doctor?"

"I've made my decision. I'll dress as a man and try to enter Medical School. Ideally, Uncle Charles will introduce me as his nephew. But I doubt he'll go along with it, that he'll take part in the hoax. He'll probably be afraid that someone would discover my true identity, which could jeopardize his reputation. I'll admit that worries me as well. I also wonder if I'll truly be able to pass as a man."

"The habit makes the nun, my dear. If you dress in mourning, you'll be a widow or an orphan; if you dress as an old woman, you'll appear ten years older than you are; if you put on an ermine cape and a golden crown, you'll be a queen. Didn't you pass as a Mameluke once upon a time?"

"Well, as your loyal paramour is fond of saying: what is meant to be, will be. Isn't that right?"

Maryse nodded in agreement and we moved on to the topics that always accompany a farewell:

Of course I'll write often.

Of course I'll come to visit.

Of course I'll never forget you. . . .

FAURIEL

IO

LIKE EVERY HUMAN BEING WHO has lived to see old age, I have the impression that I have been more than just one person. Am I really the Henriette Faber that is slowly emerging from the inkwell? I can't be sure. Even if my intention to offer a truthful account is sincere, I fear that each page I complete remains trapped somewhere between the truth and my memory. I think that between an event and one's memory of that event lies an enchanted forest; this territory, at once obscene and innocent, is called time. On the other hand, who among us could swear on a holy book that our memory is not tinged by desire? Do we not forget or remember what we choose to forget or remember? Let he who, in compiling a memoir, is certain that his writing is free of artifice, omissions, or fantasies, cast the first stone. It certainly will not be me. To begin with, my memories are as scattered as the stars in the sky. To wit: that faraway night when I met Robert and Maryse and when Aunt Margot died would be one of the brightest stars; another, the night in Strasbourg, a waning quarter moon at the expense of my virginity. Needless to say, a multitude of stars shine here and there in the darkness of my memory; points of light that I must link together, as the ancients did, with imaginary lines to form constellations—perhaps the giant Orion could represent the Russian campaign—and in such a way give, by the power and grace of words, a figurative celestial form to my past, my heaven, my existence, that otherwise, far from the orderly tale that I am constructing with my pen, would be a chaotic trail of stellar dust. My work, like any other that aspires to capture its author's life, owes a great deal to imagination, perhaps even to fiction.

More than once I have asked myself what it is that compels me to write. If there's one thing I'm sure of, it's that I do not pursue any edifying civic or educational agenda. Moll Flanders I am not. Nor do I write to improve my social position or to defend a cause; much less out of vanity, that defect so common among writers. And yet, I believe that all writing has a utilitarian purpose; it is a type of battle plan used to attain some material or spiritual triumph. And so, what forces are at work within me, impelling me to write? I believe I know the answer: I do it for the pleasure of recounting my memories, as deceptive as these may be, for the pleasure of pulling from oblivion the faces of those I loved, of reviving the magic of certain moments, of revisiting my fears, my doubts, my ambitions, my mistakes, and my successes; for the pleasure of shuffling the cards of my life and laying them out on the table as in a game of solitaire, the two of spades over the ace, the four of clubs over the three, the anticipation of placing the last king over the final queen. And what's more, I write so that all of this might last beyond my days, return like a persistent firefly to a world whose features I can't even imagine. Thanks to you, whoever you may be, the adventures and emotions laid out in front of you will shine during the hours you spend reading about them. For one moment, man or woman of another century, you will experience the illusion of looking me in the eye and of feeling my heart beat against your own. Do I play at living again? Why not? Doesn't even the most tenuous of ghosts represent a victory over death?

∝

Bundled in my traveling cloak, periodically wiping away the fog from my breath against the glass, I watched as the city I'd heard so much about paraded past my window. Uncle Charles, seated in front of me, gave a running commentary about the churches, palaces, buildings, squares, streets and houses which, because of current import or historical interest, he deemed worthy of mention. Paris! Paris, at last! A wintry Paris; damp, windy, and cold, but Paris all the same.

We rented the bottom floor of a house in an excellent neighborhood on the Rue Saint-Honoré, and we settled in quite comfortably. Our bedrooms were each a tad small, but the drawing room had a good fireplace and was quite large. The garret at the top floor of the house, divided into two rooms by a wooden partition, served as accommodations for Pierre and Françoise. (A year ago, before leaving for New York, I had occasion to explore the metropolis of grand boulevards and magnificent buildings and parks designed by Baron Haussmann. What a difference! My Paris, though the grandest city in Europe, was, in those days, still quite modest, with many of its streets still unpaved. Filthy and malodorous due to the scarcity of water, decrepit and poorly illuminated by a few thousand oil-lit streetlamps, the city was just beginning to emerge from its medieval shell thanks to the improvements being made at Napoleon's behest. And yet. . . .)

In those days, courses in the Medical School began in January, coinciding with the military draft lottery. And so, I didn't rush to tell Uncle Charles about my plans until I was certain he was happily ensconced in our flat and well immersed in the routine of his new position at the Val de Grâce Hospital. Once his life was well in order, I took advantage of the occasion of his birthday—Françoise had organized a grand dinner—to ask for his support. After listening to my well-rehearsed speech about the origins of my vocation and the certainty I held about being able to pass as a man, he sat in silence for several minutes, avoiding my gaze and tapping the rim of his wine glass with his index finger. Finally, he said: "I know from personal experience what it means to feel called to a vocation. If you want to dedicate your life to taking care of others, there's no need for you to pretend to be a man. The Medical School has begun offering courses in midwifery. What better way to honor your vocation than by helping members of your own sex through the pains of childbirth?"

I knew by his tone that he hoped this proposition would resolve the issue once and for all.

"I don't want to be a midwife, Uncle. I want to be a surgeon, just like you," I said firmly.

"So that's how you're going to be!" exclaimed my Uncle, surprised at my tone. "But what you want is impossible, Henriette," he added, extending his arms in his habitual gesture of helplessness. "The regulations for entrance into the Medical School have changed and a baccalaureate degree is now required."

"A baccalaureate . . . a baccalaureate degree?" I stammered.

"Yes, the Medical School was closed during the years of the Revolution and the profession was invaded by knaves and charlatans without the least smattering of an education, rogues who, more often than not, hastened death instead of preventing it. So now it has been decreed that anyone practicing as a doctor or a surgeon who cannot produce an accredited degree must pass a rigorous exam. As for any new entrants to the Medical School, I repeat, it is now required that they have a baccalaureate degree. Not even foreign students are exempt from the new regulation."

"But I know as much or more than anyone with a baccalaureate degree!" I protested. "You know what an excellent education Aunt Margot provided me. I can write in Greek, Latin, Italian, and Spanish; I know geometry, geography, philosophy, literature. I still have my flower and insect collections in Foix. Oh, Uncle Charles, what miserable luck! Isn't there any way around the requirement?"

"No, my child," he replied, and, seeing that my desire was not the mere caprice of an idle widow, he took my hand compassionately between his own. "The administrators at the Medical School are not fond of doing favors. It could cost them their posts. But who knows? Maybe one day the requirements will change. I'll tell you what you can do in the meantime: I have all my books in my room. You have my permission to read them and ask me about anything you don't understand. That won't be so bad, right? In those books you'll find everything you could learn at the Medical School, at least in theory. It's the only thing I can offer you at the moment. Please believe me that I am very sorry."

I thanked him for his good intentions with kisses on the cheeks and went to my room to cry. After a while, feeling the need to tell another woman about my misfortune, I took up a fountain pen and wrote a long letter to Maryse, closing with a promise to visit: "As you see, my dreams have come tumbling down. I can't get used to living without your companionship. In December, as soon as my lawyer sends me the money from the rent at Foix, I'll buy a ticket aboard the first ship bound for America."

❧

Despite my lingering sense of frustration, unmitigated even by the prospect of spending time with Maryse and Robledo, the subsequent months passed by happily enough. Our upstairs neighbors, a young married couple by the name of Orphile, were openhearted and jolly people who enjoyed my company. As their income was modest, I learned from them how to entertain myself with little money, an art form at which most Parisians were skilled and which would serve me well throughout my life. On Sundays, crowded into my new cabriolet—Aunt Margot's heavy carriage had proven a nuisance on the narrow and busy Paris streets—we would go on long rides to Versailles, Saint-Cloud, Fontainebleau, Rambouillet. When summer arrived, while Armand Orphile worked his shift in a lawyer's office, Marie-Louise, Françoise, and I would go on foot to enjoy the gardens of the Tuileries, or, employing the services of Pierre, who, by then, knew Paris as well as any of the local coachmen, we would head out to the orchards and large gardens on the outskirts of the city to buy fresh fruit and vegetables. Other times, mostly as a pretext to get out of the house, I would inspect the various construction projects underway, keeping track of their progress from week to week so I could update Uncle Charles, who only had eyes for his patients. "The great Arc de L'Etoile is complete save the paving stones. . . . They've made huge progress on the Théâtre de l'Odéon. . . . They say that the bronze bas-reliefs for the column at the Place Vendôme have already been cast. . . . The renovation of the Louvre is coming along nicely. . . . They're about to take the scaffolding down from the Arc de Triomphe de Carrousel. . . . "

In addition, I had no lack of suitors. Among the half-dozen officers Uncle Charles had introduced to me, certainly with the aim of diluting my interest in medicine, I had chosen the youngest and most original gallant of the lot: the Count Alfred Lubomirski, one of the most daring lancers in the Polish cavalry, who was serving voluntarily in the Grand Armée. My Uncle had met him at the hospital, where he'd been sent at General Poniatowski's recommendation. There he'd had various pieces of shrapnel removed from his right shoulder. I should say that if I preferred him over my other admirers, it wasn't because of his noble ancestry or his appearance, but rather because the first time we went to the theater together he told me, as we were saying good night, something that none of my other suitors had ever said: "I would very much like to see you again, Madame Renaud. I find you a unique and enchanting woman. Nevertheless, I feel it my duty to tell you that I will never ask for your hand in marriage nor allow anything serious to develop between us. I am already betrothed to someone whom no other could ever equal. Her name is Poland, my poor country, carved up three times over and now reduced to a meager duchy. I shall dedicate all my efforts, all the blood in my veins, toward her independence."

That very night, remembering his words and his beautiful voice, I had a premonition that I'd fall in love with him.

What can I say of Alfred? He was twenty-two years old and more or less of the same height and weight as Robert, although his eyes were an intense blue and he had reddish, perpetually unkempt hair. His face, dominated by that prominent and aquiline nose characteristic of many Poles, generally wore a slightly disdainful, yet somehow inoffensive, expression, which, to be sure, was quite in vogue in those days. When he was scarcely out of adolescence, he'd distinguished himself fighting in Italy with the Legion of the Vistula, then left the Legion to serve as an attaché to Field Marshal Ney. His mother, the daughter of a well-to-do princess, had died when he was nine, leaving him a fortune; his father, also a member of high nobility, was a brilliant man with an unquenchable taste for travel—in addition to traveling across all of Europe and visiting China and Mongolia, he'd seen the Islamic world, and had published his impressions of all of them. Despite his father's vast knowledge and the accolades he'd received, Alfred disapproved of the fact that he had given up the patriotic ideals of his youth to instead offer his services to Czar Alexander. But what most distanced father and son was the fact that, when the latter had been wounded and captured by the Russians, the former had gone to the Czar to beg for his freedom, promising that his son would never again wield a lance against his Crown. "It's unforgivable that he didn't consult me first, knowing, as he did, my political convictions," he complained. "I don't feel bound by the oath my father swore to that despot, but it's impossible for me to reconcile with my father." I should clarify that his feelings were ambiguous since, as a passionate reader of literature—whenever he visited me he would strike up lively discussions with Françoise—he admired his father as a writer, often comparing him to Lesage. (Years later, I had occasion to read one of the elder Lubomirski's works published in Paris under the title *Don Roque Busqueros, histoire espagnole*, perhaps part of the long novel that, according to Alfred, he was always writing in between his travels and other occupations. And I'll say that, the merits of *Gil Blas* notwithstanding, the Pole's picaresque pages seemed, to me, far wittier and more entertaining.) While he recuperated during that summer and for part of the fall, and with my Uncle's blessing, Alfred was my nightly companion. In order to give the impression that there wasn't a serious commitment between us, I occasionally accepted the arm of Jules Lavalette, a grenadier captain who had serious designs on my affections. Several times I went with one or the other of them to the circus on the Rue de Temple—whose daring equestrian numbers I described in detail for Maryse—as well as to all of the theaters, which is saying a lot if one considers that, in addition to the Opera, the Théâtre Français, the Louvois, and the comic operas of Feydeau and the Italians, there were close to twenty concert halls in Paris.

I thought it very odd that Alfred never took me to a dance, and in the middle of August, when I received an invitation to a ball the City of Paris was hosting in honor of Napoleon's birthday, I couldn't help but ask him if he planned to attend.

"Dances bore me, madame. I'm aware that they serve a social and political function, but since I'm not interested in advancing my career, nor am I a fortune hunter or a seductor, I prefer to ignore them. And really, what is a ball anyway? A press of well-dressed, sweaty people, all crowding together in order to step on one another's toes, drink warm champagne, and attempt to make witty and intelligent remarks in the hopes of landing a more private appointment later on."

"There are those who enjoy dancing for dancing's sake," I said briskly, irritated because I had hoped that he'd accompany me to the ball. "For my part, I won't deny that I enjoy waltzes and the opportunity to show off my jewels every once in a while."

"You should have told me, madame. I have nothing against music and diamonds. The next time you're in such a mood, let me know, and I'll rent out a dance hall complete with musicians, put on my full-dress uniform, and we'll waltz until dawn. Although given my clumsiness, I doubt you'd ever want to repeat the experience."

"You are incorrigible tonight, lieutenant."

"Simply abominable," he said, laughing at himself as he turned to ask Françoise for his gloves and tall, hourglass-shaped *czapka*. Where do you prefer to go, the Opera or the Théâtre Français?"

187

"To the Théâtre Français. Talma has returned to perform in *Cinna*."

"I expected as much. I've already reserved an excellent box."

This being the state of affairs, I accepted Lavalette's invitation to the dance which, since it was taken for granted that Napoleon and a considerable portion of Paris' bourgeois would be in attendance, had become a highly anticipated event. I should say that in those days, at least up until the disastrous Russian campaign, the vast majority of Parisians supported Napoleon. There were good reasons for this. Of course, the general standard of living was better than it had been under the monarchy and during the Revolution; manufacturers and merchants were making money, there was a general sense of civil order, and the numerous construction projects throughout the city provided work for many citizens. But there was something more. As all of the Empire's power was concentrated in the city, Parisians began to see themselves as France's masters. This sentiment, which, in reality, extended beyond the Rhine and the Pyrenees, was cultivated by the official press—*Le Moniteur*, *Le Journal de l'Empire*—that depicted Napoleon as the architect of the new nation and Paris as its administrative and military center, as well as the seat of knowledge about the civilized world. And so, in just a few years, Paris and Napoleon had become so intertwined that the latter's absence caused a general sense of disquiet throughout the city as though it were, in fact, and here I scarcely exaggerate, the sun that had failed to appear. During the months that he and Joséphine spent in Bayonne in order to see to the matter of Joseph Bonaparte's ascension to the Spanish throne, all manner of rumor tore through the city's streets. Marie-Louise, for example, knocked on my door at seven in the morning to tell me, aghast, as though it were a matter within her own family, something she'd heard from a reliable source the evening before: the emperor was on the verge of divorce and he'd already bought the tiara that the new empress was to wear—something which, in fact, would not occur for another two years. The unease was only heightened by the discovery of a conspiracy by a group of former military men who aimed to reinstate the Republic, and by the news of General Dupont's embarrassing defeat at the hands of Spanish insurgents. As if that weren't enough, it was said that eighty thousand conscripts would be immediately sent to fight in Spain, a rumor that caused a substantial dip in the *Bourse de Paris*. Like all Parisians, I too, began to wish for Napoleon's rapid return, and I felt sincerely happy when his balcony at Les Tuileries was illuminated. That night, on the eve of the grand ball, I understood that, were Napoleon to die prematurely or to fall from power, Paris, myself and everything that surrounded me would cease, forever and ever, to be what it once was.

I was already dressed and putting on Aunt Margot's jewelry in front of the mirror when Françoise entered my room with a note that had been left by a soldier. Since I had no secrets to hide from her, I asked her to read it to me: "Madame, I very much regret that I will not be able to accompany you this evening. Please believe me that there are grave reasons for this. With the hope of being worthy of your forgiveness, I remain at your feet, Captain Jules Lavalette."

"What nerve!" I exclaimed. "Grave reasons! He could very well have written this note yesterday!"

"The worst part of all is that your Uncle has already left in the cabriolet to pick up Madame Bagnol," said Françoise, referring to the wealthy and amiable divorcée whom Uncle Charles had been seeing regularly. "You'll have to go in a hired coach."

"Well that's that! I'm not going to the dance! These aren't the days of Cinderella, when a woman would arrive alone at a dance by royal decree," I said, kicking the air furiously, causing my shoe to fly off my foot. Agitated, I began to take off the heavy diamond and emerald necklace.

"Let me help you," said Françoise, seeing my trembling fingers fumbling ineffectively with the clasp. "Now then, let's see. There! Shall I put it in its case?"

"Oh, how I wanted to go!" I complained. "But not alone!"

"Someone is knocking at the door," said Françoise. "Settle down. I'll be right back," she said, placing the necklace in its case.

"It must be my Uncle!" I said, excited, thinking that he'd returned with Madame Bagnol to collect me so that we could all go to the dance together. "I'll answer the door myself."

One shoe on, one shoe off, I hobbled through the foyer, threw the latch, lifted the iron bar and opened the door. I stood there, astonished.

"Good evening, madame. I wonder if you'd do me the honor of accompanying me to the ball at the Hôtel de Ville," said Alfred, his voice more reverberant than ever, holding the varnished visor of his *czapka* between his fingers.

⁂

There I was again, naked, in bed with a man. I tried to think how long my fidelity to Robert had lasted. Our last night together in Warsaw had been a few days before the battle at Pultusk—the end of December, 1806. And today was the twenty-first of August. One year and eight months. How slowly the time had passed! Would it always be that way? If so, by the time I reached thirty I'd feel like an old woman. I turned my head on the pillow and looked at Alfred. He slept peacefully. The disdainful look he usually wore had disappeared and he looked even younger than he actually was. I thought that perhaps he was dreaming of his childhood, and suddenly I realized that Robert had died in the same land where Alfred had been born. Winter and spring. Two unforgettable seasons in my romantic chronicles, for, were I to make comparisons, my life with Robert had been wintry, overshadowed by death. Alfred, on the other hand, with the taut, ripe plum of his penis, covered by an unexpected cocoon that I could draw back with my fingers—that night, the mystery of the uncircumcised penis was finally revealed to me—symbolized the spring, its winged and tender beauty; a god with the face of a boy and a voice as resonant as the base-string on a guitar who, concluding the tedious geometry of a waltz, had spirited me away from the Hôtel de Ville, transporting us to that spotless white room, with its white rug, white bed, white sheets, white pillows, white canopy, white candles that burned all around us like nocturnal suns. What would the chaste abbé Lachouque say were he to discover that his lessons in Greek mythology would inspire me, that night, to imagine that I'd been reincarnated as Persephone, dragged down to the dark depths of the underworld only to emerge into the light of spring with a flower in my hand? And while I'm playing this game, how to compare Alfred's lovemaking with Robert's? Or, to ask the only question that really counts after all, with whom had I enjoyed myself more? To begin with, Alfred, staying my hands with a single motion, had stopped me from undressing myself, preferring to do it himself, slowly, standing behind me, his kisses landing like warm butterflies on my throat, the nape of my neck, my ears. The ritual complete, he'd lifted me out of the wide hoop of my dress, and placed me gently upon the bed like a precious object, fragile, as though my skin were made of flower petals, and there, kneeling before me, still dressed in his magnificent blue uniform, he had traversed my body with his fingertips, lightly yet thoroughly, avoiding my nipples and my mound of Venus, and I, my eyes half-closed, felt myself bathed in a magical rain that utterly soaked me, that transformed the bed into a boat and the rug into a clear running river, my body adrift, carried by the current who knew where, until arriving at a still pool where time and the rain ceased, though I lived yet, feeling, imagining I heard the distant music of shepherd's flutes, dreaming I was in some remote region, Arcadia, Corinth, Magnesia, and suddenly the clocks started up again and time was no longer a drop of light suspended above the boat, and I had turned to him, now naked, Olympian, his fingers encircling my nipples, describing ramparts of pleasure, now brushing the down of my pubis like furtive birds of fire, his tongue caressing my lips, his tongue on my tongue, and the boat began to spin, to careen atop a glittering wave, to roll and pitch about in the torrent, negotiating moss-covered rocks, bubbling whirlpools, and a vertiginous foam surrounded the boat as though it were nearing a vast waterfall, steaming and thundering, and then it began to take on water, to sink, to break apart, to hurl itself into an endless fall, until his Polish lance came to find me, pressing against me as I began to lose myself to the vertigo, and I grasped it in desperation, caught hold of it in the middle of the void, and anchored it inside me and felt it there, alive, rocking rhythmically through my flesh and my desire. . . .

⋙

Robert or Alfred? The winter with its Hussar cunning, or the spring with its flowering lance?

Even today I can't decide.

If I had sailed upon Alfred's enchanted boat again, or better, if the luminous orgasms with which we had celebrated Napoleon's birthday—fireworks worthy of an emperor—had been repeated, perhaps I'd have been able to decide. But they were not repeated. That was the only night we ever made love.

And it's not that we didn't see one another again. After his fencing and equestrian exercises, his body bathed in lavender water, he'd take me to the theater just as before, or simply to walk on his arm along the parapet by the river followed by dinner in one café or another, though usually it was Le Coq Audacieux, on the left bank. There, acting as though nothing had happened between us, he would speak of Poland, of his father, and of the merits of certain young English and German poets, topics that I pretended interested me greatly.

"Madame, I have something for you," he said on one occasion, taking a book of English poetry from his pocket.

"You are forgetting that I don't read English," I said impatiently, wishing he would speak to me familiarly, that he would take my hand and raise it to his lips, that he would tell me he loved me or at least make some allusion to our night together.

"Take it as a souvenir," he insisted.

"A souvenir of what, monsieur?" I said, setting the book down alongside my plate. "Of the dance at the Hôtel de Ville?"

"Ah, the dance . . . the dance wasn't half bad. It's just that, as I've told you, *dancing* isn't my favorite pastime," he said, emphasizing the word in such a way that it was clear he meant for me to understand that he was speaking of lovemaking. "But you're right. I'd forgotten that you couldn't read English," he added, retrieving the book and putting it quickly back in his pocket, not giving me the chance to say that I'd like to keep it after all.

His words wounded me. My cheeks felt hot and I imagined that I was blushing fiercely. Heedless of my pride, I said: "Clearly we don't agree on the topic of dancing. It's not that I accept just any invitation to dance, but it would be dishonest of me not to tell you that I very much enjoyed *dancing* with you."

"Surely you only say that out of courtesy, madame. I imagine myself a poor dancer. In any case, I'll not have the opportunity to escort you to another dance. My arm has fully healed and I'll soon be leaving. I found out today that the Polish lancers have already begun fighting in Spain. Now, if you'll permit me, I'll order another bottle of wine. I'd like to celebrate my reinstatement by enjoying the pleasure of your company."

After that night, there was nothing more to be said.

༝

Uncle Charles walked over to the chair in which I sat reading Madame de Staël's *Corinne*. His eyes sparkling with happiness, he held out a large package that he laid in my lap.

"The post just delivered it. It's from Maryse," he said, still standing next to me, curious, waiting for me to open the heavy wrapping.

"It's a box, a big cigar box. Look at the beautiful lithographs," I said, showing him the colorful allegories.

"Yes, yes," pressed Uncle Charles. "What's inside? I want to know how her health is these days."

"Papers . . . some engravings, a newspaper. Some documents, what looks like a letter. I'll read through it all and then pass it on to you," I said, and shut the box so I could go through its contents in my room, leaving my uncle in suspense.

And yes, inside the fragrant box there was a letter in Maryse's enormous, sprawling handwriting, but there were also many other things, among them a piece of parchment, rolled up and tied with a red cord. I opened it and spread it out across my desk. At first, I didn't understand what I was looking at, the Latin, the gothic characters, the multiple signatures and wax stamps with ribbons. It was a Bachelor of Arts diploma from the Real y Pontificia Universidad de Havana in the name of one Enrique Fuenmayor y Faber.

After recovering from the powerful emotions that had me wandering about the room like a sleepwalker, I threw myself down on the bed to read Maryse's letter in the hopes of finding the explanation for how she had managed to pull off such a miracle.

The letter began in a joking tone—"Dear Enrique"— and told of her life in Havana, a city she found dirty and boring, particularly for ladies. The theater was abysmal, though she had to admit that her Spanish was still in its infancy and she didn't understand what was being said on stage. But really, there was no need to understand. It was enough to see those poor people shouting out their lines, not knowing what to do with their arms. Luckily, she was happy with Robledo, very happy indeed, despite everything—which I interpreted to mean that he had not yet sold his estate. They were in the habit of taking lengthy excursions to the countryside, where Robledo had a house looking out over a lovely valley. It was a beautiful place full of tall palms. Later, she mentioned the presence of French colonists from Saint-Domingue who lived in the nearby mountains. There were also French people in Havana, as well as British and North Americans, but they were tiresome people whose highest form of entertainment was speaking ill about the Spanish. The native musicians were quite talented, especially the Negroes, and many had excellent voices. As soon as her Spanish improved she would probably decide to do something with them, seeing as her health was improving day by day. Finally, on the last page, she wrote of the Bachelor's diploma. It was, of course, a fake, but everything had been imitated to perfection, from the parchment and calligraphy, down to the ink, stamps, seals, and signatures. Since Enrique Fuenmayor was supposedly from Havana, she had also included a passport, a map of the city, some engravings, a visitor's guide, a newspaper, a description of the university, and information about professors and doctors. The letter concluded: "In the event that Don Enrique should decide not to pursue his studies in Paris, Madame Henriette Renaud will be welcomed in Havana with enormous affection, sympathy, and consideration by Señora Doña Marisa Polidor de Robledo y Echeverría."

What was I to do with all of that? My vocation was intact, but now I was confronted with a double risk: passing as a man *and* passing as a *Habanero*. My Spanish was fairly good, although I was sure to have something of an accent. But it was another thing entirely to pretend I'd been born in Havana. Who could be certain there wouldn't be an actual *Habanero* among the other medical students, or even someone who'd merely visited the city? I spent the remaining hours of the afternoon lying on my bed, immersed in these considerations. I would have happily stayed in my room for the rest of the evening as well, except that, realizing that the sun had already set, I remembered that Alfred was coming for dinner, and Uncle Charles would be anxious to know about the contents of Maryse's parcel. What would I say to Alfred and to Uncle Charles? I could, of course, tell them both the truth; the former would take everything as a grand turn of events and then, upon further reflection, as an unselfish act in the service of French women's civil liberties— my noble Pole understood life as a poem in which heroes fought for impossible causes. Furthermore, Alfred would be leaving any day and I took it for granted that I'd never see him again—although in this I was mistaken. But would it be prudent to show Uncle Charles the false diploma? Immediately I realized that it would not. His respect for the profession was such that he'd be affronted by it, even while knowing it represented my only chance to enter the Medical School. On the other hand, I couldn't very well hide the truth from him. Apart from the fact that I found it distasteful to deceive him, the moment would arrive when I'd be forced to reveal my intentions to him. I mulled all of this over as I dressed for dinner, and by the time I'd put the final touches on my coiffure I'd arrived at the conclusion that, for the moment, it would be best to remain silent. I put the last page of Maryse's letter under my pillow, together with the diploma, the passport and all of the papers relating to Cuban medicine and the university, and I left my room with the box in order to give it to my uncle.

❧

He didn't say goodbye. Not even in writing. One fine day I learned from Uncle Charles that he'd taken the road to Bordeaux, heading from there to Spain. Distressed by what he considered a lack of courtesy on Alfred's part, my Uncle invented various senseless excuses and passed along Alfred's supposed words of gratitude to me for having offered him my friendship during the months of his convalescence.

I won't say that his departure didn't affect me, that I didn't miss his haughty and precise manner of speech and demeanor—not even in our moments of greatest intimacy did he use a familiar form of address with me—his aura of a medieval knight, his eccentric *czapka* and that diaphanous way he'd made love to me. I won't say I didn't love him because I did, with all of my tenderness and hope that he might be the champion destined to vanquish Robert's subterranean presence. Did he love me? I couldn't be sure. If he did, he never said so. Perhaps I was, for him, a transitory love, a minor figure, a summer romance; though his unwillingness to meet with my nakedness a second time leads me to think that he was, perhaps, not so indifferent to me after all, that I did mean something to him. Perhaps he feared that, were he to allow me in his bed again, I would succeed in conquering a part of his heart. In the end, I can't fault him for loving me less than he loved his country; nor for his decision not to write to me. What would have been the point? His memory, far from having faded with time, comes back to me often, encased in two moments, one suffused with pleasure, the other with woe, like the irreconcilable faces of a coin, the currency with which we pay for our lives: the magical night of the dance at the Hôtel de Ville—needless to say— and the frozen hell of the Russian retreat, when, utterly unable to do anything to help him, I saw him shivering beneath a tattered blanket, his feet wrapped in rags, blind and groping his way along the road to Vilna. (This snowy afternoon in New York, with the wind whistling and my street resting beneath a white quilt, I think of Alfred and of his vast, anonymous grave. I think. . . .)

11

IT WAS SOMETHING LIKE ENTERING a convent. (What has become
of Madeleine Dampierre? Perhaps she's dead, or perhaps she lives
yet, seeing out her days as a reformed whore in some convent in
New Orleans, her face encased in the wimple of the Sisters of Charity; a face the good nuns had taken for yours, a face that you'd just
as soon erase from your memory, as though in ceding to her your
given Christian name you had committed an unforgivable sin. And
what sin would that be? Creating a double identity just to confuse
the celestial registry? And thinking about your name, about your
multiple and scattered names, you imagine it, above all, in Cuba,
locked away in the dusty archives of courts, magistrates, jails, and
hospitals; written on accusations, printed in pamphlets and in moth-
eaten newspapers. Who knows? If she's still alive in this world, your
name might even be stored away in Juanita's memory as well, an
old and withered Juanita, almost certainly a widow, who might be
remembering, as you are today, her years of youthful vigor in the
sultry and far-flung city of Baracoa. But why such a remorseful tone
this morning? The sun has risen in all its brilliance and yesterday's
snow has begun to melt, trickling down the windowpane. Why not
imagine that your name, Henriette Faber-Cavent, or Enriqueta, as
you were known in Cuba, might meet a happier fate, perhaps raise
its head in some old tome of medical history, noting you as a pioneer
among female doctors? Indeed, at this sun-drenched moment, with
your optimism on the rise, who's to say, my dear friend, that in the
future, that open and conjectural time for which you claim to write,
that some extravagant biographer won't be taken with your life story, or even that some novelist, yet to be born, won't discover your

memoirs in an antique book auction and decide to reinvent you as a heroine, if only for the novelty of imagining the same woman as a widow, soldier, mother, doctor, and husband, and that's assuming they don't also confuse you with our dear Madeleine and attribute to you as well the avatars of whore and Sister of Charity.) In any case, as I was saying, it was something like entering a convent:

I cut my hair.

I changed my name.

I severed ties with friends and family.

I dressed in black.

I went to live alone in a cell-like room in the Latin Quarter, which, in those days, was still a hive of *grisettes*, poets, and students.

Was I happy, accounting for the fact that there are many types of happiness, all of which are fleeting? Yes, absolutely. A happiness tied up in the joy of seeing myself capable of shattering that false sense of security that everyday life affords us, of breaking with the routines that had slowly been enveloping me in a soft and warm eiderdown quilt of hot chocolate and pastries and the *Gazette de France* at eight in the morning; a vigorous and stimulating happiness like an early-morning drum roll or the mountain air; a happiness similar to the way I felt when, leaving Maryse and my carriage behind, I saddled Jeudi and, dressed as a Mameluke, set out into the unknown.

℅

In those days, the study of medicine was enjoying a surge of popularity among educated youth, an interest linked to various changes that had been implemented in medical instruction after several years of total neglect. The conceptual bases that formed the foundation of the *nouvele école* were the incorporation of surgery and medicine as branches of a single science—until then held as separate disciplines—and the validation of clinical practice over theory. The observation of patients came to be seen as irreplaceable, and the words of Cabanis, one of the fathers of the new school, were drummed into any new student: "The true education of any young doctor is not to be found in books, but rather at the patient's bedside." Nevertheless, the Faculty did recognize the importance of theoretical study, implementing a curriculum that encompassed anatomy, physiology, pathology, surgery, obstetrics, pharmacology, chemistry, physics, natural sciences, and the history of medicine. But even within the confines of the university's classrooms, practice was favored over theory. The importance conferred on the dissection of cadavers was such that it constituted its own school, awarding students who distinguished themselves with gold medals. The instruction we received was empirical and materialist; its outlook realist and democratic, due, in large part, to our instructors' experience of the Revolution and to the surgical training they'd acquired in military hospitals.

Matriculation was open to all, although the various districts throughout the country had the right to name *Élèves de la Patrie,* local young men specially selected by means of a competition who would receive the meager support of a State stipend. In the Paris Medical Faculty there were, perhaps, three hundred of these young men. They lived in attics full of rats and old books, wore clogs and dressed in dirty, mended clothing, drank sour borage tea and sopped stale bread at all-night soup stands. Many were peasants' sons, humble people who knew well that, had the laws giving them the opportunity to study not been passed, they would never have left their towns and villages. Taciturn and distrustful, they were ferocious competitors, driven by ambition. They liked to show off their knowledge of Latin, even though in the Faculty it was already becoming a dead language: all instruction was given in French and very few doctoral candidates wrote their theses in the classical style. The rest of the students lived better; the ones from Paris, still living with their parents, did not have to pay for food and lodging; those who came from the provinces and from abroad—as was, supposedly, my case—came from families of means and received allowances that afforded them a certain degree of comfort. In general, quite in contrast with the intense and solitary "state students," they were jovial lads quite content to take a *grisette* as a lover. Because medical school was more demanding than any other discipline—in addition to the huge number of hours dedicated to clinical practice, there were no vacations, attendance lists were passed at the start of each and every class, and the oral and written exams could not possibly have been more rigorous—students scarcely had time, except every once in a great while, to attend a dance or the theater. On Sundays, weather permitting, they could be seen in the Bois de Boulogne or the Bois de Vincennes, atop a blanket spread over the grass, carefree, embracing their lovers, singing picaresque folksongs, eating and drinking. The passerby spotting them during these moments of leisure would never suspect that that very night they would be memorizing the names and functions of the muscles of the face or the bones of the foot for the next day's lesson.

Our professors were competent and effective. There must have been about thirty of them, each department chaired by one full professor and one assistant professor. Nearly all of them had served in the military, and many held positions as "interns" in the hospitals. Appointments were highly competitive, although the recipients did not always represent the best of the candidates—given that all of the medical schools (Paris, Montpellier, and Strasbourg), hospital administrations and health-related institutions were run by the State, it was not unusual for an open position to go to some influential figure's personal favorite. I should also say that, within the public health system—a vast web across the map of France—teaching was seen as a patriotic vocation, or better, as a military duty. The country had been girding for war since 1792 and, in the same way that military conscription required new blood every year, the army and navy required new doctors, surgeons, assistants and pharmacists. Since the costs of war justified low salaries, a vein of corruption ran through the entire system. In the Faculty, where Napoleon had ordered salaries to be cut in half, doctoral theses could be bought; that is, a wealthy student could always find some professor down on his luck willing to write his dissertation for him. Nevertheless, it would not do justice to my professors to fail to recognize that the majority of them were serious, talented, and dedicated individuals.

When I was visiting Paris not long ago, I was surprised to see how well preserved the Faculty's buildings still are. How many more decades will they endure? The beautiful portico with its six Ionic columns, the bas-relief allegory on the pediment, the wide entrance hall, the high windows at the back of the staircase, the library above them, the museum with its anomalous organs and fetuses floating in alcohol, the assembly room hung all around with magnificent Gobelin tapestries; below, to the left, the grand patio of the Training College, the six dissection rooms with their gray slate tables, five students per cadaver, the pungent odor of the antiseptic liquid; beyond that the second patio, the majestic round amphitheater, its terraced seats, its cupola, its lamps, its grotesque renaissance masks. . . .

Fortunately, few of my classmates spoke Spanish and none of them were from Cuba. There was one student from Mexico and one from Buenos Aires, both merchants' sons, but when we first met they had fortuitously suggested that we speak only in French to one another so as to improve our fluency in conversation. As for Spaniards, only two Catalán brothers remained, and they always spoke to each other in their own language; the rest of the Spaniards had returned to their country to take up the insurgent cause. Nevertheless, in an attempt to ward off any possible suspicion, whenever I spoke I tried to imitate the Mexican and Argentine's heavy accent. As for those who wanted to know about Havana and its customs, I had memorized all of the materials that Maryse had sent me. Quite soon I was able to manage surprisingly well, to the point that I was not only able to speak confidently about the city's castles, churches, plazas, and streets, but also about its enviable geographical orientation, temperature, rain and wind patterns and, above all, about the sugar mills, slavery and the tobacco and lumber industries. After a few weeks, I became so bold as to comment on the state of medicine in Cuba, on the institution of the Protomedicato, or about the subjects taught in the various departments at the university, or to describe my Uncle Robledo's summer house overlooking a valley full of tall palms and fruit trees whose exotic names (*mamey, guanábana, marañón, caimito, mamoncillo*) I would rattle off without having the least idea what any of them looked or tasted like. Since this promised to be a prolonged and amusing game, I wrote to Maryse telling her that my studies were off to a great start but that I needed more newspapers and some general information about the island of Cuba. One day I learned, quite by chance, that instead of calling me Enrique Fuenmayor, I was known in the Faculty as "the Cuban."

The precautions I needed to take in order to hide the fact that I was a woman were much more demanding because I had to be constantly vigilant. To begin with, there was the problem of my voice. As Maryse had said, had I decided to become a singer I would have been a mezzo-soprano. This worked somewhat in my favor since, though my voice was not as deep as Aunt Margot's, at least it wasn't shrill. At first I tried to speak in the lowest register possible for me, drawing the words from the back of my throat. But this approach, as I was soon to discover, affected my vocal chords, causing me to speak in a hoarse, muffled, and nearly inaudible whisper. As a last resort, I decided to use my Puss-in-Boots voice, which Maryse had taught me to summon from deep in my stomach rather than my throat. The situation improved, although I never managed to achieve a truly satisfactory timbre. Luckily, there were two or three students with voices higher-pitched than my own in my class.

It took me considerably longer to imitate a man's way of walking, sitting, and gesturing. To this end, I bought a full-length mirror in which I could see my entire body reflected. I had never realized how often men, even the best-mannered among them, scratched themselves, smoothed their hair, blew their noses, spit, picked their teeth, and adjusted their crotches. During lectures, I set about observing my classmates, taking note of the frequency with which they brought their hand to their faces in order to scratch their noses, stroke their chins or bite their fingernails. Not having hair on my face—one of my biggest worries—turned out not to be an issue: there were several other students who were blond and smooth-cheeked. The real problem was my breasts. Although I was naturally small-breasted, I was, according to Aunt Margot, endowed with nipples almost as long and thick as a sheep's. This anatomical aberration had contributed to my timidity since I'd entered adolescence, as they were sometimes noticeable even through thick winter garments. But ever since I'd discovered that, for Robert, my disproportion was actually an attraction—in the same way he'd been excited by the blond down on my upper lip and the curly fuzz on my thighs and buttocks—it had become my favorite flirtatious weapon, to the point that I felt disappointed if the masculine gaze didn't come to rest, at least for an instant, on the two protuberances that my blouse and dress tried in vain to flatten. Maryse had confirmed Robert's predilection: "That's how it is, my sweet, men go crazy for those perverse little details. It's well known that the Duchess of Lavallière had one leg shorter than the other and I can't remember which one of Henry the Eighth's wives had an extra finger. As for me, I've learned that my excessive lips and the deep cavity of my bellybutton constitute my greatest charms. Who could have guessed? I'd always thought that my eyes and my hands were the most attractive parts of my body." Of course, my nipples were not noticeable when I was dressed in a frockcoat and vest, but when performing dissections or assisting surgeons in the hospital, it was common to work in shirt-sleeves with the cuffs rolled up and a kind of apron that wasn't thick enough to hide them. And so, I had no other choice but to bind my breasts with a silk sash, which I would wind several times tightly about my torso—a solution I found particularly painful when my breasts swelled during the days of my period. As for the rest of it, I derived considerable satisfaction from not being obliged to adopt a passive attitude with my interlocutors, and I loved going around in pants, including the little pillow I wore sewn into my underclothes at crotch-level.

∾

Four months after I'd begun my studies, just as I was becoming accustomed to an independent life, a new war against Austria broke out. On the very same day I learned of the mobilization—several students with military experience had been called into service—I received a brief note from Uncle Charles informing me that, as he planned to join the campaign, I needed to be apprised of certain matters. We had not seen one another or written since our painful separation, although I knew from Françoise's letters—the only tie I had not broken—that he was in good health and was considering marrying Madame Bagnol. We were to meet in the Luxembourg Gardens at eight in the morning.

Eager for our meeting, I arrived early. Spring had just barely begun and it was cold and damp. I was pacing back and forth to keep warm when I saw him coming along the path, his step quick and sure, wearing his regiment's bicorn hat. He recognized me immediately, despite my pants and waistcoat, and waved as he approached. I ran to him and threw myself, crying, into his arms.

"Come now, Henriette. What will the guards at the sentry post say about us? They'll think the worst," he said in a low, gruff voice, trying to pull away from me.

"I'm so happy to see you again! You have no idea how much I've missed you! I was just asking myself if, one day, you might come to forgive me."

"I've nothing to forgive you for, my child," he said, starting to walk without looking at me. I realized that his emotions were in conflict: on the one hand, his joy at seeing me again, on the other,

203

his displeasure at finding me dressed as a man. "It is I who have behaved badly. I'd convinced myself that you wouldn't make it on your own and that you'd be back in short order. Well, at times I'm guilty of pig-headedness, although I want you to know that I had given myself until June to come look for you. Except now I'll be leaving in a few days for the war. How are you, child? You look too thin."

"It's the clothing, Uncle. Everything is fine. You have nothing to worry about. You can go in peace. At first I was a bit frightened, but everything has turned out very well," I said, taking his arm as I'd always done when walking together.

"I know, I know; don't think that I've been kept in the dark. I have friends in the Faculty," he said in a tone that hovered somewhere between comical and mysterious.

I stopped walking and let go of his arm.

"What do you mean? Someone in the Faculty knows my secret?" I said, alarmed. I'd thought many times that it would take but one word from my uncle to find myself expelled.

"No, I would never betray you. An old comrade-in-arms from my days with the Army of the Rhine. I merely wanted to know if you were having any trouble. And anyway, you have nothing to fear. I told him that you were the nephew of an old friend, now married to a Spaniard in Cuba. I was thinking of Maryse and Robledo."

I breathed a sigh of relief, although I was not pleased to know that one of my professors had been particularly attentive to how my studies were coming along. Who could it be? Possibly a surgeon of Uncle Charles' age, although there must have been half a dozen men in their forties in the Faculty who had served in the first campaigns.

"Please Uncle, whoever your friend may be, tell him that you've seen me yourself and are perfectly satisfied that all is well; tell him that it's no longer necessary for him—"

"Don't worry," he interrupted me. "I'll write to him this very afternoon. Now I must speak to you of other matters. As you might imagine, I'm extremely busy. Larrey is expecting me at ten. Just imagine, we need to organize the ambulance trains and everything is in total chaos. This time the Austrian surprised us. The Emperor is in a foul mood and Larrey . . . do you remember meeting Larrey in Boulogne, the day Aunt Margot. . . ? Well, I'll come to the point. I think it's best that we leave things as they are for now. One never knows. War is war. But you know that already. What I mean to say is that if something were to happen to me you will always have the house here in Paris waiting for you. Everything is just as you left it. Your room, your clothes, your jewelry, your cabriolet . . . Pierre and Françoise as well."

I started to cry again, this time from sorrow. I had fled from that good man's life as one embarks on a journey with no possibility of return. In my eagerness to break definitively with my existence as a well-to-do widow, I had informed him of my decision abruptly, not giving him a chance to come to understand my point of view. Two days later, taking advantage of a moment he'd gone out, I had left the house, leaving him a cavalier letter by means of explanation.

"Oh Uncle, Uncle, how I love you!" I said between sobs, and I latched onto his arm, bringing my head close to his. When I raised my face to kiss him, I saw that he was pretending to blow his nose.

I tried to convince him that it was an unnecessary expense to maintain the house, that, with him absent, there was no reason to keep Pierre and Françoise on. I had no need of their services and, while I would never dream of firing them, they could at least return to Foix. As for the cabriolet, it would be best to sell it, and really, who better than him to guard my jewelry since almost all of it had belonged to Aunt Margot to begin with? And anyway, wasn't he planning to marry Madame Bagnol? Well then, the jewelry would be my wedding present and that way it would stay in the family. I had all I needed, and more, from the rent at Foix.

"Henriette," said Uncle Charles, checking the time. "I have known good generals and bad generals. Do you know what the difference is? The bad ones always assume that they'll win the battle and they don't take the necessary precautions. The good generals, like the Emperor, Ney, Lannes, Davout, Oudinot, and so many others, hold off sending their best troops into combat because, were something to go badly, they are the ones who will have to lead the retreat along a predetermined route. So, my dear, let's be good generals. If I lose my battle, you'll remain to fight your own and you'll be well furnished with the necessary provisions; and if you're the one to lose, and you must think of the unforeseen events that may arise during your four years of study, you will have your route of retreat firmly in place. Madame Bagnol has more than enough with her own jewels and rents, and I have no need of money. And in any case, I've already paid the rent on the house and I suspect that Pierre and Françoise could prove useful to you in a time of need. Let's leave things as they are. And now, I must say my goodbyes," he added, tucking his watch back in his pocket.

"Write to me, Uncle. Françoise will make sure I receive your letters. You have no idea how much it would mean to me to have news of you."

"I'll write to you from Vienna," he smiled. "You'll see. It will be over quickly. The Emperor is impatient. He needs the troops for the mess over in Spain."

We embraced at the exit that opened out onto Rue Vaugirard. After heading off in different directions, we paused, turned, and bid each another farewell one more time.

❧

The death of Field-Marshall Lannes was gravely felt in Paris. The son of a stable boy, he was considered one of the people's most legitimate heroes; to me, he was also an old friend. The news had depressed me so that I found it difficult to be alone in my room. If Lannes and Robert had died in battle, who was to say that Uncle Charles and Alfred's lives wouldn't be equally cut short? With these thoughts weighing on my mind, I left my anatomy book on the bed and, after touching up my man's hairdo, I went out into the street to walk off my unease. Without realizing it, as dusk came on, I found myself at Le Coq Audacieux, where I hadn't been since the fall, and I took the table that I used to share with Alfred. I ordered a bottle of wine and immediately became sad all over again. I tired to think of other things, but the wine seemed to stir up all my wells of grief. I decided to let the memories accompany me as I drank.

The long march behind the Fifth Hussar Battalion.

My interview with Lannes at midnight, the compass in his hand, his penetrating gaze and beautiful mouth.

"Tell Huet to name this woman as second sutler to the 9th Hussars!"

Ma Valoin and her wagon.

The roads to Saxony, Prussia, and Poland.

Robert climbing the stairs with the leopard skin draped over his shoulder.

His fist through the windowpane.

"Ah, it's you. Doesn't it seem that spring is awfully late to arrive here in Foix?"

The bottle paid for, and my determination to manage completely on my own in shambles, I crossed the river and walked to Rue Saint-Honoré. I knocked at the door to my old house. The night was dark, and at first Pierre didn't recognize me. Françoise, in her nightshirt, sat at the table reading the newspaper by the light of the candelabra, a plate with the remains of a meal and a jug of wine pushed aside. Seeing me standing in front of her, she rubbed her eyes, blinked several times and, without a word, took me by the hands and pulled me into her lap. We talked and drank into the night. The Orphiles had moved to the *faubourg* Saint-Denis, as Marie-Louise was expecting a baby and it was simply too expensive for them to go on living on the Rue Saint-Honoré. To explain my disappearance, Françoise had told them I'd gone to the Languedoc to see to the matter of my inheritance. Lannes's death had also saddened her. "War is shit. It doesn't matter how many battles you win; in the end, you always lose," she concluded.

Françoise led me to my old bed, overcome by my memories and the wine. I slept poorly. I had to get up twice and I had my recurrent dream of Robert. I spent Sunday morning with Françoise and Pierre and, after a lunch of a traditional Languedoc stew, I said goodbye, assuring them that whenever I felt lonely I would come to visit.

12

IT WASN'T UNTIL AFTER I'D completed my first-year exams that I began to regard my classmates as regular, ordinary people. Until then, I'd thought of them as research subjects, or better, as hospital patients I needed to observe in order to learn more about them. Nevertheless, there were two exceptions who, from the very beginning, touched an emotional chord within me: Raymond Fauriel, a "state student" from the north, and Claude Bousquet, the most handsome man at the Faculty, the youngest son of a wealthy porcelain manufacturer from the city of Limoges.

Fauriel—it was our custom in the Faculty to call one another by our surnames—was the poorest of the poor; so poor that he couldn't even afford an attic room in the Latin Quarter. He lived on a tiny farmstead on the outskirts of the city. At sunup he had to help the owner milk the cows and then accompany him to sell the milk. When the milk wagon arrived at the Hospital de la Charité, he would jump off and come running into the building just in time for the class on outpatient medicine given by Boyer, one of our most popular professors. Since he didn't have enough money to buy books—he sent most of his stipend home to his mother—after classes he could be found in the Faculty library, his elbows on the table, immersed in Bichat's *Anatomie générale*, or pondering Percy's *Rapports du physique et du moral de l'homme*. He owned only one frockcoat, repeatedly mended and patched, and his wooden shoes were always covered with damp mud and straws of hay. He was quite short—a good four or five centimeters shorter than me—and he carried no extra weight on his fine-boned and agile frame. His hair, which he wore cut to shoulder length, was thick and black, like

Robledo's must have looked in his youth; we all envied it, and if anyone ever complemented him on it, he would poke fun at himself, saying it was the result of wearing it loose in the open air, since he lacked the resources to buy a hat. His only vanity was to be always carefully shaved. Allowed to grow, his beard must have been extremely thick: although one never saw actual hair on his chin, part of his face was perennially shadowed in a bluish cast. While his features were regular enough—his cheekbones perhaps a touch high and broad—his greatest attraction lay in his smile, or better, in his laugh. I had never seen anyone laugh like him; it was as though the best and most genuine of all human traits were revealed on his face. In spite of the time his farm chores took away from his studies, he distinguished himself as a student, especially in the practical courses. I had the double good fortune to count him as my friend as well as my group-mate in the Practical School, in which the dissection tables were assigned in alphabetical order. His knife cuts were always swift and clean; thanks to him, our table had been designated one of the three best in the previous year. Aware of his poverty, I bought him lunch quite frequently, and he repaid my invitations with his indefatigable good humor.

Bousquet attracted me in a different way; an absolutely animal, and therefore relentless attraction, unmitigated by morals or reason. Physically, he shared a great deal in common with Robert and Alfred. Like them, he was tall, elegant, and had a military bearing, yet he was more handsome. Although perhaps handsome isn't the word; the word could be . . . it should be, apollonian, as in Apollo. I'll explain: on one of my birthdays—I can't remember if it was my eighth or ninth—Aunt Margot had given me, among other gifts, a book of Greek mythology that my grandfather Antoine-Marie had given her one Christmas. The first of the engravings was of Zeus, depicted seated on his throne, bearded, and surrounded by zigzagging bolts of lightning, eagles, and other symbols; the next engravings were of Hera and her children, Leto with the twins Apollo and Artemis, Demeter and her daughter Persephone, and so on. The idea, I suppose, was to present the Olympian pantheon as a big, happy family in which Zeus's promiscuity, while not erased, was excused by making it abundantly clear that his fruitful romantic adventures had taken place during his youth, before he was wed to Hera. In reality, it was a children's book in which the gods appeared modestly dressed in long, loose-fitting tunics which, in accordance with Madame de La Fayette's pedagogical approach, scarcely revealed a bare shoulder, calf, or small portion of a masculine torso. When I proudly showed the book to my tutor, abbé Lachouque, he began to leaf carefully through the pages, showing his approval of its contents with repetitive little nods. Suddenly, a sheet of paper folded in quarters fell out from among the final pages. Lachouque picked it up from the table and began to unfold it, but stopped abruptly, exclaiming "Dear God!" Incapable of lying, he told me that it was a picture of a naked statue of Apollo, something that only adults could see. Noticing my curiosity, he told me to go to the other end of the library until he called me back. I did so, and when I returned, he showed me the drawing: a damp, black-ink tunic now covered Apollo's body. "Now here is something fit for your eyes," he said, and without further ado, he pushed the inkwell away and began his lesson as though nothing had happened. Having my suspicions as to the location of that which had so scandalized my tutor, the moment he left I took my penknife and scraped at the ink. My disappointment was immense: the black tunic now looked like a sort of discolored codpiece that, as I continued to scrape, became an irreparable hole in the paper. Disconsolate, I folded the drawing and slipped it back inside the book. Weeks later, seeing Laguerre's horse's member swinging back and forth, I guessed that Apollo's attribute must have been something similar. I ran to the library and found the book. Paintbrush in hand, I spent a good long time trying to reproduce my observations in watercolor. After experimenting with various colors, I finally managed something that looked, more or less, like a purplish snake escaping from the hole in the paper between the god's thighs. As I was ecstatically beholding my restoration job, Aunt Margot's powerful hands descended upon my shoulders, took the drawing, and reduced it, instantaneously, to a crackling ball of paper. My aunt had the good sense not to scold me. After offering me an impersonal smile, she left the room with the crumpled drawing in the pocket of her robe. I recount this anecdote so that it will be clear why discovering, in Bousquet, the head of my lost Apollo—his same ringlet curls, his same straight nose, his same full lips, his same smooth and harmoniously proportioned face—awakened in me the confused and elemental passion that had been dormant since my childhood days. Its power, perhaps for having been constrained all of those years, became irresistible, as though the Gorgons, Cerberus, Minotaur, and all the other creeping evils locked away in Pandora's box had joined forces against my moral equilibrium. In my nocturnal fantasies I saw myself perversely rolling back his tunic until I'd unveiled a pendulous, rosy-fleshed cylinder that, in terms of size, compared favorably with the knobby appendage that the cross-eyed Vincenzo so loved to exhibit. In the turbid scenes I would concoct in my desire, I would often kneel before the swaying phallus and, taking it in both hands, begin to squeeze it, caress it, massage it, watching as its veins swelled and feeling its juices pulsating beneath my fingers. Sometimes, in my uncontrollable deliriums, that stalk of passion would appear circumcised, in all its divine brazenness, its head an apple from the garden of the Hesperides; other times, it appeared like an umbrella made of toughened leather that, quivering, unfurled itself to reveal a gigantic ripe grape that, touching my lips, would swell until bursting in a torrent of thick nectar whose warm drops christened me the Goddess' priestess, Aphrodite's vassal, a mythic and sacred prostitute whose duty it was to eternalize all men's pleasure.

It should be said that, except for his resemblance to my Apollo, there was absolutely nothing else to admire about Bousquet. According to the date upon which he'd been admitted to the Faculty, he should have already been writing his doctoral dissertation, and yet, he was still in my class. But it wasn't his clumsiness or his lack of application that I held against him, but rather his vanity; he scarcely spoke a word to anyone, students and professors alike. He lived alone and ate dinner almost every night at the popular Café Procope. He often went to salons, dances, and theaters, and his door was like a sultan's, opening every night for a different woman. Actresses, singers, dressmakers, laborers, fine-ladies, and haughty courtesans ascended and descended the stairs to his room between six in the evening and dawn. We were not friends. In truth, as I said, Bousquet didn't have friends. Surely he believed them unnecessary for the sort of life he led. The fact that I knew about his personal life owed as much to chance as to my curiosity. When, wanting a bit more space, I moved to a different house on the Rue Vaugirard, by pure coincidence it turned out that my apartment was adjacent to his; what was more, the room I'd chosen as my bedroom was separated from his by a thin wall that made it possible to hear everything that happened on the other side. The fact that I'd already become obsessed with Bousquet only spurred my curiosity and, not thinking of the consequences, one night I pressed my ear to the wall to better hear the conversation he was having with one of his lovers. I think that, had I not made this one move, my life would have followed a different course, probably one that would have led me away from the war, rather than drawing me closer to it. But I'm a fool who doesn't seem to grow wiser with the passage of time. Though really, who can peek into the future and see the final consequences of an action? Perhaps the war was already there in the middle of my path, a morass of gunpowder and blood to which all of my steps would inevitably lead, regardless of who they were following or what direction they took; a morass I would be forced to cross in order to continue moving forward.

And so, hearing the muffled whispers coming from his room that night, I glued my ear to the wall and discovered that they were spoken in the language of pleasure. I remained there, in a state of alert, my pulse racing, until his words of farewell were followed by the sound of the door. I ran to my other room and half-stuck my head out the window: presently, a woman in a wide-brimmed hat climbed quickly into a waiting coach. I went to bed and slept clutching my pillow, pretending the warm linen pillowcase was the skin of his cheek.

When I woke up, I reproached myself for my unhealthy curiosity and moved the bed, promising myself that I'd never again enter that room at night. I would only use it to store my clothes, books, and luggage trunks. "But man proposes, and the devil disposes, my dear," Maryse would have said, had I told her that, just a week later, trembling with desire, I'd gone back to the forbidden room to listen, once again, to Bousquet making love. Soon I would become convinced that it takes only one repetition of certain actions to form a habit. In the same way that it was impossible for me to go without laudanum when my head ached or at the onset of my menstrual cramps, as night fell I was compelled by an urgent need to transform into a kind of night owl, perched on a chair against the wall, impatiently awaiting the moment of the hunt. The rest of my life continued along its regular course, outpatient clinic and surgery at the Hospital de la Charité, lunch with Fauriel at Madame Binot's tavern, botany and forensic medicine at the Faculty, dissection of an interminable thorax at table number six, walk to Rue Vaugirard, climb the stairs, open the door, wash-up and change clothes, go to the Café Procope and sit almost directly in front of him, making my presence obvious, nod my head briefly by way of greeting, spy on him as he read the newspaper between sips of wine and distracted mouthfuls of stewed beef tongue or tenderloin. After the salad and cheese course I'd let him go, almost like a cat playing with a mouse, knowing that, as night fell, he'd be mine, that I'd have him on the other side of my wall, all his sounds for me, all his words for me, all his moans for me, and then I'd take off my underclothes, hook my leg over the arm of the chair and, sinking my finger into my wetness, I'd follow the rhythm of his panting, of his pleasure, until his long cry would mount my sigh and we'd both fall against the wall, spent, sweat-soaked, breathing raggedly.

One night, after our customary greeting in the café, it seemed to me that his eyes sought me out over the top of his newspaper. I was about to leave my table, go sit next to him and do away with the pretense once and for all; tell him that I'd wanted him for weeks, that I was schooled in all the arts of love and that I was prepared to satisfy him in any way he might desire, that I didn't hope to be his lover or wish to meddle in his life, but that I wanted to have him for at least one night, just one night, and the only condition I'd impose would be that he guard my secret. The only thing that held me back was the arrival of a Hussar, his mustaches waxed, the fur over his left shoulder, the cross on his chest, the plume of his shako the colors of Robert's regiment.

"Well, *citoyen*! Haven't you ever seen an Imperial Hussar?" he said. I lowered my head, dropped some money on the tablecloth and left the place furtively, as though I'd been caught in the very instant that separates intent from the commission of a crime. I wandered the streets. I considered crossing to the other side of the river to tell Françoise of my torment, if only to unburden myself a bit. As I rounded a corner, the towers of Notre Dame, silhouetted by the light of the moon, appeared before me like an omen. I paused to look at them. How long had it been since I'd performed the duties of the religion in which I'd been raised? How long since I'd knelt before a confessional, since my tongue had received the bread of communion? But among my sins was that of passing as a man, and it didn't seem that, when it came to God, there was much room for gray areas: the Church would always accept me as a sinning widow, but never as a doctor. I sat down on a spur-stone. Several carriages passed by in the direction of the bridge; pedestrians, pairs of lovers, mounted police, men in uniform. Head down and disheartened, I went home. An unassuming *grisette* was coming down the stairs; she descended happily, a bouquet of flowers, surely a gift from him, in her hand; she had a snub-nose and her cheeks looked ruddy even in the faint light from the street lamp. I stepped to the side to allow her to pass. Our smiles met for an instant. Oh, how I envied her!

The following day, as I was crossing the plaza in front of the dissection pavilions, I heard Fauriel's clarion voice calling me from afar. I turned around. He was running toward me, his wooden clogs making a clock, clock, clock sound on the pavement.

"I'll be damned, Fuenmayor!" he exclaimed through one of his most radiant smiles. "You'll never guess what happened to me. When I put my coat on after surgery I found seven napoleons in my pocket!" he said euphorically, and he showed me the gold coins as if thinking I'd doubt his mere words.

"The genuine article," I said, after checking that the coins were good. "Do you have any idea who your benefactor might be?"

"Well, no. Whoever it was only left me the coins. No note. It's all very odd. Don't you think?"

"Extremely odd," I replied. "Well, one thing's for certain: that money was meant for you. It's yours."

"Yes, although I can't get used to the idea. Seven napoleons are seven napoleons. It wouldn't have been you, by any chance?" he said, enveloping me in another smile. "You're rich and you're my best friend," he added, putting a hand on my shoulder.

"Me! The things you come up with, Fauriel!" I said, slightly ashamed, realizing I'd never offered him money. It had never even occurred to me to give him a pair of boots or a new frock coat, both of which he could sorely use.

"Well, then, who could it be? Nuns, doctors, patients and students. . . . There's no one else in the Charité. Come on, Fuenmayor, confess. It was you."

"I'm telling you it wasn't. I'll admit that I'd thought about giving you a frock coat. But I was going to wait a bit, until winter had arrived," I lied shamelessly, promising myself that I'd do it as soon as the weather turned. "Maybe a grateful patient? Or someone you helped or did a favor for?"

"As you like. I won't insist. I ask just one thing of you, and you have to say yes. I won't accept refusals."

"Let's talk about this later. Don't forget that Monsieur X's thorax awaits us," I said, and started to walk toward the dissection pavilions.

"I'm inviting you to dinner, Fuenmayor. You can't say no. You've bought me fifty lunches. Today it's my turn."

"We'll talk about it later," I said evasively, thinking that I couldn't possibly allow him to spend any part of that money on me. Although, on second thought, it wouldn't be a bad idea to go together to the Café Procope. I'd seen him talking to Bousquet on a few occasions. Maybe he'd invite us to his table or else join us at ours. Why had this not occurred to me before? "All right then, if you insist on going to dinner, let's go to the Café Procope. And tomorrow, I'll treat you."

The table we'd been assigned in the Practical School was in the first pavilion and they had not yet passed the attendance list. We left our coats in the cloakroom and put on our aprons, permeated, as always, with the smell of the disinfectant with which they injected the cadavers. We greeted our classmates and, taking up the knives, we set about removing the intercostal muscles of Monsieur X's ever-useful body. (I won't belabor this disagreeable aspect of medical instruction. I'll merely say that, upon crossing the threshold of the Practical School, the new student was confronted full on, with no transition, with the world of death; a true trial by fire that was the cause of a good many faintings and desertions during the first few weeks of the academic year. And yet, what would we know of the human body without its *post mortem* desecration?) Done for the day, we washed our hands and arms and left the pavilion, welcoming the fresh air outside.

The Café Procope was close to the Faculty buildings, located on the Rue de l'Ancienne Comédie, a street with an interesting history. Given that Bousquet would disappoint me that night by dining elsewhere—perhaps with his most recent conquest—and that I can't remember what Fauriel and I talked about as we ate and drank, I'll describe that short and intense street so as to suspend it in time for you, reading me now, whatsoever your name may be. I'll begin with the house marked number four. It was occupied, in 1727, by Philippe Destouches, a well-known academic and dramatist with a moralizing bent. It would be his first home after returning from London, where he'd served as a diplomat while familiarizing himself with the theatrical mood of the Restoration. Among the reasons propelling Destouches to rent that particular house, we may surmise two: it was on the same street as the Comédie Française—where his works would debut—and it was nearly across the street from the Café Procope, the favored gathering place for theater types. It was no doubt an excellent move for Destouches to settle in that neighborhood. There he would write *Le Philosophe marié*, one of his most successful comedies. The house designated number ten lacked an official history despite being the oldest on the entire street. This was not the case with number fourteen. Beginning in 1550 and lasting for many years after that, that unique building housed a *jeu de paume*, an indoor game involving a ball that the competitors would strike with the palm of the hand. Purchased and remodeled as a theater, the building housed the Comédie Française from 1689 to 1770, at which point the theater moved once again. Needless to say, during that time the greatest classical works of Corneille, Molière, and Racine repeatedly graced its stages, although the most lauded new plays were those by Voltaire and Marivaux who, in those days, were the greatest exponents of the tragicomedy. In honor of the building's contribution to French theater, the street was christened la Rue de l'Ancienne Comédie. Like a witness to the building's past, its façade still displays a classical high-relief of Minerva, attributed to Le Hongre. The painters Horace Vernet, Baron Gros, and the monumental David must have seen something in that canny image, for they would all decide to set up their respective studios in that very building. How many paintings must have been created by the light of its large windows? But time is short and we must move on to the next house, number sixteen. This is where Marat lived in September of 1789, when the first issue of his newspaper, *L'Ami de Peuple*, went to press. It was there he penned his caustic articles accusing the aristocrats of conspiracy against the Revolution, becoming one of the most radical voices of the moment, an idol of the people, an open enemy of the conservatives; it was that house he would finally be forced to flee, to England, no less, upon receiving the news of his imminent arrest. Is that where he would leave behind the heavy silver ladle that would lend a revolutionary luster to Achille Despaigne's collection? Who knows? But now it's time to cross the street and enter the storied Café Procope itself. Its glorious history is as follows: in 1670, Francesco Procopio, a twenty-year-old Sicilian seeking his fortune in Paris, partnered with two Armenians by the names of Pascal and Maliban, proprietors of a small business selling coffee at two and a half *sous* per cup. When he'd become sufficiently prosperous, he parted ways with the Armenians, adopted the French name François Procope, and opened his own coffee shop on the Rue Tournon, where he remained for several years. In 1684, he came across a location he thought more providential, and set up shop in the building we see today. This move would prove fortuitous. To begin with, Procope benefitted from the clientele of two adjacent businesses: the aforementioned *jeu de paume* and Malrus' *petanque* court, which abutted the café's rear door. He was surely further pleased to learn that the Comédie Française had purchased the former. Always far-sighted, he bought the second floor of the café building, whose magnificent balcony still dominates the street today. The Procope's salons immediately filled with playwrights and actors, not to mention the patrons who flowed in after attending performances. With the daily menu improved thanks to the talents of a renowned chef, in a few scant months the Procope had become the favored spot for artists, theater critics, journalists, and intellectuals; further, it became a hub for the interchange of news and gossip; reputations were made or lost at its tables. But that was not all. It would not be an exaggeration to say that the most important ideas of the century were debated there—Voltaire, Rousseau, Diderot, D'Alambert, Fréron, Marmontel, Piron and the rest of the encyclopedists met regularly at the enterprising Sicilian's; in fact, the *Encyclopédie* itself was born of a conversation between Diderot and D'Alambert one memorable night among glasses of calvados, cups of coffee, and the diligent to and fro of the Procope's *garçons*. It was there that, in 1785, a reception was held in honor of the debut of Beaumarchais's famous *Le Mariage de Figaro*, a work that earned its author three days in jail for its critique of the privileges of the nobility. And the Revolution would arrive as well. The Bastille would be stormed and many things would change. And of course, in the new era, the café's clientele would also change. Now the hoarse and demanding voices of Marat, Danton, Legendre, Desmoulins,

Billaud-Varanne, and other inflamed residents of the *quartier* would be heard there. The red cap of the *sans-culottes* would make its first appearance there, and the cry to attack Les Tuileries would be raised there in July and August of 1792; there, toasts would be made to Robespierre and the Comité de Salut Public, the Reign of Terror would be applauded, heads yet to roll would be tallied; there, in short, the truly revolutionary years of the Republic would be born, grow, age, and die, drowned in their own blood. Understandably, the café's popularity began to wane in the days of the Directorate. The Jacobins no longer showed their faces, and the writers and artists preferred to gather in salons run by certain languid ladies, provocatively dressed in tulles with the plunging necklines of latest fashion. Yet to come were Napoleon, Italy, Egypt, the 18th of Brumaire, the Consulate, the Empire, and a different clientele, tending toward the bourgeois, began to fill the café's salons: high officials from all branches of the military, functionaries, professionals, businessmen, industrialists, and the odd student of means, such as Bousquet and myself. And finally, number twenty-one. There, at the beginning of the Revolution, lived one whose zeal for equalizing nobles and commoners before the executioner would be crowned by the most categorical and prolonged of successes: Doctor Guillotin.

⚭

Our second visit to the café went exactly as I had imagined. The ever-affable Fauriel made his way over to Bousquet's table, heedless of the fact that the latter was apparently engrossed in the newspaper. It would all happen as though in a dream: Fauriel signaled to me, I approached, Bousquet stood and politely extended his hand, then immediately invited me to sit next to him. Of course, he would say, it really was about time we got to know each other better since, after all, we lived on the same floor and ate dinner at the same café and, although I might not have realized it, he had more than once been on the verge of approaching my table and introducing himself properly, only he'd formed the opinion that I was an extremely private person or that I had exotic habits, since he'd noticed that I always drank a shot of rum before ordering dinner, not a French custom, after all, or at the very least, not a Parisian one, although it would not be an odd habit, he supposed, for a person born in

Havana, something he knew because in the Faculty they called me "the Cuban," and, in fact, he'd known of Havana since his childhood days, since his father had always received many orders for porcelain objects from there, and not the most typical objects either, but before I told him what my city was like and what sort of life I had led there, he wanted to congratulate me on my excellent French, quite superior to that of the other South Americans in the Faculty who could scarcely be understood when answering a question in class, and another thing, would I mind if he spoke in the familiar form with me since he was in need, that night, of some good friends to share his table? And Bousquet would have gone on talking, dripping ambrosia into my eardrums, if Fauriel, by nature somewhat impatient, had not interrupted him to tell the story of how, two days earlier, he'd found seven napoleons in his coat pocket, seven napoleons! And no, there hadn't been a note of any kind, only the money, and he didn't have the least idea who could have put it there, although he suspected that his benefactor was a friend, some well-off classmate, probably the very same person sitting at his side this very moment, although—

"Come on, Fauriel! I've already told you it wasn't me!" I interrupted him. "Let's talk about something else. Let's see . . . tell us how you are going to spend the money."

"Well, I don't know," he said, offering us a luminous smile.

"If I were in your place, I'd buy a pair of leather shoes," offered Bousquet.

"And a frock coat," I added.

"And a vest, and some breeches," suggested Bousquet.

"And two shirts, and wool socks. Winter's coming soon."

"And a hat."

"Never! Don't speak to me of hats!" protested Fauriel in his shrill voice, while Bousquet ordered another bottle of wine and I ordered an oyster soup and some lamb chops. "Anyway, I found all of that, plus a pair of mittens and a scarf, all barely used and exactly my size, just this morning at the pawnshop. And that's not all: I still have some money left over to share with my mother."

I was amazed at Bousquet's friendliness toward us, and toward me in particular. His greetings had always been courteous but cold, lending him a vainglorious air which, that night, was nowhere in evidence. To be sure, his conversation could not have been more superficial—I hadn't heard him utter a single intelligent word—but that was something I had already taken for granted: what Don Juan has ever distinguished himself for his wit or sensibility? As we ate, Fauriel praising the quality of the food and wine, it occurred to me that my feelings for Bousquet must have been akin to his toward his lovers; an attraction based exclusively on the appetites of the flesh, on the desire to possess a beautiful body, to touch and kiss and smell it until you'd made it yours. But no, what I felt for Bousquet was this and much more besides. Bousquet was my reencounter with Apollo and with all the dusky things that he implied, and, whatever the cost, I could not allow the hand of fate to rob me of him a second time. Unable to control my longing, I moved my knee closer to his, seeking its pressure and heat. It wouldn't last long: taking advantage of a lull in the conversation, he filled his glass and stood.

"Before continuing with dinner," he announced, "I must make a confession. You see, I, too, have something to celebrate. I imagine that you both already know of my failings as a student. I've only managed to advance to the second year and, well, it's not my studies I wish to discuss, but rather my not-studies. Gentlemen," he said, raising his glass, "a toast to my liberation. My father has just released me from academia. I am no longer required to embarrass myself in front of you two or anyone else. He's finally accepted that I'll never be a doctor. From now on, I'll work in his porcelain business, just like my brothers."

"Will you be returning to Limoges then?" interrupted Fauriel, without waiting for the toast to be over.

"God forbid!" said Bousquet, without lowering his glass. "My father's decision was aided by the sudden death of Monsieur Guichon, our longtime agent on the Rue des Lombards. Next Monday I'll take charge of the account books and the shop. It's true that I know little of numbers, but I know life in Paris like the palm of my hand. A toast to my good fortune!"

"*Santé*!" Fauriel and I said in unison.

Over dessert, Bousquet stopped talking about his family and the porcelain business and, in a confidential tone, he extended us a surprising invitation: "I must go in a few minutes. A matter of skirts. Something truly special . . . although it occurs to me that we could continue our celebration in my apartment. I have a date with two sisters. . . . There are three of us, but I could find another one of my lady friends on the way home."

"Thank you for the offer," Fauriel said immediately, without considering the matter further. "I have to walk almost two hours back to the farm and the cows wake up early."

"And you?' Bousquet asked me. "You live right next door to me. You have no excuse."

I hesitated.

"Well, no . . . I couldn't. I need to study."

Bousquet made an irritated gesture and looked at the twelve-candled chandelier that hung above our heads.

"You see! My God! Yesterday I didn't have any friends because I was too ashamed of my failure as a student. Today, just when I thought I'd found two, it turns out that they abandon me."

"How I wish I could!" I sighed. "But believe me when I say it's impossible."

"Come on, man! Even if it's just for one drink! No commitment. You can leave whenever you want to."

This time I reconsidered the invitation.

"All right. Just one drink," I said, and immediately regretted my lack of willpower. But the truth was that my desire to be in his apartment, to watch how he treated his women friends, to drink his wine, to sit on his furniture, to see his bed and the other side of my wall, simply won out over prudence. "But, I repeat. Just one drink."

❧

Their names, that night, were Mademoiselle Rouge and Mademoiselle Brune. They said they were from Passy. Bousquet had met them the previous Saturday at a costume ball on the Boulevard du Temple. No one would possibly take them for sisters—one was tall and redheaded, the other short and brunette—although they did have two things in common: each spoke with the vulgarity of a prostitute and wore a black velvet mask that covered the top half of her face. Shortly after their boisterous arrival, just as they were beginning to tell dirty jokes at Napoleon and Joséphine's expense, I finished my glass of champagne and, despite Bousquet's protests, bid them good evening. After washing up and making myself comfortable, I went to my place against the wall, ready to listen to what promised to be a singular symphony for clarinet and two violins. When the recital failed to begin, I picked up my anatomy book and started to read. Immediately I began to nod off, and I felt the book fall from my hands. In the small hours of the morning, the concert of moans awoke me. I don't know if it was because I'd awoken so abruptly but, despite my best attempts, I couldn't manage to join the threesome.

On Monday, our dissections done for the day, we went back to the Café Procope. Fauriel strutted proudly in his new leather shoes. His gray frock coat, though a touch too long in the arms, was well cut and lent him an air of distinction. Bousquet arrived late. He came from the Rue des Lombards and swore he hadn't understood a single word of what Monsieur Guichon's assistant had explained to him. He was in a foul mood, that much was certain, and he scarcely touched his food. He also appeared exhausted: bags under his eyes, a trembling in his voice, wrinkles I'd not seen before. Almost nothing remained of his Apollonian aura, and for a moment he seemed to me a mere mortal, just like everyone else. He surprised me by refusing to share another bottle of wine with us.

"*Parbleu*, Bousquet, you look terrible!" said Fauriel crossly, as though he could no longer bear to look at our new friend's lined and sullen face. "Where have you left your happiness at being a free man?"

"It will pass," replied Bousquet. "There are certain things that one does without knowing why," he said cryptically, then immediately stood and bid us farewell. When he'd made it almost to the door he turned and retraced his steps. "I have to go to Limoges. I'll see you in a few weeks."

"What happened the other night?" Fauriel asked me, as soon as Bousquet had left the café.

"Nothing in particular. I left his apartment right away. I left him drinking champagne with a certain Mademoiselle Rouge and Mademoiselle Brune. Both masked, of course."

"Maybe he wasn't up to the challenge of the circumstance," joked Fauriel. "It's not the same fighting two duels at once."

"Perhaps," I said, knowing quite well that he was mistaken. "Although I'm under the impression that Bousquet is a born Don Juan."

"You know, I don't find him attractive. He's too pretty. He

seems fake, like a doll, a statue, a painting. I don't know. He's too perfect. And in any case, his features do not bespeak intelligence. Don't you agree?"

"What do you take to be intelligent features?" I asked, intrigued.

"Oh, well, I don't really know. Let's see. . . . Some of our professors have intelligent faces. Boyer, for example."

"Boyer is an ugly man, Fauriel."

"That's true. Okay, Lacloche, for example."

"The doctor who teaches in the outpatient clinic with Boyer? Well, yes, he has a pleasant face, although it hardly compares with Bousquet's. Your problem is that you look at men with a man's eye. I prefer not to pass judgment. Now then, as for Bousquet, I can assure you that he's capable of seducing a broom. How well I know it, seeing women entering and leaving his apartment as though they were attending a show at the theater! In any case, even if he does live as though he were Casanova, I'm pleased to accept the friendship he's offered me."

"I don't have anything against him, though perhaps against his class of people, factory owners, warehouse owners, mine owners. Greedy and insensitive people. . . . But anyway, getting back to Bousquet, I'd always suspected that what everyone took for vanity was nothing more than a façade to hide his incompetence. I have no doubt that he'll excel as a tradesman. As for what you say about women, you're right. Who am I to judge their opinions about masculine beauty?"

Following the sway of the conversation, I was stuck by a curiosity to know something about his love life.

"Do you have a girlfriend, Fauriel?"

"Yes," he replied curtly. "Back in my village. And you?"

"Yes, me too. Actually, I'm engaged. Her name is Marisa Robledo and she's the only daughter of a plantation owner," I replied, using the premeditated response I'd devised in case anyone were to ever ask me that question. "We're to be married as soon as I graduate."

"Mine is poor. There are no rich people in my village, just mining families in ill health. You know, the coalmines in the north. Coal in the lungs. I'll go back there. I'll do something for them. Many die so young, you know? That was what happened to my father. I still remember him coughing," he said, making distracted piles of breadcrumbs. "But your family is rich. You can't possibly know what I'm talking about."

"There are also poor people in Havana. What's more, there are slaves. I have seen poverty up close," I protested.

"But you haven't lived it. It's not the same thing."

I knew it was true, and I glimpsed the black hole he'd come out of, realized the immense effort, given his circumstances, it must take for him to carry out his studies, and I thought how richly he deserved to have been selected as a "state student" from his district.

"The clothes you bought fit you quite well," I said to change the subject. "Although I must admit that I'll miss the clock, clock, clock of your clogs."

"Do you really think I look good, Fuenmayor?" he asked, one of his smiles beginning to spread across his face.

"Almost as good as Bousquet. Now the women of Paris will have a new threat to contend with."

"You know what, Fuenmayor?" he said, looking me in the eye. "You are the best friend I've ever had in my entire life. Who'll ever believe me when I go back to my village and tell them that I, the son of the old invalid Fauriel, dined in a magnificent café with a rich friend from Havana?"

℘

The following day I did not go to the Charité or attend any of my classes. At seven in the morning Pierre had knocked on my door to tell me that Uncle Charles had returned home. "He's wounded, madame. Françoise insisted that I come fetch you in the cabriolet."

I found my Uncle in his customary chair. His leg was resting atop a tower of pillows and cushions. When he saw me he feigned displeasure and said: "You see, no one pays me any mind around here anymore! I had wanted to wait until Sunday to tell you. That way you wouldn't miss any of your classes. But, in any event, they've already gotten you out of bed, and I'm happy to see you Henriette. Come over here and give me a kiss. You look good, my girl, you look good. Very natural, I'd say. No one would ever . . . well, you know what I mean to say."

He, on the other hand, looked terrible. He'd lost weight and his face was as weathered as a fisherman's. Of course, it had been over a year since we'd last met, but to judge by how much he'd aged, one would have thought it had been five. He'd come from Spain, where he'd been sent after the armistice with the Austrians.

"And here you have me, with British lead in my thigh. It happened in an wretched place—Ciudad Rodrigo," he said, laying a finger across the spot where the bullet had gone in. "I put myself on leave. It hurts to walk. Also to ride. I know what's happened. I'll speak to you as a surgeon. The bullet passed through the sartorial muscle, lodged in the femur and is disturbing a nerve in there. Next week I'll oversee my own operation in the Val-de-Grâce. Anyway, nothing mortal so long as the wound is debrided thoroughly. You'll see, I'll be good as new."

"Could I be there as well?"

"Don't even think about it!" he said, laughing. "I would worry too much thinking that it would trouble you to see me grimacing in pain. But I'll keep you informed. Now tell me, how are your studies going? But, before I forget, I have news to share: I've been awarded the Cross of the Legion of Honor!"

We talked for several hours. He had seen Alfred on one occasion. He'd been promoted to Captain and was recuperating from a head wound he'd sustained in Zaragoza. Some old crone had thrown a flowerpot at him from an upstairs window. The business in the peninsula was dragging on. Massena was not conducting himself well. He had brought his wife along, dressed as a Dragoon, no less. She was a greedy woman who encouraged her husband to sack and pillage. As for the British, Wellington had made a difference. He was an astute and capable man, a difficult man to conquer. "But we'll toss him out to sea nonetheless," asserted Uncle Charles. And so we passed the afternoon, Uncle Charles talking about Spain, praising its seafood, sausages, and hams. Seeing that he was tired, I said goodbye, assuring him that I'd come to visit on Sundays.

Pierre tried to insist on taking me home in the cabriolet, but it had been so long since I'd walked those streets that I refused his offer. It was a beautiful, warm evening, and twilight found me walking along the river. It was almost dinnertime and, although I knew that Bousquet was out of town, I headed for the Café Procope. To my surprise, Fauriel was waiting for me by the door.

"I was waiting for you," he said when he saw me. "Will you allow me to accompany you while you eat?"

226

"Better yet. I'll treat you to dinner."

"Oh, no, I couldn't. That's not why I've come. I need to talk to you," he said as we entered the café. "When you didn't come to dissection, I assumed you were sick and so I went to your house. When you weren't there, I thought that I'd probably find you here."

"Has something happened to you, Fauriel?" I asked, seeing his agitation. The waiter came over to take our order. He was new at the café and didn't know that I always drank rum before dinner. "Why don't you have a little rum? It'll do you some good and hopefully it'll whet your appetite."

"Thank you, Fuenmayor. I'll let you buy me a glass of wine. Any kind is fine. A glass of the house red," he ordered. "Now that I find myself face to face with you I don't know where to begin. I'll warn you, what I'm going to tell you will come as a shock."

"I'm listening."

"I know who put the money in my pocket. It's the last person you'd ever imagine. Do you know Lacloche, from the outpatient clinic at the Charité? Yes, of course you know him. We've spoken of him."

"It was Lacloche?"

Fauriel nodded.

"Did he owe you a favor?" I asked, surprised. Lacloche had graduated four or five years back and his salary as an "extern" couldn't have amounted to much; his wife even brought his meals to the hospital.

"He likes me, Fuenmayor!" he whispered after downing his glass of wine in one gulp. "Do you understand?"

"Do you mean to say that he's fallen in love with you? But he's married!"

"It's like I told you," he replied impatiently. "But now . . . now I need your help. I only have two napoleons left. Could you lend me five? I need to return his money."

"I'll give them to you right now. But tell me about it, Fauriel. I promise you I'll tell no one."

"Oh, I know, Fuenmayor, I know. It's just that it embarrasses me. This has never happened to me before. Well, there was one other time. A drunken miner from my village. I had to beat him over the head with a stick. Lacloche is another matter. What I mean is—"

"Of course he's another matter; he's a good doctor, an intelligent man, and married as well. Even if he did try to buy you, you should limit yourself to returning the money. What could you possibly gain by knocking him over the head or breaking his nose? There's no need for you to ruin your life. Look, here's the money," I said, handing him my bag. "There's enough in there for you and to pay for dinner. If there's anything left over, send it to your mother."

"Thank you. . . . Thank you. What else can I say? Oh, Fuenmayor, you're right, I can't give him a beating," he said, and started to sob.

"Come now, Fauriel. . . . We're in public," I said, alarmed by this weeping from someone always in such high spirits.

"It's that you don't know. . . . He wasn't trying to buy my favors with the money. He didn't want anything from me. He said it pained him to see me so poor, that I deserved better. The seven napoleons were part of his savings. He kissed me, Fuenmayor. He came up to me and kissed me on the mouth and told me he loved me. Oh, Fuenmayor!"

"Fauriel, get a hold of yourself," I said, taking him by the arm. "People are looking at us. Don't you have a handkerchief? Here, use the napkin."

His nose was running pathetically, and he brought the napkin to his face and rubbed at it. He stayed like that, with his face covered, for several minutes.

"Does the gentleman feel ill?" asked our waiter.

"He's received a bit of bad news," I said. "He's in shock," I added, waving him away with my hand.

"I'm all right now," he said, clearing his throat, letting the napkin fall to the table. "I've always had powerful emotions."

"Your face is redder than a cherry," I noted. It was then I realized that the shadow of his beard and mustache had run down his face like the too-wet watercolors on a painting. I looked at the napkin. It was stained a dull black. "My God, Fauriel, your eyebrows, your face . . . is not your face!" I exclaimed, perplexed, my gaze fixed upon that ruddy, distressed, unexpected face. A woman's face.

She looked at me in terror. She covered her cheeks with her hands and let out a wail that brought the patrons at the next table to their feet.

"Let's go, let's get out of here! It's all gone to shit. I knew that someone from the Faculty would find me out eventually. Hold me up, Fuenmayor. Give me your arm and get me out of here!"

I took her to my apartment and made her an infusion of coffee with an emetic. She began retching immediately and vomited the entire contents of her stomach. Still shaking, she asked me to call her a coach, saying it was getting late and she needed to get back to the farm. But when she tried to stand, beads of sweat pearled on her forehead and she crumpled onto the bed. She had no tears left, but every few seconds her chest would heave in a deep, wracking sob. I dried her forehead. I took her pulse; it was weak. Her hands were cold. I covered her in my eiderdown quilt. I insisted that she spend the night in my apartment. I would sleep in the other room, with the door open, and I begged her to call me if she needed anything. I poured an herbal tea from a pitcher into a cup and lit a new candle on the bedside table. In an effort to put her at ease, before retiring for the evening, I swore that her secret was safe with me and that she needn't feel obliged to explain anything.

Although I knew I wouldn't sleep at all that night, I lay down on the sofa with a cushion as a pillow. As always happened to me when my nerves were agitated, I had the sensation of being divided, of being two people at once: on the one hand, the woman capable of reacting to whatever the situation required; on the other, the dazed little girl who, floating in a hazy limbo, lacked a clear understanding of what her counterpart was doing. And so, oscillating between reason and emotion, I felt no curiosity about who that woman resting in my room might be. I felt only compassion for her; I felt her fear, her shame at having been discovered by someone she assumed was a man. What would our relationship be like moving forward?—asked my practical side. It would certainly never be as it had been before. And yet, if that night had never happened, or, better yet, if she hadn't needed to ask me for money, or, further, if Bousquet hadn't flustered my judgment, I wouldn't have taken her to the Café Procope and things *would* have continued just as they had been: our lunches in Madame Binot's modest tavern, the dissection table, talk of Havana. Almost without realizing it, I had started to cry, tears that were for her and for me, for what the loss of our friendship would mean for the both of us. The loss of our friendship? Yes, the loss, the termination, since the barrier between the sexes would be raised between us without her ever suspecting that such a barrier didn't exist. I didn't think further; nor did I hesitate. Impelled at that moment by my emotions, I simply stood up and removed my waistcoat, my shirt, my breeches and the silk sash that flattened my breasts. Naked and barefoot, I picked up the candlestick and walked toward the light coming from her room. I paused at the threshold. She hadn't been able to sleep either. I lowered the candlestick to the level of my stomach and walked toward the bed. Her expression of surprise began to change into a splendorous smile, the most beautiful smile that anyone has ever seen.

"It's you, Fuenmayor."

"Like you, Fauriel."

13

SHE CONTINUED CALLING ME FUENMAYOR, and I went on calling her Fauriel. If, in Maryse, I had seen a mother and a friend, in Fauriel I saw myself. We were like a mirror for one another; in front of the other, we were what we were.

From the beginning we agreed not to speak of our respective pasts. It was my idea; it would have disappointed her to know that I hadn't been born in Havana. I limited myself to telling her that my baccalaureate degree was a fake and that my name was Enriqueta. Her legal name was Raymond Fauriel. She had been raised as a boy. Her father, who had already fallen ill at the time of her birth, recorded her at the Civil Registry as a boy so that she could learn a trade and thus assure the family's subsistence. At nine years of age she began working as a blacksmith's apprentice. Her employer, an old friend of her father's, permitted her to attend school. Later, she won a competition that allowed her to continue her studies in Lille and to receive a small stipend that she sent home to her mother. Finally, she had been selected as a "state student."

After the "Night of the Napkin"—the name we had given to the night we had revealed our common secret—I managed to persuade her to move in to my apartment and to stop working at the farm. It was not easy to convince her. Though her smile and cheerful disposition were genuine, she was accustomed to solitude and an independent life. She was like a bird, one of those sparrows one sees in the parks, flitting from here to there, ever restless and sociable, that, though appearing to relish the display of its vivaciousness, at twilight becomes invisible, disappearing to some unknown retreat. In order to ease her conscience, we agreed that, in exchange for the room and board I offered her, she would see to the cleanliness of the apartment and my clothing and help me with my studies and any other matter that might arise. I, of course, was thrilled with the arrangement: not only would Fauriel keep me company, but her intelligence, pleasant temperament, and common sense had already persuaded me to extend my wholehearted friendship. Right away I noticed that she accepted her fate with less resignation than I accepted mine. Early in the morning, from my room, I would listen to her grumble as she stood before the mirror darkening her eyebrows and staining her face with the dye she bought at a theater supply shop. Given that she'd grown up as a boy, there was nothing in her body's movements that would give her away. Her breasts had barely developed; they were small and flattened; her mother had fashioned a tight-fitting bodice that she'd worn under her shirt, beginning before she'd even reached puberty. She made fun of her breasts, calling them her "fried eggs." She told me she wasn't a virgin, but she gave no further details, and I didn't ask for them. For reciprocity's sake, I told her that I wasn't a virgin either. When I asked her if I gave off the impression of being a man, she said yes, but added, laughing, that some considered me a bit effeminate. We compensated for our agreement not to speak openly of our pasts by candidly sharing the events of the present. In our nightly conversations we did not hide any of our opinions, sorrows, joys, and problems. We agreed on a great many things. We both hated the war and had republican leanings, although we differed on one important point: Fauriel was a Jacobin. Finding it difficult to hide it from her, I spoke of my passion for Bousquet and of my nights of espionage against the wall that divided our apartments. This confession seemed to annoy her. In her mind, not only did Bousquet lack in physical attractiveness, he was a blithering idiot besides.

"I can't figure out how you could lose your head over that fop. You're an intelligent woman, Fuenmayor."

I was tempted to tell her my Apollo story, but I thought better of it: once I'd opened a small chink into my past, I'd run the risk of revealing my true identity.

"I have my reasons. And anyway, emotions have nothing to do with intelligence."

"I'm not so sure," she said with an impish smile.

Bousquet returned more fresh-faced and beautiful than ever. It was as though proximity to his father's factory had somehow conferred upon him the look of a porcelain doll. He was thrilled to learn that Fauriel had moved in with me, and invited us to dinner at the café that very evening. He had gone to Limoges to consult with his father. He had wanted to be clear as to what was expected of him at the Paris office. After dinner, as though they were topics of great interest, he began to tell us about his brothers' enormous incomes and what they did with all that money; about their wives and children, their houses and furniture and his father's highly prized plate collection.

"My Uncle Achille used to collect spoons," I said, to say something. "Silver spoons. One of them came from a tea service that belonged to Marie Antoinette."

"Silver spoons, how fascinating!" exclaimed Bousquet. "People from Havana have refined tastes," he added. "We receive many orders from there. Although now, with the war. . . . Well, everything will sort itself out."

"I'm a collector too," said Fauriel, and, seeing her seriousness, I settled in to listen to one of her jokes. "I've sometimes been tempted to collect something different, but something that's also within my reach. I'd like to have time to walk through the Bois de Boulogne; I could start a collection of Parisian flowers, like the one old Rousseau is said to have had. But in the Faculty, the only thing that's free are the cadavers and, aside from the fingernails, they really don't offer much that would be practical to collect. Perhaps locks of hair, no?"

"You collect the fingernails of dead people?" asked Bousquet, his eyes widening in disbelief.

"Only from the thumb on the right hand," replied Fauriel, holding up her thumbnail. "They vary a great deal in shape, thickness and size. For example, yours, Fuenmayor, is quite wide, but yours, Bousquet, is very elongated. Did you, by any chance, suck your thumb as a child?"

"Well, no, not that I can remember," said Bousquet. "The only bad habit I had was picking my nose."

I gave Fauriel a kick under the table. It irritated me that she was pulling my Greek god's leg.

"I'll tell you what I read in an old treatise on palmistry that I found, covered in dust, in the Faculty library. According to those initiated in that arcane art form, in addition to what the lines of the palm reveal, there are messages locked away in the wrists, the phalanges, and the knuckles, as well as in the fingernails and fingertips. Of course, since I needed to study for our pathology exam, I only read carefully the part about the fingernails, since that interests me the most."

"Palm reading strikes me as a gypsy artifice," I said in order to shift the conversation away from the topic of fingernails. I suspected that Fauriel was up to something, and had chosen Bousquet as her victim. "Astrology is different. There are some who believe it to be a science. Nostradamus! Am I right?"

"Yes, of course . . . Nostradamus," said Bousquet.

"I don't share your opinion," said Fauriel. "Twins are born in the same place, at the same time, under the same astrological sign and under the same planetary configuration. Their destinies ought to be identical, but they aren't. What's more, the Greeks, the very same ones who taught us how to think, attributed very different characteristics to Apollo and Hecate."

"Well, yes, that's true, quite true," agreed Bousquet. "They are very different."

"Fingernails, however, are unique. They are strictly individual. Flexible, pink fingernails speak of good health; corneous nails of old age; colorless nails of ill health. Naturally, these are just generalizations. A closer look would offer a good many more details. Country folk, for example, have thick and blackened fingernails; washerwomen frequently have quite brittle nails. . . . Let's compare our own nails. What do we see? To begin with, my nails lack the elegant half-moon near the cuticle that yours both have. This indicates that I worked with my hands as a child. But there's more: the palmistry treatise contends that it's possible to read the future in the right thumbnail, even for left-handed people such as myself. And the most amazing thing of all is that I've been able to confirm it."

"Incredible!" exclaimed Bousquet.

I slid my hand under the table and pinched Fauriel.

"And so, my friends," she continued, undaunted, "I have observed that the fingernails of cadavers accurately reveal the way in which each individual died. This sent me back to the library to copy the pages that refer to fingernails and their relationship to the thumb, which is the most difficult part to learn because there are so many different types of thumbs."

"Do you mean to say that you have learned to read fingernails?" asked Bousquet, intrigued.

"My friend, I can read your future as easily as if I were an Israelite prophet. A good future, I might add. But bring your hand closer. I'll tell you things you'll tell your children one day, your grandchildren even, since your life will be as long and prolific as the biblical patriarchs'."

Taking advantage of the fact that Bousquet's gaze was riveted on his thumb, I knocked my glass of wine over on the tablecloth.

"Oh dear, look what I've done!" I said, as Fauriel winked at me almost imperceptibly and shot me a quick smile.

"Go on! Go on!" demanded Bousquet impatiently, once the waiter had mopped up the tablecloth with a napkin and refilled my glass.

"Well, as I was saying, your life will be long and happy. You'll have six, maybe seven children, all sons."

"That would be very good. It would guarantee the longevity of the business, Bousquet & Sons. Will my wife be rich?"

"Rich," Fauriel said soberly. "But, wait! . . . Something interesting! You'll marry a foreigner. . . . A Spaniard? It could be. . . . *Parbleu*, a woman from the tropics! It could even be a woman from your hometown, Fuenmayor," she added, looking at me.

"From Havana?" asked Bousquet.

"Quite likely. I see a fortress at the entrance to a bay that corresponds with Fuenmayor's description of the famous Castillo del Morro."

"But how can you see a castle in my fingernail? You wouldn't by any chance be pulling my leg, Fauriel?" said Bousquet in a distrustful tone.

"I see the castle just as a fortune teller would. It's a mental image, something like a memory of the future, though that doesn't make it any less exact. Don't forget that we're treading among the magical pages of chiromancy. And it's not that I'm guilty of immodesty, but the fact is, as I studied the treatise, word for word, I felt myself confronted by a great truth," she said grandiloquently, her chest puffing up. "Then, I read in an endnote that a very small number of readers, under condition they'd been born for the occult, could successfully practice palmistry using the treatise as a guide. This has been the case with me," she added, offering us a smile as modest and cheerful as a bouquet of violets.

I don't know the details of how the farce continued. Under the pretext of going to the lavatory, I left the table for a good quarter of an hour. When I returned, Bousquet's eyes and rosy cheeks reflected the most complete satisfaction.

"You missed the best part," Fauriel told me, an innocent expression on her face. "Bousquet will meet his bride in Limoges. Most likely she'll have gone there, while traveling in France with her parents, to pick out a new porcelain table service for the family. The old one will be missing several pieces due to violent causes, perhaps a hurricane or an earthquake. This will happen within two years, three at the most. We will no longer be at war with Spain and Bousquet will get married in Madrid, where his fiancée's family has a palace. Can you guess what the girl's name is?"

Furious, I glanced at Bousquet's hand and said: "Enriqueta!"

"*Mon Dieu*!" exclaimed Bousquet. "That's exactly right! Have you also studied the treatise?" he asked me. I nodded and, taking Fauriel by the collar of her frockcoat, lifted her from her chair.

"Let's go! Don't forget they are waiting for us at the theater on the Rue de Temple."

"I'd love to go with you," said Bousquet, standing up, "but I also have a date. Quite the delicacy! Fourteen years old and with a backside straight out of the renaissance!" Putting on his hat, he added: "My father collects plates, your uncle, spoons, and you, Fauriel, dead people's fingernails. Do you know what I collect? Nights of pleasure!"

Scarcely speaking, we left the café and walked to the river.

I was furious with Fauriel and, passing by Le Coq Audacieux, I took her by the arm and led her inside. We sat down and I ordered a bottle of wine.

"Do you know what?" I said huffily. "You are sticking your nose too much into my business."

"Yes," she replied.

"What do you mean *yes?*" I protested. That was the last response I'd been expecting.

"Well, yes. I realize that. What do you want me to say? That I'm very sorry, that I won't do it again?" she said, also ill-humored. "Don't you see that I'm doing you a huge favor? I want you to realize, once and for all, that Bousquet is an idiot, almost certifiably so. He's not worth your wasting your time thinking about him, spending hours with your ear to the wall and snooping from the window. You're not even sleeping with him! So what are you after, why are you so desperate to run on home so you can listen to his obscenities while you tickle yourself? Come on, Enriqueta, you're a full-grown woman. Free yourself of Bousquet once and—"

"Fauriel," I interrupted her. "You just called me Enriqueta."

"Did I?"

"My God, this is the last straw! You're jealous, Fauriel! You're jealous of Bousquet!"

She downed her entire glass of wine in one gulp and served herself another from the bottle on the table.

"Perhaps, Fuenmayor, perhaps. But I'll tell you: before the 'Night of the Napkin' I already valued your friendship a great deal. Do you know why? Because, despite being rich, you treated me as an equal. You never sought to humiliate me with your generosity; it wasn't a hypocritical gesture to allow you to feel superior to me. Then, when I left my man's face in the café, you didn't hesitate to take me home with you. You took care of me without asking a single question. And while I, lying in your bed, asked myself if the fact that you knew I was a woman would break the bonds of our friendship, you appeared before me naked so that I might see how God had made you. Yes, you revealed your secret to me, and you did so without thinking of the consequences. At the time, I was so surprised that I couldn't fully comprehend your lovely gesture. But later that night, after you'd gone to bed, I realized that you'd done it to protect our friendship. And that is something, Fuenmayor, that I might not have done for you."

"Come on, Fauriel, please! If you go on like this I'm going to start crying!"

"I'm almost finished. I just wanted to say that since that moment we've lived almost as sisters. So much so that the only thing standing between us truly being sisters was for me to tell you about my life. The suffering of my childhood, my frustrations, my efforts, my hopes. I know that you would also tell me of your life. . . . "

"Of course I would, Fauriel," I said, moved, interrupting her once again, taking her hand and squeezing it tightly as if to say that nothing and no one could separate us.

"And that moment of truth," she continued, "so important to me, was just about to arrive, Fuenmayor. It was almost here when that idiot Bousquet suddenly reappeared. What are our evenings to be like now? One needn't be a palm reader to know that we'll eat every night with that stupid Don Juan and then, while I study or read or water the plants or heat water for tea, you'll go into the other room to listen to him make love to some poor seamstress or unfaithful wife. 'I collect nights of pleasure!' he says so proudly, that halfwit. And you, my lost sister. . . . "

"Please, Fauriel, enough! I'm begging you. It isn't necessary—"

"Yes, it *is* necessary!" she said, tearing her hand from mine and pounding the table with her fist. And a new Fauriel appeared before me. Her eyes blazed, hard and flashing, her face a tight ball of deep resentment. "It's necessary for me! Today I need to say what I feel! At least today, goddamnit! I've spent twenty years being some-one I'm not! Let me be myself this one night!" she said, completely overcome. She took another long drink of wine and this appeared to calm her somewhat. "We were talking about Lacloche the other night. Well, I'll tell you. I'm in love with him. Yes, I love him. And not in the base way that you love Bousquet. I love him because he's decent, intelligent, and generous. He has beautiful eyes. When he's deep in concentration a little dimple appears on his chin. It pains me that he thinks I'm a man. You have no idea how much it pains me. But despite everything I'm in love with him and I desire him. How can it be? I think it's because I felt myself loved from within my dis-guise. Me, who nobody loves. I know, it's not easy to explain. . . . Another day. Anyway, I'll tell you something I've kept hidden from you. I had sex with him. Do you want to know how we did it? Like buggerers. We did it standing up. We scarcely fit in the latrine. It was half-dark and smelled terrible. I lowered my drawers and leaned over the best I could. Five minutes, Fuenmayor, five minutes at the most. Five minutes standing up in a latrine reeking of shit. And that was that! But that's not even the worst part. The worst part is that we went back to the latrine a few days later. There was a puddle of urine on the floor, dirty paper. He couldn't do it. I kneeled in the puddle. I kissed him. He couldn't. We both left there humiliated. What can I tell you? This sort of thing is not new for me. But since that day he has avoided my gaze. I've lost him, I know that already. It's the story of my life, Fuenmayor. It's always been this way. And all I can do is go on living the lie. But I swear to you, Fuenmayor, there are nights when I can scarcely resist the urge to put on a dress and go out whoring in the street. And don't think I haven't done it, either. The last time they beat me, tossed me in a coach, and threw me away like a worthless piece of garbage in the Bois de Vincennes. I'm tired of being a man, Fuenmayor. I try to put on a good face, to go on fooling myself, to make it all into one big joke. Oh, how nice Fauriel is, how clever! How funny that Fauriel is! But I'm tired. I know this comes as a surprise to you. And just imagine it, here you are, thinking you need me, when really it's I who needs you. You can't imagine how much it means to me to be able to talk with you, woman to woman, even if it's only for two or three hours. It means I can be myself, speak in my real voice, tell you that I'm in love with a man. And please don't think that my intention is to stick my nose in your business, as you've accused me of doing, simply for the pleasure of doing it. If you had an actual relationship, even with that fool Bousquet, I'd understand. But it hurts me to feel abandoned for a fantasy, for a fucking wall," she said bitterly. Then, resting her elbows on the table and dropping her head into her hands, she added: "I'm going back to the farmstead, Fuenmayor. I'm going back. You can have Bousquet and his harem's orgasms all to yourself."

"Come on, Fauriel, don't be silly."

"Yes, I'm going back. And it's not that I don't appreciate what you've done for me. How I wish I could repay you for it! It's just this wretched poverty! Don't you see? I'm the product of poverty! Had I not been born poor I could be married to someone, have someone's child!" she wailed.

She spoke for a good while longer, piteously vomiting across the table the accumulated bile of twenty years spent masking her true self. But as much as I felt for her and wanted to keep her by my side, I was incapable of completely renouncing my connection to Bousquet; it was, quite simply, something dark and remote that returned to me unbidden, infiltrating my desire.

"I can't promise you much, Fauriel. But I can assure you that the majority of our nights will be yours and mine alone," I offered as a means of compromise. "And I'm not just saying that to placate you, to stop you from going. It's that now, more than ever, I want us to be true sisters. I have also kept things hidden from you. I'll tell you everything, Fauriel. Everything. Perhaps it'll be for the best."

14

1811 WOULD PROVE AN INTERESTING and meaningful year in my life. It was a preparatory year, a year in which the muscles of my spirit grew strong; a necessary year. Through the course of it, the bonds that linked me to Fauriel became so close that, one day, I spoke of her to Uncle Charles. I wanted to share my small family with her, wanted her to know what they were really like—not just through my stories about them—Françoise, Pierre, and Uncle Charles, and even Madame Bagnol, who was now Madame Cavent, since my uncle had made good use of his long convalescence and married her. Once admitted into my most intimate circle, Fauriel and I went to dinner at the house on Rue Sainte-Honoré almost every Sunday. We always arrived quite early, eager to hear Uncle Charles' war stories and tales of the surgical exploits he'd performed on the battlefield. One afternoon he told us that there had always been women serving in the various armies. In Egypt he'd met a woman from Marseilles serving with the artillery. He had amputated one of her legs without complications. "What happens is that they're only discovered when they turn up in the hospital," he'd explained. When I asked him if he knew personally of other cases he'd said yes, two others, a Spaniard and a Prussian, but he'd heard of still more from his colleagues. Fauriel also asked him questions, although hers were always related to the practice of medicine. Despite the fact that several of our professors had belonged to the armies of the Republic, we had received very little in the way of instruction in military medicine. I can still see us, sitting around a huge platter of cheese, drinking Anjou wine while Madame Cavent gazed, love-struck, at Uncle Charles, seeing him as a sort of old-fashioned and dignified Knight of the Round

Table whose feats of bravery—she always insisted—should be collected in a book.

My passion for Bousquet, though it did diminish with the passing months, had not disappeared completely. Sometimes, when Fauriel was asleep, I would creep, on tiptoe, into the forbidden room. With my ear to the wall and my hand between my legs, I'd indulge in the sounds of pleasure. Since Bousquet kept us abreast of his conquests, I had learned to identify the howls of an Italian soprano named Angelina, the discrete moans of the fourteen-year-old *grisette* with the Renaissance backside, and the hoarse death rattles of Mademoiselle Rouge and Mademoiselle Brune, who'd become regular visitors. Once or twice a week, despite Fauriel's furious protests the entire way there, we would eat with him at the Café Procope. His conversation was as boring and superfluous as ever. Lately, we'd noticed that it focused increasingly on the erotic. Soon, he stopped talking about his lovers in order to offer his candid opinions on aphrodisiacs, pleasure-enhancing instruments, the virtues of unnatural intercourse, and Oriental perversions, which he detailed with an insider's precision.

"We're still in diapers here in Europe," he assured us during one of our last dinners together. "We were dazzled by Casanova when he was really nothing more than an artless fornicator. It was said that Marie Antoinette was given to a scandalous life, but it's now commonly known that the poor woman hadn't the least bit of imagination. And well, there's Sade. I won't deny his merits. But what has been his fate? The prison, the madhouse, and the monastery. What is there in the *Enciclopedia* about the passions of the flesh? A great void. In contrast, in the Orient, there are the great books, the great treatises. Let's see, Fauriel, you're a palm reader. Have you ever read sublime lust in your collection of fingernails? Surely not. The French are a prosaic race, cerebral, rationalist. We have Deuxcartes to thank for that."

"Descartes," corrected Fauriel.

"That's what I said. Anyway, I've learned, for example, that Japanese widows insert a bell into their vaginas. As they rock on their swings, the bells subtly vibrate, causing both an intimate sonority and a tickling sensation that consoles them during their period of mourning. There is also a Chinese violin, with only two strings, I believe, called an *er-hu-hu*. The sound box, tubular in shape and of moderate thickness, is affixed to the end of its long arm. It's said that some Mandarins of advanced age will have the box, smeared with stimulating unguents, inserted into their orifice. Once this has been accomplished, a courtesan begins to strum the strings with a bow of white horsehair. Custom requires that the music begin in a tempo called 'imperial elephant walk' and that, after moving through several other cadences whose names I can't recall, it must finish with the 'twitter of nightingale in spring.' It goes without saying that the vibrations pass through the rectum to the prostate gland, causing the lower regions to be engorged with blood, in turn stimulating erectile function and energizing the penis, at least for a few seconds. It's at this very moment that the nubile concubine, in the presence of a dog, offers her hymen to her master."

"Why in the presence of a dog?" I asked, repulsed.

"That I don't know," replied Bousquet. "That's what I've been told and it never occurred to me to ask."

"It must be so that it could bark in case the 'twitter of nightingale in spring' doesn't have the desired effect," said Fauriel.

"It could be," allowed Bousquet. "And speaking of dogs. . . . "

Without a doubt, something horrible had happened to my Apollo. It was as if a malignant parasite had entered through his ear and taken up residence in his brain. I say "his ear" because it was obvious that Bousquet was repeating what someone else had told him. It was enough for me to have arrived at that conclusion for me to understand immediately that this someone was, in fact, two people, Mademoiselle Rouge and Mademoiselle Brune, whose depravity had found fertile ground in Bousquet's lax Don Juan morality. The saddest part of all was that his physical appearance had also begun to decline. Having recently become an aficionado of dessert, he stuffed himself with cream puffs and pastries, chocolate-covered chestnuts and cherries. I was disappointed to discover that, underneath the sparse little beard he now wore, a double chin was beginning to appear. Even so, it was still impossible for me to ignore the call of the moans that issued from his apartment. One night not long after the evening of the risqué conversation I've just related, Fauriel caught me, my legs splayed open in the chair, my head against the wall. She said nothing. She merely looked at me and smiled in that incomparable way of hers. As ashamed as a little girl, I headed to bed, and, as I entered my room I saw her go into the front room of the apartment. I spied on her through the keyhole of my bedroom door. She was also spying, at the window. For the first time ever, it seemed she had taken an interest in the identity of Bousquet's visitors.

A week later, as I was changing clothes for dinner, she came in to my room.

"I've brought you a present, Fuenmayor," she said, holding out a key similar to my own. "Today you can enter the secret gardens of your Mandarin."

"Is that his key?" I asked, incredulous. "But how . . . ?"

"Quite simple, my little friend. Three days ago I put soft wax in the keyhole and, when I told you I was going to the library, I really went to take the mold to a locksmith who'd been a patient of mine at the Charité. He owed me a big favor. He'd smashed his finger with a hammer and I convinced Boyer to postpone the amputation until the first signs of gangrene appeared. I did to him what we always did back in my village. I covered his finger in spider webs and bandages soaked in warm water and told him to keep them moist. Miracle cure. I saved his finger."

"Not that I'm planning to actually use it, but, have you confirmed that the key works?" I asked, doubtful that it could be so easy to copy a key.

"It works," she assured me. "When Bousquet goes out to dinner, you can enter his apartment. Once inside, you can hide in his armoire and you'll have front row seats for the entire show."

"The day I do something like that will be the day I cease to be me," I declared, rejecting the key with a wave of my hand. "I'd lose all respect for myself."

"Don't be a hypocrite. You do it in your imagination all the time. Isn't that worse?"

"And anyway, I'd be invading his privacy."

"Oh, please! And what are you doing when you think I'm asleep?"

"It's not the same thing," I said, confused.

"It's worse, because it's a vice that you can't control through willpower. And in any case," she added, "you won't be running any risk."

"How do you know?"

"Because yesterday, the tables turned. While you were asleep,

244

I went into Bousquet's apartment to have a look around. There is a large armoire across from the bed. I climbed inside and looked out through the keyhole."

"I can't Fauriel. I can't," I said, trying to imagine myself imitating her actions. "I just don't have it in me. It would be immoral."

"You aren't a nun, Fuenmayor. Be truly faithful to you desires. At least on this one night. It would be best for you to do it today. You'll thank me later. Tonight your old acquaintances are coming, Mademoiselle Rouge and Mademoiselle Brune."

"How can you be so sure?" I pressed, suspecting that she knew a great deal more than she was letting on.

"Because that's what they said yesterday when I was watching from the armoire."

"Are you crazy? Bousquet could have discovered you!"

"That's true, but he didn't. I waited until his lady friends had left and he fell asleep. I already told you: you won't run any risk."

"I won't go Fauriel," I said determinedly. "Don't pressure me any more. I won't go, not today, not tomorrow, not ever."

"What a shame!" she said, putting the key in her pocket. "You would have had the surprise of your life. And not only that, but I'd have had your eternal gratitude. You can't even imagine the caprices of your Mandarin. Are you sure you don't want to find out?"

"Stop tempting me," I said, irritated by her persistence. "I've already told you. And anyway, I imagine I already know what goes on on the other side of that wall."

"Hearing is not the same as seeing, my friend. But very well, I won't insist anymore if you promise to go to the theater with me tonight. If you'll humor me on this, I'll toss the key down a sewer drain and never mention it again."

I knew Fauriel. I knew that she'd cooked up some scheme, laid a trap in which Bousquet, those perverted sisters, and I were to be ensnared. Nevertheless, this foresight wasn't enough to dampen my curiosity. After all, what physical or moral danger could threaten me in a theater?

"Any theater in particular?" I asked her.

"The Feydeau."

"We'll be late."

"We'll have dinner afterwards."

"What are they performing?"

245

"We'll soon find out."

We arrived right on time. Although I'd intended to buy tickets for box seats, Fauriel insisted that we sit in the seats closest to the orchestra pit. The opera that evening was *Ma Tante Aurore*, and I couldn't help but think of Maryse, since its author, Adrien Boieldieu, had also written *The Caliph of Bagdad*. "And now I have another favor to ask you," whispered Fauriel as the cheerful overture came to a close. "Look closely at the footmen in the chorus." She repeated this request three or four times throughout the performance. At last the curtains fell. Amid well-deserved applause and shouted bravos, Madame de Saint-Aubin and Monsieur Elleviou exited the stage, and we stood to leave.

"Did you get a close look at the footmen? " Fauriel asked again once we were out on the street. "Did you notice anything unusual about them?" she added, without waiting for my reply.

"One was very tall and the other limped a bit on his left leg."

"Exactly!" she said approvingly.

I didn't ask her why she was so interested in the men who had portrayed the footmen. I knew that, when the moment arrived, she'd move her pieces like the most accomplished of chess players and checkmate me. To hasten the arrival of the inevitable denouement, I headed for the coaches waiting in a line in front of the theater.

"Wait. It's not time to go just yet," she said, stopping me with a gesture. Soon, the street was empty of people and only a few coaches remained, no doubt waiting for the performers. The first to emerge were the musicians, followed shortly by Monsieur Elleviou, elegantly dressed in gray. Then, chattering away, arm in arm and wearing their velvet masks, Mademoiselle Rouge and Mademoiselle Brune came out the door.

"There you have your footmen," said my friend with an air of triumph. And, in fact, there they were, one tall, the other lame in the left leg. It was a devastating vision. Silently, I watched them climb into a waiting coach. Once it had left, I turned around: "Oh, Fauriel, this was all so unnecessary!" I cried out, tears in my eyes. "You could have just told me about it. I would have believed you."

"Perhaps. But I'm sure you'll agree with me that purgatives are best taken quickly, all in one gulp. Can you guess where they are headed now?"

"I don't want to know. I don't want to know anything more

about this. Don't tell me anything! Never again. Not one more word!"

But Fauriel, with the same dexterity with which she wielded the scalpel on the dissection table, made the final incision: "You don't even want to know what happens on the other side of your wall! It seems that their favorite game involves the Chinese violin," she said, mockingly.

Days later, without saying goodbye to Bousquet, we moved to a house on the Boulevard Saint-Michel. The apartment was stuffy and had only two rooms, but it was the first place we could find. More than ever, I focused on my studies, and both Fauriel and I passed our third-year exams with flying colors. While we were celebrating with a few other students in Madame Binot's tavern, Fauriel leaned in close and said: "There was a moment when I was on the verge of dressing as a woman and saying to hell with it all. You gave me the strength to keep going. I'll never forget you, Fuenmayor."

⚭

We spent the evening before Uncle Charles' birthday at his house. When the clock struck midnight, we toasted to his good health and happiness in the year to come. Then my uncle made a surprising announcement: "Now that I can congratulate myself on having survived forty-six years, I must share some unpleasant news, although, for me, it's neither good nor bad news, since it's simply a matter of duty: I'll be leaving in a few days."

Madame Cavent, who, thinking my uncle had been about to make another toast, still held her glass aloft, let it fall to the table with a little shout. The glass snapped at the stem; the rounded goblet rotated slowly upon the wine-stained tablecloth, mesmerizing us all, then fell to the floor where it shattered into tiny pieces.

"A bad omen," murmured Françoise before heading to the kitchen in search of a broom.

"Oh, what wretchedness! What am I going to do without you?" wailed Madame Cavent. "And in any case, you are still limping and Spain disagrees with you. It's a bad war."

"I'm not going to Spain, my love. I'm heading east," said Uncle Charles from the opposite head of the table. "Where both the Emperor and I have always been lucky."

"Thank goodness," I said. "For a moment there I thought they were sending you back to the war. You've given us all a good scare, Uncle."

"To the war? Heaven forbid! Larrey has been named Surgeon General of the Grande Armée and he's taking me with him to Mainz, surely in order to inspect the German hospitals," he said smiling. Nevertheless, perhaps because of what Françoise had said, I felt uneasy as I headed to bed.

I felt the same uneasiness the next day at the Faculty. There was a celebration in honor of Desgenettes, one of the founders of the new school. The Dean's speech was as insipid as ever, although he stuttered a few times and it was clear that he was preoccupied. There was something disquieting in the air in that great amphitheater, a feeling that was expressed in whispers, coughs and blown noses. Fauriel felt it too.

"There are rumors of troop movements," she told me as we were crossing the patio of the Practical School, hurrying so as to be the first ones to arrive. "But as hard as I've tried to find out, no one seems to know for certain what's going on."

When we asked the assistant to which dissection table we'd been assigned, he didn't reply. Looking at the floor, he sank his hand into his pocket, took out a sheet of paper, and held it out to Fauriel.

"Would you believe it? My number's finally come up!" she exclaimed sardonically as she read the communiqué for a second time.

❧

Uncles Charles said no, that he was very sorry but there was nothing he could do for Fauriel.

"But she's a woman, Uncle," I protested.

"Clearly this is her responsibility, not mine," he growled at my insistence.

"It's not her fault. She was registered as a male at birth. She's been passing as a man for more than twenty years."

My uncle thought for a moment and said: "My advice is that she go to the physical exam that the physicians from the recruitment commission administer at the Faculty. Since, in the case of students, the exam is a mere formality, she should disclose that she is a woman. If she does this, she'll be examined and declared unfit for service.

Then there will be an administrative procedure. Her birth certificate will be amended. I'm sure she'd be able to serve as a midwife if she so chooses."

"Very well," I sighed, "I'll tell her what you've said. Now, Uncle, tell me the truth. You know how discrete I am. Is there to be war in the east?"

"We're at peace with the Russians. Austria and Prussia are now our allies," he said, after a moment's consideration. "There is talk of a plan to invade England from the Baltic, but it's such a preposterous idea that I think it's merely a rumor started by the Emperor to confuse the enemy, whoever that may be. If Larrey knows something, he hasn't revealed it to me. He's told me only that he has orders to report to the general headquarters in Mainz. We shall see. It's true that there are huge troop movements toward the east. Perhaps Russia. . . . Most likely the Emperor plans to restore Poland's old territories. In any event, we'll soon find out. Any campaign in the east would have to begin in early summer. The Emperor doesn't like the cold. Now," he added, coming toward me, "give me a hug just in case we don't see one another again before I leave. I have certain matters to attend to. As you know, I leave the day after tomorrow."

I left the Val de Grâce hospital and took a hired coach to Madame Binot's tavern, where Fauriel awaited me.

"So, I'll go to war, like it or not," she said, after listening to the details of my conversation with Uncle Charles. "I'm not going to declare myself a woman at this late date, having just conquered my latest crisis. Anyway, I've always wanted to see Spain."

"How do you know where they're sending you?"

"Because the only war is in Spain. Surely Napoleon wants to finish it quickly. They say he's amassing a huge number of troops, including Germans and Italians, to unleash over the Pyrenees. That's why we've all been drafted."

"What do you mean?" I said, surprised.

"Oh, of course! I'd forgotten that you weren't at the Faculty this morning. Well, my dear friend, I'll tell you: every one of us fourth-year students has been called. If Leroux didn't make a general announcement in the amphitheater, it was because he wanted to handle the matter with discretion, that is, with individual notifications. Not you, of course," she added, seeing my alarm. "You aren't French, or better said, you are Enrique Fuenmayor, a subject of Spain."

"If this is another one of your jokes, I beg you to stop it now," I said, dead serious.

"It's no joke. My jokes always aim for a constructive outcome. You know how I hate war. How I wish I were in your place, or a Mexican's or an Argentine's! I would have finished this year and spent Christmas in my village. Be happy that you're staying. You have one more reason to thank your friend Maryse. If she hadn't sent you a Spanish passport. . . . Well, anyway, no one knows what war means better than you."

"Don't talk like that. You make me feel guilty."

"That's not my intention. But I would certainly love to have a passport from Havana."

"When do the physicals begin?"

"You know Napoleon. They'll start tonight. Since my name starts with an 'f,' my turn will come around nine o'clock. Why do you ask? If you'd like to come with me, you're quite welcome. We could get drunk afterwards."

But my question had a different purpose. Without weighing the pros and cons, I'd decided that if Fauriel was to be conscripted, I'd go with her. I'd offer myself as a volunteer.

"You're stark raving mad!" she cried, once I'd revealed my intentions. "Now *I'm* the one who feels guilty. And anyway, how can you be sure we'd even be together?"

"I'll go see my uncle tomorrow. I'll ask him to request us as his assistants. If there is a war, we'll march with him. We'll be part of the General Staff. I can promise you that it won't be as bad for us as it will be for some of our colleagues. I know from experience."

"Goddamned lunatic!" said Fauriel, laughing. "Who could ever have told me that I'd serve Napoleon alongside a friend who was not only a woman, but a veteran as well?"

The recruitment doctor didn't even ask us to remove our frock coats. He merely examined our tongues, pinched our cheeks and had us walk from one end to the other of the amphitheater, which had been taken over for the physicals. "Fuenmayor, Spanish volunteer, fit for service," he dictated to the clerk. Then, turning back to me, he clapped me on the shoulder and recommended that I continue attending classes until the order to join my regiment arrived.

Since it was scarcely nine-thirty, we took a coach to my Uncle's house. We didn't stop joking the entire way there, Fauriel saying that for once she was going to have new clothes and a new hat: "A bicorn, no less!" When we arrived at the house on Saint-Honoré, we were surprised to see that the windows were dark. We knocked several times. Above us two heads poked out through the little attic window: it was Pierre and Françoise. Uncle Charles had left at noon, taking Madam Cavent with him. There was a letter for me. They had been instructed to place themselves at my disposal beginning the very next day.

While Pierre and Françoise made their way down the stairs to open the door for us, Fauriel looked at me appreciatively. "You're no longer under your Uncle's protection. Just look at the fix you're in because of me."

It was cold in the house and Pierre lit several logs in the stove. I read Uncle Charles' letter, which was really no more than a note. He had left earlier than expected because Madame Cavent had insisted on accompanying him and she wanted to say goodbye to her mother in Blois. I was not to worry. Everything would go well. He had just paid another full year's rent, my room was exactly as I'd left it, my jewelry had been entrusted to his lawyer, Monsieur Dubreuil, and the cabriolet and the horses were in a stable in the *faubourg*. He closed by apprising me of the fact that Françoise and Pierre had begun a relationship and, although the decision was, by rights, mine, he thought that I should allow them to return to Foix so that they could marry.

While Françoise served us the last of the wine from an open bottle, I asked Fauriel to give us a moment alone.

"My Uncle tells me that you and Pierre are in love. Is he mistaken?"

Françoise shrugged and sat down next to me.

"Little by little, we've been getting closer, Henriette. I am grateful to him. He saved me from burning to death in Germany. Do I love him, well, I don't know. . . . He's good company up there," she said, referring to the attic room they shared. "I taught him to read. What can I tell you? He's like a big child. He's a good man, Henriette. He respects you a great deal. He says he's seen the world thanks to you. You should see how he struts about when he gets together with the other drivers!"

"Would he marry you despite . . . ?" I said, leaving the question hanging.

"Despite Claudette? Well, yes. It's not that he's spoken to me of her but he has told me more than once that if he were in Foix he would like to marry me and have children. His mother and brothers live there, as perhaps you already know."

"Will you be happy with him?"

Françoise nodded. By the light of the candelabra a few gray hairs shone in her red tresses. I thought that like me, she also had a story to tell. Would she remember her days as Aunt Margot's housekeeper? Perhaps they seemed as distant to her as they did to me. For an instant, I saw her at my aunt's bedside, reading her to sleep with one of her favorite novels.

"I'm very happy to hear it," I said contentedly. "Tell Pierre to come in. I want to hear from him what his intentions are."

And so, the wedding was arranged. I gave them the cabriolet and the horses, which, together, were worth at least three thousand francs. They could use the money from the sale of them to establish themselves back in the village. I also gave each of them one hundred and eighty francs in gold. Finally, I told Françoise that she could take all of my clothes from the armoire except the black dress, my mourning dress for Robert, which I'd kept as a kind of keepsake since Warsaw. Of course, I told them, they could leave whenever they saw fit, but when they found out that Fauriel and I would live in the house until we were called up, both insisted upon staying in my service as long as I remained in the city.

❧

After a few days, our lives went back to normal. We continued attending classes and, though more than two-thirds of our classmates were called up relatively quickly, it appeared that the authorities in charge of conscription had forgotten about us. Nor did the newspapers reflect any military unrest. They made a great deal of Napoleon's visit to the new beet sugar factory and, although there was a shortage of bread, the celebrations for carnival were the most joyous of any I'd seen since my arrival in Paris. At my insistence, Fauriel agreed to accompany me to the students' ball at the University. We made grand preparations for the event, including the dancing lessons I gave my friend. Powdered and rouged by Françoise, we wore women's domino costumes and masks. Our audacity reached such a point that we even joined in a quadrille with the Spaniards from the Americas. Fauriel's movements lacked feminine grace, but her smile, now highlighted by lipstick, proved irresistible, to judge by the half-dozen young men who asked her to dance. At the end of the evening, I found myself having to liberate her from a veritable blockade of admirers.

"You were a complete triumph," I said as we were entered the house. "Don't your feet hurt?"

"Everything hurts," she said, collapsing in Uncle Charles' soft armchair. "But I had such a good time. I'll even tell you that a daring hand found its way between the buttons of my costume and pinched one of my fried eggs. How was it for you?"

"My bottom must be covered in bruises. Although I feel it's quite content," I laughed. "Don't you think we could do this more often? There are still several days of dances left," I proposed, throwing my domino costume on the sofa.

"No, Fuenmayor. It's too dangerous. Soon you'll want to do it every night."

"Come on, Fauriel. Just one more time. Do you know where I'd like to go? To one of the dances at the Temple."

"And what if Bousquet asks you to dance?"

"Oh, my Apollo! What has become of him?"

"He's probably been completely devoured between Mademoiselle Rouge and Mademoiselle Brune."

"Seriously, though. Why not go to the Temple tomorrow night?"

"I already told you why not."

"You talk as if you're not headed off to war. Come on, woman!"

"Fine, we'll go on the last night of the season. That way we won't be able to relapse into the sin of being women."

Dolled up once again by Françoise, we took the cabriolet to the Boulevard de Temple, where there were several dances being held that evening. We went into one called the Bal Frisson, where, to judge by the menu outside the door, a good meal could be had. The dancehall was absolutely packed and we danced until we could dance no more. I noticed that Fauriel was moving with ever more suppleness, and that she appeared to be as at home as a goldfish in its bowl. Invited to dine by two good-natured centurions with solid-looking calves, we sat at a table away from the music. In the middle of dinner I felt my centurion's hand come to rest on my thigh and begin to climb slowly upward. On any other occasion I would have slapped his hand away, but the mask had a curious effect on me, making me feel that it covered my entire body like a protective talisman, a magical cape that made my body invisible, as well as my virtue. I opened my legs and allowed the hand to do what it would. My eyes half-closed, I looked over at Fauriel: she was reading her companion's left palm. Immediately I corrected my assessment. Her mouth was partially open, her tongue lolled in a kind of sweet panting, as if she'd fallen into an ecstatic trance. I realized that the man's other hand was under the tablecloth. I thought that if she were to look at me, she'd see exactly the same thing that I was seeing: a thick open mouth, damp with pleasure. . . . Seeing myself reflected in her masked face, in her yearning lips, I suddenly wished it were my hand caressing her and her fingers roaming my privates. I felt the tremor of an orgasm arriving and the table began to shake. She looked at me. For an instant, we were one.

"I told you it was dangerous," she said, back in the cabriolet.

"Yes," I sighed. "It must have been the mask. I'll never put one on again. I will tell you though that while he was caressing me under the table, I wanted it to be your hand between my legs. That never would have occurred to me if I hadn't been wearing the mask," I added, a bit surprised by my own frankness.

"It wasn't the mask," she said. "Deep down, it wasn't the mask. It was the real person that you wear under your everyday mask. I've wanted you too. Come here. Come closer."

"Mesdames!" shouted Pierre from the coachbox. "The other drivers swear that there is to be war with Russia. The stock market fell three francs and the National Guard has been enlisted."

"So much the better," said Fauriel, ill-humored, withdrawing her embrace.

❧

One morning before breakfast we heard a loud knock at the door. It was a sergeant accompanied by a pair of soldiers. Fauriel was to report for duty in the courtyard at the Val de Grâce hospital at two o'clock that afternoon. There she would receive her assistant to the Surgeon General's uniform and the following day she would head for Germany aboard a Guard train.

"At least you're in the Guard," I said, seeing that she was depressed at having been given notice. "I expect they'll call me any day now. Surely I'll serve with you. Luckily my uncle—"

"Leave me alone, Fuenmayor!" she said curtly.

"Aren't you going to have breakfast with me?"

"Leave me alone, please."

After breakfast, I got dressed and went to see her in her room, which was actually Uncle Charles' old room. When I opened the door, I saw that her expression had changed. It was the same Fauriel as ever.

"Fuenmayor, if there's one thing I hate in this world it's good-byes. Go to the Faculty just like any other day. Let's say goodbye right now," she said quickly, taking me by the waist and hugging me tight.

"I wanted to go with you to the Val de Grâce," I protested.

"It's better this way. Believe me."

"You'll need money," I said.

"Whatever you think to give me, leave it on the table. Now go. As I told you, it's easier for me this way."

She hugged me again and pushed me out of the room. Deeply saddened, I put a bag of napoleons on the table and left the house. I wasn't in the mood to go to the Faculty. I wandered aimlessly until I came to a café. I was cold and ordered some wine. Suddenly I felt an urgent need to be with her, even if only for a few minutes. I paid the bill and headed back to the house. I went as quickly as possible, half-running, half-walking. But when I arrived, Françoise told me right away that she had gone, scarcely saying goodbye and carrying a bundle of clothing under her arm. An uncontrollable sob exploded from within me and I threw myself into Françoise's arms.

At dinnertime Pierre called to me, distressed, from the other side of the door.

"What's happening?" I asked him.

"Get dressed, madame! There are some soldiers outside who want to search the house. Françoise is arguing with them."

When I came out of my room, I recognized the sergeant who'd come to the door that morning. He told me that Fauriel had not appeared at the Val de Grâce or at the Faculty, either. He had orders to search the house. "It's in your friend's best interest, *citoyene*. If he doesn't turn up before midnight he'll be declared a deserter."

Overwhelmed, I gestured my consent and returned to my room. The soldier who came in to search my room shot me a recriminating look, as though I were an accomplice to a crime. He looked under the bed and opened the armoire. In frustration, he threw all of my clothes to the floor. "The Emperor is not popular here in the Saint-Honoré *faubourg*," he muttered as he passed by me.

Confused, not knowing what to think, I began to pick up my clothes and to hang them back up. As I was closing the armoire, I had the feeling that something was missing. I looked at the clothes again, my pants, my frockcoats, my vests. My mourning dress wasn't there.

I called Françoise.

"She was wearing it, Henriette. I told her to take it off, that it was important to you. I tried to stop her. I didn't want to tell you today and make you even sadder."

"I understand," I said, knowing I had lost her.

Her name appeared on the list of deserters and she was expelled from the Faculty. I never saw, or heard of her again.

Five days later, I went to war.

NADEZHDA

15

WE SAW THE MOSKVA RIVER directly beneath us as we reached the top of the rise. Just beyond a large, hook-shaped bend, we could make out the golden towers, the fortresses, and rooftops of the Russians' venerable capital. The sun was setting at our backs, bathing the domes of the city's innumerable churches in a russet glow. For a few moments, the city sparkled like an enormous, twinkling, jewel-encrusted, golden crown, captivating us. But when the sun disappeared beyond the road to Smolensk, a blast of cold air blew in and, like a magic spell, Moscow was transformed into an ashen shadow in the dusk.

"A breathtaking spectacle," said Uncle Charles, turning to me.

"Peace, at last," I said, fed up with pursuing an enemy who, defeated over and over again, always found a way to double back upon itself, drawing us ever farther into the interior of that vast country, sinking deeper and deeper into the mud of autumn, forcing us to leave large detachments of troops as a rearguard to watch over cities, towns, villages, bridges, crossroads, provisions depots, ammunition stores, prisoners, hospitals; and, worse yet, detachments of the dead, wounded, sick, stragglers, deserters, bogged-down wagons, broken carriages, lame horses. . . . I was fed up with riding exposed to the sun and the rain, with the abusive stinginess of the *Intendance* that, instead of providing us with ligature, bandages, and medicine, denied us the weapons of our trade. The exhausting march to Königsberg was still fresh in my memory, me in my bicorn hat displaying the colors of Joseph Bonaparte's Regiment, Spanish Volunteers, Almeras' Brigade, Broussier's Division, 4th Corps, Prince Eugène, attempting to combat the tedium by copying down in my notebook the irreverent oaths of our colonel whose foul-mouth went unrivaled among the troops: "I shit on God. I shit on the Virgin. I shit on the whore who gave birth to him." Still fresh as well were the river crossings at the Neiman and the Viliya. Napoleon had fallen from his horse at the former, and, at the latter, two Polish squadrons were dragged under by the current, horses and all, shouting *"Vive l'Empereur!"* before their heads disappeared beneath the water. Still with me was the occupation at Vilna, where the diplomatic retinue, representing twenty nations and adorned with gold braid and medals, had remained, deciding to await the overthrow of Czar Alexander while attending balls, banquets, and salons, while we slogged ahead with empty rucksacks under interminable downpours. I could still see the siege of Vitebsk, where I'd reunited with Uncle Charles and, my transfer arranged, entered into service with the General Staff under the orders of Baron Larrey, and where, for two weeks, I'd visited the hospitals along the Dvina, the sick wracked with fever and diarrhea from influenza and bad water, among them a young girl from Burdeos who'd enlisted as a drummer-boy. Still present for me was the battle of Smolensk, where I saw a single cannonball level a line of twenty-two soldiers, where we'd counted our casualties in the thousands, only to discover a deserted city, reduced to smoking ruins. Still with me was the terrible battle of Valutina-Gora that would claim the life of General Gudin, leaving his decimated troops, shattered men with torn-off limbs and scorched faces, standing in proud formation among disemboweled horses in order to receive Napoleon's crosses and promotions and useless words such as "You have fought for the glory of France like no other army before you." With me still was my return to Smolensk with the ambulances brimming with men pleading and moaning, and the horror of finding the only hospitals still remaining filled with thousands of unattended men lying in their own excrement, crying out to be seen by the few doctors who had remained there. I could still see the formidable battle of Borodino, an endless battle that dragged though hours and hours of savage attacks led by Ney, Murat, Poniatowski, and Prince Eugène, and hear the incessant sound of cannon fire against the strongholds, against the stubborn left flank, against the stubborn right flank, against the stubborn center, that battle in which, through flashes of artillery fire and clouds of smoke, we glimpsed Kutuzov surrounded by patriarchs and orthodox priests, like furious bearded saints, hoisting standards, holding aloft huge icons with images of madonnas, crosses, censers, crosiers covered in gold and silver and gems and dark offerings of old Russia, his troops bleeding piteously but refusing to surrender, defending their territory inch by inch while a lethargic, sallow, irresolute Napoleon dragged his feet back and forth in front of his tent as though mourning the dozens of his generals who'd fallen, dead or wounded, and, not far from him, just ahead of the Imperial Guard regiments, Larrey and my Uncle and me and every other able-bodied surgeon incessantly amputating an arm at the elbow, an arm at the shoulder, a leg at the knee, a leg at the hip, a Cuirassier's foot, a Hussar's hand, cutting and cutting through flesh, sawing and sawing through bone, sewing and sewing up stumps, bandaging and bandaging wounds, seeing the repulsive heaps of human scraps accumulate around us like piles of garbage, and all of that thankless work done without sleep, without food, sticky and encrusted with blood, and at sunrise on the third day, the battlefield deserted, the same story as always, the silent nocturnal retreat that left us victors without victory, without truce, without armistice, without pronouncements, without prisoners, with nothing else to do but count up the more than seventy thousand dead, thirty thousand of them ours, and fill the Kolotskoïe abbey with the wounded so as to begin the cutting and sawing and sewing and bandaging all over again, leaving the most gravely wounded there and loading the rest into whatever ambulances and wagons could be found and then, only then, close our eyes for a few minutes, drink a slug of vodka, and chew a mouthful of stale bread before continuing on. All of this was still with me that evening as the sun set over Moscow, and as I stood there, sick of the war, exhausted, numb, hungry, dirty, no longer moved by the suffering of others, I cursed the day when, passing myself off as a volunteer from Havana, I'd surrendered my body and intellect to Napoleon's ambition, and all for Fauriel, and I shit on her mother and her father and their poverty and the northern mines and the "state students," and all for the Café Procope, and I shit on every one of its tables and chairs and on the "Night of the Napkin," and all for Bousquet, and I shit on his whore of a mother and on his son of a bitch father, and all for having pressed my ear to that accursed wall, and I shit on its bricks and on the miserable mortar that held them together, and all for that damned picture of Apollo, and I shit on Zeus and on Leto and on Mount Olympus too, what the hell, because only a signed peace treaty with Russia and my return to Paris, safe and sound, would persuade me to stop cursing the entire world.

❧

We entered Moscow the following night. It was true what people were saying: save for a few bands of thieves and commoners, almost all of them drunk and boisterous, and a handful of Frenchmen and foreigners who'd remained behind, hidden, the city had been completely abandoned. Riding slowly through the deserted streets, we could see, illuminated by torchlight and perfectly intact, the beautiful wooden houses, humble thatched-roofed huts, businesses and brick storehouses, churches and stone palaces. I was tempted to leave the General Staff retinue in order to kneel before an altar and thank God for the good fortune of having come across that abundance of habitable houses. The thought of spending two or three weeks there, well-bundled and well-fed, as we awaited the peace accord, brought the first smile to cross my lips for many days.

"Thank God, Surgeon Major," I said to my uncle, addressing him as would any other assistant. "The campaign is over."

"Perhaps," he grunted. "It makes me uneasy that the city should have been evacuated. It's the same thing that's been happening all along."

There was room to spare in the deserted city, and Larrey assigned us a solid, two-story stone house near the Kremlin, where Napoleon had ensconced himself. We left our horses in the stable, where we found hay and water in the trough. Then, we broke open the lock with musket-shot and entered the mansion: everything was exactly as though the owners and servants hadn't left, as if upon our arrival they had all become silent, invisible presences in the house. The candlesticks in the lamps and chandeliers had been carefully snuffed before burning themselves out and, when lit, they illuminated an enormous table set with solid silver, Sèvres china and etched Bohemian crystal, complete with a centerpiece of pears and apples, still good enough to eat; in the music room, decorated with cheerful paintings and porcelain figurines, it seemed as though we could still hear the echo of the final chord of the fugue for piano, violin, viola, and flute laid out on the music stand; in the library, lined up on dustless shelves, their white calf-skin spines imprinted in gold lettering, were volumes by Voltaire, Rousseau, and Raynal, Montesquieu's *L'Esprit des Lois*, dramas by Molière, a history of Russia by de Clerc and Levesque, and many other books whose seriousness contrasted with the banal and incomplete shopping list, written in perfect French, left forgotten on the writing desk (taffeta and flannel, leather gloves, wool mittens, nightshirts for the servants); in the six upstairs bedrooms, nearly all belonging to women to judge by the dressing tables and the bedspreads, we found not a single portrait, nor any jewels, nor coins in the coffers—only some paper rubles—though the armoires were full of clothing for all seasons, including woolen vests and magnificent overcoats and fur caps made of sable, mink, and Siberian fox; the wine cellar was so well-stocked that it could have been the Café Procope's—reds from Bordeaux and Burgundy, sparkling wines from the Rhine and the Don, tokay from the Danube, whites from the Costes de Moselle and Costes de Meuse, ports and sherries, and even a tower of champagne crates alongside barrels of beer from Prague and casks of vodka, cognac and rum; the larder, the door to which was flanked by an enormous earthen jug of fresh water, caused us to cry out in amazement, as the shelves and cupboards were filled with bags of sugar, salt and pepper, chili powder, cinnamon, cloves and bay leaves, bars of chocolate, biscuits, tins of tea and coffee, tempting, glossy fruit, cheese and eggs, crocks of butter, mustard and caviar, jars of pickled mushrooms and cucumbers and, up above, hanging among the pots and pans, a large ham, smoked bacon, a wineskin swollen with oil, and several strings of sausages and garlic; near the back wall were five barrels half-filled with white flour, rice, dried beans, noodles and brined fish, not to mention the piles of turnips, potatoes, beets, cabbages and golden onions that rose out of the corners of the room. That entire gastronomical treasure, which seemed straight out of *A Thousand and One Nights*, exuded a warm and appetizing vapor that made my mouth water and immediately brought to mind Aunt Margot's beloved pantry. The only thing that prevented us from pouncing upon the ham or from snatching a pair of sausages or from sinking our hands into the brined fish or from biting off a corner off a bar of chocolate was Larrey's imperious voice ordering that nothing be touched.

"You are intelligent people and, as such, you understand that the condition of our stomachs is hardly good. We shall eat and drink from all of this, but in moderation. Otherwise, we'll fall ill, and you well know what the hospitals are like these days," said Larrey pointedly. "Do any of you know how to cook?"

Antoine Petit, the other assistant, said that he did.

"I do, too," I said, not intending to be separated from the provisions. It was, of course, only half-true, since, although I'd spent a fair part of my childhood helping in the kitchen, the only thing I'd ever actually cooked on the stove was water for tea.

"Prepare a light supper in an hour," he ordered, before going off to take a bath.

"I'll wager a napoleon that you don't know how to cook," said Petit, with his usual bitterness, a defect made even more insufferable by his nasal voice.

"I know some things, but I'm not betting anything. And what do you know?"

"I know how to fry, boil, and roast," he responded smugly.

Limiting myself to working with the knife, we managed to prepare a plate of cold cuts and a thick ham, onion, and potato omelet, which we carried to the table before the appointed hour. Uncle Charles, a great lover of toasts, raised his glass to the peaceful conquest of Moscow, to the Grande Armée, and to our health. The food, though strictly portioned out by Larrey, tasted glorious to us.

"Very well, Fuenmayor. Have you learned anything from this campaign?" Larrey asked me.

"Yes, Surgeon General. In Borodino I learned that it's possible to perform two hundred amputations in fewer than thirty hours," I said to flatter him, although truth be told, his proficiency had amazed me, especially at night when, by the tremulous flicker of candlelight I'd seen him suture arteries with the same dexterity he'd displayed by day.

"It's a matter of practice, Fuenmayor," he said, downplaying his prowess. "I've been practicing for many years. You'll do the same one day, although it would be better for the need never to arise. And you, Petit," he added. "What have you learned?"

"An important lesson, Surgeon General. I have learned that the wounded should be treated according to the severity of their wounds, and not according to their rank."

"Unfortunately, it's not always done in this way," said Larrey.

"It was common practice in the armies of the Republic, isn't that so, Cavent?" My uncle nodded and Petit, not taking into account the enormous gulf between himself and Larrey, a divide that ought to have precluded him from asking questions of a political nature, said: "Surgeon General, when will the Emperor make peace with the Russians?"

Larrey, taken aback, blinked and stiffened in his chair. Furrowing his brow, he looked at Petit in silence. Perhaps feeling compassion for that coarse peasants' son whose studies in Strasbourg had been interrupted, he softened his gaze and replied: "That is something only the Emperor knows. Our job is to save lives. Tomorrow we'll inspect the hospitals. I certainly hope we'll find them in the same condition as this house!"

The conversation was interrupted by a knock at the door.

"Let's all go answer it," said Uncle Charles. "It's likely someone hoping to stay here. If he sees us all together, surely he'll look for a different house."

When we opened the door we were met by an aide-de-camp from the General Staff and several grenadiers from the Imperial Guard. The aide said: "Baron Larrey, I've come to alert you that we've discovered fuses and explosives in several houses. Yesterday there was an explosion at the Exchange and several arsonists have been arrested. I advise you to inspect the stoves and chimneys."

Once they had departed, we discovered a bundle of sulfur and tarred oakum fibers beneath the large stove in the dining room. After inspecting the entire house, Larrey asked if we felt comfortable staying there. We all said yes. Where would we find another house as comfortable as that one? Before he and my uncle went up to their beds, Larrey ordered that we stand guard until six the following morning, with me taking the first shift and Petit the second, and told us to wake him should any urgent matter arise.

After devouring half a bar of chocolate and three biscuits soaked in wine, I decided to stand lookout on the balcony, the only vantage point from which I could observe the goings-on in front of the house. Wearing my greatcoat and armed with a musket, I stepped out into the cold. Almost instantly, a reddish glow and a thunderous explosion forced me back inside. An arsenal must have blown up, because the explosions continued for three or four minutes and I could see the trails of flame coming from several rockets as they arced across the sky. The smell of gunpowder was thick in the air and, almost simultaneously, my uncle and Larrey appeared on the balcony, barefoot and wrapped in sheets. Other, smaller explosions reverberated from distant parts of the city, and suddenly we realized that we were surrounded by fires. In the reddish glare that now illuminated the street, we saw, to our surprise, people shouting and running out of houses we had supposed abandoned. They were Russian families, mostly women, children, and the elderly. They were carrying coffers, bundles, boxes, and valuables; they had been in hiding but were now running hither and thither like frightened barnyard fowl.

"We must get dressed, Cavent!" said Larrey. "We must put ourselves at the Emperor's disposal!"

"Saddle the horses!" my uncle yelled to me, running toward his room.

On the first floor I knocked into Petit who, completely drunk, was coming out of the wine cellar with an oil lamp in his hand, and an idiotic smile on his face.

"What's all the noise about?" he sputtered.

"¡*Vete al carajo*!" I said in furious Spanish. It had been over eighty days since I'd slept in a bed and I'd had my period for over a week. "Don't you realize, you idiot, that the ball is over before it even started?"

❧

When we arrived at the Kremlin, the soldiers guarding the rampart gate refused us entrance, despite having recognized us. "The Emperor is asleep, Baron Larrey," the Captain told us. "We're under orders not to disturb him."

On the way back to the house, the sky now completely red, we witnessed several of our own soldiers in the act of looting. Despite the fact that only elite troops had been admitted into the city—the Imperial Guard and the Italian Royal Guard that served with Prince Eugène—certain officers looked the other way and allowed their men to take whatever they wanted from the palaces. Coming across a squadron of Italians, Larrey, indignant, confronted their commanding lieutenant: "Aren't you ashamed to permit such chaos? What has become of discipline?"

"The city is lost, monsieur. Before fleeing, the Russians destroyed their fire trucks and hoses. If all of Moscow is to burn, we might at least take some small souvenirs with us."

"Some souvenir!" said my uncle, watching a soldier carting off a giant basket full of wine.

"What can you do? These are the spoils of war," said the lieutenant, shrugging his shoulders. Then, turning in his saddle, he indicated two men who stood, their hands tied to a sergeant's horse, watching expressionlessly the scene unfolding around them. "They're arsonists. So you see, we're still doing what we can. We entertain ourselves with trifles here and there, but we always carry out our orders. Here you have them! They'll be interrogated and strung up on a lamppost!" he shouted, surely hoping to frighten them.

"Have you seen any hospitals?" asked Larrey.

"Why yes, just around the corner, five or six hundred meters down the road. But I warn you, there's a fire in that area."

Following the lieutenant's directions, we came to some wood and straw huts, now nothing but fuel for the flames, where we were met with a horrifying sight. Wounded men were hurling themselves out the windows of a large brick building on the other side of the street. They were Russian soldiers who had been abandoned in the sudden evacuation. Among them were five or six men who dragged themselves along with amputated arms or legs, their stumps open and bleeding.

"Let's find a wagon," said Larrey. "We must save those men."

We returned to the Kremlin, again in vain. When we arrived, the guardsman assured us that Napoleon had been awakened and would be leaving any minute to take up residence in a palace on the outskirts of the city. Any wheeled vehicle was already spoken for. "If I were you, Baron Larrey, I'd join the Emperor's entourage. From the looks of it, the city will burn to the ground."

"We will stay. Stone does not burn," said Larrey, darkly.

I was so exhausted that I gladly accepted Larrey's mandate. I simply couldn't go on, and I cared not a whit that Moscow was going up in flames around me. But it was destined that nothing was to turn out well that night. When we arrived at our house we saw that it had been looted and that the wine cellar had been reduced to a huge pool of wine and frothy beer, upon which floated empty bottles and barrel staves, and that the larder floor was now a trampled mat of flour, grains, herring, and macaroni, and that, in the armoires, there were no longer furs, and that in the dining room, not even the cloth remained on the table.

◌

What none of France's enemies had yet achieved, Napoleon accomplished in the five weeks he stayed in Moscow: the disintegration of the Grande Armée's discipline and morale. A great deal has been written about the military disaster of 1812 and I've little to add, except to say that the majority are works intended to correct events by means of conditionals such as: If Napoleon hadn't lost the initiative at Borodino. . . . If Napoleon had withdrawn from Moscow by the middle of September. . . . If Napoleon had set up winter barracks in Moscow. . . . If Napoleon had marched toward Saint Petersburg. . . . If Napoleon hadn't believed himself invincible. . . . If Napoleon hadn't so overextended his supply chains. . . . If Napoleon hadn't waited until October 19th for an offer of peace that never arrived. . . . If Napoleon had retreated by a different route. . . . If Napoleon had launched the Grande Armée first against Wellington and then against Alexander. . . . If Napoleon this and if Napoleon that.

Not one of these speculations interests me, and I'm quite certain that they would be of no interest to the two hundred thirty three thousand soldiers that the Russian peasants found in the fields when the snow melted that spring, nor to the innumerable others who, devoured by wolves and dogs on the steppes, or lost in the forests, or fallen into the icy waters of rivers, or burned in the villages and hospitals, disappeared from this world without a trace.

The campaign of 1812 *was* an irreversible fact and no politician or historian's *if* will ever remedy it. Nor would it serve as an example or lesson so that nothing like it would ever happen again in the future—even the most immediate of futures, since any petty incident was all it took for France and Prussia to try, once again, to settle their rivalry by force of arms. The old refrain: "One can't learn from another's mistakes," one of Aunt Margot's favorite sayings, is most especially applicable to men of war. And so, I'll limit myself to describing my memories of that campaign, and I'll begin by saying that I'd suspected we were beaten even before we'd retreated from Moscow. Why did I suspect it? I could see it in myself, thinking of nothing but finding something to eat that wasn't horsemeat and brown bread, and I could see it in the conduct of the Old Guard Grenadiers, Napoleon's pride and the *crème de la crème* of the Grande Armée's elite units. I'll explain. The Imperial Guard was, for practical purposes, divided into two corps: the Old Guard and the Young Guard. The former was comprised of the 1st, 2nd, and 3rd regiments of Foot Grenadiers, the 1st and 2nd regiments of Foot Chasseurs, the Mounted Grenadiers, the Mounted Chasseurs, the Mamelukes and the 1st and 2nd regiments of Light Cavalry. But most emblematic of the Old Guard were the Foot Grenadiers of the first two regiments, veterans with profuse gray mustaches, hair pulled back in a queue, and gold rings in their ears; men hand-picked from front-line battalions, who had fought in the revolutionary campaigns in the Wars of Liberation, at the Rhine, in Italy, in the Pyrenees, in Egypt. To be selected to join their ranks, a soldier was required to know how to read and write, to have served for more than ten years, and to have received decorations of valor during that time, to be no shorter than 1.84 meters, and to be in possession of a ruddy complexion. Their pay was double that of the other Grenadiers and it was customary to address them as "monsieur." Their most distinguishing feature was a tall bearskin cap adorned with a gold badge embossed with an eagle; on the battlefield they wore wide trousers and blue greatcoats. They were men of few words who joked only among themselves and who carried themselves with a parsimonious deliberateness that contrasted sharply with the Hussars' cheeky vanity and the Cuirassiers' boisterous bravado. Their drums and bugles were the best in the entire Grande Armée and, with a serene and disdainful *porte militar*, as though in formation for an inspection, they marched to their rhythm onto the battlefield, singing *On va leur percer le flanc* in a single, unified voice.

In any event, with Napoleon now in retreat, I saw those venerable lions bivouacking in the muddy squares, beneath the pyramids of their muskets, their shoes torn open and their uniforms in tatters, roasting some bloody piece of horsemeat on their campfires, sitting on mahogany and satin armchairs, sheltered beneath improvised lean-tos cobbled together from doors, Chinese folding screens, windows and wall hangings, surrounded by bottles of wine, samovars, silver candelabras, violins, grandfather clocks, marble statues, fine porcelain, paintings, bolts of silk, and Oriental brocade. I saw them in the markets, their hands black from digging through the city's charred remains, exchanging plunder for gold coins—easier to carry in a rucksack or ammunitions pouch—or buying half a kilo of coffee or sugar or Turkish tobacco at astronomical prices. Napoleon, no longer able to hold the disorder at bay, normalized it, granting one day of pillage to each regiment.

Certain grains were abundant during the first week and, above all, there were the enormous cabbages and beets that grew on the outskirts of the city. The regulation meal, dispensed in the canteens, was beet and cabbage soup, thickened with oats or rye. The horses also had food, as our commissaries forced the peasants to sell them their hay and fresh forage. Many believed, Larrey, Uncle Charles, and myself among them, that Napoleon would spend the winter in Moscow, as at least a fifth of its buildings had been spared from the flames: almost all of the churches and many houses and other structures built of stone or brick, including two of the city's biggest hospitals. But almost from one day to the next, everything became scarce.

As always, work was the one thing I had plenty of. The first order of business was to get all of the wounded and sick that we had brought in the ambulances settled; then, to treat them. Fortunately, in addition to the Imperial Guard surgeons, we had the disinterested assistance of several Russian doctors who'd remained behind in the city. Since our stone house had lost its charms—the armoires, the wine cellar and the larder—we grew accustomed to sleeping at the hospitals, one of which was commanded by Larrey, the other by Uncles Charles. The number of patients, far from diminishing, grew day by day, and we soon had more than five thousand. This was because, despite the evacuation order, a substantial portion of the population had not left their homes. After these were destroyed by the fire, it took no more than a glance out the window to see entire families wandering the streets and not a soul offering to help them. Seeing this sad spectacle, I remembered Maryse's story about the destruction of Cap-Français, especially the part about how the women, and even the girls, had begun to prostitute themselves in exchange for a crust of black bread and a swallow of wine. Although we did admit into the hospital all those who, faint with hunger or fever, had collapsed in the streets, soon enough there was no longer room for all of them. Despite our very best intentions, there was simply nothing we could do. We were military surgeons, after all, and our first responsibility was to attend to the Grande Armée.

Many priests had also stayed behind, perhaps with the intention of protecting their ornate churches. They would fare no better than the rest. Thrown into the streets, their altars looted and their sacred places converted into barracks and stables, they could be seen in slow procession with their icons and crosiers, intoning grave hymns and offering what meager consolation they could muster. I had no doubt that they prayed for us to be punished. Surely they damned us for our greed and for our paltry fear of God, beginning with Napoleon, who had ordered the dismantling of the enormous gold and silver cross that had crowned the Kremlin, right down to the Grenadier who, armed with an iron rod, had seen fit to pry the bas-reliefs depicting the stations of the cross off a church wall.

By this point, there was scarcely any food left in Moscow. Bands of Cossacks prowled the outskirts and, emboldened by their successful attacks on provisions wagons en route from Smolensk, they drew ever nearer to the city, drawing out our Dragoons and Chasseurs, only to turn and ride away on their little horses. What's more, the nearby mills no longer had grain to grind and not a single blade of grass grew for several kilometers all around. Everyone's ire turned toward the *Intendance* Commissaries, who, under the pretext of storing up provisions for the winter, sold the lion's share of what they'd acquired or confiscated at many times its value. Noticing that the nights were growing ever colder, I went to buy an overcoat in the market that had sprung up in the vast square adjoining the Kremlin. With my own gold, I bought an astrakhan coat and matching hat, a pair of otter-skin gloves, felt boots, and a beautiful cashmere shawl that, judging by its odor, must have been previously used to wrap up fish. I also bought a kilo of Chinese tea, a box of dried figs, a tin of caviar, and two bottles of rum. The main customers were no longer the merchants, but rather the highest ranked officers who, paying in francs as I had, bought objects sold at high prices in France—pearl necklaces, pocket watches, diamond brooches—as well as provisions for the winter months. Silver was, by now, worth almost nothing, and I saw a Grenadier sell a sack of forks and spoons for a few scant napoleons. But, while the situation in Moscow grew worse by the hour, the immense majority of the Grande Armée was even worse off; the five infantry and four cavalry corps which, billeted in neighboring villages, or in pursuit of the elusive Russian army, or sent to reconnoiter this or the other route, lived almost exclusively off the land, met with nothing but hunger and ambushes, and would end up finishing off their already exhausted horses.

In the hospital where I worked with Larrey—he had preferred my services to Petit's—things were going from bad to worse. An epidemic of dysentery had been unleashed, and we could scarcely take care of the sick. One afternoon, seeing me pale and exhausted to the point of near collapse, Larrey pulled a folded piece of paper from his pocket and held it out to me. "It's an invitation from the General Staff. A French theater performance. I've decided not to go. It's been four nights since I've written in my diary."

I'd heard that part of a French acting troupe had stayed behind in Moscow, and that its members, living, by now, in the most complete indigence, had been taken in by certain well-accommodated officers. They'd been in Russia since the Treaties of Tilsit, in honor of which Napoleon had sent them to Czar Alexander, as a gesture of friendship. Reading the program, I was pleasantly surprised to see that I was familiar with both works from my time with Alfred: *Le jeu d'amour et du hasard*, an old comedy by Marivaux that had remained popular in many companies' repertoires, and *Amant, auteur et valet*, a one-act play by Ceron. The performance was to take place at six in the evening on the Posniakov palace stage, the only theater that had survived. Thanking Larrey for his kindness, I washed up, put on my new astrakhan coat, and headed for the palace. An enormous chandelier of more than a thousand candles, brought in from some church or another, illuminated the refurbished theater, its luxury contrasting sharply with our filthy uniforms, reeking of smoke, as did everything in Moscow, from the flour used to make bread down to the writing paper used by the *Intendance*. Officials from every service occupied the two rows of box seats, and the finest soloists from the Imperial Guard's marching band were featured in the orchestra. The actors' lavish costumes had been furnished by Count Dumas, the Quartermaster General. The performance was excellent and the evening closed with Madame Louise Fusil performing multiple renditions of *Plaisir d'amour* to endless applause and tears of nostalgia. She was a still-beautiful woman, and her generosity and ease on stage reminded me of Maryse, back in the happy days of the Théâtre Nomade, days I'd let pass me by, never realizing that, amid Andrea and Piet's flirtations, Kosti and the Pinelli Brothers' acts, the roulette table in Baden-Baden, and the romances between Françoise and Claudette, and Maryse and Robledo, I'd left my youth, and the most carefree moments of my life, behind forever.

16

I SAW HER BY THE side of the road. She lay across a dented silver samovar and a rolled-up oriental rug. She had fallen face-up and, as the carriage passed alongside her, I felt the desire to possess her well up within me. We were going so slowly that, handing the reins to Petit, I jumped to the ground and rescued her from that luxurious garbage heap.

"What are you doing?" shouted Petit from the coachbox. "It's too big to take with us. It'll just slow us down," he added, urging the horses forward.

"This is my business. Stop the carriage for a moment," I said, approaching with the painting balanced atop my astrakhan cap.

"The last thing in the world we need is a painting," he growled.

I opened the door, lay her across some bundles of provisions, and returned to the coachbox.

"If its owner threw it away, it's because it isn't worth anything," said Petit, handing me the reins. "They should have left it back in Moscow!"

"Just yesterday you grabbed a box full of obscene novels."

"That's true, but I'm not planning to keep them. After I've read them, I'll throw them away. Not exactly the case with you."

"¡Vete al carajo!"

"If you start speaking Spanish to me again I'll stop speaking to you altogether!"

Lieutenant Belliard's heavy Russian wagon came to a halt half-way up a hill and I had to pull back suddenly on the reins. The Lieu-tenant's skeletal horses had given out. I tried to merge with the line of wagons passing to my left, but they were huge *Intendance* box wagons, each pulled by six horses, so I stayed where I was.

"That cretin! He's stopped again! Doesn't he realize his wagon's too heavy?" whined Petit. "Well, I'm not helping him this time! What kind of idiot travels with a piano?"

Belliard was coming over to us. "I'll have to relieve myself of a few sacks of flour. Would you like them?"

"No, thank you," I said.

"If I were you, I'd relieve myself of the piano," said Petit.

"It's the last thing I'll part with, "said Belliard. "It's for my wife."

"Your horses can't go on," insisted Petit.

"It's because we're going uphill," said Belliard, throwing open one of the bolts that secured the wooden plank across the rear of his wagon. Seeing the look of disgust on Petit's face, he added: "I'm not holding anyone up. All the wagons in this line have stopped."

We had left Moscow on October 19th. Carrying out their orders, the Commissaries had set fire to their famed winter store-houses. Millions of rations of hay and wheat had burned, leaving me with the bitter knowledge that the hunger my horse and I had suffered during the previous week had been pointless. First we marched to the South, toward Kaluga, but the Russians cut us off and attacked near a village with an unpronounceable name. As always, they abandoned the battlefield after killing more than two thousand of our men. Knowing that it would be pointless to pursue them, Napoleon decided to turn north and to make our retreat along the road to Smolensk. Uncle Charles and Larrey marched with his retinue, alongside the Dutch Lancers of the Imperial Guard and the officers of the General Staff. When we'd parted, they'd left us with one of the carriages assigned to the medical corps, an elegant two-horse coupe, to the rear of which Petit and I had hitched our own horses.

"He should have jettisoned the piano," said Petit, watching Belliard carefully place, as though it were a beloved object, the fourth bag of flour by the side of the road.

"I'm tired, Petit. I'm going to sleep a bit. When you get tired, wake me up," I told him. The truth was, I wanted to go inside the coach so I could look at the painting. There was something irresistible about it, something not meant for Petit or for anyone else but me.

Were I to describe the painting, I'd say there was nothing spectacular about it. Certainly, it was a fine piece of work and there could be no doubt that the artist had been a true professional, but it had that domestic yet remote quality that one sees in family portraits, those paintings that hang in palaces and castles alongside those of mild-mannered old women with white coiffures, rigid prelates, and sanguine military men encrusted with medals. In any event, she was a beautiful woman of about my age. She was wearing a red jacket embellished with a bearskin collar. On her head she wore a black shako, similar to the ones the Prussians wore, except with a cockade of the most unlikely colors—orange, green, and purple—certainly of the painter's own invention, affixed by a chain of hammered gold. She was shown in profile, facing to my right, and the distant expression on her face, accentuated by the Byzantine line of her nose, contrasted with the deliberateness of her military attire. Her eyes, intensely green, appeared to be witnessing events yet to come, but they kept these secret from me. The artist had painted her, life-sized, only from the shoulders up, but it was easy to imagine her slender and well-proportioned body. The frame had been finished in red Chinese lacquer—a common Russian predilection—dulling somewhat the red of her jacket and the lavishly colored insignia. In the right-hand corner of the canvas there was a brief inscription written in Cyrillic script, incomprehensible to me.

It was not the first time I'd been attracted to an object, such as the cuckoo clock I'd bought in Munich, a certain hat, or even the cashmere shawl I'd bought in Moscow, despite its distinct odor of herring, to replace the tattered sash I used to flatten my breasts. But this was different; very different. I had the impression that the painting had once belonged to me, if only in dreams; that it was something very dear to my heart that I'd lost without even realizing it and that now had come back to me, making it known that her destiny and mine were in lockstep. But what destiny might await us on that monumental retreat which, ten times longer than Xenophon's *Anabasis*, could well have been called The Retreat of a Hundred Thousand, a retreat that, in its Biblical proportions, had made of Napoleon a new Moses, certainly quite worse for wear in his gray cloak, his Swiss hat sideways over his thick, circumspect face, a meager caricature of the Prophet, who, in place of the Ark, was custodian of Ivan the Great's celebrated cross, along with whatever gold and other treasures he had found in the Kremlin, his nation a vast and disorganized caravan of dirty and ragged souls, on horseback and on foot, in wagons, coaches, carriages, artillery trains, and all manner of carts, large and small, that crawled at a snail's pace along the road to Smolensk?

The carriage stopped and Petit's large crooked nose appeared in the door. "I'm freezing. Come out of there so I can warm up a bit."

I turned the painting face down and said: "Don't you dare touch it, or I swear to God you'll regret it!"

I climbed up to the coachbox and took the reins. It must have been about three in the afternoon but the sky had clouded over and a cold wind was blowing from the north. As if that weren't enough, it began to drizzle and the road, already trodden by countless shoes, hooves, and wheels, soon became impassible. Belliard's wagon came to a stop. I huddled inside my fur. Leaves were falling from the birch trees on both sides of the road, denuding their branches and white trunks, leaving them sad and stripped, like rows of spinal columns cleaved to the earth.

⚭

The sound of a nearby explosion ripped me from a dream in which Maryse and Robledo were offering me tastes of delicious, animal-shaped fruits. The little yellow cow was a *mamey*, the *mamoncillo*, a green kitten. . . .

"What's going on?' I asked, startled. It was already nighttime.

"The powder wagons have been exploding for a while now. I don't know how you could have slept through it," said Petit, at my side. "Look!" he added, pointing to the carriage window, through which a thunderous flash briefly illuminated the steppe. "I've counted more than ten," he grumbled. "They could just as easily have blown them up in the daytime."

"Let's move!" a gendarme shouted, passing us on horseback. "Come on, to your feet, it's after five o'clock! It'll be light soon!"

In keeping with my plan to conserve our provisions, I chewed one voluptuous spoonful of caviar while Petite made short work of a hard-boiled egg. I drank a bit of cold tea, tossed back a shot of rum and, taking advantage of the predawn dark, stepped off the road to relieve myself.

278

"Let's move, let's move!" shouted another gendarme.

I climbed up into the coachbox, allowing Petit a few more hours of sleep. Stretching like a long worm of iron and wood, the convoy began to move with a great creaking, crunching, and neighing, accompanied by the occasional distant howl of wolves on the steppes. The sun rose at our backs and Belliard's covered wagon began to roll forward. What might the woman in the painting's name be? Why had she chosen to be portrayed as a soldier? What did the inscription say? Her name? The painter's? And what if it were some kind of message, a message meant especially for me? But who could translate those words into French? Well, somewhere in the convoy were Madame Fusil and the theater troupe, and those Jewish Muscovites and merchants who, fearing retaliation, had decided to join us, and also the girls who'd taken up with the officers and, of course, the interpreters with the General Staff. As soon as Petit woke up, I'd copy the characters into my notebook and saddle my horse. I'd see what opportunity might present itself.

Belliard's wagon came to a halt at mid-morning. The sky, now covered by dense, grayish clouds, foretold of snow. To entertain myself, I started reading one of the novels Petit kept under the seat. It was about five French prisoners guarded by a sturdy and abundantly fleshed Austrian woman. My reading was interrupted by Belliard, shouting furiously. One of his weakened horses had collapsed and two gendarmes were using their sabers to poke at the remaining horses' haunches. Six other gendarmes and a captain joined them.

"Push the wagon off the road," yelled the captain.

Belliard, without thinking, put his hand on the hilt of his saber.

"Unsheathe that goddamned blade and you're a dead man!" said the captain, aiming his pistol at Belliard's head. "Come on, help push the wagon!"

"You there, stop staring and give us a hand!" said a gendarme, pointing at me with his saber.

"There are two of us," I said, and climbed down from the coachbox. "My friend is inside the carriage," I added, so that Petit would also do his part.

Fifteen minutes later, we were moving again. Belliard had been left behind with his toppled wagon and useless horses, his piano just one more piece of junk in the cemetery of castoffs that lined both sides of the road.

Now we were traveling behind a coupe almost identical to ours. As had been the case with Belliard, the coupe had no extra horses in tow. When the convoy was stopped for the third time, I went to introduce myself to our new neighbor. (I already knew that the carriage behind us, driven by an orderly, carried the belongings of an artillery major with the Young Guard.) It turned out to be the tenor Tarquinio, whom Napoleon had invited to the Kremlin so he could hear some music in Italian. He was traveling alone, surrounded by boxes covered in swathes of gold brocade fabric. But, since he couldn't read Russian, I saddled my horse and headed out cross-country. I was immediately reminded of my ride on Jeudi alongside Lannes' column. But no matter how my memory might have amplified the number of wagons traveling with the 5th Corps, that number paled in comparison with the dense tide of vehicles that, the road too narrow to accommodate them—and they were three, and even four abreast—spilled over onto the plain, scattering into lines as far as the eye could see, mixing with cavalry squadrons and entire regiments whose faded colors could now scarcely be distinguished from the sparse, yellowing grass of the countryside. Resisting the urge to spur my horse into a gallop, I held him at a trot until we reached one of the groups of gendarmes who were in charge of the road. I learned from them that Napoleon had ordered that a great deal of powder and munitions be exploded in order to use the horses to transport artillery.

"The Emperor doesn't want to leave the Russians even a single cannon that he might show off as a trophy," one of the men told me. I also learned that, during the previous night, the Cossacks had attacked several wagons that had fallen behind, taking a fair number of prisoners.

"Always have your pistol at the ready, doctor. Don't allow the Cossacks to capture you."

"You'd be better off blowing your brains out," said another. "The Cossacks would sell you to the peasants. You don't even want to know the horrors they'd inflict upon you before they killed you."

"The Emperor is too kind," commented another gendarme. "Instead of setting fire to the villages with those dogs inside, we're required to drag them out of their huts first. Why treat beasts with such consideration?"

"I'm with the medical service of the Imperial General Staff and

I need to see Barron Larrey," I said, to change that disagreeable topic.

"Ah, Baron Larrey, the one who'd recommend I blow my brains out," he said reverently. "He cured me of a lance wound in Aboukir. He's sure to be traveling with the Emperor's retinue, about two leagues ahead."

I was surprised by the distance that now separated us from Larrey and Uncle Charles. They must have driven on through the night, sleeping in their carriages. Four leagues was too far for my emaciated horse. It was necessary to conserve his strength for the weeks ahead. As they had given him to me without a name, I simply called him Cheval.

"Have you seen the wagon carrying the theater troupe that came to Moscow?" I asked. They looked at one another in silence.

"The woman who sang *Plaisir d'amour?*" asked the eldest among them.

"Yes, Madame Fusil," I replied.

"She's quite near. Perhaps half a league from here," he said, pointing down the road. "She's traveling in a *dormeuse* in the farthest right-hand column."

Thanking him for the information, I set off in the direction the gendarme had indicated.

It was easy to find Madame Fusil, since there were very few *dormeuses*—as the narrow, elongated carriages that allowed one to stretch out on a folding bed were called—in the column. I began by telling her how much I'd enjoyed the performance at the Posniakov Palace. Although she couldn't have been much older than thirty, I asked her if she knew Maryse Polidor.

"Maryse Polidor . . . Polidor," she repeated. "I heard of her when I was a child, but I never heard her sing. Do you know her, monsieur?"

"Well, yes. She's married to an uncle of mine who lives in Havana."

"You're from Havana? Who'd ever have guessed! Your French is excellent."

"Thank you, madame. I had a very good teacher," I said, realizing that it had been some time since I'd bothered to imitate the Spanish accent. "But, speaking of languages, perhaps you might do me a favor. You see, in Moscow I acquired a painting with an inscription in Russian. I've copied it here," I added, taking out my notebook. "Do you speak Russian?"

"A little, monsieur. A barbarous language, to tell you the truth. Nothing like French, although after four years, I have learned some. Let me take a look."

I handed her my notebook through the carriage window.

"Woman . . . ," she said right away. "You see, I can read something at least. And this word could mean several things: dress, garb, suit . . . and this one means . . . battle. Now let's add the prepositions."

"Woman . . . in . . . battle . . . dress," I said.

"Voilà! *Woman in Battle Dress*. That's the title! Is the woman dressed as a soldier?"

I nodded, smiling, for the painting's title filled me with joy. The column came to a halt and I stopped Cheval. The air began to fill with snowflakes, small as fish scales.

"It would never have occurred to me to have my portrait done dressed as a soldier. And it's not that I've never dressed as a man, either. But the theater is the theater. Why don't you come inside, monsieur? It's snowing. There's plenty of room and I'd love to know what moved you to buy that painting. Perhaps you're drawn to fierce women?"

This last Madame Fusil said in a dangerously flirtatious tone and, insisting that I needed to see Baron Larrey, I bid her farewell, promising that I'd take her up on her offer sometime soon.

❧

It's never ceased to amaze me how the snow can render unrecognizable a street or landscape that ought to be familiar. And so I didn't realize that we were crossing the battlefield at Borodino until I saw, half-covered by that vast white cloak, the countless bodies of the men and horses we'd left unburied. So they had fallen by the tens of thousands on the 8th and 9th of September, and so we would find them seven weeks later. The low temperatures had staved off the process of decomposition to such an extent that it was still possible to see individual features on some of the faces, except that the skin had turned brick red, save for the cheeks, which were now blue. Many of them had been half-eaten by wolves and dogs before freezing, and crows could yet be seen trying to peck some scrap of cold-hardened bloody flesh. Despite my training at the Practical School, the spectacle nauseated me. I was able to avoid retching, but the tenor Tarquino wasn't as lucky. Coming to the bridge, I saw Genlis, one of the assistants who'd worked with us during the battle. He was opening and closing his arms, trying to stay warm. I assumed he was there waiting for me and Petit, and I called out his name. Recognizing us, he spurred his horse in our direction.

"The baron needs you at Kolotskoïe. When you reach the fork, take the road toward the abbey. I've been waiting for you a long time in this cold," he complained.

I guessed that Larrey and my uncle had gone to the abbey to arrange for the evacuation of the twenty thousand wounded we'd left behind with the monks.

"And our wounded?" I asked.

"A terrible thing," said Genlis, grimacing as he moved away.

When we arrived at the great compound of walls and towers that formed the abbey, we found a train of ambulances in the yard. Almost all the wagons were overflowing with cadaverous men, and my uncle was personally instructing the orderlies into which wagon to deposit each man.

"Where have you been?" he asked when he saw us. "You should travel closer to the General Staff," he scolded. "A terrible tragedy has occurred here. The monks left a month ago, abandoning our men to their fate. Go to the stable and tell the orderlies which of those wretched men are still alive! One out of every three they bring out is dead," he said, indicating two long lines of motionless bodies behind the wagons. "Hurry, it will be getting dark any minute."

The stable looked like a rotting garbage heap. The stench was unbearable. The living and the dead shared the same roof, the same straw, blackened with blood and diarrhea. Larrey had secured Napoleon's permission to enlist two companies of the Württemberg light infantry to assist in transporting the survivors. The soldiers, irritated by the extra effort being required of them, carried out their work without showing the least modicum of compassion. Petit and I, at opposite ends of the stable, indicated not only which men were still alive, but also those who had any hope of recovering. Even so, the ambulances were soon completely full. Just when it seemed we would have to leave more than a thousand unlucky souls behind,

Larrey arrived, leading a train of wagons, carriages, and supply carts. By Napoleon's order, they had been diverted from the main road so as to transport at least one or two of the wounded per vehicle. Seeing that a chance at survival had arrived, those unfortunate men began to joke and sing. Buoyed by their mirth, some on stretchers and others supporting themselves on a comrade's shoulder, they made their way toward the men they took for friends. Days later, we found out that almost all of them, over the nights that followed, had been tossed into the road and crushed under wagon wheels. Napoleon, enraged, ordered several of those responsible shot.

The next horror awaited us a bit further down the road, as we entered the village of Ghjat. We found several hundred dead in the middle of the road. They were Russian prisoners. The Portuguese who'd been escorting them had forced them to lie down in the snow and had dispatched each of them with a bullet to the head. The crows that had been following us began immediately to peck at their remains. "This is a bad sign, Larrey," said my uncle.

"Yes, and this is only the beginning," sighed Larrey somberly, recording something in his notebook. Then, turning to Petit and me, he said the same thing Uncle Charles had told us: "Don't let anyone get ahead of you on the road. March directly behind us, as though you were our aides-de-camp. Petit, give this message to Gourgaud, the Emperor's chief orderly! We must bring this to his attention. If discipline continues to deteriorate, we'll never even make it to Smolensk. The true test of a soldier lies not in conquering his fear before a battle, but rather in resisting the demoralization of retreat."

I remembered the morning I went to the hospital in Passau, where Robert was convalescing. When I'd asked him how he'd been wounded, he said: "The Prussians were retreating and we were ordered to go after them with our sabers. It was a bloodbath. They had flung down their muskets and their rucksacks and were running ahead of our horses. I must have left ten or twelve of them lying in the dirt, but when I turned Patriote to finish off an officer who'd fallen to his knees, the rascal took advantage of the fact that I had my saber raised and he slashed my right thigh. It was a moment of carelessness. I'd taken it for granted that he'd lost the will to fight. Out of every hundred men in retreat, only two or three return blows. The others allow their throats to be slit like geese."

This was what worried Larrey.

It was already well into the night when Petit returned from his assignment. He said he was frozen near to death and, while he drank one of his bottles of wine, he told me that he'd seen Napoleon, wrapped in animal skins, mounted on his gray horse. "The first thing he asked me was if his orders with regard to the transport of the wounded had been carried out, and then he asked if it were true that a company from Baden had killed the Russian prisoners. I told him that the culprits were not from Baden, but from Portugal. He said: 'Well, then that was a different incident,' then dismissed me."

We'd just tied Petit's horse to the coupe when we were surprised by a series of explosions. To our right, the wooden houses of Ghjat began to burn, the flames cutting off our passage. We veered off the road, hoping to find a place to ford the river so we could rejoin Larrey and my uncle, but our wheels got bogged down in the mud.

"We'll have to wait for daylight," said Petit.

For once, I agreed with him.

We awoke at mid-morning. The horses were calmly grazing the still frost-covered grass. We cut a good deal of chaff with our sabers and allowed them to eat their fill. Taking advantage of our proximity to a small stream, we watered them from a bucket and filled all of our water vessels. Then we made a fire with the wood we'd stockpiled, comprised mainly of broken pieces of furniture, and we heated tea and oatmeal. Finally, with the help of our extra horses, we freed the coupe and entered what remained of the village of Ghjat. We could see a large number of charred bodies among the ashes and cinders. Still in the village, we heard sustained cannon-fire from the direction of the abbey and we guessed that the Cossacks were attacking the rearguard, in which Field Marshall Davout's battalion was conveying thousands of vehicles—ambulances, convoys of ammunition and provisions, artillery trains, and wagons filled with women and Russian refugees. The sound of the battle lasted for some time. I thought that, were I a Cossack, I'd limit myself to attacking those convoys, whose wagons were too numerous to be well defended. Apparently, Petit was thinking the same: "Let's get moving. I don't want to become part of the rearguard."

❧

The road was now overflowing with stragglers. Almost all were sick or limping because of a frostbitten foot or a poorly healed wound. It was rarely possible to determine to which regiment they belonged, since they had layered other clothes over their uniforms, sometimes even women's clothes, or they had wrapped themselves in wool blankets or brocaded cloths that covered them from head to toe. The most prudent among them had acquired overcoats and fur caps back in Moscow. Almost all of them walked without muskets, some carried a chunk of horsemeat, the only food they could find, under their arms or slung over their shoulders—every so often a horse head and a smattering of tripe and bones would appear along the road. There were also men sitting or lying down. Seeing us pass, they would raise their hand, begging us to take them along; the majority of them appeared to be suffering from the stupor brought on by extreme fatigue. Since it was only possible to fit one other person in the coupe, and even this was difficult, we had agreed that we'd only pick up someone we knew or who inspired our trust. We picked up a recruit who still had his musket. I had been moved by his smooth, hairless face, and by his youth. He was so weak that when we lay him down across our luggage, he let out a sigh and fainted. Near sunset, a band of Germans descended upon us, intent on stealing our horses and carriage. One of them managed to grab Cheval's tail, but the horse kicked him with both hooves and I saw him fall, twisting in pain, while his cohorts cursed us in German. After this incident, we decided not to stop again until we found one of our battalions. We had no idea in which order they were marching. We knew only, from the occasional explosion of an ammunitions wagon, that they were not bivouacked far from where we were.

Sometime after three in the morning, we came across some artillery carts. When we stopped the coupe, we saw that the recruit had died and we left him by the side of the road. We spoke to the men standing guard, a corporal and a soldier, and I made tea for everyone over their fire. They belonged to the 3rd Corps, under the command of Field Marshall Ney. They had crossed the Niemen with forty thousand men, and now scarcely numbered eight thousand.

"We left four garrison battalions in Kovno, three in Vilna, and we lost the rest at Borodino and in the battles along the road," lamented the corporal, a fierce-faced veteran named Grenelle. "Your ambulances must be overflowing with our men."

"We aren't traveling with the ambulances," said Petit. "We're with the General Staff."

"With Baron Larrey," I added, knowing that his name was well known throughout the Grande Armée.

"I've heard of him," muttered Grenelle.

"The Emperor is far ahead of us," said the soldier.

"We'd be farther ahead as well were it not for Davout," protested Grenelle, with a gesture of irritation. "His men march with lead feet."

"They are being attacked by the Cossacks," I said, by way of excusing them.

"So are we. When a horse dies, we blow up the wagon so that they can't take advantage of it."

"If your carriage is captured, you'd be better off shooting yourselves," advised the soldier.

"We've got our pistols at the ready," replied Petit.

"So much the better. If you're taken prisoner, they'll strip your clothes and turn you over to the peasants."

"The word for peasant in Russian is *moujik*," said Petit with his customary pedantry.

"Whatever you want to call them, they'll put out your eyes and cut off your tongues and your hands. And then they'll leave you in the fields, at the mercy of the wolves and dogs," the soldier assured us.

"We will not allow ourselves to be taken alive," I said. "Do you know which troops are up ahead?"

"The Old Guard."

"A true disgrace," lamented Grenelle. "A plague of rats who eat and drink everything they find, without a thought to those marching at their backs."

When we entered Viazma at dawn, I saw that the old artilleryman had been right. Despite the fact that they already had food enough for five days, the Guard had sacked the storehouses of provisions being saved for the wounded, disobeying Napoleon's orders.

The village had also been burned and, while we were talking with a light cavalry officer, a powerful artillery blast exploded from the rearguard.

"The Cossacks!" shouted Petit, frightened.

"If only it were!" said the officer. "That's forty or fifty cannons.

It's the Russian army attacking Davout. Soon enough they'll be attacking us, since we've been given orders to support Davout. They've chosen a fine moment, too; my horse is on its last legs," he added with disgust, before turning the emaciated animal around.

We fled Viazma in a frenzy of whips and spurs. The stragglers also picked up their pace, leaving anything they'd been carrying behind. Suddenly, in the distance, we saw a cavalry formation heading toward us. Terrified, thinking they were Russians, we got off the road. Since the terrain was covered in brambles, we abandoned the coupe and climbed up a ravine, dragging our beleaguered horses by the bridles. From the highest rock outcropping we could see the battle that Ney, on the outskirts of Viazma, and Davout, further to the East, were waging. Turning my head in the opposite direction, I saw that the cavalry troop advancing along the road was the Italian Guard of the 4th Corps, easily recognizable by their white uniforms. From the looks of it, they were coming to prevent the rearguard from being cut off. Other cavalry troops could be seen in the distance. Presently, Ney's cannons began firing at the Russian artillerymen from a small wooded area. Nevertheless, the latter continued bombarding Davout's wagons. From our perch, it was possible to see the entire battle unfolding, almost as though it were a game or a field exercise devoid of cruelty and blood. I would happily have stayed right there but Petit, quite rightly, insisted that we return to the coupe. Except when we climbed back down, it wasn't there. The stragglers had appropriated it, taking everything we owned—or almost everything: they'd left our muskets, cartridges, and firewood, the indecent novels, and my painting. Petit, disconsolate at the loss of our food and clothes, began blaming me.

"It was you who said the Russians were coming!" he reproached me for the third time.

"And you who said we should run!" I said, furious and, not looking at him, I cut the canvas from the frame, folded it in quarters, and put in under my coat. Then I mounted Cheval and set off without a word.

❧

I learned an important lesson from Aunt Margot when I was a little girl. "What did Abbè Lachouque teach you today?" she'd asked me at dinnertime once, perhaps hoping to show me off to her guests. I responded, quite proudly, that I'd learned all about the solstices and equinoxes, knowledge that I aptly demonstrated with the aid of an apple and a grape I'd found on the table. The next day dawned cold and, while we had breakfast, she asked me what season it was. I said it was autumn, since the date of the winter solstice had yet to arrive.

"But it's as cold as if it were winter, isn't it?" she'd asked. I replied that yes, it was cold. "Do you know why?" she pressed. I tried in vain to come up with some geographical explanation.

"I don't know, Aunt Margot," I said.

"Well, neither do I, but it does seem that, this year, winter has arrived before your solstice."

That day I learned that the seasons, marked by the equinoxes and solstices, expand and contract in accordance with the mysteries of nature.

I suspect that Aunt Margot's intentions went beyond planetary considerations. But here I'll take them literally: the winter of 1812, at least along the road to Smolensk, did not arrive on the last week of December, but rather at the beginning of November, and it did so amid great windstorms, fog, and ton upon ton of merciless snow.

It took only a few days for the Grande Armée to lose a third of its already much diminished numbers. It's easier to understand this if one takes into account that it was an army exhausted by hundreds of kilometers of marching—thousands, in the case of the Portuguese, Spanish, Italians, and French from the South—an army that was retreating along the same route it had come two months before, burning towns and villages, killing the livestock and robbing the peasants of anything of value; a famished army, insufficiently dressed, forced to bivouac in the open air, continually harassed by the enemy, almost without ammunition or horses and, above all, on the verge of total demoralization.

What do I remember of that terrible march through the snow, wind, and ice? I was surprised that the road disappeared into the white of the steppe, that the wine froze in the bottles, that iron seemed to burn on contact with our hands. Many wagons and cannons were abandoned over those first few days. Those who were poorly shod—particularly among the light infantry—watched as their feet went purple, then blue, then turned from the color of tobacco to coal-black. It was not infrequent for a man to sit down to rest and, a few minutes later, to hear him cry out in fear because he couldn't get up again. Others, possessed by a strange euphoria, began to laugh and to jump about like clowns before falling down lifeless a few steps later. Many died silently; they fell and got up again until the moment came when they refused to go on. It's true that the pines provided firewood, but it was green wood; when its resin was burned, instead of flames, it emitted huge clouds of smoke that caused coughing and streaming eyes. In any event, the cold was so intense that even the dry wood from the wagons and the huts was of little use. It was common to find dead men clustered around the remains of a fire, their shoes charred and their heads and torsos frozen. The horses died just as easily, although perhaps not so much from the cold as from thirst, since the surfaces of all the creeks, ponds and wells were frozen and picks and hatchets were scarce. Further, it was necessary to melt a great deal of snow to yield a bucket of water. And, in any case, where were the buckets? No one had thought that they were irreplaceable objects, and most had been smashed to use for firewood or had simply been left behind with the wagons, along with everything else that was considered useless. A similar thing happened with the cooking pots, tossed along the road, together with the muskets and tools, because they were too heavy to carry. No one carrying a pot ever had to worry about eating. All he needed to do was to carry it on his back, in plain sight, and he'd receive dozens of invitations. A few still had the odd bottle of rum or cognac, or a bit of sugar, tea, or coffee, some flour or rice. But in order to enjoy these provisions one had to leave the road, go to a nearby forest, and make one's own fire to eat in private. The only food at hand—and this not always—was horsemeat, and a piece of liver, or a repulsive-looking pudding made from boiling horse blood with a bit of flour, became truly gourmet meals. And so, when reveille sounded each morning, the first order of business was to slaughter the horses that had fallen during the night, even those that were not yet quite dead. When one died on the road, the nearest men would set upon it immediately; voracious as crows, they would disembowel it in the blink of an eye, looking for the precious liver, while others butchered the haunches, torso, and legs.

How did I survive those first few weeks of November? Purely by chance. After riding for two days, passing alongside scene after macabre scene, I came to the bivouac of a regiment of Polish lancers from the rearguard of the 5th Corps, Poniatowski. Dying of hunger and exhaustion, I asked to see an officer. Luckily, one of the lancers spoke some French. Faced with his sullen expression and his reluctance to offer me any help, I made up a fantastical story: "I'm carrying a message from the General Staff for Count Lubomirski," I said firmly. I was certain that Alfred was in Spain, but I thought that perhaps his name would be familiar to someone in the regiment and that it might serve as an *entré*.

The lancer, without saying a word, walked off toward a wagon at the side of the road. A short while later, he returned with an officer who adjusted his *czapka* as he approached.

"Josef Ostrowski," he introduced himself.

"Surgeon Major Cavent, from the General Staff, invites Count Lubomirski to dinner tomorrow evening," I said with the same naturalness as though we were in Paris. "I had a note from Baron Cavent with me, but I was attacked by some stragglers and I lost everything."

"But Count Lubomirski is not with us," said the Pole, in good French.

"Baron Cavent had understood that he was."

"You've come from Headquarters looking for Count Lubomirski?" asked the Pole, finding it difficult to believe that anyone would have ridden an entire day to deliver a message of such little importance.

"That's correct," I said, with as much confidence as I could muster. "The Count is an old friend of the Baron's, and mine as well. We cured him of a wound to his right shoulder when he was stationed in Paris. Tomorrow is the Baron's birthday and—"

"But Count Lubomirski is with one of the Vistula regiments, assigned to the Imperial Guard, quite close to headquarters," said the lieutenant, cutting me off.

"What?" I said, genuinely surprised.

"Well, yes," smiled the lieutenant. "He's right under the Baron's nose, if you'll pardon the expression."

"I'm speaking of Count Alfred Lubomirski, Legion of the Vistula, General Staff to Field Marshall Ney, Cross of Honor, wounded at Zaragoza," I said, incredulously, thinking that perhaps the lieutenant was referring to a different Lubomirski.

"Yes, the very same. I see that you know him well. I do not have the honor of calling myself his friend, but there's not a single officer in the Polish cavalry who doesn't know his name. He is one of our heroes. He could be in his castle or traveling the world and instead, well, you know. . . . He's sacrificed his life to our cause since he was a boy."

"If only I'd known!" I said, thinking how close I'd been to him, of the opportunities I'd had to run into him in Moscow.

"Yes, it's a pity you didn't know. It would have spared you the exhaustion of all that riding. But, please, let's go to my wagon. I have some good furs and something left to toast to Count Lubomirski's health. Tomorrow I'll introduce you to the colonel."

The time I spent with the Polish lancers was quite pleasant, under the circumstances. Accustomed as they were to the cold, I learned from them how to sleep in short intervals with the goal of moving all of the body's bones and muscles every two or three hours, especially the legs, arms, and feet. They also taught me to sleep barefoot, with my feet, after a vigorous rub, wrapped in rags, while the frozen mud melted from my boots by the fire. Given Ostrowski's generosity in sharing his wagon and its amenities, I availed myself of the opportunity to wash with hot water. Presented with the gift of clean clothes brought from Moscow, I removed the cashmere shawl and allowed my bruised nipples to breath, their raised forms now hidden by the thick winter uniform that had once belonged to a Russian footman. No one took better care of their horses than those lancers. They wrapped them up at night as though they were children, and they fed and watered them as best they possibly could. Before reveille had sounded in the other corps, they had already sent a squad armed with pickaxes to the nearest stream to break through the surface layer of ice. There, men and beast would drink before setting off on the day's march. Because their well-cared for horses could travel farther than any others in the Grande Armée, the parties they sent ahead in search of food and forage visited villages far afield from the road, villages that had never been sacked, and they were able to make themselves understood by the villagers because of the similarities between Polish and Russian. Cheval, the object of all of those attentions, appeared completely rejuvenated within a matter of days.

At last we arrived in Smolensk. I say at last because the rumor running through the entire army was that we would set up winter barracks in Smolensk, the third largest city in Russia. There, receiving provisions from Poland, Prussia, and Germany, we would recover our strength and, with proper reinforcements and supplies, we would march to Saint Petersburg in the spring to put an end to the campaign. There is no question that this was, in fact, Napoleon's plan, but in order to carry it out it was necessary to hold Vitebsk, a city to the west of Smolensk. In order to guarantee possession, Prince Eugène's corps had received orders to leave the main road and march to Vitebsk, where it would unite with the troops garrisoned there. And so, for both the Poles and for me, when we saw the city walls of Smolensk and the tall tower of its cathedral through the mist, it was as though we were seeing the gates of heaven. Further, in my case, it was there I'd surely find not only Uncle Charles and Larrey, but also Alfred, to whom I hoped to give the surprise of his life.

17

WE ENTERED SMOLENSK AFTER BIVOUACKING against the rampart. Napoleon and the Royal Guard were already there, and this time the city looked like a replica of Moscow, but on a smaller scale. Like Moscow, it had it been burned and evacuated by the Russians before being sacked by our own troops, and was now swarming with vendors and buyers conducting their business in improvised markets. Since it had been chosen as a hub for communications between Moscow and Vilna, I knew that it would be heavily fortified, with convalescent hospitals, and large stores of ammunition and provisions. Although it was now much more crowded, its appearance was every bit as lamentable as a few months before. Its colors were the black of charred ruins, the gray of stone walls, and the white of snow that blanketed its streets and rooftops.

It all happened very quickly. I was on my way to the General Staff Headquarters when a mob of foot soldiers wielding battle axes and fixed bayonets streamed into a side street and began assaulting a provisions depot with such violence and clamor it was as through they were attacking an enemy position. Cheval spooked, I tried to bring him under control, he reared up, slipped on the ice and that's where my memory goes blank. I came to in a hospital ward, lying on a straw-stuffed pallet situated between a wall and a Russian with compresses over his eyes. My astrakhan coat had disappeared and I was covered by a green cloth which, once upon a time, had lined a billiard table. My head hurt horribly and I could barely move my left arm. I was also cold and nauseated, but above all I could feel a growing panic rising within me: had the doctor who had attended to me discovered my secret?

Uneasy, I nevertheless drifted back to sleep, awaking in the middle of the night with a terrible need to urinate. I raised myself up on my good elbow and lifted my head, which still hurt terribly. I noted that it was bandaged and I could feel a large swollen place above my ear. The ward was poorly lit, but I could make out various women attending to the patients. I called out several times and one of them hurried over to me, almost at a run. She helped me to stand and took me to the latrine. Walking brought on such dizziness that, without her help, I would never have managed even a single step. She asked me my name and to which regiment I belonged. I didn't answer. At that moment I could remember only that my name was Henriette Faber-Cavent and that I shouldn't say so. She continued talking without pause, speaking in a classical, old-fashioned French. She wore a faded ball gown, very outdated, with a chestnut-colored velvet bodice, and over that, nothing to keep her warm but a silk shawl wrapped about her head and neck. Her name was Nadezhda and she told me that my arm was not broken; the worst of my injuries was the contusion on my head, although I was fortunate that the skin had not been broken. I guessed that my hat had cushioned the blow, and I asked after my coat and horse. She claimed to know nothing. They had brought me in along with two others who'd been wounded and, like them, all I had been wearing were the clothes currently on my back.

"Did they, by any chance, leave a painting, a portrait of a woman wearing a shako?"

"I'm sorry," she said. "Those who brought you here left nothing."

I remembered that my fictitious name was Enrique Fuenmayor, from Havana.

"My name is Enrique Fuenmayor, from Havana, on the island of Cuba. I'm with the General Staff. I'm an assistant to Baron Larrey."

"We shall sort everything out tomorrow. I'll see to making the proper inquiries," she said, smiling tenderly, then gave me a sip of water and a spoonful of cognac.

⅋

I awoke before dawn. The Russian was also awake. He was humming the same song over and over again. He didn't seem to feel the cold. He was a sergeant with an Uhlan regiment. My head and arm still hurt and, although I wasn't hungry, I felt a dull ache in my stomach. Trusting that the day would bring good news, I sank lazily into a torpor, quite placid, despite the delirious cries of someone in the center of the ward who carried on a conversation, almost at a shout, with his wife and children.

I saw him come in with Nadezhda, navigating the rows of pallets, and I thought I might weep with happiness.

"Henriette . . . dear girl! Thank God you're alive!" he exclaimed. Abruptly, he dropped a large bundle to the floor, held out his arms in his customary gesture of resignation, and squatted down next to me. He was wearing an enormous bearskin coat and a hat with earflaps. He looked well.

"Oh, Uncle!" I whispered and, unable to control myself, I began to cry.

"I've found you at last, my child! Oh, thank goodness!" he said, clearly moved.

"Here I am," I said, trying to smile through the tears. "I fell off my horse."

"I've already spoken with the doctor who attended to you. It could have been worse," he said, beginning to remove my bandages. "A contusion. Are you nauseated? How is your vision?"

"It's not serious. I was able to get up last night. My arm hurts too."

"I'll bleed you a bit. Then we'll have a look at your arm. I'll be right back."

With Nadezhda's assistance, he let blood from a vein in my wounded arm. Afterwards, he gave me wine from his canteen and we talked awhile, catching up. Petit was alive. He had managed to join with the General Staff and was now traveling with Larrey, transferring wounded Guardsmen to hospitals. Doubtlessly, we would soon see them arrive here. The campaign was going from bad to worse. Vitebsk had been lost and it was no longer possible to stay in Smolensk.

"We are only waiting for Prince Eugène to return before we begin our retreat," he explained. He was surprised to learn that Alfred was with the Vistula Legion and he asked me if I wanted to see him. I said no. I preferred to go see him myself, once I had recovered. I begged him not to send for him. I didn't want him to see me like that.

"When will I be better? Tomorrow, the day after?" I asked.

"You don't appear to have broken anything, but the blow to your head was powerful. We shall see, child. We shall see. You should stay warm. I've brought you my cloak and a wool blanket," he said, indicating the bundle he'd brought with him.

"One more thing, Uncle," I said, feigning nonchalance. "Has my secret been discovered?"

"That's not important now. The important thing is that you recover."

"Tell me, Uncle. Please."

"The doctor said nothing to me about it. As you know, it's not that unusual to see women dressed as soldiers. If a problem arises, I'll speak with him. The woman who came to find me, the one who helped with the bloodletting . . . she knows. But I'll pay her to stay quiet."

"What will become of me?" I said, dejected, ignoring his words. "They'll throw me out of the army. I won't be able to finish my studies. This is a disaster!" I wailed.

"I already told you," he insisted. "Everything will be all right. I'll have Larrey put me in charge of this hospital. You must calm down. The most important thing is that you recover quickly," he added. Then he folded the green cloth several times, placed it under my head, and covered me with the blanket and cloak.

But after he had gone I couldn't stop thinking of the consequences my unmasking could bring. If only the Uhlan would stop humming that same song!

Nadezhda came at noon with a cup of horse broth and a small piece of sweet bread.

"This is all you should eat for now. Doctor Cavent gave me wine, caviar, and peach compote for you. . . . Perhaps tomorrow."

"Tomorrow I'll be leaving here," I muttered, scarcely looking at her.

"Very well. We shall celebrate the occasion," she said in a low, soft voice, a voice that Enrique Fuenmayor would have liked to have. "The doctor will be by to see you in a little while, Henriette," she added, raising her eyebrows in a signal that it was useless to go on pretending. "Doctor Muret."

"I suppose he knows everything."

"Doctor Cavent has already spoken with him. You have nothing to fear from him."

"And from you?"

"Of course not. Consider me your friend, an old friend. I know what difficulties you've had to overcome. . . . But here comes Doctor Muret."

Suddenly, upon seeing her face from a different angle, I recognized the woman from my painting. The same Byzantine nose, though the green of her eyes was not quite as intense and maybe the corner of her lip. . . .

"Enrique Fuenmayor. Am I correct?" said the surgeon, stopping at the foot of my pallet. "How do you feel?"

"I feel fine," I said, grateful for his tact. "Although my head still hurts . . . and my arm."

"I have some tobacco. It helps with the pain."

"No, thank you."

"Cognac?"

"Cognac is fine. But I'd sell my soul to the devil for a bit of laudanum."

"So would I," he smiled. His outfit made him look like a buffoon in a theater company: Russian boots made of black felt, a Dutch lancer's red *culottes*, a sheepskin jacket and a white cape like the ones worn by our cuirassiers, except with an insignia from a corps I didn't recognize. He laid his hand across my forehead and said, "You don't have a fever. Eat sparingly and stay bundled up. The arm is nothing. Tonight I'll bleed it and massage it with arnica."

"When do you think—"

"Three or four days if all goes well," he said, abruptly concluding his exam, crouching now over the Uhlan.

"Ask him if he remembers his name yet," he said to Nadezhda, who immediately began speaking in Russian.

The man shook his head no. Then he said a few words.

"He has remembered another song."

The Uhlan began humming the same tune I had been hearing for hours on end. A sad and monotonous melody, in a minor key.

"It's a lullaby," said Nadezhda, surprised. "A Siberian song that I know well," and she began to sing it quietly in her beautiful voice.

"Well, something's better than nothing. That's six songs, counting this one. I'd appreciate it if you'd translate the words and record them in my notebook. Perhaps they'll provide us with a clue," said Doctor Muret. "Now, bring me some fresh compresses."

299

While Nadezhda went to carry out the order, the doctor delicately uncovered the man's eyes. I expected to see empty eye-sockets or a scar from burns or shrapnel, but no, his grayish-brown eyes appeared healthy. When he turned his head toward me, I saw his pupils slide across mine and fix upon the wall beside me. His Asiatic face became animated and he whispered something.

"What is he saying?" Muret asked Nadezhda, who had just returned.

"More or less the same as always."

"Tell me exactly."

Nadezhda looked at me and raised her eyebrows, warning me of something.

"He says he has just greeted a French Hussar, a handsome young man, and a tall, plump woman with gray hair. It's the first time he's seen them and he assumes that they are new on the ward."

I was startled.

"Are these people you know?" Muret asked me, anxiously. "Answer me, please!"

"Two loved ones I've lost forever," I said, trembling. Muret returned his gaze to the wall and shrugged his shoulders. Then he poured a musk-scented oil onto the new compresses and placed them over the Uhlan's eyes. He stood up and said to me: "A fascinating case. I am keeping this man under my protection. He complains of pain in his eyes. He says it's from seeing. . . . In any case, do not be afraid. He won't bother you. Try to sleep," he advised me, and continued making his rounds with Nadezhda.

გ

After the bloodletting and the warm prickle of the arnica, already deep into the night, I felt a body at my side. I turned. It was Nadezhda. I was happy to have her near me, lying next to me; I couldn't sleep and now at least I'd have someone to talk to.

"I need to rest for a while," she said. "I feel a bit weak at night."

I propped myself up on one elbow. "It doesn't surprise me. It must be late, although I've slept so much that I'm not tired." The clairvoyant Uhlan had stopped humming. No one was ranting, snoring, or coughing, and an icy silence floated around us.

"Do you feel any better? " she asked me.

"I think so."

"You loved the Hussar, didn't you?"

"Very much. He was my husband. How is it possible for this man to know?"

"There is nothing physically wrong with him, but his vision reaches into the world of the dead. He doesn't know who he is. He has no memories. Only songs. He was already here in the hospital when Doctor Muret and I arrived. He complains of pain in his eyes. He says it's from seeing the dead. It's not so rare a case as you might think. I have met people with similar gifts. Usually it's poor people, monks and peasants. Although sometimes. . . . These things have always happened in Russia. They will go on happening."

"What are you doing here, among the French?"

"I learned French as a child. Almost my entire family died in Smolensk. I wanted to come see them before they died. The youngest died at the other end of this ward. I have remained here because I am waiting for something. Something is coming. Something that will arrive accompanied by wind and light. It will arrive after you have already left. You would understand me better had you been born in my country. . . . I've always wanted to go to Paris. Hopefully I'll go one day yet. Have you been to Paris?"

I nodded. I was cold. I couldn't understand how the Uhlan could sleep uncovered. I touched Nadezhda's cheek. It was frozen.

"Aren't you cold?"

"Why did you look at me so strangely, you know, this morning? Do I remind you of someone?"

"You look like the woman in my painting. It's of a woman wearing an officer's shako. But I've lost it. Someone stole it from me. That painting meant a great deal to me. I liked the title the painter had given it."

"*Woman in Battle Dress*," she whispered.

I felt a chill run down my spine. I felt my arm hairs stand on end. I looked away from her and lay my head back against the pallet. It occurred to me that I was dreaming, that Nadezhda didn't really exist, and that the Uhlan who had seen Robert and Aunt Margot was part of the dream as well.

"I have frightened you," she said, brushing my forehead with an icy finger. "Do not be afraid. If I am here beside you it is because it is meant to be this way."

"Are you the woman in my painting?"

"I am Nadezhda Ivánova. I come from far away. I have nothing to do with the woman in your painting," she said, in a teasing tone. "They are selling your painting in the square, right here, in front of the hospital."

"Is that true?" I said, sitting up again.

"I'll buy it tomorrow. Your uncle gave me some money. It's a beautiful painting. Very striking. Do you really think that I look like her?"

The Uhlan sergeant took up his tune again. But this time it was all right. Now everything about the night was just fine.

"Your hands are very cold," I said. "If you want, you may put them under my cloak."

"Yes."

I felt her frigid fingers above my heart. I felt them skillfully unbutton my vest and seek out my nipples through my shirt. I felt my nipples swell. I moved closer to her, face to face. Her breath caressed me. I kissed her.

༄

Though it's true that for some time we had counted our losses by the thousands: thousands dead, thousands wounded, thousands taken prisoner, thousands of deserters, thousands of stragglers, thousands of horses, thousands of carriages . . . until the Battle of Berezina the Grande Armée, despite flagging discipline, was still a more or less functional army. After Berezina it became nothing more than a roving pack of wolves that stayed together out of pure instinct, a band of starving and desperate vagabonds dragging themselves through the snow in time to *La Boîteuse*.

But I shouldn't get ahead of myself. The time of La *Boîteuse* had yet to arrive. First, I should relate our retreat from Smolensk through the Krasnoye gate, all of us together again in a caravan of ambulances: Uncle Charles, Larrey and Petit, and me, with my painting and my magical memory of Nadezhda and the Uhlan's song, my head still swollen and my arm in a sling, furiously disappointed at not having found Alfred. I had just learned that his regiment was a day's march ahead, escorting the twenty-four carriages that held Napoleon's treasury.

Kutuzov had spread his army out along the length of the road on the right hand bank of the Dnieper; the Cossacks were on the other side, with their little horses and small cannons mounted on sleds. We fought at half a dozen places, losing more men, more horses, more cannons. We lost cities to the north and to the south, Polotsk, Minsk. . . . And so, dripping trails of blood, and followed by tens of thousands of stragglers—some of them deserters who, upon learning of our retreat, now hurried to rejoin the ranks they had abandoned during the summer—all of the companies began to converge on Berezina. Plainly, I have nothing good to say of the deserters. The stragglers were a different story since, in general, they had fallen behind involuntarily. A wound, a frozen foot, or the pitiless combination of cold, hunger, and exhaustion could prevent even the most loyal of soldiers from keeping up with his regiment. First he would lag a few hours behind, catching up to the bivouac at seven or eight in the evening; the next day he would lag four or five hours, finding the bivouac near midnight; the next day he would be unable to rise at the sounding of reveille, and little by little, he'd be lost. First he'd see his company's rearguard pass by, the cannons and the supply wagons, the ambulances, the various conveyances full of women, children, and the elderly, merchants and refugees; then he'd join the long and ever-narrowing line of forgotten men, men who survived by any means necessary, even stealing from one another, and finally, he'd disappear to the east, amid fog banks and whirling snow.

After Krasnoye we went by foot—even Uncle Charles, whose limp was not too painful—aided by walking sticks fashioned from pine branches. Larrey had observed that those who traveled by horseback or carriage succumbed first to the white death. In order to survive, one had to walk and walk and walk, and sleep as little as possible, since very few ever awoke from a slumber that lasted longer than four hours. We traveled with the Old Guard. This was not a matter of coincidence. We could do nothing now for the wounded in the ambulances and, after a brief deliberation, Larrey and my uncle decided it would be advantageous, as their names were not only known, but revered in the Guard, to march with the company in which they had both served for so many years.

"We'll fare better alongside those old rapscallions than anywhere else," said Larrey.

"The Emperor will protect them; without the Old Guard he'll never be able to build a new army," pronounced Uncle Charles. "The new officers will come from its ranks."

Suddenly, the temperature rose. First the water melted, followed shortly by the wine, which until then had been but a dark block of ice that had to be hacked into pieces so that it could be melted. It seemed miraculous that such a thing should happen in the middle of winter. But then came days of rain and then the cold returned, fiercer than ever, and the wet mud turned to stone in the wheels and axels of carriages, wet clothing froze stiff, icicles hung from beards and mustaches, and then the pneumonia set in, the incessant coughing, fever, chills, and chattering teeth. Then there was nothing left to do but lean against the shaft of an overturned carriage and await death, or hasten it with a bullet to the head.

We entered a town where we found stores of flour and barrels of cognac. There I learned that the cavalry of the Vistula Legion was marching just ahead of the Old Guard and, again, I let myself hope that I might see Alfred. We made bread, drank, and continued on.

It was snowing when we reached Studienka and three Russian regiments, on both sides of the Berezina, threatened to surround us. Our engineers constructed two bridges to span the gray water, now nearly frozen and churning with heavy chunks of ice. The larger bridge was as wide as an officer's carriage; the smaller one was a precarious footpath suspended above the river. Neither had side rails. The first to cross were Oudinot and Ney's battalions, followed by the Guard's artillery command. The next day, from our bivouac, we saw the Vistula regiments passing at a distance, the red pennants on their lances parading slowly by, with Alfred surely among them, leading his horse by the reins. I almost asked Larrey for the telescope he was using to watch the bridges, but decided against it. (Larrey also had, among other implements, a Réaumur thermometer hanging from his buttonhole, which allowed him to later record in his memoirs the exact daily temperature during our retreat.) Presently, we began to move out toward the river. Stragglers and the provisions belonging to the columns that had already crossed blocked both ends of the bridge, and the Guard had to open a path with sabers and bayonets drawn. Confusion reigned, although it was nothing compared to the mayhem that was about to ensue. Having made it to the right bank, we gathered rank at the edge of a snowy forest of birch and pine, and began to wait for Napoleon. Completely exhausted, I spread my cloak over the snow and sat down, wrapping myself from head to toe in the billiard cloth. I took a long swig of cognac and immediately began to doze inside my green refuge. I don't know how long I stayed like that, sitting cross-legged, hovering between sleep and wakefulness, my imagination producing the faces of strangers that would appear for an instant and then vanish, only to be replaced by others; brief visions that were not quite dreams, they would disappear with each nod of my head, until little by little I sought out the image of Alfred, gloriously naked beside his white bed.

I should say that my mysterious night with Nadezhda was marked by tenderness. Although it's true that our kisses and caresses were driven by erotic desire, more than anything we were moved by a mutual longing to give and to receive a mother's love, the love of the Madonna, the love of Demeter for Kore; the love that is distilled from rage, grief, adoration, belonging. That night I felt that ancient and secret love manifest in me and I knew that all women are mothers and daughters, and that every mother holds her daughter within her, as every daughter holds her mother, and that every woman extends backwards in time through her mother and reaches forward into the future through her daughter. First I was mother to her, sharing my blanket and cape, and offering her my breast while I stroked her head with my good arm; in turn, she offered me hers, which I delicately bathed with my tongue while the Uhlan hummed his distant lullaby. That night we were Mother and Daughter; Daughter and Mother. And the woman in my painting is the symbol that unites my two sides, She and I, I and She, forever. (Where could you be, Nadezhda Ivánova, my beloved *matrioshka*? Did you go to France as you wanted, or did you remain forever in your Russia of icons and church bells, of servants and princes and troikas and empty steppes? Why didn't I take you with me? Why did I leave you, serious and enigmatic, your hand describing a slow and immense cross in the air, meant to bless me for all my days? Oh, Nadezhda, my Nadezhda, how I would have loved to see you sing and dance, how I would have loved to show you Paris, the Arch du Carrousel and the grand Arch de Triomphe, the rose window at Notre Dame and the Théâtre Le Temple and the Rue de l'Ancienne Comédie, to dine together at Le Procope and drink at Le

Coq Audacieux, to take a boat along the Seine and then stretch out by the fire to make love, oh, and so many other things! Why don't I ever dream of you? Could it be that the moment of our encounter is complete, that you already were my dream, and I, a part of yours in that frigid hospital in Smolensk, peopled by bizarre doctors and intimate visions?)

Comforted, consoled, caressed, and suckled; now integrated and complete, my desire for Alfred had became an obsession, just as it had with Bousquet. I took it for granted that, seeing me now as a defender of his cause rather than an obstacle, he would be eager to repeat the night of the dance and the fireworks. Knowing that he was so close, perhaps only a few hundred meters away, perhaps in the forest or posted with the Guard's cavalry, only heightened my ardor. My desire for Alfred became so intense that there, upon the snow in the minimal privacy afforded me by the green cloth, I sank my hand between my thighs, something I hadn't done since my days in Paris. I would have continued like that too, had the sound of cannon fire not begun to howl over my head. I leaped to my feet.

"They're firing at the bridges," said Larrey, extending his telescope.

In the distance I saw a cannonball fall into the water, followed by another. "Did the Emperor already cross?" I asked.

"A little while ago," answered Petit.

"Damn it all to hell!" exclaimed Larrey, passing the telescope to my uncle. "What a disaster!"

"This is going to be a bloodbath," murmured Uncle Charles. "Many will never make it across."

"If you'll allow me to look for a moment, Surgeon Major," said Petit impatiently. But Uncle Charles, pretending not to have heard him, passed the telescope to me. Terrorized by the Russian cannon fire, throngs of people were running toward the bridges. Unable to withstand the weight, the larger of the two sank into the river, taking everyone who had been crossing along with it. The people still on the bank ran to the other bridge, tangling with those who were already there waiting. Men and horses fell into the river and struggled to stay afloat among the blocks of ice. I raised the telescope a little; the sun was already setting, and I saw thousands and thousands of stragglers crossing the steppe like rows of ants, forming a line that got wider and wider the closer it came to the river.

"Let me see!" said Petit, yanking the telescope from my hands. He had only looked through it for a moment when Larrey asked for it back.

"The ambulances won't be able to cross," said Larrey, his eye glued to the lens. "No, they won't be able to cross," he repeated, resolute, and passed the telescope to Uncle Charles.

"We'll lose all of the wounded and many more besides," sighed my uncle. "And worse still, all of our crates of bandages and medicine, and all of our surgical instruments. With what knives and saws and probes are we to operate now?"

"*Vive l'Empereur!*" shouted the men of the Guard, repeating the cry again and again. It was Napoleon. He was riding an Arabian horse and was wearing white breeches and a leather hat with a feather. I had never seen him so close, not even in Borodino. His face was a pallid mask, a tad soft, yet determined. Larrey hurried off to speak with him and Napoleon leaned down from his saddle to listen. Whatever it was that Larrey requested, it was met with an immediate nod from the Emperor. Napoleon turned directly to Field Marshall Lefèvbre, the Commander of the Old Guard, who was riding alongside him. After issuing him an order, Napoleon continued on, impassively surveying the troops, as though the shouts of "*Vive l'Empereur*" were meant for someone else.

"The Emperor has granted me a small squadron of men to accompany us to the left bank tomorrow," Larrey told us. "We'll go across to the ambulances as many times as we can and bring back as much as we can carry.",

๛

What had seemed utterly unimaginable would prove possible after all: we crossed the river three times, salvaging what supplies we could. How did we manage it? I don't know. I remember only the fear and the urgency of making it to one bank and then to the other. I see only fragmented, explosive scenes, as when I try to reconstruct that afternoon in Germany when Claudette died; hazy scenes smudged through with the fur caps of the Old Guard, blue greatcoats and snowflakes and bayonets, and further off I see the blood and the gaping mouths, and the terror and the fury and the pain in the faces. In my memories, I don't hear what I know I heard: the screaming, the neighing, the pleading, the shells exploding, the hissing of the shrapnel, the undulating creaking of the bridges, the thud of cannonballs hitting bodies and carriages. I hear only a general noise, confused, disorganized, continuous, dominated by the thundering of cannon fire, which sounded as if many people were playing organs all at once inside an echo chamber; a sound with texture, three-dimensional, like a box or a drum. And through the center of this all-consuming cacophony float what scenes I can remember.

There, on the left bank, the military police can no longer detain the carriages trying to reach the bridges, plowing a path through men and horses until forced by the sheer multitude of their own numbers to stop. . . . In the water, to my right, I see people swimming and cavalrymen trying to ford the river, struggling against the current; among them I see the camp-follower who gave birth on the road to Krasnoye, holding her baby above her head with one hand. . . . I don't see the ambulances, only the men of the Guard who open a path for me through enraged faces and the enormous eyes of the horses. . . . The wounded men in the ambulances think that we are coming to save them and some even help us with the crates of sutures and bandages. . . . There, on the right bank, cannon fire thunders, and the Swiss and Polish soldiers move into the snowy forest to try to push back the Russian onslaught. . . . And there, on the left bank, more cannon fire and bullets rain down on the human sea plunging toward the bridges. . . . Near the ambulances, a wounded man with a long beard and rabid eyes seizes Uncle Charles by the throat and a foot soldier chops the man's hand off with a single blow of his saber. . . . Crossing back with the crates I see a battalion of the Guard open fire against the Russian positions on the bank I've just left behind. . . . The iron bullets penetrate the dense mass of people and open bloody furrows in the snow. . . . My arm hurts worse and worse and I can barely hold onto the crate I am carrying tight against my chest. . . . The bridge we are heading for collapses again and we turn back, aiming for the other one. . . . There, on the left bank, I see the head of the useless bridge, ringed by a semicircle of crushed bodies lying on the blood-stained snow. . . . With sabers and bayonets drawn, the foot soldiers clash with the people coming in the opposite direction; Larrey falls to his knees and gets up again, never dropping the crate he is carrying. . . . The Russian musketeers open fire and the foot soldier to my right raises his hand to his forehead and disappears from sight. . . . I leave a box of bandages next to the pile we've already brought over, turn, and run toward the bridge again. . . . The dead and wounded make the way nearly impassible and in front of me there is a woman on horseback carrying a little girl between the reins; the animal becomes tangled up with other horses dragging a cart behind them; one of them falls, its eye shattered by musket fire, and another bullet lodges in the woman's thigh, causing a spurting gush of blood. . . . Some of the wounded have thrown the crates down onto the snow and are sitting on them; they wait for us, hoping we will take them with us; I try to help a Cuirassier who has lost both an arm and a leg and is hopping grotesquely, but my strength gives out. . . . The Russians spray grape-shot and the bridge begins to sink until it hangs a few scant centimeters above the water; it rocks and jostles with the impact of huge floating pieces of ice. . . . On one side of the river I see a line of nearly submerged horses, their riders already drowned; they have gone over there to await an icy death, their heads resting on the wooden slats of the bridge. . . . Larrey is pushed into the water and manages to grab onto a cross-timber; two foot-soldiers drop their weapons and rescue him. . . .

We did not cross the river again.

At nightfall, the remnants of Field Marshall Victor's battalion, charged with protecting the rearguard, passed by. At dawn, Napoleon ordered the bridges destroyed and a massive segment of stragglers and provisions remained on the other side of the Berezina.

18

PLAGUED DAY AND NIGHT BY the Cossacks, we reached Zembin, a village surrounded by swamps, the icy surfaces of which broke under the weight of the cannons that were traveling off the main road. When we arrived, I recognized the treasury wagons and, hurrying toward them, I went to look for Alfred. But now Prince Eugène's Italian Guard was in charge of the treasury, and no one could tell me where the Vistula cavalry was.

As we bivouacked that night, Larrey calculated that we'd have to march some fifty leagues to make it to Vilna, and eighty to reach the Niemen.

"We're going to have to carry out this entire march in temperatures between fifteen and thirty degrees below zero, or perhaps even worse. The slightest carelessness, the smallest lack of vigilance, means death. We must combat the drowsiness produced by continual exposure to low temperatures; we must resist the temptation to lie down alongside the road. The only remedy is to walk and walk and walk," he warned me and Petit, huddled near the already struggling fire we'd managed to make that afternoon with green wood, gunpowder, and sparks from our pistols. The snow melted from the heat, the flames and embers had been sinking until, half a meter down, they met the sand of the square. The smoke, thick and harsh, issued from down there, like a chimney burning wet rags.

Uncle Charles had gone in search of dry wood. The Guard had demolished several houses and we were waiting for him with a jar of sweetened cognac and melted snow. After a while we saw him coming, carrying several lengths of board and accompanied by two women. These turned out to be Madame Fusil and a young actress with her company. Both had lost their carriages in the Berezina and were traveling, insufficiently clothed, by foot. The fire stoked and our dinner finished off in two sips, we stayed up talking about our misfortunes. They slept next to us, wrapped in my green billiard cloth and in a wolfskin of Petit's, who, imprudently, had begun flirting with the young woman, despite the fact that he knew that her father, along with several other French actors, had been sent to Siberia by the mayor of Moscow. When reveille sounded, the women went off in search of any vehicle that would take them and they didn't return.

The next day, the Cossacks attacked the rearguard and made off with a large number of wagons. The following day, a Guard patrol found a hundred deserters who'd managed to cross the Berezina and had been hiding in the forest. They had two *Intendance* wagons filled with mounted Grenadier uniforms, caps, and boots, and another loaded with food and barrels of vodka. Since we were assigned to the General Staff, we were given boots. Mine were too big for me, but I cut my cashmere shawl in two and wrapped up my feet. Then we traded our old boots for pieces of boiled horsemeat. Even this foodstuff had become scarce, since the number of horses, alive or dead, was now so greatly reduced. We continued walking in the snow and the cold.

We came to a large village called Smogorni on December 5th. I remembered it well. We had stopped over there in July. The immense forests that surrounded it were full of bears. They were hunted for the high prices their skins fetched, and their paws were considered the finest of delicacies. They were also captured alive for the purpose of training them and selling them to gypsies and buyers from other countries. Seeing them dance in the square, our soldiers had spared them their lives, though they sacked every last storehouse of its furs or food. Now the village was deserted and encased in frozen crystal. Translucent icicles hung from the cornices and rooftops, and vapor escaped from under the doors as though the houses were breathing. In the adjacent forest, the tree branches were bowed under the weight of the ice; the heat from the campfires made them glimmer like garlands in an enchanted wood. Here and there were frozen birds, like alabaster statuettes. As campfires came to life, the birds began falling from the trees like ripe fruit. The sky was completely clear and, for some reason, the stars seemed to have multiplied, changing the configuration of the constellations. In the distance, wolves howled endlessly at the crescent moon. I thought of Hecate, the sorceress. I'd always felt like a foreigner in Russia, but never as I did in that small village. That night Napoleon, traveling with a retinue of three carriages and accompanied by a small entourage, abandoned the Grande Armée to its fate.

I heard the news while I was helping Uncle Charles probe a wound to a sergeant's buttock. "The scoundrel left last night for his castle in Paris," said the man, face down on a table. "He left us behind, just like he did in Egypt. Do you remember, doctor? You were there." As the news spread, I found out that he had taken as an escort several Chasseurs of the Guard and two squadrons of the Vistula that had been bivouacking in the forest. Alfred commanded one of them. Once again, I'd come close to him; once again, I'd lost him.

I searched anxiously for him when we arrived in Viednicky two days later. There, Napoleon had changed escorts and horses and, after many inquiries, I arrived at the decimated stable where I'd been told some Polish lancers had made camp.

"Lubomirski? He's still on the road, monsieur," Captain Wonsowicz, a small man with a war-hardened face told me. "When we left, we were more than six hundred men, and when we arrived here there were thirty-six of us. The Emperor has fresh horses; we do not," he explained with a strange smile.

My legs went weak and I began to tremble.

"Might he still be alive? We're friends. I'd very much hoped to find him," I said, breathing deeply and bracing myself against a beam.

The captain thought for a moment. Through the holes in the slats, I could see delicate snowflakes floating slowly through the air. "Good snow. Fine and dry," he said, not looking at me. After a while, as I was getting ready to repeat the question, he turned his head toward me and added: "Men like Lubomirski don't just die. Had I been in his place, I'd have tried to band the men without mounts together so they wouldn't fall behind. I think it would be possible to unite four hundred or so, possibly more. They would form a battalion of men on foot, and they'd follow the forest in the direction of Lithuania. They would not die from hunger or cold. Of that I am certain. The spent horses would provide meat, and the forest, wood. I doubt that the Cossacks would dare to attack a battalion marching in formation and without wagons to steal."

I sighed with relief, knowing that Alfred, whose knowledge of the life of the soldier went back to his adolescence, had managed to do everything that his friend had told me. "Where do you suppose he is now?" I asked.

"Probably marching a route parallel to Ney or Victor's corps. . . . A day's march ahead of us, a day and a half, at the most. Don't worry, we shall see him in Vilna."

I couldn't sleep that night for thinking of Alfred. At dusk the day before, I had seen people camping off the road, alongside the forest. I'd had no reason to think that Alfred might have been among them. And suddenly the idea came to me that if I didn't go in search of him, we'd never see one another again; that even if we both arrived in Vilna on the same day, something would happen to prevent us from meeting. Shortly before dawn, while my companions were still asleep, I shouldered my rucksack, wound my blanket about my head, and started down the road with a swift gait. I had thought of leaving a note for my uncle. But what could I have told him that would not have seemed an act of utter madness?

⁍

The wind began just after noon. At first it was only a frigid breeze on my cheek that was barely strong enough to stir the snow that had fallen the day before. In front of me, I could see how it swept the white powder, lifting it just below the level of my knees and creating a kind of mirage only visible six or seven meters in the distance. The stragglers approaching from the west came toward me with their feet sunk in that fine-spun cloud and, at times, seemed like ghosts suspended in the wind. "You're going the wrong direction," one said to me, passing to my left. Suddenly, the wind intensified and its gusts, clothed now in all the snow of the steppes, blew from one side of the road to the other, pausing on high, or down low, to describe spirals and odd shapes. I could now barely make out the forms of the stragglers and the wind began to howl. I was as cold as if I were walking naked. With my chin sunk into my chest and my arm protecting my face, through slanted eyes I saw a man, like a weak shadow, covered in a swath of window curtain. Almost directly in front of me, he stepped off the road and turned his back to the wind. I saw him walk quickly away until he faded into the clouds of snow. I decided

314

to follow him. I took a few steps, but the force of the wind threw me face down. I managed to stand up, only to fall again, this time directly behind the straggler's boots. I considered staying like that for a moment, stretched out on the snow, except that the gray bulk of the man became covered, within minutes, in a white blanket. Without yet standing up, I figured out how to turn around. I was able to get to my feet with the help of my walking stick, and I bent over at the waist so as to encounter less resistance from the windstorm. The blasts of pulverized snow choked me and I soon fell again. I groped blindly for my walking stick. In reality, it was of no use to me at all, but as I searched for it, patting the snow desperately, I felt the frigid bite of terror rise in my stomach. My heart began to pound in my chest and I started to scream, knowing full well that my cries were snatched away by the storm like wisps of smoke. I screamed until I could no longer hear my own voice. But, by means of those screams, and without meaning to, I managed to purge myself of fear. I threw myself face down and thought that I was going to die; I thought this with a sense of resignation, as though it were something unavoidable that no one could prevent from happening. I prepared to die in peace, and immediately I saw how Ney's men would see me when they passed by this stretch of road: a low, rounded burial mound, scarcely a tiny wave in that vast sea of snow. That would be all they would see. I myself had seen, and even unintentionally stepped on, many of those imperceptible tombs. I knew how I would die. Larrey had explained to me the changes that occur in the human body when it's exposed to low temperatures. First, the circulation to the capillaries is arrested; then to the small veins. My fingers, ears, nose, cheeks, and eyelids would go numb, and I'd discover that I could no longer close my eyes. The idea that, come spring, my cadaver would emerge with open eyes seemed intolerable to me, and I closed them. Now they wouldn't find me ridiculously awake. Now I wouldn't be a wooden doll with glass eyes. When they threw me on the bonfire to dispose of me, I would no longer seem to look on impassively as I was reduced to charcoal and ash. This certainty gave me peace of mind. And now it was only a question of letting go. Where would I go? To what place? Would I see Robert there, and Aunt Margot, as the Uhlan appeared to have seen them? Would I come to know my mother there, with her copper-colored hair, or my father, who had shown me my first rainbow? Who could say? Because now I could sense *presences* beyond my closed eyelids and the hours of my life swirled vertiginously like the roulette wheel in Baden-Baden, and, little by little, that snowy niche transformed into a forest clearing, ringed with mushrooms and yellow dandelions, and of course, I couldn't see it but I could sense it, I was in the woods back in Foix and I heard the gardener's daughters laughing as they folded up the tablecloth and put the leftovers from our picnic away in Aunt Margot's big basket, the heel of bread, the chicken wings, the pâté, the blackberry tart, the bottle of lemonade, the clinking of the silverware and the glasses as they were settled into their places, and everything seemed perfectly fine to me and I was happy to be able to die in peace, and just when I was quite contentedly stretched out on the soft grass, Fairy Godmother held out a golden key, something like a fishhook that yanked powerfully on my consciousness, pulling it free, and I could feel how the cold and the whistling wind and the sound of my blood and my own will were returning me to my body. How many times had I awoken at the sound of reveille with two feet of snow piled on top of my cloak? The storm would soon pass and the most important thing, the truly important thing, was to cover myself well and curl into a little ball and allow myself to be entombed so as to hoard any heat my still living body could produce. Determined to survive, I fought off the drowsiness by moving my fingers and toes and thinking of the things I'd like to do one day. One by one, I went about accumulating wishes until, simply and diaphanously, the desire to have a child came to me. It was then I knew who had yanked on that fishhook: Maryse, ever determined to triumph, to always give her best possible performance; Nadezhda, suckling at my breast and revealing my capacity as a mother and, above all, the woman in my painting, the Woman, the sum of all women, whom I carried folded against my breast and who showed me the road I had yet to travel. What would my child be like, where and when would it be born, who would its father be, my second or third husband, as the gypsy woman had predicted? And so I passed the time until I realized that I could no longer hear the whistling of the wind above me.

I knew exactly what I needed to do. I knew that if I tried to stand all at once I'd fail and the fear would return and I'd be lost. I knew that I must first move my hands, rotate my wrists until I could feel my forearms again; then try to move my elbows using all the muscles in my arms and shoulders. I was soon able to draw my hands out of my cloak, and I began to dig. Luckily, it was a dry snow, as fine as corn meal. I dragged myself upward until I could stick my head out, and I took a few anxious breaths of the clean air left behind by the storm. The effort exhausted me so that I had to stop moving. My face was numb, but I could raise my eyelids and look toward the road. A few stragglers were already walking it, with that lead-footed, erratic gait that was so common among them; others, still buried, poked their hands up through the snow like pitiful tulips. It was still impossible for me to smile, but I did so internally, thinking that if any of those men were to look my way, they would see a face deposited on top of the snow like a discarded mask. And then I saw him. He was blind. A scrap torn from a shirt covered his eyes. The blood, dried on the bandage and on his cheeks, was the color of the red enamel often seen in Spanish depictions of Christ on the cross. The Cossacks or the peasants must have blinded him when they stole his clothes, for he was walking covered only by a tattered blanket and with his feet wrapped in rags. He walked alone. Someone must have helped him, guiding him to the road and dressing him in those pathetic garments; they had also given him the shaft of a broken lance to use as a walking stick. He bore his misery and pain with a poignant dignity. Testing the snow with his cane, he walked in a straight line with his head held high. When he passed in front of me, I could see that he was trembling and that his lips were moving, and for a second I heard him reciting one of those English poems he liked so much. I screamed and screamed his name, but they were mute cries. I tried to get out of my snow trap, to no avail. I watched him head west, mumbling stanzas that I couldn't understand, his red hair extinguishing little by little, like the last flame in a candelabra. I saw him go, knowing that I'd lost him, that I'd never see him again and that it would be useless to look for him.

"Are you alive or dead?" a straggler asked me around sunset, without a doubt trying to ascertain whether or not he could rob me. I had managed to draw near to the road, but, my energy sapped, I'd sat down to wait for the sugared cognac to revive me. My clothes were completely covered in a dusting of snow and I must have looked like one of those who, exhausted, had resigned themselves to death, knowing that their bodies, as hard as stone, would serve as relics of that miserable war until spring came. I looked up. The man who'd spoken was Grenelle, the veteran artilleryman whom I'd met at the entrance to Viazma.

"I'm alive," I replied. "Do you recognize me?"

"Yes."

I gave him the last of the cognac I had left. Then we joined with two other artillerymen who had made a bonfire alongside an abandoned wagon. Like me, they all had frostbitten feet, and I advised them that, in order to avoid gangrene, they should not get too close to the fire. Then it started snowing and we all lay down to sleep under the wagon. I was so tired that it wasn't until I awoke that I realized I'd been robbed. My cloak was open and my pockets empty. Seeing Aunt Margot's locket on the edge of my blanket, I realized that I was no longer wearing the gold chain that had held it around my neck. I said nothing to Grenelle and his friends. I'd decided that it would be best if I acted none the wiser. We warmed our hands over the embers that remained of the fire and, despite the fact that it was still snowing, we began to walk. We were all limping, and I was trying not to step on the burial mounds that had arisen in the fresh snow and the silence.

❦

As you'll have no doubt noted, I prefer not to speak of my feelings of sorrow, of those desolate pilgrimages among cathedrals of grief. What purpose could it serve to illuminate with words that which ought to remain dark, secluded; that which ought to remain a requiem, the concern of darkness, of the ashes within? Nevertheless, it's obvious that I don't shrink from speaking of my dead. I couldn't do so, for with them, I made love or marched to war; they were—they remain—the salt of my life. I evoke them, my dearly beloved, and they come to me, ever reliable and accommodating, regardless of my mood or the time of day. At other times it is they who seek me out, who find me and, transparently, superimpose themselves on another's face or gesture. And for a moment, Robert's eyes become confused with those of the corner barber, a man with long eyelashes whose gaze seems to spread across one's skin; or I see a perfect replica of Claudette diligently filling a parcel with peaches for a man with an umbrella tucked under his arm; or I pause to watch Alfred, slightly overweight, as he tries on a hat in front of the mirror in a shop on Broadway while Aunt Margot, at twenty, the living image of the portrait I wear around my neck, looks on, enchanted. It's true what they say. It's true that, in old age, the body likes to drink from the pools of its own memory. And it's not just that it hopes to recapture the time swept away by gray hairs and wrinkles; it's that we find it difficult to forget those we so loved. It is they who impose themselves over time, who invite us, insistently, to join them in their houses of mirrors. And what else can I do but sink my pen into the inkwell, as one crossing a threshold, and meet them there? What better proof of fidelity can I offer them but to request their company on my firefly's flight?

∝

Nearly dragging one another, we arrived in Vilna. There were no longer battle corps or battalions or regiments. With the exception of a few hundred men with the Old Guard, almost all of us had descended to the sad condition of straggler. The lighthearted and elegant retinue of officers, nobles, and diplomats we'd left there in the summer had fled, terrified at the news of our approach. When we entered through the long, narrow gateway to the city—where a situation similar to the one created by the bridges across the Berezina had arisen—we discovered that the hospitals were already full to overflowing, as many of the ambulances dispatched from Moscow, Borodino, Smolensk, and countless other places we'd waged battles, had come here. It was necessary to force the monks, under threat of death, to abandon their monasteries in order to make room for the wounded and ill. Like a plague of rats, we dispersed across the squares and streets in search of a café or an inn, where we might buy a plate of food and drink a glass of wine by the fire. Then we went to the storehouses of the *Intendance*, as we'd been told that we were to be reprovisioned. But the lines were so long and the bureaucratic administration so slow and, upon seeing that the provisions were muskets, cartridge cases, and two kilos of bread, the majority went off to find lodging anywhere they could. The locals wanted nothing to do with us; they had locked themselves in their houses and precious few offered us shelter. Only the merchants, the tavern keepers, the Jews, and the civil servants paid us any heed, and this thanks only to the gold we brought in our saddlebags. We were a louse-ridden, starving, limping, sick, dirty, and foul-smelling herd if there ever was one. Suffice to say that the rooms we occupied had to be fumigated after we left.

It had been easy for me to find Uncle Charles and Larrey. It had not been a joyful reunion. The first was suspicious of my motive for desertion and was hurt that I'd left without telling him; the latter thought that I'd straggled on purpose, neglecting my duties as assistant surgeon. His voice took on an acidic tone when he told me that Petit had been captured by the Cossacks as he was driving the medicine wagon. I made my apologies, but did not offer any explanation as to my departure for the rearguard. Although I could barely stand, I willingly helped them the best I could. There were fourteen hospitals and very few doctors. More than taking care of patients, we became heralds of death, pointing to the lifeless bodies that could be tossed into the patio, or indicating which were sick with typhus so that they could be transferred to the largest of the monasteries. When we learned that the Russians were on their way, we abandoned thousands of those poor devils to their good graces.

∝

Despite the fact that spring has already begun to color the streets of New York, the physiological mechanism that drives my body has not yet taken note of the new season; for the first time ever, I'm aware that the calendar is moving in one direction, and I in another. Have I been permanently trapped in winter? I fear so. "It's been days since you've left the hotel, madame," Milly said just a while ago. "It worries me to see you working so much, writing since dawn." A good girl, Milly, only she doesn't understand that I resent every hour I spend away from my papers. But no, she must understand. Aside from being the only witness to my struggle with the pen, she copies, in her flawless hand, each and every completed page I hand over to her. She's witnessed how what was, at first, the bittersweet labor of converting memories into paragraphs, has now become a dangerous obsession. So dangerous, in fact, that lately I've been asking myself if I'll survive it—I work with the feverish steadfastness of a machine, stopping only when, exhausted, my eyes close over the paper. And when I think of everything I have yet to tell, of the years I've yet to grind out, I'm struck by the fear of leaving my work unfinished.

Today I realized that, in my race against the inevitable, I'm scarcely gaining ground. As my past becomes ink, I'm proportionally losing my fire, my internal combustion. It may be that what has kept me active and healthy was the accumulated heat of all my summers; one might say that I was bursting with hot air, like a balloon heading toward the clouds. But now, after I've burned up so many memories, I have the impression that I'm getting colder and that I'll end up a poor exhausted skin, deflated, hanging uselessly from a flagpole or laid out, full of wrinkles, on a rooftop spattered with pigeon shit. What I gain through my writing, I lose in life force, something like the race between Achilles and the Tortoise. No doubt about it, this is not going well; I scarcely sleep, my digestion is poor, and my left leg is worse than ever—I can no longer do without my cane. Another symptom: I've always been curious about what's happening in the world or I've had a plan or two up my sleeve; a trip, a new way of increasing my fortune, or even the search for trustworthy inheritors to whom to leave it. But now I don't even follow the war in Cuba in the newspaper, or what's happening in France, which is saying something, and if I heard about the Suez Canal it was only thanks to Milly. As for traveling, I get tired just thinking of more boats, more hotels and cities, more trunks to pack and unpack. It also seems pointless to acquire more properties or stocks—what for? After making out five, no, six wills, I've found no better beneficiary than the Red Cross in Geneva. If only I were visited by a hopeful dream or some vision that would ignite my spirit, I'd have something to delay my fall, a pair of wings or a providential influx of hot air that would allow me to float until I finish my narrative. But I no longer dream and, no mater how I search, I don't see anything beyond the page I'm writing. What's worse, a few minutes ago, as I was thinking about all of this, I felt tempted to set down the pen and simply be quiet and alone; to send Milly back to her Yorkshire of moors and stone fences and lie down to die in this sumptuous mausoleum of marble, wall-hangings, and hydraulic elevators. Except that, reluctant to surrender, my memory has called up Larrey's words in Russia: "We must combat the drowsiness produced by continual exposure to low temperatures; we must resist the temptation to lie down alongside the road. The only remedy is to walk and walk and walk," words that Maryse surely would have applauded. Very well, Doctor Larrey, I'll set my pessimism to walking. Something will come to me; something will happen. I'll start by reading the newspaper from cover to cover. I'll go to the theater with Milly, and to dinner at Delmonico's now and then. For the time being, although I'm feeling wintry, I must admit that I'm still sparking like a dry wick. Who knows? Maybe, in two or three weeks' time, I'll manage to catch up with spring.

※

Walking as best we could, we took the road to Kovno, the first city we'd occupied back in the summer, now the final leg of our retreat. Of the hundred thousand of us that left Moscow on October 19th, there were now only five thousand, almost all of us lame. It was then that a black musician, the horn player with a regiment of mounted Chasseurs, composed the song that suited us precisely. He didn't give it a name, but it immediately became known as *La Boiteuse*. Never had a military march so perfectly described the gait of the soldier at the point of collapse. It was not even two minutes long, and it had no lyrics, but its simplicity was its greatest virtue. Otherwise, it never would have won us over. In the first few bars, orchestrated for brass, the notes seemed to drag along like a cripple's leg; percussion dominated in the next bars, the clacking of drumsticks played the downbeat, the upbeat rounded out by the bass drum, as though limping along on a lame foot. We adjusted our step to its rhythm, limping and laughing at ourselves, making a joke out of the miserable spectacle we made. It was a march of life and of death. And while its spirit of parody helped a few of us make it through, its distant horns heralded the hour of death to many, the time to sit down, one final time, on the side of the road.

Of all the marches, I felt *La Boiteuse* to be the most mine, the ragged rhythm limping along with me and all the rest of us. Nevertheless, its gruesome brilliance was short-lived. Besieged by the Russian light cavalry and the bands of Cossacks, there were fewer and fewer of us every hour that went by. And so, the day came when *La Boiteuse* was nothing more than a distant horn and drum, somewhere back in the rearguard, where Ney was still battling. Somewhere near Kovno, I ceased to hear it altogether. (Count Dumas, the Quartermaster General, was drinking with some friends in a café when he saw a peasant dressed in a shabby beige overcoat, and a black man with a bugle approaching. The peasant had a huge red beard and frostbite on his forehead and eye-sockets. "I've finally made it to Kovno," he said. "But Dumas, don't you recognize me?" he added. "Well, no. Who are you?" he replied. "We're the rearguard of the Grande Armée, and I'm Field Marshall Ney.")

Years later, under the title *La Boiteuse-March des Eclopés*, the score was published in Paris. The date given for its composition was correct: 1812. It was unattributed. It said, in parenthesis, that it was anonymous, and I thought that was as it should be. That march had belonged to everyone, to the few of us who had survived, and to the last of our dead.

CHRISTOPHER

19

MADAME CAVENT WAS EXPECTING US in Danzig, where she'd waited out the campaign in a comfortable apartment. Under her care, we recovered quickly. The bluish color of my left foot faded day by day, and Uncle Charles was able to avoid having his bad leg amputated, although his limp would be more pronounced than ever. But the terrible things we'd seen and suffered had left their mark, even on my uncle, accustomed as he was to the horrors of war.

"There will never be another military disaster or retreat to equal ours," he told me bleakly when, unable to talk of anything else, we'd begun again to grieve the cold, the snow, the Borodino, the burning of Moscow, the Cossacks and the Muzhiks, the wounded and the prisoners we'd left behind, Alfred's death, and the deaths of so many others we'd seen marching to music and pomp toward the Niemen. The most painful part was that half a million of our men had died for nothing. But while Uncle Charles blamed this on the wickedness of France's enemies, I blamed the debacle on Napoleon, though I kept this to myself in order to spare him any further distress. I felt like that soldier in Borodino whose case, much discussed at the time, had been considered extraordinary. Having lost both legs and been left for dead, he'd managed to survive by eating moss and raw horse entrails. Weeks later, as Napoleon was crossing the battlefield, he'd dragged himself to the road in order to confront him, throwing his own sorry condition in the Emperor's face and cursing him in the name of the thousands of French citizens who had died there.

"And all in only five months," my uncle went on, now addressing Madame Cavent who, looking at us over her crocheting, nodded sympathetically. "So many years to build the Grande Armée, and in five months everything went to hell! And not only that, now we're worse off than before. As soon as spring arrives, the Russians will descend upon us and, mark my words, so will the Austrians, in spite of Empress Marie Louise, and I wouldn't be at all surprised to see the Swedes follow them, now that they've got Bernadotte. And let's not even mention the Prussians. We've been abandoned." My uncle was referring to Prussia's recent declaration of neutrality, a truly hypocritical gesture, since Friedrich Wilhelm was already raising a volunteer army. "And just what do you think will happen to the Confederation of the Rhine? Well, I'll tell you. It will turn against us as soon as the war reaches the Elbe. The only ones who'll stand by us are the Bavarians and the Hessians, those from Westphalia, Baden, and Württemberg, and I can only say that because I saw them die all around me. In all honesty, our truest allies are the Poles. We will always be able to count on them, although if you really think about it, the Spaniards weren't half-bad at Borodino; nor were the Swiss at Berezina. In any case, if I were the Emperor, I wouldn't negotiate any further with the Russians, or with the Austrians and Prussians, or with the Saxons either. I would simply forget about them. Let them ally with England! I'd be content to hold on to half of Germany and to Holland, Italy, and Switzerland. And Spain as well, since as far as Portugal goes, I'd leave it to the British. But Spain is Spain. It's our safeguard. Atlantic ports. . . . We have a Bonaparte there as king, troops, and some support. We could defeat Wellington if we sent in a hundred thousand reinforcements. . . . So, what do you think of my ideas as a statesman?" he asked me. "You'll soon see that the Emperor will think the same as I do. Oh, but of all our allies, I'll stand by the Poles. Poor Alfred! I can still see him. . . . We must figure out how to take some territory from the Russians and the Prussians and give Poland its independence."

As the situation in Prussia was rapidly becoming more complicated, and we were in desperate need of a respite from the war, Uncle Charles put his experience on the Iberian Peninsula to good use and arranged to be sent to inspect military hospitals in Spain, with me, of course, to go along as his assistant. I should mention that this news came at a moment when I was weighing two alternatives: continuing to be Enrique or going back to being to Henriette, with the intention of returning to Foix or of visiting Maryse or of doing whatever I felt like that didn't involve practicing medicine. To enact the latter, the only thing I'd have to do would be to dress as a woman; Enrique Fuenmayor would instantly vanish, his name appearing, in the f's alongside Fauriel's, on the long list of people disinclined to risk their hides for the whims of one man. Except Uncle Charles was so happy to have arranged for a sort of vacation in a warm and sunny clime that the balance tipped in his favor. But there was something else as well. My uncle—even Madame Cavent—no longer thought of me as an ordinary woman; to him I was both Enrique and Henriette, and he took pride in being able to count on me as a niece, colleague, and comrade-in-arms. And that recognition of my complex roll in life filled me with satisfaction. As for Madame Cavent, I couldn't help a wry smile when, one afternoon when my uncle had gone out to a café, she came into my room to tell me, quite tenderly, how fortunate she felt to have me by her husband's side. "Though I can't be present in those horrible battles, I know that you'll take care of him just as I would."

Given that we weren't expected in Madrid until the 30th of May, we planned a trip that would take all of our interests into account. My uncle needed to be in Paris for a few days in order to collect his back pay, and I would take the opportunity to recover my jewels from their safe deposit box. Madame Cavent wanted to visit her mother in Blois, and I wanted to arrange a meeting in Toulouse with my lawyer, Monsieur Lebrun, to put my will in order—until then I hadn't thought that, statistically speaking, my chances of dying during a campaign were the same as a soldier's—and, while there, pay a visit to Françoise and Pierre. And since I'd be near my country estate, I could take advantage of the opportunity to meet my renter, a certain Monsieur D'Alencourt, and ride horses through the woods, and especially, return to Fairy Godmother's clearing, that magical circle of games and picnics that had revealed itself to me in Russia as the sweet space that separated life from death. And so, to save time and energy—the journey overland would have been too tiring, particularly in winter—we would board a ship-of-the-line serving in the blockade against the British that would dock at Brest. From there we would travel by carriage, stopping over in all the places I've mentioned, and finally enter Spain along the road from Perpignan to Barcelona.

It was not the best time of year to travel by boat and we all suffered terribly from seasickness during the crossing. But, as Aunt

Margot, always so fond of refrains, used to say: "Every cloud has a silver lining." Forced to lie down through most of the voyage, Uncle Charles and I both had the chance to rest our injured legs.

‰

After dropping Madame Cavent in Blois, we arrived in Paris on a Saturday in the beginning of April. I remember the day of the week because Uncle Charles wanted to attend a grand military review which, presided over by Napoleon, was to take place at the Place du Carrousel on Sunday. We went first to the house on Saint-Honoré and opened the windows to air it out after a year of being closed up. Nevertheless, it was impossible to rid the rooms of a dense aroma of dead flowers—quite inexplicable, as all of the vases were empty. It wasn't even all that similar to the stench of decay that pervaded the battlefields, but it put us off anyway, perhaps because it was, in some way, sad to be confronted by the perishable nature of beauty. The concierge, a woman quite competent with domestic affairs, sent her daughter to buy incense, but the new scent was still unable to displace the other in the corners of the rooms and inside the armoires. As I was hanging my *Woman* in her new frame—the canvas had begun to deteriorate from having been folded for so long—I found, above the fireplace, a brief letter that Françoise had written to me before she left. Nothing in particular. Very grateful for my gifts, she'd sold the cabriolet, the horses, and my women's clothing for almost five thousand francs. She and Pierre would travel to Foix in a postal wagon and, after the wedding, would try their luck in Toulouse. Pierre planned to buy a carriage, and she would open a small seamstress' shop. She would leave their new address with my lawyer, Monsieur Lebrun, and she closed, wishing all the best to Uncle Charles, Madame Cavent, and me.

After our disastrous defeat in Russia, the Parisians' political sentiments were not what they'd been when I left. As before, the majority of the residents of the Saint-Germain and Saint-Honoré *faubourgs* detested Napoleon, even as the poor and working classes continued to idolize him. But now, the bourgeoisie's loyalties were divided. Until then, that class had not been directly affected by mourning for those who hadn't returned, since it was common practice for manufacturers and businessmen to pay for substitutes to fight in the place of their sons. But now this was no longer possible. In accordance with the new directive, they were to join the ranks of the National Guard, inciting great unrest among these families. (Upon his return from Russia, the first thing Napoleon had done was to take measures to raise a new army of three hundred and fifty thousand men. Of them, one hundred thousand would be from the 1814 conscription, one hundred thousand from the National Guard, and one hundred fifty thousand from the 1813 conscription, for which the enlistment age had been lowered to include young men of sixteen—called "Marie-Louises" after a proclamation made by the Empress. Also called up were the invalids whose wounds had healed enough to allow them to march and to bite open cartridges. The truth was that all human resources were utilized, and volunteers even up to sixty years old were accepted. Because the Grande Armée had lost its cavalry, an appeal to the generosity of the general population was issued, requesting donations of draft and riding horses.) Nevertheless, that said, I would venture that the majority of Parisians were still afflicted with "Napoleonic fever." The night I went to the theater to see *L'Abencérage*, Napoleon and Marie-Louise occupied the imperial box to raucous cries of *Vive l'Empereur!*

After Uncle Charles agreed to my idea of applying for French citizenship for Enrique Fuenmayor, an alter ego that already felt very much my own, we decided to consult with his lawyer, Monsieur Dubreuil. In the end, we had to visit his office three times. For the first visit, to collect my jewelry, deposited under the name Madame Renaud, I wore women's clothing, a beautiful black-haired wig, and Uncle Charles' reading glasses. Not that this was even necessary, because Uncle Charles himself had deposited my jewels, and could have just as easily taken care of collecting them. It was just that I was so curious to see if anyone would be able to discover my double identity, for the following day I would have to return as Enrique Fuenmayor to attend to the matter of his change in citizenship. In case the hoax were to be discovered, I would engage Monsieur Dubreuil as my lawyer, who would then be professionally obliged not to divulge his client's secrets.

Now wearing my dress uniform, blond pigtail hanging down beneath my bicorn hat, I called again on Monsieur Dubreuil, accompanied by my uncle who, fortunately, had good-naturedly agreed to go along with the farce, treating it as though we were attending a costume ball. After he'd examined the documents Maryse had sent me from Havana, along with my student and military credentials, Monsieur Dubreuil, an incredibly fat man, said: "Everything is in order. The only difficulty is that there are thousands of applications in process and it could take months, if not years, for your paperwork to go through. In addition, they've lowered the salary for public functionaries. . . . What I mean to say is that, if the application were presented with a little gift. . . . There's even a sort of price list with variable rates: 'extremely urgent,' 'very urgent,' 'urgent,' 'less urgent.' It's up to you, Don Enrique," he added, using the Spanish form of address, surely to flatter me, never suspecting that in affirming my masculinity he did so in another sense as well.

"It's 'most urgent,'" intervened my uncle. "Don Enrique, Madame Renaud, and I must leave for Toulouse as soon as possible. How quickly can we obtain the certificate of citizenship?"

"Four days, five at the most."

"And the gift?" I asked.

"For 'extremely urgent' the price is seven thousand francs, an amount that includes my fee as well, naturally."

"But that's an enormous amount of money!" protested my uncle. "It's more than I pay in rent, as you well know, maître Dubreuil!"

The lawyer shrugged his shoulders, causing his jowls and lardy cheeks to quiver.

"It is what's required," he said. "Don't forget that there are several functionaries whose pockets must be lined. Evidently, there are those prepared to pay this amount. 'Very urgent' is five thousand francs. That will take about two weeks."

"It's a lot of money," said Uncle Charles.

"We haven't even received our salaries yet," I said, disappointed.

"Ah, but there is one solution I've just remembered," said the lawyer, tapping his temple with a chubby finger. "If someone were willing to serve as guarantor. . . . "

"Guarantor? I don't know anyone in a position to do that. It's a sum beyond any of my friends' capacities. Were we in Havana, it would be another story."

"Undoubtedly, Don Enrique. But, unfortunately, we're in Paris. Perhaps you'd be interested in 'urgent,' three thousand five hundred francs; there's also 'less urgent,' about four months, maybe five."

"What about Madame Cavent as guarantor?" said Uncle

Charles. "She's quite fond of Don Enrique and I know she'd be thrilled to do him a favor."

"Of course, but didn't you tell me when you arrived that she was in Blois visiting her mother? We'd need her signature, doctor."

"And Madame Renaud?" I said with a wink at my uncle, thoroughly enjoying myself. "She's also fond of me and she's available."

"Madame Renaud? Well, yes, of course. Some of her jewels would be worth more than 'extremely urgent.' We can take care of everything this afternoon. If it suits you, we can all meet here after lunch."

My heart sank. I cursed my idea of accompanying my uncle as Madame Renaud. I'd have no choice but to reveal my disguise, a situation that, in addition to humiliating me and compromising my uncle, would not amuse Dubreuil in the slightest, since the fact that he'd failed to see through my trick would mark him a fool in our eyes.

"Don Enrique had planned to meet with some of his old professors this afternoon," said Uncle Charles providentially. "He does not wish to lose contact with them. After all, he'll return to the Medical School once the war is over."

"Yes, that's true," I affirmed. "It's already set. I'm having lunch at the Café Procope with my anatomy and surgery professors."

"No problem at all. We can put the application papers in order right now and when Madame Renaud has a moment she can stop by."

And so everything was resolved. Enrique Fuenmayor y Faber requested French citizenship under the name Henri Faber and, hours later, Madame Renaud became guarantor of a loan in the amount of seven thousand francs on his behalf. When the lawyer recorded Madame Renaud's maiden name, he paused at the coincidence of the surname Faber, but he quickly acknowledged that it was a common name in Switzerland, Italy, Germany and Spain, and even in France, where it had taken the form Favre.

Four days later I received, from Monsieur Dubreuil's voluminous hands, my certificate of citizenship, which would remain in his files together with Enrique Fuenmayor's other papers. That very morning I took him on as my lawyer, putting him in exclusive charge of Henri Faber's affairs. My lawyer in Toulouse was already the executor of those of Henriette Faber-Cavent, Renaud's widow.

And so, my double identity, now legalized, was recorded separately in Paris and in the Languedoc. Having collected his salary and recuperated his travel expenses, my uncle paid a month's rent in advance and we left the house on Saint-Honoré, still permeated with the smell of dead flowers. That same day Napoleon left Saint-Cloud, bound for Germany. According to the latest rumors, the Russian and Prussian armies were already advancing on the Elbe.

❧

The weather improved steadily as we traveled. Uncle Charles had enlisted the services of a postilion, a colorful Italian who drove the horses at a comfortable pace, singing ballads all the while. Now deep into an auspicious spring, full of birds and bumblebees, the landscape seemed abuzz with glee, glory, and resurrection and, suddenly, strangely, I felt certain that a man was awaiting me somewhere. Yes, without a doubt, this would be the gift of the new year; more than just sensing him, I could actually feel him breathing next to me, his hands caressing me, his lips kissing me. Where would I find him? In Toulouse? Barcelona? Madrid? Who would this new love be, this passion as yet without a name or a face, a mere ethereal body, evoked in a flash of intuition? Would he be the Second Husband, the Father Husband who would give me the child I'd longed for in my snowy niche? But life is not prodigal. It gives with one hand and takes away with the other. What would it rob me of this time? And if it were to take him, and Robert all over again, and Alfred, whom I could still see before me, walking his *via crucis* along that terrible road to Vilna? Perhaps it meant to give him to me only to take him away again in the blink of an eye? Would it always be like this, continually shifting from lover to mourner, never even having enough time to fully understand for whom I wept? But what was the point in anticipating the end of an imaginary union, and a tragic end at that? Why not imagine that everything could go smoothly? Hadn't I confirmed by now that nothing can been foreseen or taken for granted, not even death, since at the last minute someone can pull the cord and yank a person out of the Garden of Delight, setting her once again upon life's path? Why not concur with Robledo, why not accept, without banging my head any further against the wall, that what is meant to happen, happens?

Toulouse appeared unchanged since my last visit. We stayed in a hotel along the river and while my uncle and Madame Cavent rested, I dressed as a woman, took my box of jewels, and went off to see my lawyer, whom I'd only met through letters. Because he'd been the executor of my inheritance and greatly trusted by my Aunt Margot, I'd expected to find an elderly man with ink-tinted fingers, dandruff on his jacket shoulders, and a kind of provincial eloquence. But the man who received me in his office couldn't have been more than forty years old and, if not exactly handsome, quickly revealed certain unmistakable charms.

"Ah, Madame Renaud, have a seat, I beg of you," he said, after elegantly kissing my hand, an appreciative smile on his face.

"Monsieur Joseph Lebrun?" I asked, incredulous. As he nodded, I remembered that the name of the firm was Lebrun & Son. Surely this was Aunt Margot's friend's son, who shared a last name with his father. "How is your father?" I asked, sitting down, intending to tell him that I'd prefer to conduct my business with the other Lebrun.

"My father?" he said, taken aback. "My father died over seven years ago. I wrote to you of this sad turn of events."

"Oh, do forgive me! I didn't know. I'm very sorry. He was such a dear friend of my aunt's. I'm truly sorry. . . . As for your letter, I never received it. That explains my confusion."

"You've nothing to apologize for," he said, with an expressive gesture of the hand. "It's not the first of my letters to be lost, particularly when they're sent to another country. At that time you were living in Bavaria . . . Munich, I believe. Just after my father died, I handled the matter of your dowry, a triangular operation through a banker in Vienna. . . . Kessler, wasn't it?"

"My God, maître, what a good memory you have!" I exclaimed, surprised.

"Actually, I don't. In truth, I'm rather forgetful. The fact is, about a week ago, when I received word of your visit, I went over your file," he said, indicating a safe standing next to the bookshelf. "Which reminds me, Monsieur D'Alencourt, your renter, wishes to extend his lease for a five-year term. If you've decided to settle in Paris, I think it prudent to do so; we could raise the rent a touch. I already have the paperwork ready, along with his rent for the year. By the way, I've just paid off a promissory note of yours in the amount of seven thousand francs. But tell me, what can I do for you?"

"My will, maître. I'd like to take advantage of my stay in Toulouse to draw up my will, and I'd like to deposit my jewels with you. I'm just passing through. On the way to Spain, actually. I'll be accompanying my uncle and his wife. I don't know if you have the time—"

"I congratulate you, madame," he interrupted. "It's an intelligent decision. Very few people of your age stop to consider that we aren't immortal. Especially, as in your case, when one is so healthy and beautiful."

I thanked him for the compliment with an idiotic smile. It had been so long since anyone had flirted with me that I'd forgotten the language of coquetry. But his flattery was all it took for me to consider him more closely. His charm lay in his gaze. Nothing appeared to escape him. Those black, Southern eyes, looked on with the keenness of a sharpshooter, the best marksmen in the whole of the Grande Armée. Their mission was to fire at special targets, usually high-ranking officials, aides-de-camp at the gallop, ammunition carts. . . . His hands, his long and agile fingers, moved gracefully up and down, from left to right, with a language of their own that almost rendered words superfluous. He was wearing a woman's ring, but on his pinkie rather than on his ring finger, and I wondered if he were a widower. It also occurred to me that he would make a fine actor, although, in reality, he already was one, except his stage was that somberly furnished office, done in mahogany and bronze, with its olive green drapes, rows of law books, an antique mariner's clock, a grand portrait, à la David, of a beautiful woman dressed in the style of the Directorate. Suddenly, I felt my nipples swell. Without lowering my head, I looked down through my eyelashes. There they were, quite noticeable, especially the one on the left.

"Very well, madame. Have I won your approval?"

"What do you mean, monsieur?" I asked dryly, hiding my embarrassment at the realization that my scrutiny had not gone unnoticed.

"Your approval as a lawyer. What else could I have meant?"

"Oh, yes, of course, maître. After all, we've been writing to one another for years. We're already old friends," I allowed.

"You were talking about your will. But before we go on, I should tell you that, no matter whom you should designate as beneficiaries today, you are free to change your mind next week or whenever you see fit. It is the final document, and not those that precede it, that is legally binding."

"Understood, Monsieur Lebrun. Well then. . . . My jewels, which I will leave in your custody tomorrow morning, I leave to Madame Anne Cavent, my uncle's wife. Here is the address of her house in Blois, where her mother currently lives," I said, holding out the paper to him. "And any amount of money that I have with me, or with which you are entrusted in my name, should be given to the Manches, Pierre and Françoise. Perhaps one of them has already left their address with you?"

"Yes, yes, I have it here," he said, looking through a leather portfolio. "I often take Monsieur Manche's carriage to attend to some errand or another, especially when my business affairs require me to travel to other cities. An excellent coachman, Monsieur Manche. I should say that he holds you in very high esteem. He speaks of you often. It wouldn't be an exaggeration were I to say that, when I saw you come into my office, I felt I already knew you."

"I appreciate him a great deal as well," I said. "We went to the war together. Then he went to work for the traveling theater company we had back in Germany."

"The Théâtre Nomade," said Lebrun, and his hand described a grandiose spiral as though he were introducing a circus act. "Oh, madame, there are many here who would envy you your life! Vienna, Berlin, Warsaw, Rhineland, Westphalia, Bavaria, Baden, and, of course, most recently, Paris. I, on the other hand, a modest provincial lawyer. I haven't even been back to Paris since my years as a student."

"Believe me, maître, my life has been more difficult than you might imagine."

"Of course, Madame Renaud. Please forgive my lack of tact," he said, resting his hand over his heart. "I understand, I have also been widowed," he added, fixing his gaze on my indomitable nipple, closing one eye as though taking aim with a musket. Then he raised his hand weakly toward the portrait. "My wife. . . . Many years ago now."

"Very beautiful, Monsieur. I'm sorry for your loss. How nice that you were able to preserve her image. I have the impression that the painter did her justice."

"Do you like it?" he asked, getting up from his seat to move closer to the painting. Then he took a few steps away from it and examined it carefully, as though he'd never seen it before.

"The work of a fine artist," I assured him.

"Thank you, madame. I am the painter," he said, turning back around to face me, giving me a sad smile as he forced himself not to allow his gaze to linger over my breasts.

His confession impressed me. Suddenly, I couldn't think of anything to say. Finally, I said: "How is it possible that an artist of your talent should have changed professions?" Although, had I been more honest with him, I would have asked him why he had traded in his paintbrushes and palette for an occupation as prosaic as the administration of real estate.

"Oh, madame, I never was a true artist, I mean, a professional painter. I studied at the Academy as a young man. But my father convinced me of the benefits of working here with him. I wanted to marry. Have a family. I imagine you know well the risks assumed by those who live off the arts."

"I understand. Did you paint that canvas in Paris?" I asked, curious to know more about his past.

"Yes. It was my last painting. Afterwards, I swore I'd never paint again. And well . . . here you find me."

"Do you have children?"

"Camille. She's just turned fourteen. But getting back to your will. As for your properties. . . . "

"Yes," I said, in light of his reticence to discuss his life in further detail. "I think it would be best to leave all of my properties to my uncle, Charles-Henri Cavent. But with one condition."

"Forgive me, allow me to make a note."

"That upon his death, the château shall become a school for the daughters of disabled veterans, to be operated off the profits brought in from the cultivation of the lands. The school should be directed by a capable woman. . . . Another thing. I would like to use the money accumulated through my rented property to buy the house I use in Paris, you know the one, on Rue Saint-Honoré. It isn't urgent. The rent is paid through next April. I wish to leave that house to Madame Nadezhda Ivánovna. The last I knew of her she was working as a nurse in a military hospital in Smolensk. I beg you to investigate her whereabouts and inform her that the house will always be at her disposal. Furthermore, in that same house I have a painting of a woman in a shako. My wish is that it be hung in the school."

"Very good, Madame Renaud. A question: who is to inherit the house if Madame Ivánovna doesn't turn up?"

"My uncle, but I implore you to do everything in your power to locate Madame Ivánovna. In addition, should she lack funds to travel to Paris, these should be provided as well."

"I'll do the impossible to find her. And now, as for the school . . . you must name a board of trustees."

"What does that mean?"

"Individuals to see to the administration of the lands, the maintenance of the building, the hiring of the school's personnel and the director and, above all, to ensure that she perform her job well."

"Well, in that case, I'd like you to chair the board of trustees and to organize it according to your own good judgment."

"Thank you, Madame Renaud. You truly honor me with your trust. But, if I were unable?"

"What a nuisance, maître Lebrun! Couldn't you designate someone serious and dedicated to the task?"

"I could, it's just that you must authorize me to do so."

"Yes, yes, of course. I'd imagined my will would be a more straightforward matter," I protested.

"It's not as complicated as it seems," he said, erasing the difficulty of the legal requirements with a carefree wave of his hand. "It's just that, in terms of the law, it's best to leave things as absolutely clear as possible. But very well, everything is quite clear now. You can come by tomorrow afternoon to sign the will, the inventory list for your jewels, and the new rental contract," he said in a tone of voice that suggested our conversation was over. But then, as though he hoped I'd stay a while longer, he added: "I can give you further details. Or if there's anything else I can offer you. . . . "

"Thank you, maître Lebrun," I said, standing up. "It has been a pleasure to meet you in person. I need to think about the new lease. Five years. . . . I don't know. I may wish to return to Foix before that."

"The pleasure has been all mine. I know now that the captivating

339

image I've held of you in my imagination corresponds with the real person."

"In that case, you could paint me without my even being present."

"Perhaps," he said, running his intense eyes over my features. "But as I've already told you. . . . "

"Going back to painting could alleviate some of the pain of her loss," I replied, trying to prolong our meeting. I felt that, before going, I needed to be sure that he wasn't the man of my premonition.

"My pain will be with me as long as I live," he murmured, looking again at the painting.

"But you have a daughter, someone to live for."

"I won't deny that it's crossed my mind more than once to pick up a brush and paint our famous bridge, though it's been done a hundred times already. Also, to marry again. But if that is to happen, the moment has not yet arrived."

"I understand," I said, disappointed, and I turned slowly toward the door, giving him time to come open it for me. "One last thing: do you know what play is showing at the theater? I'd very much like to see something interesting before I leave France. I'd also appreciate the name of a good place to eat."

It was my final attempt. If he invited me out, Joseph Lebrun could well become my second husband.

"I can't tell you anything about the theater. I only rarely attend a show. You could ask my assistant, Ducharme, on your way out; he'll know, because his brother works as a prompter. As for a meal, I recommend La Chasse au Sanglier, just around the corner. Although, if you saw fit, I'd be honored to invite you to dine with me. But no, pardon me, I remember now that I can't. Another time," he said, retreating to his desk. "Tonight I must draw up Madame Larraz' will. She's quite ill, the poor thing."

(And now, Joseph Lebrun, as I raise you in my memory, I realize how close you were to opening a new destiny to me. Because we came so close that night to sharing a *cassoulet* with wine from Avignon, to talking and talking for hours, and I'd have watched your hands flutter about like skylarks until I felt them over mine, stretched out across the tablecloth, offering themselves up to your caress, your eyes fixed on my nipple, setting it firmly in your sights so that it couldn't escape you. Oh, Joseph Lebrun, what a pity that you weren't on my path, because it would have been so easy for me to leave it all on that night that never happened, to tell Uncle Charles that I'd be staying in Toulouse dressed as a bride because I'd found the One Foreseen, the Father Husband, and we'd have done so many things together, you'd have painted me and our children and Camille, and I'd have accompanied you on all your business trips, Montauban, Carcassonne, Montpellier, Nimes, Pierre taking us in his carriage, and we'd have spent Sundays in Foix and I'd have shown you my forest and my magical circle of mushrooms and dandelions, and we'd have spent holidays and Christmases there and, little by little, you'd have grown accustomed to living without the city, and, at first, you'd have stopped working on Mondays, and then Tuesdays and, over time, you'd have left Ducharme in charge of certain matters, and later, assuming that he'd marry Camille, since that's how things often work in the provinces, you'd have given him a share of the firm and you'd have dedicated yourself to painting the Ariège and the Garonne, the headlands and gorges, and the narrow valley of the Pyrenees, the village women with their headscarves and flowered aprons, the gypsies who tell fortunes and dance, showing off the colors of their many skirts, and the mule drivers and peddlers and smugglers with pistols at their waists and blunderbusses over their shoulders, who leave with scissors and blades and pocketknives from Marseilles and come back with peanut brittle and marzipan and handkerchiefs and sandals from Aragon. . . . And it wasn't only that night we lost. There was still the next day. More dressed-up and perfumed than ever, my hair done and re-done and with my bosoms almost completely exposed, I walked into your office to sign the papers. I know that, for a moment, you were on the verge of making a move. You kept silent as I signed the will and the inventory list for my jewels and, after the witnesses had gone, there remained only the matter of the lease for Foix. I know you had chosen this moment to move your pieces; I, too, had saved it to advance my own. I paused with pen in hand. "Five years without returning to Foix," I said, and raised my glance so that you might respond with a word, a gesture, at the very least, with your eyes. And I know that your plan to dissuade me began to take shape, that you considered taking the paper away from me and proposing any old thing, a café in the square, a carriage ride. But you came up short, you stood there with your mouth half-open, your hand in the air, your expression falling to pieces from pure impotence; you remained there, forever silent, watching as each letter of my name drew us further apart, standing before your dead wife, and she was more powerful than I. If only you knew, maître Lebrun, how close you were to changing my life!)

※

Françoise had put on weight. She'd given birth to a son scarcely a month earlier. Two girls were working in the front room of her house—filled with bolts of cloth, spools of thread, boxes of buttons, newsprint patterns, and dresses on hangers. In one corner, behind a curtain, a long mirror was affixed to the wall, and a stooped old woman was trying on a mourning dress. The next room was the bedroom, with an enormous walnut bed, quite old, surely from some inn from the time of Louis XIV. Next to it was the cradle. The baby slept on his side, red hair highlighted against the white of the sheet. To one side was a small courtyard with a fig tree and a few potted plants, clothes and diapers hung out to dry and, in the back, the tiny outhouse. The last room was the kitchen, with its pleasant odor of sautéing herbs and garlic. Françoise set a plate of bread and cheese on the table, along with some glasses and a bottle of local wine.

"What is the boy's name?"

"Pierre-Henri. Pierre, after his father and Henri, after . . . can you guess?" she smiled. "I don't have any milk. I'm raising him with goat's milk mixed with water. They say it's good for the stomach. He likes it."

"I'm happy to hear it. Look at you, Françoise, a mother! Can you believe it?"

"I was afraid at first. I never thought. . . . But now, Henriette, I'm very glad I had him. And Pierre's crazy about him. Really, we're not so bad off: he has his carriage; I have my shop and my son. You'd be surprised to know that I barely read anymore, not even the newspaper. I work ten times harder than before and I don't have time for anything. But it's all mine. And I owe that to you," she said, taking my hand and kissing it. "And now, some bad news: Pierre's been called up. He's to appear in four days. Many people have been drafted."

"That's how it is this time around," I said, almost to myself, thinking that, this time next year, there would scarcely be any men at all left in France. "You must resign yourself, Françoise. There's nothing to be done about it."

"Yes there is. Pierre is from Foix. He knows the Pyrenees. He has a brother who's a smuggler. He thinks he'd be better off in the mountains, in Andorra, or even on the Spanish side. His ideas have changed. He's gone back to being a republican. Oh, Henriette, I don't know what to advise him! He's asked for my opinion and I don't know what to tell him. What do you think?"

"Do what your heart tells you. But do consider that desertion is severely punished," I said, chewing on a piece of bread. "What time will Pierre be home? I don't want to leave without saying hello to him. Especially now."

"He almost always comes home for dinner. You'll eat with us, won't you?"

"I'm afraid not. I already have plans tonight with my uncle and Madame Cavent. We're meeting at La Chasse au Sanglier."

"They have the best *pâté de foie gras* in the city. Delanoix is an excellent cook. I didn't say anything before, but you should eat more. You look quite thin to me."

"It's the uniform. Also, wearing my hair in a pigtail sharpens my features."

"It's not the uniform or the hair. I've known you since you were a child."

"Well, the Russian campaign. . . . It's too long a story . . . and too sad. Do you remember Count Lubomirski?"

"How could I forget? He preferred English writers to my beloved Chateaubriand!"

"He's dead."

"Goddamn this war!" she said. "Well, now you see, I've decided! Pierre will desert!"

"But today, he's here," said Pierre from the kitchen doorway.

We talked for a while. Pierre had the latest news of what was going on in Spain. He'd met with his brother, Jacinthe, the night before at their mother's house. According to him, it would be impossible to win that war.

"Andalucía is already lost, and the guerrillas control the mountains in Aragon and Navarre, as I well know, since Jacinthe is

343

planning to join up with them. What's more, next month, the British will cross the Duero and begin their summer campaign. King Joseph is waiting for them in Valladolid, but he'll be defeated. He has the support of the wealthy, but not of the people. If I were you, madame, I wouldn't go to Madrid. Madrid is nothing. It's been taken before and it will be taken again."

The thought of finding myself caught up in another retreat worried me, although I thought that Pierre, or rather, his brother, was exaggerating the danger of the situation.

"But we have two hundred thousand soldiers in Spain!" I protested.

"I'm not sure how many there are," replied Pierre. "My brother says that they're scattered among the villages and along the roads because, otherwise, they'd lose all possibility of communication." Even if I didn't completely share his pessimism, it was enough to see his furrowed brow, his gray eyebrows so prolific they nearly covered his eyes, to understand that this business with Spain was serious, that the pleasant summer excursion my uncle had in mind was unrealistic. According to Pierre, the guerillas functioned something like the bands of Cossacks; they attacked convoys, robbed them, took prisoners, and retreated. From what he said, there were guerillas in every province throughout Spain. Suddenly I realized that it would be much better for Pierre to drive our coach than that carefree Italian who'd brought us to Toulouse. The advantages were obvious: aside from almost being family, he spoke Spanish and knew the road through the Pyrenees; what was more, his brother Jacinthe could prove quite useful to us in a difficult moment, on account of his relationships with the guerillas and smugglers. Since I was certain that Uncle Charles would agree with my reasoning, I proposed that he accompany us. He fell suddenly quiet, lowered his head, and began to crumble some crumbs of bread with his hands, calloused from so many years at the reins. It was Françoise who spoke first: "Do as you wish, but think of our son."

After emptying his glass and clearing his throat, Pierre looked at me.

"Madame Henriette, if you asked me to, I'd follow you straight into hell. But given my own choice, I'd prefer not to go with you. I have my own ideas. I'll share them with you, and you'll forgive me if they aren't the same as yours. The tyrant who governs us has been no better for France than the kings and nobles were. Those of us who are poor continue to be poor, and what's worse is that, for years now, we've been dying like flies everywhere from Russia to Spain. I believe in the Republic and in liberty for those who work the land and for those like Françoise and myself, who work to survive. I speak to you with my heart in my hands. I'd rather desert to the mountains than lift a finger in support of Napoleon." And, turning to Françoise, he said with a villager's pride: "*Parbleu*, I'll leave my ideals to my son!"

We dined at La Chasse au Sanglier. Madame Cavent wanted to sample a local dish, so we ordered the *cassoulet*. Naturally, I didn't tell Uncle Charles the details of my conversation with Pierre and Françoise. Why provoke a useless argument, since I knew that nothing would change his mind about Spain? Noticing me lost in thought, he interrupted his lively gastronomical conversation with Madame Cavent to tell me: "Forget about Russia. You must forget each campaign so that the next one will be like the first. We've already ruminated long enough about the retreat from Moscow. What was lost must remain buried. It's springtime. The day after tomorrow we'll be in the country with the best ham in the entire world."

∞

We spent only a few days in Barcelona because my uncle, greatly disappointed at the news of the crisis confronting King Joseph's throne and the nasty war Spain was waging against us, wanted to arrive in Madrid as soon as possible. The military hospital was on the western end of the city, in a huge Benedictine convent called Jonqueres, near the city's outer wall. Everything there was clean and in good order. There were a few cases of fever, and a handful of knife and bludgeon wounds, which lent the place the feel of a civilian hospital. Nevertheless, after we'd completed our rounds of the wards, the chief surgeon, a bespectacled man dressed in a smart uniform, said to my uncle: "Don't be fooled, inspector, we're as hated in Catalonia as in the rest of Spain. Despite the annexation decree, this is a far cry from France. Suffice to say that some of the new prefects are afraid to assume their posts. The munitions arsenal in Lérida was blown up a few months ago, and right here in Barcelona the garrison at the Citadel was poisoned. Just imagine, arsenic in the bread ration. Luckily, it didn't go any farther than vomiting and diarrhea, although it did keep us quite busy. Of course the city's been pacified and a few of the wealthy are collaborating with the Civil Government, but they do so with a grumble of discontent; the English blockade has ruinously paralyzed trade with America. Many a dawn finds a soldier stabbed or badly beaten and left in an alleyway. On the one hand, Intendant Chauvelin tries to win the Catalonians over by telling them that their customs are similar to ours. On the other hand, we've taken over their churches and convents to use as barracks, storehouses, and stables, forgetting that religion is ten times stronger here than in France. And so we are faced with two enemies: the Junta and the Holy Trinity. And that's not even taking into account the Virgin of Montserrat, who, in addition to working miracles, appears to be every bit as patriotic as her sister, the Virgin of Zaragoza."

"Are the roads to Madrid safe?" I asked, hoping that an answer in the negative might dissuade Uncle Charles from continuing with the trip.

"No Spanish road is safe at night; by day, one should only travel with a large military convoy. And even so, there are ambushes from time to time. I confess that I'm frightened every time I have to leave Barcelona. You'll soon see what I mean."

"Monsieur, you are speaking with veterans from the Russian campaign," said my uncle, irked and, after bidding the surgeon a cool farewell, we turned on foot toward the palace where we were staying.

Seeing his limp growing worse, I suggested we sit for a spell on a park bench. I'd never seen him so upset, not even during the worst moments in Russia. He dropped down onto the bench, his breathing ragged. After a while, he said: "Now then, while we were walking I was thinking. It seems that the roads to Madrid are not safe. . . . Come now, don't think you're fooling me. I know you don't want to go ahead with the trip. I don't blame you, of course. And there's Madame Cavent to think about as well. I'd imagined it completely differently. Things are not looking nearly as promising as I'd thought. Last night I spoke with the palace guard. You know, catching up on all the rumors. The Emperor ordered King Joseph to leave Madrid. The battles will take place in the north . . . Wellington. I know Wellington. A tough man to fight. I owe him my limp.

Madame Cavent is not made for war. It's my fault. I'd imagined it would be different. What can I tell you? I was wrong. But I'm a soldier. You know this. A soldier like Larrey, like Robert and Alfred were. Something that Madame Cavent simply cannot understand. The war is my life. That's why I've been so decorated. And I have my orders . . . Madrid. Get to Madrid and, from there, organize an inspection of the hospitals. It's not my concern whether or not King Joseph returns to Madrid. Although once we've defeated the British. . . . In any case, Henriette, do as you wish. I'll say the same to Madame Cavent. You could return together in my carriage. After all, Paris is Paris."

"Do as you wish," I repeated to myself. But what was it I wished? I certainly did not want to go to Madrid, an abandoned capital not worth the risk of the journey. Much less did I want to stay in Barcelona. If the war was to be waged in the north, the British could cut off our retreat, and I knew all too well how prisoners were treated. Instinct told me to go wherever King Joseph was. The lion's share of the army would be with him. If it were defeated, it would retreat over the Pyrenees, and I had no doubt that this would be the best way for me to return to France. On the other hand, if I were to succumb to my uncle's insinuations, I'd be forced to desert, dress as a woman, accompany Madame Cavent to Paris, abandon my final year of medical school and set about attending dances in search of a husband. No, thank you. My premonition that a man was awaiting me in Spain returned, stronger than ever. Would he be in Madrid after all? At last I broke my long silence: "If what you're trying to do is convince me to return to the Rue Saint-Honoré with Madame Cavent, I'm sorry to tell you that I won't do it. I am also a soldier and I, too, have my orders. My orders are to follow you. If you want to stay in Madrid, I'll stay there, although I think our place is with King Joseph's General Staff."

Very rarely have I seen a person's mood change so quickly. My uncle's face lit up with a smile that even Fauriel would have envied.

"You're a good soldier, Henriette," he said, throwing an arm over my shoulder. "With people like us, we might lose some battles, but never a war."

❧

After a journey replete with rumors of defeat, the majority of which we made in the company of a convoy transporting money from Valencia, we arrived in Madrid in the middle of May. Madame Cavent did not come with us. My uncle convinced her to stay in Barcelona, whose ramparts and fortifications guaranteed safe lodging.

Madrid reminded me a bit of Moscow. A Moscow without domes, naturally, but a city that, despite its palaces and boulevards, still had the feel of a large village. It was quite dirty and lethargic, the gardens untended, here and there a fragment of a mirror, a staved-in guitar, a pile of broken plates that testified to the successive sackings it had suffered—the French, English, and even the *Madrileños* themselves had vied with one another for its spoils. One needn't have been a local to see that disorder and improvisation reigned, a fact that immediately vexed my uncle.

When we presented ourselves to General Leval, the garrison commander, he treated us almost as though we were lunatics, making it plain that he found it difficult to believe that we had traveled all the way from Barcelona with the sole objective of organizing an inspection of hospitals throughout Spain.

"This never was Paris. But in any case, there's nothing to organize here except our retreat. The General Staff is in Valladolid, and any day now I'm expecting the order to join up with His Majesty's forces," he said acidly. But, realizing that we could be of some use to him in the evacuation effort, he added, addressing himself to my uncle: "Of course it goes without saying that we are in sore need of experienced men such as yourself. I'm naming you interim chief of medical services for my troops. You're in charge of requisitioning the wagons necessary to transport our sick and wounded, and do be sure that everything is carried out as efficiently as possible." And without further ado, he sent us off with an aide-de-camp to see General Hugo, who was acting governor.

The evacuation order came at the end of the month and, at dawn the following day, we began to march. My uncle's bad mood worsened with the arrival of the news that Wellington had taken Salamanca and was threatening both Madrid from the South and Valladolid from the North. By then, he scarcely spoke to me and I noticed, worried, that he was drinking continuously, to the point that, by nightfall, he was completely inebriated. He did almost nothing in the hospitals, limiting himself to inquiring after the number of wounded who were fit to be transported in the wagons provided by the governor. Once the ambulances were full, he disregarded everything else. He took a large carriage for himself in which, in addition to two hams and several cases of wine, he installed the widow of a royal functionary who, almost without preamble, had agreed to become his lover. Not having been invited to share his living space, I made room for myself in an ambulance carrying seven wounded men and a surgeon major traveling with his library. The last French families remaining in Madrid fell in behind Leval's infantry, as did many of the Spanish ministers and courtiers who'd served King Joseph. The locals called them "Frenchifieds," and hated them even more than they hated us, the invaders, as is usually the case with those who've betrayed their own country. They'd refused to leave the city with the convoys in March and April. They remembered all too well their miserable flight the previous summer, when Wellington had advanced on Madrid, and they'd delayed their departure until the last possible moment in the hope that their Exodus wouldn't be repeated. But it was to be repeated and now, traveling by coach, wagon, mule, and horse with their most prized possessions in tow— including manservants and wet nurses—they prepared, weeping and wailing, to cross the Guadarrama mountain pass. (Is it even worthwhile for me to give the details of that retreat, to revisit the insufferable slowness of the march, the overturned wagons by the side of the road, the children begging for food and drink, the uncertainty and the hardships we suffered over four long weeks? I think not. Even though I believe that history brazenly repeats itself, I've read enough to know that novels do not benefit from repetition. It might seem odd that I speak of novels and not memoirs. It's just that, after spending a week calmly reading over my papers—I've had no choice but to prescribe myself a restorative tonic and stretch out to rest by the window as though I were a plant in need of sunlight—I've reached the conclusion that this manuscript I'm so obsessively writing, cutting and re-cutting into parts and sections, rereading and editing, tuning and fine-tuning, is, definitively, a novel. To wit: I've left out hundreds of people, friends as well as enemies, who never managed to take shape as characters; I've omitted countless experiences, impressions, and episodes whose excessive foliage overshadowed certain passages I wished to highlight; I've imagined dialogues that perhaps never took place, and reconstructed meticulously detailed scenes based on memories by now so blurry they could well be taken for dreams; I've hidden, like one sweeping dirt under the rug, my hypocrisies and pettiness, anything that seemed imprudent to reveal. Haven't I silenced the fact that, one afternoon, to spite Robert, I went to bed with his best friend Constant, and that for many, many days I allowed Andrea and Piet Vaalser to lick me from head to toe in the dim light of my carriage, and that Fauriel and I, after living first as friends, ended up living as husband and wife until the very day of her desertion? I've silenced all of this, and so many other dubious adventures. And why have I done so? I've done it—I see it clearly now—in order to be the woman I never managed to be, to present myself as I wish you to see me, you who have bought my book for a moment's entertainment; I've done it in order to survive as the protagonist of my own story, in order to balance my behavior as though I were walking with a long pole across a tight rope, poised between two fatal falls, since in novels heroines are equally damned for being overly indecent and overly chaste; it's all a matter of a slight adjustment to the right or left, Madame Bovary or Jane Eyre, although deep down they're the same, paper acrobats, or better yet, obliging prostitutes sold for ten francs per read. And it's not that it's too late to turn myself in, exactly as I've been, to the tribunal of the printed word. I've saved all my rough drafts right here in this drawer, and it would be easy for me to resuscitate the material I've censured. It's just that, without being aware of it, I've chosen a course that adheres more closely to fiction than to my reality, and I see no reason to backtrack now. I'd rather adorn myself with the trappings of a fable and unfold myself along the lines of *Tom Jones* or *Gil Blas*, than display the inconsistencies and irremediable complexity of a flesh-and-blood person. In the end, the only spontaneous lines that shall go to the printer will be the ones I wrote when, expelled from Havana, I was traveling to New Orleans; notes that, like my tiny portrait of Aunt Margot, seem to have a will of their own that insists they not be lost, that follow me stubbornly across the years and dusty roads. In honor of their perseverance, I shall give them to Milly to copy down. I'll decide later if they'll go at the beginning or at the end of my manuscript.)

20

WITH THE BRITISH FORCES ADVANCING, Valladolid was no longer defensible and King Joseph determined that our convoy, joined now with his artillery trains and numerous other wagons—including those carrying his personal fortune—would follow his troops to Burgos. But it proved impossible to defend that city as well and, after taking on more wagons of refugees, ammunition, and provisions, we continued on toward Miranda, on the banks of the Ebro. The king set up headquarters there, but, fearing for the safety of our enormous caravan, he ordered us to keep moving toward the northeast and to set up camp on the outskirts of the village of Vitoria, on the edge of the Basque Country. I took the announcement of this new retreat as good news: not only would I be getting closer to France, but, consulting the map that I carried in my rucksack, I saw that the road to Bayonne went right through Vitoria.

A curious incident befell Uncle Charles on the way from Valladolid to Burgos. The convoy had stopped for the night and my uncle came down from the coach-box to have dinner with Doña Pilar, his traveling companion. When he opened the carriage door, he was surprised to find it empty and dark inside, though he quickly realized that his lover must have gone to the side of the road to relieve herself. So he lit the candles and began to arrange some cold cuts on his folding table. But the minutes kept ticking by, and still, Doña Pilar didn't return. Then, while he was looking for a bottle of wine beneath the seat, he noticed that his friend had left the dress she'd been wearing on top of her valise. This did give him pause, but he still wasn't overly concerned. It was obvious that Doña Pilar intended to continue traveling with him, otherwise, she'd have taken her clothing and valise along with her. Finally, after he'd finished the bottle of wine, he decided to ask a postilion working for a "frenchified" family traveling in the column. To his dismay, the man told him that about two hours earlier, while my uncle was climbing down from the coachbox, he'd seen a nun leaving from the other side of the carriage. Uncle Charles went from carriage to carriage inquiring after Doña Pilar, but received only threats and insults for having awoken their occupants. As he was too worried to sleep, he walked alongside the column until he came across a Royal Guard squadron bivouacked under a tree. The only clear piece of information he could gather was that, some distance ahead, and moving in the opposite direction, were several wagons carrying priests and nuns who'd chosen to leave their convents rather than face the risks of the British occupation. Along past midnight, my uncle came to the wagons carrying these devout souls, but when he tried to open the canvas covers enclosing them, he was beaten back by stick-wielding priests and their servants. It wasn't until arriving in Burgos that he learned the truth, or, at least, the clerical version: Doña Pilar was, in reality, a devout nun who, according to the ancient priest he'd asked, had lost her mind amid the upheaval of her convent's evacuation. Having regained her composure, she'd repented her irrational behavior and had returned, like a contrite lamb, to her traveling congregation.

And it was also as a contrite lamb that Uncle Charles came to me in Vitoria.

"I don't know where to begin, Henriette. The older I get, the more stupid I become," he said, hanging his head, after bidding me a good morning. "I curse the moment I met that woman. If I've put off coming to see you it's only out of shame. Just think of it, Madame Cavent in Barcelona. . . . So far away, the poor thing. And you. . . . You whom I love like a daughter. What you must think of me!"

He went on, interrupting himself every ten or twelve words to call himself a miserable idiot, telling me all about his adventure with Doña Pilar, from the afternoon he'd met her in an inn in Madrid, until the moment of her disappearance.

"It sounds like a story fit for the stage," I said, to diminish the matter's importance. The truth was, I couldn't blame him too much for having abandoned me. I knew that his behavior was a result of frustration and that, sooner or later, he'd come looking for me. Further, though I'd missed him, it hadn't been at all unpleasant in the ambulance, thanks to the wounded men's good humor and the surgeon's library. "But tell me, Uncle. Wasn't there anything about her that reminded you of a nun?" I asked, intrigued.

"More like a whore. If it's true that that fine pearl is a nun, she has a lot of Our Father's and Hail Mary's to pray before she'll be back in God's good graces."

⬥

After two or three days camped under a suffocating sun behind Vitoria's city walls, I learned happily that King Joseph and Jourdan's troops had abandoned the front at the Ebro and were taking up positions in the hills to the north and west of the city, including at our rear, along the road to Bayonne. I was now certain that the King's plan was to retreat to France in an orderly fashion without giving battle to the English.

"What do you think?" I asked, passing the map to my uncle.

"I think that, if what you're saying were true, the Emperor would have to dethrone King Joseph for having lost a good part of his army in Spain. No, Henriette. The war is not yet over for us," he said, spreading the map across the seat on the opposite side of the carriage. "We have troops in Navarre, in Aragon, and in Catalonia. If we retreat from the Basque Country now, Wellington will descend from the north and destroy them all in a few short months."

"But, Uncle Charles," I said, refusing to be convinced, "you won't deny that the war here is lost. We've done nothing but retreat since the moment we arrived in Madrid."

"It's true," he sighed, "but in the future, we won't be fighting to win Spain, but rather, to defend France. Although we'll lose anything we have left here, the time has come to make the enemy pay dearly for any attempt to cross the Pyrenees. Otherwise, Wellington's troops and their allies will invade us with full force across the Bidasoa, the Maya, the Roncesvalles, and the Jonquera," he said, pointing on the map to the various passes through the Pyrenees. "Luckily, the Emperor is winning battles in the east and he'll soon extract peace with the Prussians and the Russians. Then he'll send us a hundred thousand men to put an end to this matter. What's

353

more, the Emperor himself will come with them. As I've said, my opinion is that those troops you see taking up defensive positions will confront Wellington tomorrow or the day after."

"You'll forgive me if I doubt that," I said, gesturing toward the disorganized spectacle of the wagons surrounding ours, in whose shade the women sat fanning themselves, while the men, the sleeves of their sweat-soaked shirts rolled up, played cards or dozed. "The fugitives' wagons are all mixed up with the artillery trains, the ambulances, and the provisions and munitions carts. The convoy is in complete chaos. If they were expecting a battle, there wouldn't be such disorder and the cannons would already be moving out to set up batteries. You'll see: the order to continue the retreat will arrive any minute."

Deep in thought, my uncle didn't reply. A while later, after single-handedly finishing off a second bottle of wine, he said: "I'm going to see what news I can find out from the General Staff. There will be a battle and I should know what preparations are being made to attend to the wounded."

"It's very hot, Uncle. The sun won't be good for you. Why not wait until early tomorrow morning?"

"It's only a short walk," he replied, pointing toward Vitoria's two tall bell towers. Even so, the simple act of climbing down from the carriage left him panting.

"I'll go," I said anxiously, seeing how sweaty and red-faced he was. "Stay here and guard our things," I added, jumping down.

"You stay. This is my business," he growled.

"Your health is also my business," I replied, pushing him gently toward the carriage door.

"*Parbleu*! I said I'm going!" he exclaimed, pulling away from me.

"As you wish, Uncle. But please, go slowly."

Half an hour later, I saw him coming back, his arms draped over two artillerymen's shoulders, his feet dragging, his face parched and purple with pain.

"Bleed me, Henriette! You must bleed me!" he gasped, as we lay him down on the grass. "It's . . . my heart," he murmured, just before fainting.

❧

"It was quite thrilling to meet your old friend," said Milly as we reached the hotel. "I expect you'll describe the encounter in your novel; he's a character of some importance, after all."

And so, my dear Milly, as you'll see, I've decided to humor you. You are my first reader and this gives you as much right to suggest that I add pages as to remove them. Although, were I to use you as my sole guide, my book would be longer than the *Thousand and One Nights*. In any case, perhaps that chance encounter has gotten me back in the game, causing me to jump, like a knight on a chessboard, from a white square to a black one, to the square of the improbable, the square of France in New York. It happened last Monday. It was a sunny afternoon of clear blue skies. The breeze was inviting and I didn't resist Milly's suggestion: "Madame, what do you think of taking a carriage ride through Central Park? And you should get out and walk a bit, too. You know better than anyone that exercise is good for your leg."

It had been days since I'd been out in a carriage, but not even the traffic and the many buildings under construction—this city grows bigger by the day—could rouse my curiosity. My attention was continually drawn away from the scaffolds and bricklayers with their wheelbarrows, lapsing into thoughts of the past as I tried to put my confused memories of Spain into some semblance of order. Before we reached the park, we got down, asked the driver to follow us, and started walking along 5th Avenue. As we were crossing 59th Street, I felt a sharp pain in my leg and I stopped, under the pretext of watching some workers who were planting bushes at the park's entrance. As I rested, leaning on my cane, I heard someone speaking French off to my left. I turned my head. It was a young man of not more than twenty, a good-looking boy with the air of a romantic poet. The man he was speaking to could well have been his grandfather, and oddly, when I looked closely at him, his lean face and prominent, crooked nose seemed familiar to me. Much time had passed, of course, but I thought I recognized Petit. Could that old gentleman really be him, or was the resemblance simply coincidental? It was impossible really; Petit was dead. Or, what amounted to the same thing—he'd been taken prisoner by the Cossacks. But who besides Petit could have that long, twisted nose, and be speaking French in that same nasally voice? A Petit with hunched shoulders, to be sure, but wearing a top hat and a dignified bearing. The traffic lessened at that moment, and I saw that they were about to cross the street. Since, at my age, I no longer let opportunities pass me by or worry about making mistakes, I decided to head over to him.

"Monsieur!" I called out. Both men stopped and turned to look at me. "Monsieur Antoine Petit?"

He didn't recognize me, of course, but he approached me nonetheless. I felt my emotions rise as I saw that he'd responded to my call, and I realized that I had no idea how to even begin to explain to him that I was the same Enrique Fuenmayor who'd been alongside him during the Russian campaign.

"Madame?" he said, looking at me fixedly, searching his memory for some recollection of my face.

"We knew each other when we were young," I said in French, still shocked that he could truly be Petit.

"It's been so long!" he exclaimed, pretending to recognize me out of pure politeness. "I'm pleased you're well."

"Not as well as I'd like to be," I said, half-raising my cane. "Are you visiting or do you live here?"

"I left France many years ago. We met in Strasbourg, didn't we?" he said, feigning certainty. Milly, without letting go of my arm, turned to us.

"Emily Barrett," I introduced her. The young man's name was Daniel Petit.

"He's my grandson. He's studying medicine," he said with the pride of my old comrade-in-arms. "A chip off the old block."

"Are you still practicing?" I asked, to prolong the conversation.

"I left medicine some time ago. At the beginning of the Civil War I volunteered as a surgeon in a Union military hospital. But when I realized that my hand was no longer steady, I returned to my business. I sell French-made medical instruments and equipment. My shop is near Madison Square. In any event, madame, I am at your disposal," he said with an easy fluency quite different from the aggressive way he'd spoken years before. Clearly, life had smoothed the rough edges from his old temperament.

"I'm happy that you've done so well, but . . . " I said, and hesitated, deciding if I should reveal my identity to him. "But we didn't meet in Strasbourg. It was in Russia."

"In Russia? In Russia. . . . I really don't remember. . . . In Russia, you say? Of course! You were one of the actresses in Moscow!

We met one night in a village on the other side of the Berezina. Isn't that right? Of course I remember you," he said, taking me for the young actress he'd courted in Zembin, the one he'd given his wolfskin.

"We had a friend in common. Enrique Fuenmayor."

"Yes, yes, Fuenmayor. I haven't forgotten him," he said, smiling sincerely now, perhaps remembering the adventures and travails we'd shared. "We served with the General Staff. He was from Havana and sometimes spoke to me in Spanish, which infuriated me. We were always arguing, but he was a good person. Very competent, to be sure. . . . Fuenmayor. . . . What could have become of him? He disappeared unexpectedly. Perhaps he went into the woods searching for firewood and was left behind. Surely he died, like so many others. What a catastrophe Russia was! A total catastrophe, and all for naught," he lamented. "I was fortunate. I was captured by the Cossacks, but I saved the *hetman's* son's life and was kept on as their doctor until the armistice was signed. You must have stories yourself. We can both count ourselves lucky to have made it to our age. But tell me about your life. How long have you been in New York? I see that you have some difficulty walking. . . ."

While Petit was recommending a complicated treatment of baths, massages, and daily exercises that had worked wonders for him, I realized that it wouldn't be fair to tell him that I was Enrique Fuenmayor. I shouldn't erase the fine memories he had of me as a man and colleague and replace it with the dubious image of a female impostor. Seeing that our conversation was to continue, Milly moved discreetly away and began to watch the workmen at their labors. The young man, however, remained at his grandfather's side. He'd been listening to our conversation with great interest.

"If you only knew. . . . Enrique Fuenmayor didn't die. I saw him in Paris not more than a year ago," I said, determined now to keep my secret.

"What are you saying!" exclaimed Petit, almost at a shout, and he raised his hand to his mouth as if trying to excuse his surprise.

"It was a chance encounter, like ours today. We were staying in the same hotel. He's quite well off, although retired now. His sons run the business these days . . . something to do with . . . I think with ships or with trading. I don't remember exactly. He lives in Marseilles. It was quite moving to talk with him. We'd been good friends, Madame Fusil, Fuenmayor and me, as you'll no doubt recall. Don't you find it incredible what's happened to me? Fuenmayor in Paris and now you in New York, after so much time knowing nothing of either of you?"

"More than incredible! What a small world, indeed!" he said, amazed. "Now that I know he's alive, I'd love to see him. What a pity we're so far away. There are not many of us left from those times."

"I'm certain that it would please him a great deal to see you as well. Perhaps he thought you were dead. Naturally, I'll write to him to tell him that I saw you and that you're in good health. In any event, I'd love to talk more with you. What would you say to meeting in the dining room at my hotel on Saturday? I could reserve a table for seven o'clock. I live in the Fifth Avenue Hotel. In case you don't remember, my name is Henriette. Henriette Faber-Cavent."

"Magnificent. I'm grateful for the invitation, madame. It will be a pleasure," he said, bowing politely.

"I'd like to meet your family."

"That won't be possible. I'm a widower and Danny's mother, who's French like us, is with my granddaughter in Bordeaux. A matter of her inheritance. Of course, I'm quite worried about them. I don't know if you're read the newspaper today; France and Prussia have mobilized their armies. Well, we shall see. Perhaps it won't go any farther than that."

"From your lips to God's ear, monsieur. I hate war."

"As do I. Danny's father, my only son. . . . My only son died in the Civil War. At Fredericksburg. Of course you know how things go when the enemy wins the battle. His remains were never found," he said, not allowing his sadness at speaking of his son, a sadness I could sense inside him, to alter his affable expression. "I never tire of telling Danny about the horrors of war. It would break my heart to ever see him in a uniform."

"I'm going to be a children's doctor," said Danny with a smile. "That way you won't have to worry. The only things that interest me about war are the stories you tell me."

"In that case, you should come with your grandfather to have dinner with me," I replied. "Perhaps you'd be curious to know what it was like to cross the Berezina."

"Thank you, madame," said Danny. "My uncle has told me about his life with Napoleon, but I'd find it fascinating to hear what you remember of the Russian campaign: Smolensk, Borodino, the burning of Moscow, the Berezina. That's right, isn't it?" he said, turning to his grandfather. I liked his attitude. His French was very good, although with a slight English accent.

Finally, we exchanged cards and said goodbye.

On the way back to the hotel, moved by my meeting with Petit, I began to cry.

"Is something the matter, madame?"

"It's just life, Milly. Life is complicated. Sometimes even happiness hurts."

☙

Uncle Charles awoke from his deep slumber at the sound of the dry tac-tac of musket fire. After bleeding him twice, I hadn't dared move him. He'd spent the night stretched out on the grass next to the carriage, with me watching over him, taking his pulse every little while, and changing the compresses on his forehead.

"Did the battle start?" he asked me after drinking a glass of watered-down wine.

"I don't think so. Perhaps just a skirmish. But tell me: does your chest still hurt?"

"Almost not at all; the worst of it has passed. I just have a small pain here," he said, laying his hand on the upper part of his stomach. "I see that you bled me in both arms."

"You're having a heart attack, uncle."

"I know. It runs in the family. But I'll survive this one, you'll see," he said, trying to smile and struggling to lift his head from the cushions I'd taken from the carriage.

"Don't try to get up. Your heart must remain as calm as possible. You know this better than I do. Let me take your pulse," I said, taking out my watch. "I need to bleed you again. I'm going to look for the basin and the lancet."

"Wait until midday, my girl. It's better to bleed me during the heat of the day. How long ago did the battle start?"

"I don't think it's a battle. I haven't heard even a single cannon shot. The sound of the musket fire is coming from the hills. I heard

359

the first shots around eight o'clock, about fifteen or twenty minutes ago. It must be a skirmish with some band of guerrillas."

"It's possible. . . . I feel weak, Henriette. I think I'll close my eyes. The light is bothering me. Let me rest until it's time for the bloodletting."

I took advantage of Uncle Charles being asleep to go to the ambulances, all the way on the other side of the encampment. I needed a stretcher and someone to help me. I wanted to settle my uncle inside the carriage; even if it wouldn't protect him from the heat, it would at least keep him out of the sun, not to mention that the order to move out could come at any time. Ricart, the surgeon with whom I'd traveled since Madrid, offered to help me. He told me that we were fighting Wellington's troops, a fact he'd learned from an aide-de-camp whose mission it was to move several pieces of artillery into positions in the west. We agreed that the British attack wouldn't amount to much. There were more than one hundred cannons in our convoy, all of them immobile and mixed in with the fugitives' vehicles. Nevertheless, the noise of the battle was getting nearer, which meant we were losing ground. The sound was no longer coming only from the mountains, but now also from the plains and, now and again, as we wove through the wagons with the stretcher, we were met with the acrid smell of gunpowder. This change in our situation raised alarm among the people in the convoy, especially among the "frenchifieds," who started collecting their tables, chairs, and blankets from the grass, saddling their horses, and gathering their families into the wagons. Unfortunately, because we were camped behind the city, we couldn't see anything that was happening on the other side of it. Then, just as we were arriving at our carriage, the artillery fire began.

"The ball has begun," said my uncle after Ricart, two Spanish guards and I managed to get the stretcher settled on the carriage's seats.

"I should get back to my wounded," said the diligent Ricart, marching off with scarcely a goodbye and almost being run over by one of the carts that had already started off down the road.

"Uncork a bottle, Henriette. I'm thirsty," said my uncle, his voice hoarse. Seeing my hesitation, he added: "Don't make me beg. You'd do well to open one for yourself as well, since I fear that, as soon as the order to retreat comes, we'll find ourselves in a predicament just like at the Berezina: all of the carts converging along the same road." I carried out his wish and we began to drink in silence, a silence all the more noticeable against the sustained thundering of the cannons. After a while, he said: "If we lose the battle you must promise me something. Many of the wagons will be captured. It's quite possible that we, too, will share this fate. Doña Pilar's valise is underneath the seat . . . or whatever her name was. Promise me that you'll dress as a woman and—"

"Don't even think about it, uncle!" I interrupted him. But I didn't have time to explain myself: the order to retreat had been given somewhere in the encampment and, spreading out, the wagons began heading toward the road. As soon as I climbed up into the coachbox, I knew there was nothing to be done. In front of me was an impenetrable mass comprised of all manner of vehicles. If I tried to move forward, the horses would trip over other carriages' horses, putting me in danger of being crushed in a heap of broken wheels and suffocating animals. To make matters worse, hundreds of stragglers had come down from a nearby hill and, like birds of prey, were descending upon the wagons intent on plunder. Following my instincts, I tried to steer the wagon to the right, moving as far as possible from the bottleneck of vehicles blocking the road. A tremendous screaming made me turn my head: several squadrons of light cavalry, breeching the walls of Vitoria, were coming toward us, the sun glinting off their sabers. They were English Hussars. Obviously, our center had not held, and Wellington had unleashed them on the rearguard. Panic spread instantly. Powerless to escape on wheels, both "frenchifieds" and soldiers leapt to the ground and, running as fast as they could, scattered toward the scrubby hills that surrounded the plain on the Pyrenees side. Terrified, since no one knew better than I the Hussars' mission with respect to an army in retreat, I raised the whip and lashed the horses' flanks and heads with all my might. But the terrain, in addition to being rocky, was uphill, and the poor animals' hooves slipped, scarcely advancing. Finally, they came to a halt at the base of a rock wall. When I climbed down from the coachbox, I saw that many of the English had dismounted alongside the abandoned wagons, surely in order to pillage them. My nerves were so undone by fear that my trembling hands made it impossible for me to open the carriage door. Uncle Charles kicked it open from the inside. I found him sitting up on the cot, his pistol in his hand.

"*Merde*! I thought you were an Englishman!," he shouted. "I thought you'd escaped. Now we're really in a dire situation," he said, grimacing in irritation and lowering his pistol. "If we try to defend ourselves, they'll kill us."

"They'll kill us anyway," I said, and burst into convulsive sobs.

◈

Although it's never easy to praise one's enemy, I must acknowledge that the English soldier of my era was the least cruel of all the warring nations, including the French and her allies. On second thought though, I shouldn't extend this laudable judgment to the entirety of British people. In reality, I should limit my opinion to the soldiers fighting under Wellington, since I can't actually speak about the others. Perhaps the fine behavior of those Hussars who took me prisoner had to do with what Christopher once told me: "What happens, Ketty, my darling, is that Wellington, instead of flattering us, insults us continuously, even after we've won a battle. As for us officers, he admonishes us with irony and indifference, making it quite plain that we're still a long way from being as gentlemanly as he is. He tells the common soldiers to their faces that they're the dregs of England, accusing them of being lazy, cowardly, stupid, undisciplined thieves. The result is that, out of the mixture of hatred and respect that we have for him, we strive to behave as though we were members of the royal family; that is, we take our revenge, telling him with our actions that we are not lesser men than he."

As it happened, when a squadron of Hussars arrived at our carriage, the lieutenant in charge used one of Doña Pilar's shawls to carefully wrap up the money and gold items with which we were trying to buy our lives. I say "trying," because it proved unnecessary to pay for them. All prisoners were treated with consideration, to such an extent that many of the women were allowed to leave in their own carriages. As for the "Frencifieds," not only were they set free, but they also enjoyed the compassion of Wellington himself, who wrote letters to the Spanish authorities begging that they not take reprisals against them. The only dead prisoner was Monsieur Thiébault, the king's treasurer, who had the unfortunate idea of trying to defend the hundred thousand pesos he'd been transporting in his private safe. The plunder taken in that battle was enormous:

362

forty-five million francs, equal to the entire payroll of the French army; King's Joseph's treasury, in addition to enormous sums of money, included the Crown jewels and numerous works by Rafael, Murillo, el Greco, Rembrandt, Velázquez, and other great masters. Added to this were more than one hundred and fifty cannons, hundreds of provisions wagons and ammunition stores, thousands of carriages, horses, and mules, and everything of value that the "Frencifieds" had been carrying.

Five days after our capture, after Uncle Charles and I had already been transferred to the hospital at Miranda de Ebro, I was informed that I would serve there as surgeon until a peace accord was reached with France.

21

OUR FIRST ENCOUNTER WAS DISADVANTAGEOUS for both of us; Christopher was overwhelmed with the task of admitting four thousand wounded into the hospital, and I was beside myself with worry over Uncle Charles' heart. My nerves had settled somewhat during the journey to Miranda and, satisfied with the treatment we were receiving at the hands of the British—almost none of them spoke French, but many could make themselves understood in Spanish—I was no longer the child overcome with emotion (perhaps the frightened little girl from Lausanne?) who arose within me during times of great stress.

"Surgeon Major Cavent is recovering from a heart attack," I said in Spanish to Christopher who was, at that time, nothing more to me than a tall man wearing a bicorn hat, gray pants, and a red frockcoat adorned with white fringe. "I implore you to treat him with consideration. His condition is still critical."

"I have thousands of men in my hospital," he responded, scarcely looking at me. "Speak with Doctor Thorn."

"Zorne?" I repeated, unable to pronounce the name properly.

"Thorn, sir!" he exclaimed impatiently, indicating a short and prematurely balding man who was issuing orders to a group of assistants in one corner of the room. That said, he dismissed me with a nod and went off to inspect the next ward.

Our second encounter was more promising. Uncle Charles had been settled in and I'd received my instructions from Surgeon Major Thorn as to my duties and responsibilities, when an orderly came looking for me in the ward where I was attending to a hundred or so wounded Frenchmen.

"The Director wishes to speak with you," he said.

I followed him through the building's beautiful cloister and, after climbing a steep and narrow staircase with a single banister that rose into the cupola, he showed me into a semicircular chamber awash in sunshine streaming through a large skylight. A medium-sized telescope perched on a tripod pointed out from one of the two windows. In one corner was a washbasin on a sideboard, a cot, and a lantern; near the opposite corner, an armoire and a traveling trunk; in the center of the room, two backless leather chairs and a sturdy table of black wood, upon which sat books, papers, and two copper candlesticks. He stood alongside the wall to my right, arms crossed behind his back, examining the rows of books visible behind the glass of a bookcase.

"Good morning, Señor Faber," he said in Spanish, noting my arrival. "I've sent for you because, in our profession, a watch is an indispensible object. Thorn has told me that you've lost yours."

"I gave it to the Hussars who captured me, Director."

"I guessed as much," he said, walking pensively over to his table. "Please, take a seat," he added. "I've spoken to General Grant and his boys have returned a few watches. They've just arrived in this box here. See if you recognize yours."

He turned the box over carefully onto the table. There were more than twenty watches. I spread the pile out with the palm of my hand. First, I saw Uncle Charles' stopwatch, easily recognizable for its large face. Then I saw mine, of Swiss make. I separated it from the rest.

"I'm very grateful. I never thought I'd get it back," I said, a bit surprised at the courtesy of a man supposed to be my enemy.

"You may take Señor Cavent's as well. If it's not in this batch, take the one you think best, and offer him my apologies. As for any of your other belongings: money, jewels," he said with a shake of his head. "Spoils of war. Please believe me that I am very sorry."

"Thank you, Director," I said, perplexed by his amiability.

"I'd prefer that you called me by my name," he said, placing the watches back in the box one by one. "Moving on to another subject, I understand that you know Doctor Ricart."

"Has he been taken prisoner as well?" I asked, surprised, since I hadn't seen a single other French doctor in the hospital.

"He's among the wounded. Nothing serious. The ambulance he'd been traveling in lost a wheel. He broke a heel when he fell out.

You haven't seen him because you're only in charge of the serious cases. He's in one of the basement wards."

"Well yes, of course. I know him. We traveled from Madrid to Vitoria together."

"So he told me. Surely you've seen the many books he brought with him from Madrid."

"An entire library," I affirmed.

"Grant's boys aren't much for reading. What I mean to say is that the books were left behind on the battlefield. Fortunately, it hasn't rained and perhaps they may yet be recovered."

"I hope so," I said, remembering the multitudes of books I'd seen alongside the roads in Russia.

"In any event, seeing that our cavalry was approaching, your friend took a few of the books and put them in his traveling case."

"I'm glad to hear it," I said, amazed at the turn the conversation had taken.

"Yesterday afternoon, as I was making my rounds on his ward, I saw that he was reading an interesting book: *Del ingenioso hidalgo Don Quijote de la Mancha*. I wonder if you're familiar with it."

"One of the first books I read in Spanish."

"Unforgettable, don't you think?" he said, looking at me intently, pausing so that I could corroborate his words. "Cervantes and Shakespeare. No one writes like them anymore."

"Indeed," I managed to say. "Unsurpassable authors, each in his own right."

"I'm very interested in the volume your friend has, and I'd like to borrow it for a few days, or a least a couple of hours. It's a first edition. Naturally, I told him this, but he's formed an erroneous judgment as to my intentions. He suspects me of wishing to steal his book. What nonsense! If you will help me to convince him otherwise, I'd be most grateful."

"I'll do what I can, Señor O'Gorman."

"Do you speak English, Mister Faber?"

"No, sir."

"Oh, I thought I'd understood that you'd read Shakespeare."

"Only in translation. Even so, his works are magnificent."

"Once our work settles into a routine, we'll find time to chat a bit more. I'll see you soon, Señor Faber. It's been a pleasure," he said, standing up and extending his hand.

That night, after I'd finished my rounds on the ward, I thought about how much of Alfred there was in him. Even though they were different physically—to begin with, Christopher was forty-two years old and, in addition to being not a slender man, his blond hair had already begun to turn gray at the temples—he shared Alfred's love of literature, his careful manner of dress, and his habit of expressing himself with the utmost respect and correctness. Nevertheless, Alfred's courtesy could, at times, wound in its disdainfulness, something I did not detect in my captor's character. I wondered if Christopher O'Gorman would be the man of my premonition. I decided not. And not so much because I'd seen a wedding ring on his finger, but rather because at no time had I experienced the burning attraction I'd felt for Robert, and neither his voice nor his words had elicited any feelings toward him beyond friendship.

❧

Uncle Charles took a turn for the worse in the middle of July. Christopher took him on as his patient and, for a short time, he seemed to improve. His blue eyes shone more brightly than ever and absolutely everything made him laugh. But there was a false note to his laughter, a shrill, bitter note, an ill omen that spread through his guffaws until ending in a coughing fit.

One morning he was dead.

I closed his eyelids myself.

❧

Yesterday I had the pleasure of dining with Petit and his grandson, an enchanting young man, to be sure, who couldn't take his eyes off Milly, causing her to blush. We scarcely spoke of Russia. We spent the evening discussing the alarming news reported over the past few days in the newspapers. After a series of foolish telegrams, myopic speeches, and communiqués, France and Prussia are preparing to attack one another like a pair of enraged bulls. Because it will prove impossible to find a real justification for the conflict, in the future it will be said that it was one of the stupidest wars in history. But aren't most wars stupid? One province loses its flag and years later gets it back. Today an oasis or a river is won in Africa and tomorrow a port or an island is lost in the Caribbean. Borders have advanced and retreated throughout the centuries, but the French go on being French, the British go on being British, and the Germans, German, each with their own languages, religions, and customs. Europe has changed very little since the Crusades. Thousands of battles and millions of dead have made history so that the maps might remain almost unchanged. And even so, I ask myself, what would my life have been without war?

❧

Christopher's declaration of love—if one could call it that—was so unexpected that it seemed to fall from the sky like a piece of the moon. It happened at summer's end, by which time our friendship had already grown quite close, just when, through his telescope, we could see grapes being harvested bountifully across the river. We were drinking port in his room. Wellington had invaded France from the Biadosa and Christopher, filling our glasses, asked me: "What will you do when the war ends, Señor Faber?"

"The war? I think the war will last quite a while longer, Señor O'Gorman."

"I don't think so. Five, six months at the most. All of Europe is descending upon Napoleon."

"Six months is long enough," I said, thinking that he was mistaken, that France would fight with the same tenacity as it had during the revolutionary wars.

"Do you know what I'd like to do? I'd request a leave and I'd go to La Mancha. I'd try to follow Don Quixote's route, according to the information Cervantes provides," he said without raising his eyes from his glass. His words did not surprise me. Don Quixote appeared to be his sole passion. I had served as intermediary between him and Ricart, arranging for the latter to sell his copy of the book at a very good price. Christopher told me once that he'd like to translate the work into English, as the available editions were not one hundred percent loyal to the original. I had no doubt that he'd succeed. I knew enough Spanish to appreciate that his was not just fluent, but erudite as well.

"I think that would be a very interesting trip, very creative. I,

369

on the other hand, do not want any more adventures. I'd return to Paris. I still have one year of school left to obtain my medical diploma."

"Yes, of course. Although, in your case, it would be a mere formality. We're all in agreement here that you are an excellent surgeon."

"Thank you, Señor O'Gorman. As you know, in Russia I had excellent teachers. And, unfortunately, a great deal of practice."

"Such are the rules of our profession. You should take comfort in the thought that, thanks to the lives you were unable to save, to-day we have better weapons with which to combat death."

He stood up, walked over to the telescope, and put his eye to the lens. "The moon is beautiful. What a pity we can't know what her other face looks like," he said distractedly. A few minutes later, still at the telescope, he added with the same neutral inflection in his voice: "I don't suppose you'd be inclined to postpone your studies for a few months."

I didn't know how to respond. The war could go on for another year or two and my studies weren't exactly foremost in my mind. I was primarily concerned with Madame Cavent, awaiting news in Barcelona, my name and Uncle Charles' on the list of the missing. I had written to her, of course. It was just that the city was still under French occupation and it was extremely possible that my letter had never arrived.

"I'd very much appreciate having you as a traveling companion," he continued without moving his head from the apparatus.

"I don't think it would be feasible," I said, recovering from my surprise. What did that man want from me? Why had he singled me out among the other doctors in the hospital, why did he constantly invite me to dine in his room under the pretext of looking at the planets or singing the praises of Cervantes and Shakespeare, me, a prisoner of war, separated from him by such enormous distances (nation, rank, age) that not even his telescope would be enough to render us equals in size? Could it be that he was attracted to me as a man? Rumor had it in the Grande Armée that the British were quite given to pederasty, even married men with children, as was the case with him. Abruptly, I decided to nip this in the bud, to stop his attempts to draw me closer right then and there. I stood from my chair and picked up my hat. "Furthermore, monsieur, I don't much fancy the idea of playing the role of Sancho Panza," I added dryly in French, a language he understood.

"Sancho Panza?" he said, moving away from the telescope. "It has never crossed my mind that you could embody our dear Sancho," he smiled. "If I've asked you to come with me, it's for another reason."

"What reason?" I asked defiantly, prepared to break off the friendship he'd extended to me.

"Now that you've made reference to *Don Quixote*, I'll tell you. You are my Dulcinea."

Not saying a word, I turned my back to him and headed for the door.

"Don't go, Madame Renaud. We should talk tonight."

Hearing my name, I stopped dead, my hand on the doorknob.

"Your uncle told me your story. He knew he was going to die and he honored me with his trust. He was afraid for you. Don't go, I beg of you. At least allow me to tell you face to face that, since the moment I learned that you were a woman, I haven't been able to stop thinking of you."

Without turning my head, I opened the door and ran down the staircase as if pursued by flames.

∞

Naked atop the sweat-soaked sheets, I watched him go over to the washstand and rest his reddened member on the edge of the basin. While he soaped it, I reflected that it had taken but a week for his desire and mine to find one another in his narrow bed, he allowing me everything, delegating all libidinous responsibility to me, permitting me to ride him at a slow march, then at a trot, and finally at a wild gallop, as if I were leading him into a cavalry attack. My desire for him had begun to grow the very night he'd said my name, as though the fact of my knowing that he was the master of my secret had lifted the barriers that had been blocking my womanly instincts. Possibly, under any other circumstance, I would have fought against my own nature. But Uncle Charles represented the last thread tying me to my family; his death had left me facing a torrential river of sorrow and insecurity, and Christopher looked like the only bridge that might allow me to keep moving forward.

"You were wonderful, Ketty, my love," he said, returning to the bed. "You must forgive my passivity these first few nights. It won't always be this way. It's just that, in my fantasies, I always saw you on top of me. It's usually that way for me, surely because looking up from below is so much more exciting than the inverse. Don't you agree? You'll note that it's an architectural principle employed as far back as Ancient Greece. The Colossus of Rhodes, the Pyramids, the Parthenon. A principle used in the Romanesque and the Gothic. And not only in order to beautify bell towers and façades, but also the vaults of the ceilings. Take, for example, the frescoes in the Sistine Chapel. The view from above tends to flatten things, to diminish them, make them irrelevant."

"You weren't nearly as diminished or as irrelevant as you suppose," I said from the bed. "Not to mention that you're forgetting about the Roman circus. The action is observed from above."

"Action! A few poor gladiators killing one another off. People devoured by wild beasts. Just think of the trails of intestines and innards. Saint Peter crucified upside down. What decadence!"

"And right here in Spain. What do you have to say about bull fighting?"

"Reminiscences of barbarity," he said dryly.

"All right, but what about the theater? Aren't the kings' and emperors' boxes on the uppermost level, high above the stage and the orchestra?"

"Only so that their majestic forms may be admired from below," he said, sitting down on a footstool and crossing his legs, hiding his parts between his thighs to indicate to me that the time for carnal pleasures had passed. "It's for the same reason that the gods were placed on Mount Olympus or in high temples. Above is for blessed immortality; below, for tremulous sinners and demons prodding the damned with their pitchforks."

"You know what, you obstinate Irishman? Everything of value in the world comes from beneath the ground: gold, silver, diamonds and rubies and sapphires and other gems, pearls from the bottom of the sea, which is more or less the same thing. And now that you mention hell, I'll tell you that I've seen icons in Russia in which the condemned, instead of burning in flames, shiver naked and blue between mountains of ice."

"What can you expect from the people of the North? Think

of the differences Shakespeare delineates: on the one hand, *Hamlet* and *Macbeth;* on the other, *Othello* and *Romeo and Juliet.* Madness and blind ambition correspond to Denmark and Scotland; passion, jealousy, and love, to the cities of Italy."

And so we would spend our nights, making love methodically, as though by medical prescription, then talking for hours, both of us naked and content, united by a tolerance brought on by loneliness, embracing the freedom to talk about our loves, our dreams, our strange or significant moments, he in Spanish and I in French, the law of the path of least resistance always engaged between us.

❧

Oh Christopher, my dear Christopher, how right I was not to fall in love with you, but also not to hesitate to speak to you of Robert, of Alfred, of Fauriel, even of the foolishness with Bousquet and the engraving of Apollo; to tell you about the mysterious Nadezhda and the clairvoyant Uhlan in exchange for your stories of Dublin, the one about the faceless woman you'd seen next to your bed as a small boy, or the one about those strange people who seemed to be staying in your grandfather's manor and how when, one morning, you'd asked your aunt about them, she'd made you point them out and describe them until she began to beat you, shouting that you shouldn't lie to your elders and, of course, from that day forward, you never again saw a ghost. And you met my story of the lascivious Vincenzo with yours of a gypsy woman, and I, in turn, learned that your father had sent you to Old Castille, to an Irish seminary, no less, and that you would have become a priest if you hadn't happened to look out of your cell window one evening and seen a gypsy caravan detour off the road and stop beside the edge of the forest, and if, as they played their instruments and sang around a bonfire, you hadn't been captivated by a young dancer who, noticing you watching her, had let down her hair, black as the wings of a crow, I remember you described it, exaggerated her undulating movements and beckoned you with the impatient arabesques described by her hands, and I'd interrupted you to tell you proudly that I'd known the gypsies from the East, those who played nostalgic violins and jubilant zithers and who knew all there was to know about horses, and you'd picked up the thread of your story to thank God for having sent you that

373

burning temptation before it was too late, and to tell how that very night you'd jumped the monastery wall and lost yourself in the scent of smoked goat that emanated from between that gypsy girl's thighs. And so we'd continued for many nights, and I learned of your jovial grandfather, who made four different kinds of beer and was the only one in I-don't-know-how-many generations of O'Gormans to have made any money, and I learned of your medical studies in Edinburgh and of when you embarked aboard the *Golden Dawn* as ship's doctor, and how much you'd learned about fevers in the islands of the tropics, and of your black and mulatta lovers, and of your wife, the daughter of a Jamaican planter, who, ever inventive, had once painted a little face on the tip of your penis purely for the pleasure of watching it swell. And, of course, the war continued and we discussed its progress as well; Napoleon's defeat at Leipzig at the hands of Schwartzenberg, Bernadotte, and Blücher, the Saxon and Bavarians' betrayals, Wellington's victory in Nive, another in Nivelle close on its heels, and then Murat signed the peace accord in Italy, the Prussians invaded France, and the Austrians and Russians as well, and then there were three armies organizing a march on Paris and now it was merely a question of guessing in which month the war would end.

"Now then, my dear friend, prepare yourself for the surprise I've brought for you," I said, entering his room one gorgeous April evening. "Guess what it is."

"Today's mail brought two important pieces of news, one good, the other bad," he replied without raising his head from the page on which he was writing. "Napoleon has abdicated at Fontainebleau. The war is over. You are no longer my prisoner."

"Yes, I know. The news has just swept through the entire hospital, and everyone is ecstatic. Even the French are singing and dancing. What's the bad news?"

"I've been transferred to London," he said, throwing the pen down on the table, splattering ink on his nose and forehead.

"I see," I said, feeling my soul sinking all the way down to my feet. Nine weeks had passed since my last period and, three days earlier, I'd vomited before breakfast. My belly didn't appear to have swollen, but as I'd finished heaving, a small interior voice had assured me that a small life was growing inside me. I'd decided not to tell him anything until I had a clear idea of what I was going to do, but that afternoon, upon learning of Napoleon's surrender, a plan had suddenly come to me. To begin with, I didn't want to have my child alone, but rather together with Christopher. I'd accompany him on his journey across the countryside of La Mancha and, when I neared the time of the birth, we could stay in some village on the plateau. We'd live there for a few months, just long enough for his child to come to recognize him as his father. Then we'd bid one another farewell and I'd return to the Languedoc. Henri Faber, gone missing in Vitoria, would never reappear. To hell with medicine. I would raise my child in Foix, just as Aunt Margot had raised me.

"You are the very portrait of desolation," said Christopher. "I'd gotten my hopes up as well. I'm sure that I would have managed to convince you to follow me to La Mancha. A pity. . . . We would have had such a wonderful time looking for the ruins of windmills and the genealogical trail of the Knight of the Doleful Countenance."

"You have ink on your face. You look ridiculous. Let me clean it off," I said, drawing near to him. I dampened my handkerchief with the tip of my tongue and wiped away the tiny drops.

"Thank you, Ketty darling. Give me a kiss."

I kissed him.

"We'll celebrate the peace, at the very least. Enough dried salted cod and lentils! I've ordered chicken fricassee and a roast suckling pig. Amazing how, with a flash of gold, everything suddenly becomes available. We have three or four nights left together. We'll make love seven hundred times."

"I'm very sorry to disappoint you. The surprise I've come to give you is that I'm leaving for France at dawn. I'm going with Ricart and a few other Frenchmen."

"And so this is goodbye? You're slipping my cage tomorrow?" He came over to me and hugged me tightly. "I'm going to miss you very much," he whispered in my ear. "You are an extraordinary woman. Oh, Ketty, my darling Ketty. I'll remember you until the day I die."

His words were sincere. As we released one another I saw that his eyes were damp.

"Come on, Don Quixote. Enough of this nonsense. I'll always be your Dulcinea," I said, trying hard not to cry.

"Who knows? Perhaps we'll meet again. Sometimes the world can be a very small place. Wait," he said, and crossed to his traveling case. He opened it and rummaged around inside. "For your trip," he said, handing me a pouch of money. I took it and kissed him again. This time his lips did not return the kiss.

"I have things to do, Ketty, my love. I need to see to my replacement. I'll leave Thorn in charge of the hospital."

"One last thing. Tell me a name you like, one that you'd want for yourself, or for a dear friend."

"That's easy. Dunsinane. Do you remember the prophecy in *Macbeth*? It's the most beautiful name I've ever heard. I would have loved to be named that. Dunsinane O'Gorman. But why do you ask?"

"Something to remember you by."

22

I ARRIVED IN TOULOUSE IN mid-May, by which time Napoleon was already on Elba Island and Louis XVIII ruling from Paris. Wellington and Soult had fought in the hills on the outskirts of the city, not knowing that the war had already ended. Thousands of men fell on both sides in that useless battle, and yet no one seemed to notice. Everyone was celebrating the peace and a return to Bourbon times as though the past twenty years had never happened. Françoise and Pierre were beside themselves with joy at the sight of me. They had taken me for dead. Although they made no mention of my woman's clothing, I could tell that they approved of my decision. Madame Cavent had sent them a note a few months before from Perpignan. She was on her way back to her mother's house in Blois. As she hadn't received any of my letters—in the last of which I'd given word of Uncle Charles' death—I set about the sad task of writing to her again. Fortunately, called by my motherly instincts, I was able to entertain myself with little Pierre-Henri. He could walk on his own now, and tottered around the patio yanking leaves off plants and putting them in his mouth. He learned to call me "Aunt" right away. After a week's time, I realized that my presence interfered with Pierre and Françoise's privacy, so I took up residence in the inn above La Chasse au Sanglier.

When I went to see Lebrun in order to collect my rent payments, he was not in his office.

"He's away on a trip," his assistant, Ducharme, told me as he handed me the money and a long letter from Maryse. "Monsieur Lebrun got married and is on his honeymoon in Paris."

My curiosity piqued, I asked the name of his new wife. She was Madame Larraz' heiress. Since there was still a good deal of time left before the rental contract at Foix would be up, I asked him if he knew of a villa in the area that might be available. I wanted to have Dunsinane in the countryside, someplace secluded and pleasant.

"Not that I'm aware of, madame."

"It doesn't necessarily have to be a villa. Any country house would be fine. I need only four walls and a roof, a peaceful place, even if it's small."

"I can't think of anything, madame. If I hear of anything, I'll let you know."

I was about to climb into the carriage when Ducharme came out into the street and stopped me. "I don't know if it would suit you . . . after all, it's on your own property," he said, uncertain. "It so happens that Monsieur D'Alencourt, your tenant, has dismissed the gamekeeper. It's just an old stone cabin, quite small. I don't know if you remember it."

Of course I remembered it. How many times had I played near it with the gardener's daughters? The ivy that climbed its walls gave it a somewhat wild look, and sometimes we'd called it Bluebeard's Castle or the Beast's Palace. It was exactly what I was looking for.

Pierre took me to my château the following day. I'd never met Monsieur D'Alencourt personally, and he turned out to be a good-natured patriarch, surrounded by daughters, sons-in-law, and grandchildren. The property, including the gardens and stables, was extremely well kept, and I couldn't help but thank him for it. When he learned that I wished to stay in the gamekeeper's house for a few months, he offered to make some repairs to it and to lend me some furniture. Although my belly had scarcely begun to swell, I was certain that he suspected my reasons for wanting to leave Toulouse. During dinner he continuously praised the air at Foix, insisting that it was responsible for his grandchildren's excellent health. I had further reason to be grateful for his tact—when one of his daughters made a derisive comment about Napoleon, whom she called "The Corsican Monster," he ordered her to be silent with a gesture. Surely he assumed, given that I'd returned from Spain and that I was Uncle Charles' niece, that I was a dyed-in-the-wool Bonapartist. "We beg God that the peace may last," he concluded diplomatically.

The next day, as we said goodbye, he asked that I keep him in mind should I ever wish to sell the estate at Foix.

"I'm afraid that will never happen. Furthermore, Monsieur D'Alencourt, I'm very sorry to tell you that I'm not planning to renew your rental contract."

"That's unhappy news, indeed," he sighed. "I already feel as though this place were mine. But, in any event, we still have three years ahead of us here, more than enough time for you to change your mind."

❦

As the time for the birth approached, Françoise left her shop in the hands of one of the seamstresses and, along with little Pierre-Henri, we went to live in the cabin. Thanks to the course I had taken in obstetrics, I knew all that needed to be done, even were complications to arise. The lying-in transpired amid a benevolent autumn. As we had back in Aunt Margot's days, we struck up long conversations lying in the forest clearing, covered now in a splendorous carpet of golden leaves.

"So Christopher was the man of your premonition," decided Françoise, after I'd told her why my son would be named Dunsinane.

"Yes, in the end, he was. Although he never knew," I said thoughtfully.

"Have you heard from him?"

"No. Before I left, I gave him Lebrun's address. If he writes to me one day, I'll tell him about our son. But I doubt he will. He's a man of many interests. And in any case, he only loved me as a friend, for which I'm glad."

"How do you know that you'll have a boy?"

"I've known since Russia. It's too long a story to explain. But in any event, if I have a girl, I'll still name her Dunsinane."

"Pierre doesn't love me anymore," she said suddenly.

"What are you talking about?" I said, surprised, since I hadn't noticed anything amiss except, perhaps, how late he came home in the evenings.

"He has a lover in Foix, in the village, I mean. Sometimes he doesn't come home for days at a time. He tells me that he's gone to take some people to Carcassonne or some other place. But he's a

379

terrible liar. I've done some checking. He met her in the mountains, in Andorra, when he went off with his brother. I think she's a cousin of his."

"How does he behave with the boy?" I asked, shifting my gaze to Pierre-Henri, sleeping peacefully atop the leaves.

"Oh, I have no complaints there. He loves him and spoils him to death. He's a good father."

"Well, that's enough. Perhaps the business in Foix will prove a passing fancy. Do you still love him?"

"I love him as the father of Pierre-Henri. We no longer do anything together."

"Are you telling me this so that I might do something about it?"

"No. I'm telling you as a friend. Life is strange, Henriette. Like a rope that gets tied in knots only to be untied later."

"It's true," I said, thinking of all the things I'd gained and lost, "but though the knots are untied, they remain knotted in our consciousnesses. Surely you haven't forgotten Claudette."

"I remember her. Lately I think of her quite a lot. You never knew her well. Maybe not even Maryse did. She was a very special person."

"Speaking of Maryse, I've had a letter from her. She and Robledo are both well. She's learned Spanish. She got her way, after all; Robledo sold his sugar mill. Now they live almost full-time in the countryside, in the mountains. They were in Prussia. A business trip. She said in closing that they are thinking of taking a long trip . . . a trip . . . around . . . a trip around the world. Oh, Françoise, I think it's time!" I exclaimed, caught somewhere between pain and happiness. "Scoop up Pierre-Henri and let's get back to the cabin quickly."

❧

Dunsinane came out of my body with difficulty, as though it was hard for him to leave my womb. He must have weighed about three kilos and he looked more like Christopher than like me—his same gray eyes and thin lips, although everything in miniature. He latched on to my breast immediately, with the appetite of a little lamb. In order to spare him future complications, I told the parish priest a half-truth: I had gotten married in Spain to an Irish doctor, Christopher

380

O'Gorman, who would be joining me again as soon as his assignment in London was over. I gave this same explanation to Monsieur D'Alencourt and his family, who attended the baptism and filled his cradle with toys, little gowns, colorful ribbons, tiny sheepskin boots, and diapers with his initials embroidered in blue thread.

No matter how happy I'd dreamed having a child would make me, Dunsi more than exceeded my wildest expectations. Seeing him move his small arms and legs in his cradle, changing his diapers, noting how perfectly formed his tiny fingernails were, a feeling of pride and belonging hastened me to pick him up, caress him and coo at him, even to sing him the folksongs from *Puss in Boots*. I don't remember ever feeling more complete, more alive, more a woman.

As winter fell, Dunsi became congested and started sneezing. The weather had turned damp and cold. A continual drizzle matted the dead leaves along the forest paths, mixing them in with the mud. I assumed that Dunsi had a cold and I wrapped him up snugly in his cradle, but one night he began to cough and to struggle for air, and I decided that it would be better to hold him upright so that he could breathe better. Françoise and I spent hours and hours walking with him from one end to the other of the cabin's three rooms. He scarcely slept; when he wasn't coughing, he was crying. Nor did he eat properly. He would take four or five sucks from my nipple and then vomit the milk onto my shoulder. Suddenly, he spiked a high fever. I had bought various remedies at the pharmacy in Toulouse, Peruvian powders among them. I mixed them with my milk in a teaspoon and made him swallow it. But then he would vomit the foamy liquid. I tried the whole process again several times to no avail. His fever went up and we no longer knew what to do. I wrapped him in my blanket so that he would sweat, and I lifted him to my shoulder again. Françoise appeared with a jar of cherry conserves and a piece of cheese.

"You have to eat something, Henriette. You can't go on like this," she said.

I ate a small bite and told her I was going to sleep a little. I remember that the wind blew a window open and I felt her get up to close it. Then I fell asleep in the armchair with the baby in my arms. I awoke when the rooster started crowing in the henhouse. Dunsi, who had slid down to my lap, was calm and his eyes were closed. I lay my hand on his forehead to check his temperature. It was damp and cool. The crisis seemed to have passed and I stood up in order to settle him in his cradle. It was then I realized he wasn't breathing. Screaming and begging God, I rubbed his body, I took him by the heels and swatted his bottom, I hugged and kissed him. But my Dunsi was no longer breathing and would never wake again.

I didn't take him to the cemetery. Pierre dug his small grave just outside the clearing, next to the blackened trunk of an oak tree. I had his tombstone engraved with the prophesy from *Macbeth*:

'Till *Birnam Wood do come to Dunsinane.*

It would have pleased Christopher.

❧

Snow covered the clearing and the tree branches. My footsteps left imprints in the silence and I wept.

The grass began to turn green and the thrushes returned from the South. Berries ripened on the bushes and still I wept.

The forest bustled with caterpillars and grasshoppers. A snail left its laborious slow trail upon August's clover. A spider swung on a ray of sunshine and I wept more than ever, seeing that the thousands of life forms I saw surrounding me were not enough to revive my heart. The black squirrel that lived in a hollow oak tree stopped scurrying about amid the foliage and jumped into my lap.

"You wouldn't have a nut by any chance?" it asked me.

And suddenly it was Fairy Godmother, my old friend, enveloped in black tulle, her dragonfly's wings beating softly, as young, slender and beautiful as ever.

"It's been so long, Fairy Godmother!"

"Not so very long."

"So what happened in Russia wasn't my imagination?"

"Of course not."

"I felt like I was here, in your magic circle."

"You may come here whenever you are feeling lonely."

"No matter how far away I am?"

"The only thing you need to do is wish for it very hard."

"I'm sad, Fairy Godmother. My Dunsinane died. I have nothing left. The months go by and I don't feel any better. I cry and cry and I don't know what I'm going to do with my life. My soul aches, Fairy Godmother."

"I know. That is why I am here. Today you are a child again. Otherwise, you would not be seeing me. You would think I was a squirrel."

"Was I also a child on the road to Vilna?"

"You were a tiny thread of life. Scarcely even a little girl."

"Was it you who pulled me back from death?"

"Me? Such nonsense! I don't exist outside of this clearing. It was your desire to live that brought you here, a desire you have always had. Once I heard your aunt telling Françoise how you managed to escape the flames that were engulfing your house. You were five years old and you refused to speak after the fire. How well I remember the first time you laughed! You still limped a bit and you would let the candies your aunt gave you fall from your hands. You were thinking of your mother stretched out alongside you on a big white bed. You were sitting very near to the spot where you are right now. The other girls were gathering blackberries and mushrooms, but you didn't move and you wouldn't eat anything. I felt such pity for you that I stopped being a hare and began twirling around in front of you and making silly faces. I stuck my tongue out at you. I crossed my eyes. I stood on my head. Then you laughed. For the first time you laughed and your dear aunt was so happy. It was I who taught you to laugh."

"I don't remember, Fairy Godmother. But if you say so, it must be true. Did the gardener's daughters also see you?"

"They never saw me. They were happy girls and they kept each other company. You always felt alone. Even when you were playing with them."

"I remember some of your stories. . . . The one about the greedy squirrel who never stopped eating nuts, the one about how the caterpillar who wanted to fly turned into a butterfly, about the snail who was afraid to leave his house. . . . "

"You also told me things. You told me about your walks with your aunt, about abbé Lachouque, about Pierre, about Françoise, and sometimes you even came here with Laguerre so you could show me how well you could ride a horse."

"But then suddenly I didn't see you anymore."

"As I have already told you, only lonely children can see me. You grew up and didn't need me any longer. Today you have gone back to being a lonely little girl. That is why I am here," she said, her eyes looking at me now as though they were the eyes of the entire forest.

"The last time I saw you, you gave me a key. A golden key. Which doors should I open with it, Fairy Godmother?"

"You will know. But it is getting late. I am starting to get cold and I must change myself into something that will warm me. After all, I am more than six hundred years old."

"Tell me, Fairy Godmother. Please. I don't have anyone left. Only you. Tell me what I am to open with the key."

"The doors to yourself," she said. And then, beating her wings swiftly, she rose from my lap. "The doors to yourself," she repeated, her tiny voice now almost inaudible, her wings becoming indistinguishable among the swarm of dragonflies flying above the clearing.

"You were gone so long!" said Françoise, seeing me arrive. Spoon in hand, she was feeding her Pierre-Henri a stew made of peas and carrots. Suddenly, I felt hungry.

"Is there anything for me to eat?"

"Why, yes," she replied, surprised at my appetite. "I'll fix you a plate right now. You must have walked a long way in the forest. Your cheeks are rosy."

At the end of autumn, after putting my affairs in Foix and Toulouse in order—the modification of my will among them—I took the postal wagon, headed to Paris.

❧

Submerged in my sorrow, I had scarcely paid any attention to the events of the previous few months. It wasn't until I arrived in Paris that I understood the scope of their historical importance: the defeat at Waterloo, Napoleon's ultimate fate, the return of Louis XVIII and the vengeful *émigrés*. I only went to the house on the rue Saint-Honoré to find my *Woman in Battle Dress* and to pack up Uncle Charles' things so as to send them to Madame Cavent, who had decided to stay in Blois. Dressed again as a man, I rented two rooms in a guesthouse on the boulevard Saint-Michel, and paid a visit to Monsieur Debreuil so that he could arrange for my discharge for reasons of disability.

"Ah, Monsieur Faber, Madame Cavent told me you weren't dead," said the lawyer, fatter than ever, indicating a chair with a certain coolness.

"I would like to leave military service so that I might complete my medical studies," I said, coming straight to the point. "Perhaps Madame Cavent also told you that I was wounded in one leg. I still limp a bit. I was held prisoner until the armistice. I didn't want to leave Spain until I felt fully recovered."

"Almost two years, isn't that right?" he said, an absent look on his face.

"More or less."

"I don't suppose you have any letter or document that might verify your words," he said almost impatiently, as though I were wasting his time.

"I only have money. I received a large sum from Havana. I'm only just settling in here."

His eyes sparkled and a smile broke open his fat face.

"It will be arranged, Monsieur Faber. Don't worry, just a small gift and all will be arranged. No one has any money. Not even the king. These are difficult times for all of France. I've never gotten myself involved in politics; I have friends for that. Nothing like friends, Monsieur Faber. Might you have available . . . let's say, five hundred francs?"

"I can have it to you whenever you like."

"Tomorrow would be fine. The sooner the better. Your name will be moved from the list of the missing to the list of the permanently disabled. Of course, with a little more, let's say six thousand francs, you could become a Spanish citizen. That wouldn't be so bad. Your Bonapartist patriotism would be erased, something that many are trying to accomplish. Who would ever have thought that Ney and Murat would end up before the firing squad? We could even negotiate some sort of title of nobility. I have a colleague with contacts in the Spanish Court. Things are bad there as well. The war has taken everything. Of course, you know this better than anyone. Oh, but nothing's worse than our disgrace. As you know, the British have taken advantage of the situation. We've lost Savoy, the Sarre Basin, seven hundred million francs in indemnization, Alsace is occupied. But you are young, the son of a well-to-do family. This is your moment, Monsieur Faber. Houses, lands, palaces, castles . . . everything is for sale or under dispute. It's the perfect time to invest, to buy cheap that which once commanded a high price. I am at your disposal."

"Thank you, Monsieur Dubreuil," I said, hiding my disgust at his words. "It will be enough to obtain my discharge. I need to matriculate immediately. Classes are beginning soon."

"Don't worry. You'll have your leave papers in a few days. There are also opportunities to avail oneself of a favorable marriage," he continued, showing me his ring, nearly encased in the flesh on his incredible finger. "The vast majority of the *émigré* nobility is now returning with no capital other than their titles and marriageable daughters. Perhaps I could be of some use to you in this delicate matter. Of course, it would be easier if you had a Spanish title, or Italian, at the very least. All of this could be arranged for no more than—"

"Another time, Monsieur Debreuil," I said, standing up from the chair. "Another time. I'll see you tomorrow so that we can formalize the matter of my discharge."

"Don't give it another thought, Monsieur Faber. I'll take care of it right now," he said unctuously. "But remember: everything is for sale and I am at your service for any opportunity that might arise."

Back in the guesthouse, I was happy to have resolved a matter that had felt so crucial to me. Before traveling to Paris I'd tried to imagine myself in the future, in three or four years, an exercise I'd recommend to those who tend to think only in terms of an immediate tomorrow. Of course, the future seldom corresponds to our imagined vision of it, but in the act of imagining it, life at least takes on a direction so that one might cease to feel like a leaf in the wind. In any event, having cried my grief down to the last tear, I'd come to the conclusion that, despite the difficulties it might mean, I'd prefer to see myself as a doctor than as an idle *rentière*. Although my medical vocation had been battered, not only during the war, but also from seeing both Dunsi and Uncle Charles die in my very arms, something still remained of my old enthusiasm. Also, I remembered Christopher's words: "You should take comfort in the thought that, thanks to the lives you were unable to save, today we have better weapons with which to combat death." And so, I decided to complete my studies. After all, returning to Paris and to the Medical School was like retracing an old road, something that lent continuity to my steps. Once I'd graduated, I'd do what the majority of doctors did: I'd open a private practice—I could run it out of the house on rue Saint-Honoré—and I'd work in a hospital two or three times a week. Before that, however, I'd give myself a graduation present and go visit Maryse in Havana, something she'd begged of me in every one of her letters. Finally, there remained the question of love. Would I fall in love again? Would I have clandestine lovers, as had happened with Christopher? Would it be true that I still had two marriages ahead of me, both in foreign countries? What would I do were I to fall in love? Would I leave my profession? I left the answers up to time.

∾

Throughout the course of my life I have seen the rise and fall of various idols of medicine, each within his own branch of specialization. About two years ago, during my brief stay in Paris, I got to thinking about them as I passed by the busts lined up in the Medical School's gallery of honor. Some of my old professors were there. Their ideas and theories, once taken as definitive truths, had been branded as erroneous by those who'd succeeded them, physicians whose own discoveries would, in turn, meet the same fate ten or twelve years later. It was there, looking at the bust of Broussais, the man who had so revolutionized both the theory and practice of medicine during my last years at the Faculty, that I finally understood that there are no absolute truths, but rather, an interminable chain of half-truths. In exchange for his efforts to illuminate the mysteries that shroud the human body and to discover methods to prolong life, Broussais achieved recognition, fame, and medals of honor, but, who today remembers his name, his writings, his principles? If I've been reluctant to speak in depth about the particulars of my profession it's because I know that the works I read with such enthusiasm and the treatments I administered to my patients would today—whatever the date of that convenient "today" might be—seem misguided, when not outright laughable. Nevertheless, in defiance of the voice that gives council to the most vulnerable part of me, the part that wishes for a kind of immortality, I've decided to come clean. I shall speak about Broussais, my first guide in the difficult occupation of combating disease; I shall speak of him, my now-forgotten teacher, whose career I've just reviewed in a tome entitled *French Medicine*, which Petit had recommended so highly during the most recent of our weekly visits.

The son of a surgeon, François-Joseph Broussais was born in 1772 in Saint-Malo. After serving in the revolutionary army during the Guerre de Vendée, he went to work as a doctor on the pirate ships that were disrupting British trade in the English Channel. In 1798 he went to Paris, enrolling in the recently opened Medical School. There he studied with the luminaries of the *école nouvelle*, Cabanis, Corvisart, Chaussier, Pinel and, especially, Bichat, whose theories he would apply, in his thesis, to the study of pernicious fevers. After graduating, he served as a doctor in campaigns in Holland, Italy, Austria, Germany, and Spain, alongside figures such as Larrey and Desgenettes. Owing to his experience performing autopsies between battles, he was able to publish his *Histoire des phlegmasies ou inflammations chroniques*. It was here he noted that a principle cause of death derived from fevers caused by inflammation to the lungs and gastrointestinal tract. The work was highly esteemed by Desgenettes, Pinel, and other "sacred cows," even if Laennec, his rival, criticized his stubborn refusal to distinguish pneumonia from tuberculosis. Named as a professor at the Val de Grâce military hospital, he immediately became a favorite among the students, not only for his superior rhetorical skills when compared with certain of his colleagues, but also for the bold trajectory of his ideas, a trajectory that would radically transform the practice of medicine in his era. With the publication, in 1816, of his *Examen de la doctrine medical généralement adoptee*, Broussais was transformed overnight into the new Messiah of medicine. His point of departure, which he termed "anti-ontological," relegated to the stuff of novels those detailed matrices of symptoms that described the different diseases, symptoms that appeared to be causes in and of themselves but that were actually nothing more than the superficial effects of important physiological changes. In order to understand these changes it was necessary to first subscribe to his theory of life. What was life, after all? According to Broussais, life was made possible only through stimuli or irritations, whether of the internal or external order. The principal stimulating force was oxygen, which produced contractions, or "vital erections," in different organs, experienced sensorially by the individual. In the case of disease, certain organs were overstimulated by various disruptive agents, either the "ingesta" variety—cold air, food and drink, drugs and noxious gasses, for example—or the "percepta"—moral or psychological influences. The overstimulation caused inflammation which, in turn, caused damage to one organ or another. In this way, any pathologic damage was caused by an irregularity produced by inflammation. Therefore, the object of pathology should be the study of these irregularities. "The nature of disease depends, for the physician, upon the observation of physiological changes in the organs," he used to say. "My doctrine is physiological because it does not consider the disease to be a foreign element, a common mistake made by ontologists, but rather simply as a change in the function of the organism." If an organ was irritated, that irritation would propagate through "sympathy"—by way of the nervous system—to other organs which would then immediately become inflamed and present irregularities in their own function. According to Broussais, there were no specific diseases. Smallpox and syphilis were simply inflammations; cancer was the consequence of inflammation; tuberculosis was nothing more than a chronic pneumonia or pleurisy. In reality—he asserted—almost all disease began or ended as gastroenteritis, since it was the stomach's destiny to be always irritated by the "ingesta." Drugs or medicines taken orally were counterproductive, as they tended to increase irritation to the gastrointestinal system. Thus, the physician should focus his attention on the irregularities of the stomach. Changes in its functioning could spread rapidly to other organs, including the brain. For all intents and purposes, gastroenteritis was the only disease. "This is so much the case," he explained, "that even malarial fevers may be explained as a periodic gastroenteritis." What, then, was the proper treatment to relieve the ill? In light of the fact that almost all suffering was the product of inflammation caused by an overstimulation of the stomach, the treatment was "antiphlogistic," that is, the application of leeches that would drain blood from the abdominal region, and a strict diet of liquid emollients and acidifiers. And suddenly, a substantial number of prestigious physicians, beginning with Broussais, swore that they had cured typhus, syphilis and gonorrhea, cancer and tuberculosis, smallpox and measles, with the simple use of leeches and an intelligent diet. The price of leeches went through the roof and so-called "physiological medicine" erupted like an enormous comet in the firmament of medicine. Naturally, being a comet, after all, the day arrived when it would disappear altogether. All that would remain of Broussais was his bust and a statue erected by his colleagues and students in the Val de Grâce. For good or for ill, the first years of my medical practice, as was the case for all the doctors of my youth, were based on Broussais' ideas.

❧

Save my enthusiasm for Broussais' novel ideas, nothing extraordinary happened during my final year of medical school. In parallel fashion, nothing extraordinary, aside from boredom and rancor, occurred in Paris during the early days of the Restoration. It wasn't only France's form of governance that had changed with Napoleon's fall. Despite the buildings and monuments that Napoleon had erected four years earlier, Paris now had an entirely different spirit. It was as though a new personality had been grafted onto the same body. To be sure, the Bonapartism of the common folk and of the old soldiers had not been erased, but it had been suffocated. Out of fear of reprisal, few dared to publicly praise the days of the Empire. The merchants and businessmen, once so allied with Napoleon, were now the first to call him the Tyrant, the Usurper, the Ogre of Corsica. A new class—new, at least, to me, born in the second year of the Revolution—composed of aristocrats, courtiers, and priests, had swiftly installed itself in the city, laying claim to lands and forests, titles and pensions and, what was more, demanding reparations for damages. They could be seen arriving from England, Germany, and Russia, the women in their grand flowered silk dresses, the men in stockings and generously cut frockcoats, worn open in front to reveal vests that fell to their thighs. They were the same people I'd seen in Baden-Baden back in the days of the Théâtre Nomade, playing roulette and *rouge et noir*. They arrived triumphant, treating anyone outside their class as a discredited rebel; they came, to hear them tell it, in order to return things to the way they had been before and to put the rest of us in our place. The priests also returned victorious, ordering masses for the Royalist martyrs and processions of atonement for the death of Louis XVI. With their return, Paris ceased to be a city of parades, dances and tri-color flags, becoming instead a city of preachers, church bells, and white banners embroidered with the *fleur de lis*. The political landscape was so narrow that only two factions had room to breathe within it: the Royalists and the Ultra-Royalists.

And as if that weren't enough, it was the latter that took control of the Chamber of Deputies.

One night, drinking alone in my room, I realized, almost to my horror, that I preferred Napoleon's France, in which some of the Republican liberties had been maintained, to the obsolete and sterile country offered me by the Restoration. Having already defended my thesis, which applied Broussais' principles to tertian fevers, and now in possession of my degree as Doctor of Medicine and Surgery, I decided that the time had come to pay Maryse a visit.

JUANITA

23

THERE WAS HAVANA, STRETCHED ALONGSIDE the sea like an exotic garden of green palms, red-tiled rooftops and white, blue, and yellow houses. Leaning against the gunwale of the ship, shoulder to shoulder with other spellbound travelers, I saw with enormous satisfaction that the actual city, beginning with the noble promontory from which the Castillo del Morro rose, was much more beautiful than the one depicted in the engravings Maryse had sent. As we entered the majestic bay, occupied by dozens of vessels, from modest brigs to lofty ships-of-the-line, cries of admiration rang out from the deck of the *Helvetica*. Transferred to the dock in a dinghy canopied with enormous leaves, I stepped foot on land and threw myself into my friends' arms, covering their faces in kisses and tears. Unable to articulate coherent sentences, we spoke in random fragments, brimming with emotion: "Oh, I'm so happy! You look wonderful! It's about time! We'll never let you leave! So now you're a doctor! Here you have me! What a beautiful couple, it's as if no time had passed!" As we walked toward a calash with enormous wheels, I noticed that Robledo, still welling with emotion, was holding a red silk parasol over my head, forgetting that, in the eyes of those surrounding us, I didn't merit his gentlemanly attentions.

Once we were in the carriage and I'd had a chance to recover from the emotion of my arrival, I realized that the city smelled bad and that its narrow streets were unpaved, making for slow and uncomfortable progress for vehicle and pedestrian alike. I observed that many of the city's inhabitants were Negro, their skin ranging in all shades from darkest to lightest. I also noted how important commerce was there: vendors filled the plazas and porticos, and it seemed as if everyone were selling something—bread, sweets, milk, water, flowers, vegetables, fruits, and a great deal of native produce I'd never seen before. The heat didn't bother me particularly, although Maryse was quick to tell me that we were not yet in the hottest months. It was a different story with the dust which, kicked up by the carriage wheels and horses' hooves, required me to incessantly fan myself with my hand, reminding me of the summer, twelve years back, when I'd marched to the Rhine with the Grand Armée.

Robledo's house was on a corner and had two stories, both with high balustrades. From outside, the house appeared austere, if not exactly ugly, but its interior was enchanting: through the main door was an inner courtyard, the stable on one side and barrels and crates of provisions on the other; to the rear, three arches supported by rectangular columns, and beyond those, the fragrant foliage of a patio filled with rose bushes and lemon trees, the only vegetation I could identify. Finally, two stone staircases, one ascending to each of the house's two wings, and then the mezzanine with the kitchen—whence scents of stews and fritters; higher up, a large foyer, clean mosaic-tiled floors beneath a blue coffered ceiling, furniture in dark mahogany, paintings of Spanish vistas and serene landscapes of Scotland and North America, an alabaster Ceres and a set of shelves filled with porcelain figurines and strange idols made of wood and clay—surely souvenirs from Robledo's travels—a French piano alongside a formidable Chinese vase, everything caressed by the soft, rosy light filtering through the leaded glass that, fan-shaped, crowned large balustrade windows, closed against the heat of the street below. At right angles to the shady corner of the room was a verandah set with high-backed wicker chairs and decorated with a multitude of large earthen flowerpots and cages of spectacularly colored birds, including a parrot that called out, oven and over, in a croaky voice with heavily rolled r's, "Marrrryse, Marrrryse." More than a dozen slaves of both sexes served the household, moving from one room to another with great familiarity, talking and laughing among themselves as if there were no one else there. Unlike the postilion, whose extraordinary hat and elegant livery had surprised me, the rest of them went about in simple, loose-fitting attire, their heads covered in brightly colored kerchiefs. I learned that they slept in the mezzanine and in rooms off the inner courtyard where the carriages were kept. Having seen, from the outside, numerous similar, or even larger houses, I realized that Havana was swimming in money.

Nevertheless, the room I was offered was extremely simple: a narrow canvas cot covered with a mosquito net, a nightstand, and an armoire. A side door opened into the bathroom, where, in anticipation of my most urgent needs, I found awaiting me a marble tub filled with steamy water and a luxurious bronze-encrusted, ebony privy.

"What do you think of my house?" Robledo asked me at dinnertime.

"I like it very much."

"And Havana?"

"I like it too."

"Don't be so diplomatic. It smells like manure, dried codfish, cured tobacco, and *tasajo*. And some other things too," he smiled. Seeing my gaze pass over his gray wig, he said: "We're among family here, Henriette. And anyway, you're a doctor. I'm guessing that you're asking yourself how my head finally turned out. I'll show you now, before Maryse arrives," and, with the same childishly vain gesture with which he used to exhibit his Absalom's mane, he removed the wig. A few white tufts sprouted from his wrinkled skull; of his right ear, nothing remained but an opening in a stretch of skin that looked tough as wood.

Not knowing how to respond, I made an empty gesture that he interpreted as a signal that he could cover up again.

"Don't think that I wear the wig out of vanity. It's only to spare others an unpleasant sight. It was Maryse's idea."

"What is *tasajo*?" I asked, pretending that it hadn't pained me to see his scars.

"A type of cured meat, usually horsemeat, eaten by slaves and the poor. It has a very strong taste. I doubt you'd like it," he said, sweeping an invisible plate away with a wave of his hand. He began filling the glasses set in front of my place at the table with various liquids. Once the jugs had been removed by a thick-waisted Negress, he added: "Juices made from native fruits: this one is pineapple, this one is tamarind, this is coconut water, an excellent diuretic, this whitish one is *guanábana,* very good against the heat, this one, I think, is *mamoncillo,* this one is . . . this one is. . . . " he said, pointing at a pink-colored liquid. "Tomasa, what's this one?" he asked the slave in Spanish.

"It's guava, Master Julián."

"Guava, of course. I don't know how I could have forgotten the name of one of my favorite fruits. Well, there you have it. Stir them with the spoon before you taste them. There's a pinch of sugar at the bottom of the glasses."

I set about tasting a sip from each of the glasses. They were delicious, and quite distinct one from another. I thought that, in Cuba, it would be a blessing to be on a diet. In the midst of the tasting, Maryse arrived and sank into a chair, freshly bathed and wearing a new wig of dangling curls and an embroidered linen robe. Her scar, covered by several layers of white powder, was invisible, although her left eye did look smaller and more almond-shaped than the right. As for the rest of her, no one would have guessed that she'd already turned fifty.

"Why don't you dress as a woman, my love? You'd be cooler. I have several robes and some of my dresses could be altered to fit you." Seeing me shake my head, she said: "Who could give you away?"

"Your servants."

"They are discreet people. Not one of them would dare tell what goes on inside the house. An old Cuban custom."

"If you'll allow me to make a suggestion, perhaps it would be better to dress as a man one evening and as a woman the next," said Robledo, lighting a cigar. "That way you'd be free to accompany me to my favorite café and to the gambling houses. The next day you could go with Maryse to the shops on Muralla Street and go for a drive in the *quitrín* along the Prado."

"Forgive me for asking so many questions, but what is a *quitrín*?"

"It's a light carriage pulled by only one horse. It has two wheels and a collapsible hood. Made for vain ladies. My *chiquita linda* has one. I prefer my calash, for obvious reasons."

"Two carriages?" I said, impressed.

"We're rich, my love. That's the truth of it, though I'll tell you that I still haven't gotten used to it," said Maryse.

"We've planned several outings and trips for you," Robledo put in. "We'll be in Havana for only two or three weeks, more than enough time for you to see what the city has to offer. Then we'll go to my old coffee plantation in El Cuzco. We'll pass through several little villages and you'll see for yourself how beautiful our country-side is. Oh, how you'll love it! I understand that you like to ride horses. Well, you'll ride so much you'll get bored of it. Maryse will come with us on our excursions, isn't that right, *chiquita linda*?"

"On my mule, Adolfina," my friend replied. "I'll come with you as long as you go slowly."

"We'll hunt, fish and have just a wonderful time," Robledo went on. "In two months, when the milling season begins, we'll visit a sugar refinery. There you'll see how sugar is made. But the best part will be the coffee plantation. We'll live there during the dry season. We have French and German neighbors, jolly people who love to dance and play cards. I'll teach you to play . . . oh, for heaven's sake! What's that card game called?"

"Monte, my love."

"Right, we'll play lots of Monte. And we'll dance until we collapse. I'm reserving the first dance with you right now."

"That's enough, baldy," Maryse said tenderly. "Are you trying to make me jealous?" Turning to me, she added: "Come on, Henriette, go put on a dress! We'll take a ride along the Prado before dinner, that's what all the ladies in Havana do."

"Just this once. Things are less complicated when I go as a man."

⚶

Traveling by *quitrín* was like riding on a gun carriage, albeit somewhat more comfortable. It was well-designed for the poor condition of the roads. The enormous wheels rotating on either side of my head and the two long planks of flexible wood that supported the leather chassis upon which the carriage's box rested made it possible to ride without being ejected from the seat. The Paseo del Prado was outside the city walls and led down to the sea, ending just at the entrance to the bay, very near a fort that, together with the Castillo del Morro, protected the entrance to the harbor. The Prado was traversed in both directions by numerous *quitrínes* seemingly identical to our own, all carrying women adorned with fans, wearing flowers in their hair and ruffled dresses and, astride each horse, Negro postilions dressed in tall hats and long boots. A few discreet gentlemen on horseback also rode along, generally in pairs, with whom

399

Maryse exchanged almost imperceptible greetings chiefly involving her fan. The spectacle seemed somewhat ridiculous to me in its rustic formality, although on our ride toward the sea I'd been captivated by the landscape at twilight, by the layers of oranges, pinks, and violets that streaked the sky as the sun sank sumptuously in the distance, to the left of the city. On the way back, a sweet, lilac dusk upon us, Maryse took my hand and said: "Now you've become who you wanted to be: a bona-fide physician with a diploma. And since I know that nobody ever ceases to want things, I ask you: what is it that you desire now?"

"Exactly what I'm doing: spending some time with you. You don't know how often I've wanted to come see you. In the midst of everything, especially in the darkest moments, you were always with me. Oh Maryse, if you only knew how much I've needed you!"

"You have lived through a great deal, my child, you've seen more than enough for your years. Some of your letters made us cry. Ah, Henriette, if life could be expressed in numbers and you were to add up all that these Creole ladies you see enjoying the cool of the evening have lived, the final tally wouldn't come to half of our combined sum. I've missed you a great deal too, you know? No one to talk to," she sighed. "Not a single true friend, I mean to say. Here no one knows anything of wars or revolutions or travel or operas or books or anything else. They aren't even aware of their own boredom. They haven't awoken yet. Their moment in history has yet to come. In any case . . . how long are you thinking of staying?"

"I don't have any plans. I only know that I don't want to go back. At least for now."

"The situation is bad in France, isn't it?"

"It couldn't be worse, really. Everything is in complete confusion and, since the war had at least offered a means of making a living, now only a very few have any money at all. Even the king is in debt. But the thing I resent the most is the lack of freedoms. Every single letter that gets printed has to pass through a censor. But there's censorship and then there's censorship, and what's happening in France today is insufferable. Even romantic novels are looked down upon. What's not an affront to the divine right of the monarchy is an immorality that won't be tolerated by the church. It's as though the Republic had never existed."

"But it did exist, my love. One day it will come back."

"Yes, but not in the near future, which is what really matters to me. You'll be surprised to learn that I, who never was a Bonapartist, would be inclined to exchange Louis XVIII and his *émigrés* for Napoleon, even with his thirst for glory and all his defects. We've reverted to the last century, plain and simple."

"Well, my sweet, as far as that goes, I'll tell you that Cuba is a perfect disaster. The reality is that any law here is made purely at the governor's whim. The one we have now, an Artillery General, isn't so bad. But even so, there are times I want to flee this island."

"Haven't you been thinking of taking a long trip with Robledo?"

"Would you come with us?"

"I wasn't thinking about me."

"We'll talk about that later. Robledo is no longer the same man you met in Baden-Baden."

"Yes, I know. He showed me his scars. But I think he's quite strong for his age."

"Strong he is, my dear. He makes love to me twice a week. But he's seemed very distracted these past few months. At first I thought he had another woman on his mind or that he was preoccupied by something. He's losing his memory, Henriette. And there's something else. He enters and leaves places without seeming to realize what he's doing. Other times he says things that don't make any sense, although his words are always beautifully strung together. The other morning I found him weeping in the garden. He doesn't want to see a doctor. Perhaps you know of some remedy."

"I'll observe him more closely. This does happen sometimes, although generally in people of more advanced age. How old is he?"

"Sixty-four."

"How is his stomach?" I asked, thinking that perhaps Broussais's recommended treatment could be useful in the initial stages of senile dementia, since, unfortunately, this is what he seemed to be suffering from.

"He could eat a horse."

"I can't tell you anything yet," I lied mercifully. "Perhaps his retirement has been bad for him. I remember that sugar production was very important to him. Try to see that he's occupied with something."

"I've thought of all that. But he sold his sugar mill, with all its lands and slaves, in order to placate me. I wrote to you about that.

It's not that he's renounced sugar completely. He's invested some of his money in Prussia, in beet sugar factories. He swears that soon it will be an excellent business in Europe. What's happened here is that Spain signed a treaty with England in exchange for a huge pile of pounds sterling. Soon, slave trafficking will be illegal. It's thought that this treaty, even if it doesn't put an end to slavery, will contribute to its escalating cost. The day will come when a strong man will be worth more than a thousand pesos and the cost of sugar production will rise precipitously, in turn raising the price of sugar. According to Robledo, the price of beet sugar will become increasingly competitive. The only bad part is that he has nothing to do with the management of the factories. He has also invested part of his capital in a shipping company, steamships that will soon begin making the trip between New Orleans and Havana. The coffee plantation he bought in El Cuzco is not functioning; it's just to live in. The truth is, he doesn't have anything to keep himself busy."

"Well, then, the trip around the world you mentioned doesn't seem like such a bad idea. It would keep him interested."

"I'm scared, Henriette. Do you know what he did the other day? He went into a gambling house and, after winning a sizeable sum, left by the back door. Francisco, the Negro who drives his calash, waited for him for three hours to no avail. Finally, he went into the establishment and discovered that he'd left. He found him at sunset wandering about in the square. He came to his senses when he sat down to dinner. He talked and behaved completely normally, as if the lapse in time during which his mind had been blank had never happened. If this could happen to him in Havana, his hometown, what might happen to him in a foreign country where nobody knows him? Over there he wouldn't have a Francisco scouring the streets looking for him."

"Yes, you're right," I agreed, now convinced that Robledo's was a veritable case of early senile dementia. "I've noticed that the slaves in Havana are quite free to move about. I'd imagined it rather differently. You know, crushing work, lashes of the whip, shackles, terrible food."

"Unfortunately, all of those things do happen, but only on the plantations. House slaves aren't so mistreated. You won't see foremen carrying whips in the houses. House slaves are often sent out into the street to deliver a letter or to buy or sell something. In general, they are used like servants, particularly the coach drivers like Francisco. It's the most envied job among them. It's not uncommon for the house slave women to take in laundry or sewing on their own account, though they give the lion's share of their earnings to their master. Sometimes they are even allowed to go to their *cabildos*, which are houses where they get together to sing and dance with free negroes, gathering according to their common tongues and places of birth in Africa. Of course, it all depends on the master's particular disposition. But nothing even similar exists on the plantations. There they do brutal work and endure cruel punishments. If a house slave steals something from the master or misbehaves, he or she will be sold through an advertisement in the newspaper or will be sent to work for a few months on the plantation. This is their greatest fear. But even within the limited parameters of the domestic world, slavery can be as low and abhorrent here as anywhere in the world. There's nothing to stop the master, Robledo, say, and his son, should he have one, from making free use of a slave's body, even if she's just a little girl. What happened to Claudette happens here with equal or greater frequency than in old Saint-Domingue. It's the same odious type of society. Here, just like there, the slave is responsible for all wealth; the slaves' work is in everything that you can see. A truly shameful thing. It's true that Robledo hasn't wanted to free the slaves working in the house, but, in truth, it wouldn't really make much sense to do so. Despite the fact that he has no more than twenty slaves, he'd be accused of belonging to some abolitionist conspiracy and run out of Havana, and that's assuming they don't also confiscate all his assets. Don't forget that Cuba is a colony. The Spaniards from here are precisely the ones who've gotten the richest through trafficking in slaves. They're the ones in charge. Slavery reigns on this island. No one can escape that sad reality. Wherever you are, slavery surrounds you. When I married Robledo, when I moved to Cuba, I fell into a trap from which there is no escape. Yes, I could have left him; I could have gone back to France. There's opera and theater there and surely I could have made a living as a singing or acting teacher, at least in the provinces. But what sort of life would that be? Do I not owe him my very life? Do I not love him and feel loved by him as never before in my life? And so, I've become a prisoner of my own conscience. I don't know if I'm making any sense."

"Perfect sense," I said dully, reproaching her, my heroine, just a bit for having accommodated her ideals to suit the interests of a slave colony. I was sympathetic to her situation with respect to Robledo, but the truth was that she allowed herself to be directly served by slaves. "I've been wondering . . . . Isn't there any concern that a great rebellion like the one in Saint-Domingue might occur, or even a revolution like those in South America?"

"Ah, my dear, you've hit the nail on the head. Here everything revolves around those two questions, though always in *sottovoce*. But I've no head for statistics. I'll let Robledo explain the situation to you. It's a question of numbers. Any independent conviction you may have will be met with irrefutable numbers: so many slaves, so many whites, so many plantations, so many thousands of pesos, so many Spanish soldiers. As I said, it's a trap. The entire business of sugar, slaves, and politics is a labyrinth that no one I know has been able to find a satisfactory way out of. May whatever is meant to happen, happen. Yes, yes, I know. You'll think I've changed, and I can't say that you're wrong. Sometimes I don't even recognize myself anymore. It must be the years I've accumulated and my love for Robledo. That, more than anything."

Over the course of dinner on the verandah I revised my first impression of Maryse. She hadn't changed as much as I'd supposed. Her convictions were the same as always, it was only that she'd sacrificed a part of them to her feelings for her husband. Hadn't I gone to extremes that many would condemn when I had a child with an enemy of my country? All of a sudden I felt completely at home in her company, as if we'd gone back to the days of the Théâtre Nomade. Seeing her smile, her expression reflecting how happy my arrival had made her, I had a premonition that my stay in Cuba would be longer than I'd initially imagined. When I went up to my room, I took the rolled-up canvas of my *Mujer* out of its cardboard tube and spread it over the bed to have a look at her. Her military attire complemented the austerity of the room's furnishings. She seemed quite pleased to be there.

❧

If I stayed nearly a month in Havana it was due less to the modest attractions the city had to offer—bullfights, a circus that included equestrian numbers, a New Orleans theater company's performance of *The Caliph of Bagdad*, no less—than to the dances and dinners to which I was invited. The first of these, organized, of course, by Maryse, was intended as my introduction to society. As word spread that I had studied at the University of Paris, a halo of prestige began to appear over my head. The men were all eager to shake my hand and to ask me about the treatment used in the French colonies for yellow fever, an illness that was besetting many travelers and ship's crews on the vessels in the harbor. I would invariably offer my pat response, which seemed to amaze them: "Malignant fevers are always treated with leeches applied to the stomach and a liquid diet." After dancing with Maryse, who made fun of me the entire minuet, I found myself surrounded by a cluster of young women in plunging necklines, their shoulders and faces white with powder, all too eager to teach me the fandango and the quadrille. Almost all of the musicians were Negroes. They played loudly and well, drawing each piece out interminably. What most fascinated me was the informality with which the members of that society, old-fashioned in so many ways, treated one another. All of them, including the counts and marquises, called one another by the most comical names I'd ever heard in Spanish, all with diminutive endings: Cuquito, Chichito, Toñito, Pepito, Lalita, Mimita, Cachita, Lupita; or else, as was the case particularly with husbands addressing their wives: *mi chinita* or *mi negrita*, or even *mi viejita*. By the end of the evening some people had begun using the informal form of address with me; for others, my name had changed from Doctor Faber to Don Enrique, settling at last, encouraged by Maryse, who was dying of laughter behind the unfurled peacock feathers of her fan, on Don Enriquito.

At a dinner organized by one of Havana's great families, I met three of the most notable and well-admired people in that city: Intendant Ramírez, champion of arts and letters; Bishop Espada who, perhaps because he was among the rare survivors of yellow fever, was very interested in knowing my opinions on public health and personal hygiene; and Tomás Romay, the country's preeminent physician and a man of liberal ideas and great erudition. Since the attendees at those dances and dinners were generally the same from one to the next, I had ample opportunity to talk with Romay. His friendship would be a great source of support for me a few years later, when all the rest of that frivolous sugar aristocracy would turn its back on me. Among his many merits was the fact that he had introduced to the island a vaccine against smallpox, which he tested on his own children in order to persuade those who were hesitant to use it. Of the many works he had published, I was familiar with those on the topics of yellow fever, the unsanitariness of slave ships, and the benefits of building cemeteries on the outskirts of towns.

Romay's candor also afforded me an inside view on the prevailing political and economic opinions held by the educated Creoles.

"It's a well known fact that Baron Humboldt greatly influenced Simón Bolívar's independentist thinking," Romay said as we strolled by the light of the moon through the jasmine-scented garden of some well-off landowner whose name I no longer remember. "But the Baron, despite his unquestionable knowledge and the fact that he actually came here for a visit, didn't discern any major political differences between Cuba and the colonies of South America. It's a pity that Señor Arango is away traveling. No one could better explain to you the unique characteristics of this island. Hundreds of wealthy families in Havana owe their fortunes to his astuteness, to such a degree that many compare his genius to that of Aranda or Floridablanca, although in my opinion, the latter has more in common with the English, in his calculations as much as his utilitarianism."

"I'm thinking of staying on in Cuba for a while. Perhaps I'll have the opportunity to meet him."

"In any case, when Arango received the news of the great Negro rebellion and irreversible destruction of the plantations in old Saint-Domingue, he convinced the Spanish officials that Havana should fill the sugar vacuum that these events had created in the market. To that end, he secured the unhindered introduction of slaves and all manner of benefits for sugar production, including local refinement and exportation by way of ships belonging to friendly and neutral countries. But even though the proliferation of sugar plantations brought enormous wealth and triggered the general blossoming of Havana, some continue to see slavery as a problem. Please understand, when I say a 'problem,' I'm not referring to the immoral character of the institution, which I condemn without reservation, but rather to the fact that the increasing importation of Africans will soon create dangerous conditions on the island, conditions similar to those that provoked the disastrous revolution on Saint-Domingue; that is, a significant imbalance between the white and black populations. According to last year's census, the number of Negros in Cuba already considerably exceeds the white population. Arango himself, the man responsible for this state of affairs, has begun to defend, in private, the idea of bringing white people into Cuba. Naturally, I am in favor of this idea, although I'm not harboring much hope."

"It's rumored that Bolívar plans to send a liberating expedition to Cuba. Is there any truth to it?"

"Gossip. It will never happen. If Cuba weren't an island . . . perhaps. But we are surrounded by water, my friend. The best defense there is. And in any case, except in the minds of a few foolhardy individuals, the idea of independence won't find fertile ground in Cuba. The situation in South America, as I was telling you, is different from our own. Here we depend entirely upon slavery and sugar, something that never happened down there. If the plantation owners, following the example of Bolívar's revolution, decided to free their slaves so that they could fight against Spain, not only would they ruin themselves financially, but the freed slaves would join with the free Negro population in a war against whites, making no distinction between Creoles and Spaniards. I don't know if you've heard about the discovery, just a few years ago, of a dangerous conspiracy of free blacks that, aided by Haiti, would have had serious ramifications for the island. Fortunately it was nipped in the bud just in time. So, you may rest assured that no plantation owner will feel inclined to initiate a war that, in addition to landing him in the poorhouse, could also cost him his head, and not only his, but those of his family and friends as well. Frankly, I don't see it ever happening. In reality, the most certain ally that Cuba's sugar producers have is the Spanish Crown. It's precisely the Spanish troops, deployed in every city and town, that prevent slave rebellions. And it's not that they haven't happened. Every so often a particular group of slaves will rebel and kill three or four whites on their plantation, but the uprising is always suffocated before their pernicious example can contaminate a neighboring plantation. Without the presence of those Spanish troops, we'd be lost. But there's something else: the plantations' property lines are circular, and the land between them belongs to the King. As we say here: the King is everyone's neighbor. His presence is as permanent as the land itself. On the other hand, the Creole landowners also depend on the powerful alliance between slave traders and businessmen; the former supply the manpower essential for the growth of their sugarcane and coffee crops; the latter, the loans needed in order to buy provisions and machinery from abroad. This formidable group, which even our intendants and governors fear, is comprised almost exclusively of Spaniards. As you can see, Doctor Faber, we Creoles simply lack the strength to separate from Spain. Like it or not, the King's throne is firmly planted on our island."

"You've painted a truly hopeless portrait of your situation. And yet, I still think that once South America is liberated it will become very difficult for Spain to prolong its dominion over Cuba."

"You're mistaken, my dear friend. The solution to our political situation shall not be found in Cuba or in the hypothetical independence of the South American colonies; the solution lies in Spain itself. It is crucial that the liberals triumph there, decisively and definitively. Only then will the Constitution of 1812 be reinstated, giving us a chance at autonomy: a local Government with a permanent delegation to the Spanish court, free press, secularization of university education, roads, canals, ports, schools, laws favorable to us. Once the situation here changes, Cuba will honor its treaty with England to the letter and slavery will gradually disappear. This would be the best-case scenario for us."

I took my leave from the good doctor under the impression that it would be nearly impossible for his political opinions, instilled in him by the radically unequal society into which he'd been born, to escape his well-intentioned fatalism. Perhaps, as Maryse had so astutely observed, Cuba's moment in history had not yet arrived.

༄

In a little convoy comprised of Robledo's calash, Maryse's *quitrín* hitched with an extra horse, two saddle horses and two pack mules, we left the walled confines of Havana behind. Along the way we were accompanied by many peasants—called, in accordance with subtle differences, *guajiros, monteros,* or *sitieros*—who were returning to the countryside with their strings of pack animals after having delivered their goods, before dawn, to the markets in the city. In the place of frock coats, which not one of them used, they wore blue-striped shirts that hung down, smock-like, over a similar style of pants; they wore hats woven from a fiber called *yarey*, kerchiefs around their necks, and shoes of yellow leather. They were scraggly-looking men with sun-worn faces. Their horses were of a small but lively breed; they walked with a quick, short gait, so sure-footed that some of their riders dozed in their saddles. We passed through several villages, really just tiny hamlets with a few rough stonemasonry houses clustered around a square. The most common type of dwelling was the *bohío*, a kind of hut with an earthen floor and peaked roof made from tightly bundled dry palm fronds. This humble sight contrasted with the entrancing landscape of the countryside, with its abundance of small brooks, gentle, tree-covered hills, and the green of palm trees, cornfields, banana groves and dense cane fields that stretched out along both sides of the road, from which the chimneys and rooftops of the sugar mills appeared like tiny islands.

After spending the night in a village popular with city folk for its medicinal spring waters, we arrived at a place called Caimito, which is also the name of a purple-fleshed fruit. There, while Maryse and the carriages continued along the main road, Robledo and I followed a path that led up into some mountains of white rock. From that height, facing north, we could see the ocean, Havana off to the right, and to the left, an impressive mountain range that stretched, palely blue, toward the west, finally disappearing into a fog that seemed to emanate from its own peaks. Extending his arm, Robledo indicated Mariel bay and pointed out the sugar mills that surrounded the small town. We dismounted and drank rum from his silver owl flask. At my friend's insistence ("In Cuba, all men, and not a few women, smoke; people would think it strange if you didn't"), I lit a cigar, and tried, amid choking gasps and bouts of dizziness, to follow Robledo's instructions on how to savor and exhale the strong and aromatic smoke. We rejoined Maryse in a village near the foot of the mountain, where a delicious suckling pig awaited us, prepared in the rustic style of the countryside (roasted in a hole dug in the ground over a grill made from green branches). We ate so much that we decided to spend the night there.

Starting out again early the following morning, we entered the intense natural world of a region called Vuelta Abajo, a land of gorgeous accidents and intricate virginal vegetation; a kind of Eden furrowed by deep paths and rocky streams, the banks of which were overgrown with watercress, pomarrosa, and bamboo, which the locals called *caña brava;* we passed through gorges whose rock faces were riddled with caves, shrubs, and creepers growing straight out of the limestone walls; we descended into hidden glades, upholstered in ferns, liana, and flowers I'd never seen before, about which fluttered butterflies of the most extraordinary colors and birds that Robledo recognized immediately: "That's a mockingbird, it has a long and beautiful call and distinct mannerisms. That's a *tomeguín,* a kind of finch that also sings. Look at those parrots, they're the same type as the one I have in Havana. We call those little ones *bijiritas,* and those over there, black as crows, are *totíes.*" We entered forests in which, unlike in Europe, so many different types of trees grew that they looked like authentic botanical gardens: "Cedar, pine, trumpetwood," said Robledo, ticking off names: "*Guásima, yagruma,* mahogany, *majagua, paraíso, quebracho,* ceiba, and the palm, always the palm."

We decided to spend the night in a rustic inn in a tiny mountain village, Maryse in high spirits because Robledo's memory had not faltered even once since we'd left Havana.

"It must be the country air," I offered, to say something.

"I think it's his desire to show you all the wonders of his country. As I'm sure you've noticed, he's quite proud of them," said Maryse. "Oh, if he would only get better! Then the three of us could go on that trip. I've wanted to take a trip around the world for years: Veracruz, Acapulco, cross the ocean, Manila, Canton, Bangkok, Singapore, Rangoon, Madras, Bombay. . . . I've learned all these name from travel memoirs. I have it all planned out. I'd love to see those ancient Buddhist temples up close, and of course, in Arabia we'd travel by caravan to the Nile, and then we'd go to Cairo to see the pyramids and the sphinx. We'd have to go to Jerusalem, obviously, and to Damascus and Bagdad and Istanbul and Samarkand, don't you think that Samarkand is a fascinating name? Sa . . . mar . . . kand, it sounds like an exotic fruit. But I've forgotten about Greece and Japan, and, well, there are the islands of Captain Cook and Monsieur de Bougainville. Yes, my love, I have it all planned out. I've wanted to see those places since I was a little girl, and then the operas, as you know, many of them take place outside of Europe," she added with the dreamy enthusiasm of other days. "Be honest with me: do you think that Robledo will ever go back to how he was before?"

"No one can ever go back to who they once were," I said cautiously. "Perhaps his disease won't advance, or will progress slowly. His current state is not hopeless."

"Tell me the truth, Henriette," she pressed. "I've faced worse things in my life."

"The truth is that he suffers from an erosion in his brain, something that usually occurs in people of very advanced age," I said frankly. "We occasionally see it in people of Robledo's age, and even younger, although that is extremely rare. It's possible that the damage began with an inflammatory fever, but the workings of the human body remain a mystery. Sometimes our organs heal themselves. In any case, when we get back to Havana I'll treat him with leeches and prescribe a special diet for him. His memory has been clear these past several days. That's a good sign. Perhaps, as I said, the country air does him some good. It seems to me that it would be an excellent idea for us to spend some time at his house in El Cuzco."

But we wouldn't make it to the mountains of El Cuzco, which we could already make out in the distance. Maryse's panicked voice drove me out of my cot at seven in the morning. At dawn, while she slept, Robledo had left the inn. According to the *guajiro* who saw him leave, he'd gone off on foot by way of the same road we'd been traveling. We all went in search of him. We found him sitting on the banks of a little stream, sunk in a deep stupor, his bare feet in the water and his pockets filled with flowers. Bees had stung his right hand. He allowed us to lead him back to the inn like a child and, once there, I used my smallest pincers to remove the stingers from his hand. At noon, while Maryse helped him to drink some broth, he came to his senses, buried his head in his arms and cried silently, ashamed. A short time later, after he'd recuperated a bit, Robledo himself decided that we should return to Havana.

∞

Cuban apothecaries were prohibited from selling leeches to anyone not a doctor and, as the druggist didn't recognize me, I had to go back to the house to look for my diploma.

"Here it is," I told him, spreading the parchment over the countertop.

"I'm very sorry sir. This isn't valid here," he said after reading it closely.

"What do you mean it isn't valid? It's a diploma from the University of Paris," I protested.

"I don't doubt it, but in Cuba foreign doctors are forbidden from practicing without the authorization of the Protomedicato."

"The Protomedicato?"

"Well, yes. It's a tribunal of doctors."

Suddenly I remembered that among the papers Maryse had sent me in Paris was information about medical instruction in Cuba and the Protomedicato. The apothecary told me that I would have to pass two exams, one in surgery and the other in medicine. "But it would be best for you to inquire yourself," he added.

When I returned in a foul mood and without leeches, Maryse guessed what had happened.

"It doesn't surprise me a bit, my love. We used to complain about the French bureaucracy, but here it's ten times worse. In order to resolve any public matter, no matter how minor it may be, one's petition has to pass through the hands of at least four or five pen pushers, each of whom orders further investigations or asks you to submit letters of recommendation or declarations of good conduct signed by your neighbors, or copies of your birth certificate, or an inventory of your assets or your marriage license. You're in the city of red tape, signatures, and rubber stamps. And how those miserable little bureaucrats put on airs! They're the earls of the inkwell, the marquis of the *escritoire*. Forget it, they're a herd of asses! Don't worry, I'll speak with Doctor Romay about the leeches."

I treated Robledo for three weeks. Fruitlessly. He docilely accepted the liquid diet I prescribed, but, seeing how quickly he was losing weight and that his health was not improving, I discontinued it.

"I can't do anything for him," I told Maryse sorrowfully. "I think the deterioration of his brain is irreversible. You should speak with Doctor Romay."

"I already have," she sighed. "He believes there's no cure for his disease. He says there are several cases like Robledo's in the Insane Asylum. Oh, Henriette, such a strong and kind-hearted man! He's given me everything! Who could ever have thought that he'd end up mad? Do you remember when we met him in the roulette room?" she said, starting to sob. "How striking he was with his

412

mane of hair and his pearl, all in black. The number nine. I was instantly captivated by him. Do you remember? A madman, my God! How can it be possible? Tell me the truth: will he die soon?"

"No. Or, I should say, not because of his dementia. He'll get worse bit by bit. I've seen advanced cases in the Salpêtrière. The time comes when they are no longer aware of their own disease. They don't suffer," I said, hoping to console her at least a bit. "They burn out slowly like a wax candle. He could well outlive you."

I couldn't sleep that night. I thought of what Maryse had said during our ride along the Prado in the *quitrín*. Why was it that certain people, like she and I, were destined to lose the ones we loved the most? Would my life continue down that same path? I'd traveled to Havana in order to leave my sadness behind and now, instead of feeling happy and at peace within myself, I felt despondent and nerve-wracked by Robledo and Maryse's misfortune. My head began to hurt terribly and I closed my eyes, resigned to the many sleepless hours ahead. Suddenly, from somewhere beyond my closed eyelids, appeared the resplendent face of Fairy Godmother. I was back in her forest clearing, stretched out on the grass, the autumn leaves falling slowly all around me.

"I can't help my friends, Fairy Godmother. I feel as hard and bitter as a green apple."

"That's why you are here," she said, sitting down next me. She was naked and as big as any full-grown woman. I had never seen her that size. Seeing my admiring gaze, she coquettishly unfolded her wings, now so large they nearly filled the clearing.

"I don't know what I'm going to do. My medical knowledge is useless and I feel terrible."

"Don't talk like that. Medicine is not my strong suit, but I know that you have healed many people."

"How do you know that? I don't remember speaking to you about it."

"In dreams, Henriette. Sometimes, when you're asleep, you come to visit me."

"I've been thinking that Maryse and I will never be happy. Just when we start to be, something terrible always happens."

"I know. I've heard your complaints. The only thing I can tell you is that things are as they are. Do not complicate the world any more than it already is."

413

"I need your help, Fairy Godmother."

"I've already given it to you. Don't tell me you've forgotten the golden key?"

"You said I should use it to open my own door."

"That's right."

"And have I done it?"

"Of course you have. Thanks to the key you went to Paris to study. Thanks to the key you've come to Cuba."

"And now I've nowhere to go. It frightens me to see my friends suffer. It's like suffering myself. I don't want to stay, but where am I to go?"

"Suffering is not so bad as you think. One learns a great deal."

"I'm tired of suffering, Fairy Godmother."

"Well then, you could always turn yourself inside out. You know, as though you were a glove."

"What do you mean?" I asked and, looking in her eyes, I felt myself moving deeper and deeper into the heart of the forest, as though a path that only I could traverse were opening up in the dense thicket.

"I mean that if you keep all of your suffering trapped inside yourself, you'll choke on it. But if you turn yourself inside out, the suffering will be on the outside. It's the same with love. You no longer even think of Bousquet. Do you know why? You choked yourself on loving him in secret. But the ones to whom you gave everything, those are the ones who will live in your heart forever. To love is to surrender oneself. To suffer is to surrender oneself. You must turn yourself inside out. Otherwise, you'll choke yourself, and your sorrow will become guilt and your love will turn into fantasy."

"Are you insinuating that I should stay with my friends and surrender up the suffering I feel for them?"

"I'm not insinuating anything."

"Sometimes it's not so easy to talk with you, Fairy Godmother."

"The things you come up with! It's the same as talking to yourself. But now you must leave me. It's time for you to go back to your bed. I have an appointment with a little girl who fell off her horse and has been left crippled. She should be arriving any minute. She's already begun to dream."

"Goodbye, Fairy Godmother. You have no idea how much I love you."

"I love you too," I just heard, as I shot out of the clearing and flew toward the brilliant flash of a lightning bolt.

⁂

It turned out to be much easier than I'd imagined. I found two bottles of rum and knocked on the door to Maryse and Robledo's huge bedchamber, in the other wing of the house. They greeted me in their nightshirts and I told them that I couldn't sleep and had come to drink with them, a proposition they welcomed without hesitation. The bottles and glasses arranged on the bedside table, we immediately began to reminisce about the night of the phallus when, gathered in my room in the guesthouse in Fulda, I'd had my first taste of rum, Maryse trying to convince me not to accuse Vincenzo, Robledo taking her side and appealing to me to take pity on those without the good fortune of being beautiful, untying the ribbon that bound his magnificent mane of hair, telling us of his worldly adventures in the islands of pearls, me talking with unaccustomed ease about my Mameluke disguise, my days in Austerlitz, and the explosive campaigns in Prussia, Vienna, Berlin, and Warsaw, although not about the dark days in Pultusk, and the glasses of rum filling and emptying, and Maryse remembering the grand theater at the Palais Royal and the salon in Talma and the learned conversations with Señor Olavide, though she did not mention Justine or Portelace, and Robledo describing the various buildings on his plantation, the process by which sugarcane was converted into juice, the juice into molasses, the molasses into sugar, though he said nothing of his previous life as a married man, or of the cause of death of his first wife, all of us showing joy on our faces and hiding the black ribbon of our mourning, and the glasses of rum filling and emptying, and Maryse, putting up almost no resistance, singing, *a capella*, an aria by Gréty, followed by renditions of the latest popular songs in Havana, *El Caramelo*, and *Tata, ven acá*, both well-received on stage at the Teatro Principal, and then, keeping my words light, as if in passing, I broached the subject of Robledo's illness, yes, senile dementia with all its symptoms, down to the last detail, what we should and should not expect, always speaking in the first person plural, as if we were all suffering from the disease, Robledo quite agreeable, shrugging his shoulders as if the topic didn't concern him, saying, "What can you do, we all have to die of something," and the glasses of rum filling and emptying, and me replying, "There's no reason for us to be too down about it, we still have many months ahead of us, we have years yet, if you ask me," and Maryse thanking me for including myself in that plural with an appreciative look, and me ratifying my pledge to them with kisses on both their cheeks, and the glasses of rum filling and emptying, and Robledo drawing me and Maryse to his side, assuring us he'd bring us up to date on his beet sugar and steamship concerns, excellent businesses, he insisted, we wouldn't lack for money, and he thought it perhaps best to make his condition public, that way he'd feel more comfortable, not having to feign a perfect state of health, and Maryse responding that there was no reason to go overboard and announce his illness to the newspapers, for example, and me agreeing with Robledo's proposal that we invite all his friends to a grand banquet, "and, at midnight, I'll take the floor and explain the circumstances in which I find myself," and Maryse conceding with a gesture of resignation, "Just so long as you don't mention the name of your illness, because you're neither demented nor old," and me suggesting a new name, something like amnesia fever, "a recurrent fever like malaria," and Maryse saying that she disliked the word "fever," but that "recurrent" wasn't bad, although, on second thought, we ought to come up with some exotic cause, perhaps a slowly progressing illness that he'd contracted in China or in the Pacific Isles, and Robledo enjoying himself immensely, the glasses of rum filling and emptying, and me in favor of not offering too many details, Pinel Disease, for example, "named for a famous Parisian doctor who specialized in disorders of the mind," and, after agreeing with me, Robledo commencing to repeat the word "pearl" twenty or thirty times, standing up from his chair, his face smooth with the bliss that sometimes accompanies madness, and wandering about the room looking for something, something that he wouldn't find and that wasn't inside the armoire or in the dresser drawers or under the bed or beneath his wig or inside one of his shoes, and Maryse emptying the last of the bottle into his glass and approaching him, "Here, my sweet baldy," putting the glass in his hand and raising his elbow until the rim brushed against his lips, and Robledo beginning to drink in tiny sips, holding the rum in his mouth until I instructed him to swallow it, and, the rum finished, allowing himself to be led to bed, where we all flopped down together, drunk in each other's arms, thinking that we could manage because things weren't really that bad. But we were mistaken.

24

To DESCRIBE MY LIFE DURING the year that followed would be the same as describing Havana, with all its virtues and defects. (The cathedral with Christopher Columbus's tomb, the Golden Lion café with its refreshments cooled with ice brought in from Boston, the University, the Seminary, the women's hospital, the orphanage, the Bishop's Garden, the new cemetery, the tobacco factory, the palaces, the churches and convents, the bustling plazas, the fortresses and towers, the slums outside the city walls, the river called the Almendares or La Chorrera, the nearby village of Guanabacoa and other distinctive characteristics.) With nothing else to do but share in Robledo's resignation—which grew more vociferous as the days wore on—we would set out early in the morning, usually in his calash, and I would listen carefully to everything he had to say about his city, which was quite a lot, especially with regard to the British occupation of his childhood, an event he obsessed over and which I came to know in all its details. At noon, Maryse would be awaiting us for lunch and, after a coffee with rum and a cigar, the smoke and flavor of which never did manage to win me over, we'd stretch out to sweat through siesta time until five o'clock. Then, the aforementioned *quitrín* along the Paseo del Prado, or a walk along the Alameda de Paula, dinner with a small group of trusted guests. These were friendly and well-spoken people, though always cautious with their opinions, as though the walls had ears, at times daring to criticize Cuba's lack of schools and poor public health, or the vices of gambling, idleness and prostitution, but never venturing onto the themes of independence and the abolition of slavery. The evening usually ended with Maryse at the piano or strumming the strings of her guitar to the tune of a nostalgic love song that she'd dedicated to Robledo.

And so we spent those days, my life taking on a routine as predictable as it was during my years in medical school, my stay extending indefinitely, more an unassailable duty than a true choice. The city grew ever narrower to me. At times I had the impression that its walls were closing in on me, suffocating me, imprisoning me within its four sides like a dungeon, and then I would saddle a horse, ride down the Paseo del Prado, and set out along the coastal road until I came to the Chorrera Tower, situated next to the river mouth. But then the next morning I'd awake to my habitual tedium, go down to breakfast with hot chocolate, and then off to the calash, Robledo speaking without pause, trying to preserve Havana in his hazy memory by naming its stones, by incessantly traversing its streets. There wasn't a port, corner, plaza, or fortress whose history he didn't know, from the legendary times of Tejada and Antonelli, through to the era of Count Albemarle and the larger-than-life Bishop Morell. Things with Maryse weren't going much better. Whether in the *quitrín* or with a bottle of rum, I felt that our past was being exhausted through so many retellings: my childhood in the Languedoc, hers in Paris, Robert and Portelance, Justine and Dunsinane, Russia and Saint-Domingue, the white death and yellow fever. When she realized that that we had already exhausted all that we had to tell, she compared our conversations to rehearsals for an opera. After that, it wasn't uncommon for us to ride or walk along scarcely speaking, our gazes on the fading colors of twilight. As if that weren't enough, Robledo's condition worsened after a bout with a malignant fever that left him wrecked; his periods of lucidity grew shorter and his personality became erratic: at times he would refuse to leave the house, and at others he'd decide to climb naked into the calash, lashing out at us, as we tried to stop him, with the worst expletives he could come up with in the Spanish language. Without the moral restraint imposed by lucidity, his instincts burst out of control, and he would run after the slave women, trying to grab and touch them. One night I heard him trying to open my door. Much to Maryse's displeasure, it became impossible to invite anyone over for dinner. She also decided it would be inappropriate to go on accepting invitations to dances and soirées and, little by little, her friends began to forget about her. The moment arrived when the doors to the house opened only for the ever-loyal Doctor Romay and for a certain Nicolás Jerez, the manager of Maryse's estate—Robledo had already been declared incompetent. Deprived of the opportunity to show off the livery of which he was so proud, Francisco, the postilion, became sullen and disrespectful, a mood that quickly spread among the rest of the servants.

"Go back to France, my love," Maryse told me after I'd complained of a roast made inedible by too much spice and salt. "I am aware of the sacrifice you're making. I thank you for it with all my heart and I will miss you a great deal, but it's simply not fair for me to keep you here with me. And I say 'with me,' because my poor Robledo scarcely even counts anymore."

"I couldn't, Maryse. I could never leave you alone in this condition. I'd regret it for the rest of my life. We need to look for a solution."

"There is no solution. I will be with Robledo until he dies."

"I'm not suggesting anything different, it's just that I think you've allowed yourself to be dragged too far down by his illness and that it isn't good for you. You could say the same of me."

"I do what I feel, Henriette. I live as I do because it is not possible for me to live otherwise. Do you think that I could go to the theater or to a dance knowing that he's here, locked up like a recluse and at the mercy of his madness? And anyway, there are still moments when he is himself, moments when he suffers and he needs me. We're together and we remember things and we laugh and we cry. What do you know of what goes on in our bedroom?"

"His illness is advancing very rapidly. Within a few months he'll no longer recognize you," I said, deliberately harsh. "He won't have any memories and he won't even know who he is."

"And how can you know if he will recognize me or not, if he will have memories or not?" she said coolly.

"I'm a doctor, Maryse."

"Oh, a doctor! How admirable! Haven't you yourself told me that the human body is a mystery and that sometimes the organs heal themselves?"

I remained silent. There was no point in continuing that disagreeable conversation. While Maryse drank her rum without looking at me, a plan formulated in my mind, one I'd considered more than once before.

"I will not leave you alone. You know me too well. Nothing you could say or do will change my mind. However, I have a profession. In order to practice here I must request an exam by the Protomedicato. I've hesitated to do it out of a question of pride, but I think that if I felt useful, my mood would improve. It would do all of us some good, don't you think?"

At that moment Robledo appeared on the verandah, elegantly dressed in black, recently shaved and his wig powdered.

He looked as dignified as a chamberlain, and he reminded me of Talleyrand taking his seat in the imperial box in the theater in Vienna.

"You look gorgeous, my sweet baldy," said Maryse, amazed.

"As befits the occasion, my dear Aurora. Here is my anniversary present for you," he said, setting a small silver box alongside Maryse's plate. "Open it. They're earrings. I hope you like them. I had them made with the most beautiful pearls that I brought back from Tahiti."

Maryse, biting her lip so as not to cry, opened the little box and pulled out a bit of snuff, spreading it carefully across the tablecloth.

"Do you like them, my Aurora?"

"They're lovely," replied Maryse, her voice breaking.

"You haven't introduced me to your friend."

Incapable of participating in that pathetic scene, I said goodbye with a wave and went down to the stables.

⁙

With the help of Doctor Romay's kind intervention, it was arranged that the doctors of the Protomedicato would come issue me their exams in four weeks, which was, for them, an extraordinarily short time. When the date arrived, I saw to my satisfaction that Havana's inconsistent winter offered a mild and sunny morning, reminding me of Paris at the end of spring. I took the splendid weather as a good omen and, since the mud in the streets was dry and hardened, I decided to go to my appointment on foot.

After waiting for more than an hour, my two examiners arrived dressed in long cassocks and wigs, as though they were attending a high-ranking official ceremony. Both were more than twice my age and, after another hour, they deigned to receive me in a dimly lit chamber, the walls of which were covered with portraits of somber prelates and diplomas with elaborate signatures. After some twenty or thirty minutes, during which time I gave an account of my studies and of my experience in hospitals and on the battlefield, one of them, the regent of the tribunal, asked me the first question: "Suppose that the wheel of a heavy carriage has shattered a pedestrian's leg. When would you amputate?"

"As soon as possible," I replied without hesitation. "Ideally, one would perform the operation *in situ* or in a house close to the site of the accident."

"Why?"

"For two reasons. In the first place, the state of agitation that generally comes immediately following an accident desensitizes the person and the operation will not be as painful for them. I've seen cases in which the wounded person hasn't felt any pain at all. But beyond this, my teacher, Baron Larrey, has observed that during this state of agitation, one bleeds less than after it has passed, and it is, therefore, easier to suture the arteries."

"Very good, Doctor Faber. Even here, we know of Doctor Larrey and his famous amputations. We are pleased to have the opportunity to meet one of his disciples. Let us continue. What treatment would you prescribe for dysentery?"

"I would prohibit solid food. I would recommend a diet of acidic liquids. I would administer some sort of astringent to combat diarrhea, and I'd apply leeches to the abdominal region in order to reduce inflammation."

"Leeches on the stomach?" said the other doctor, surprised.

"As I mentioned, I studied with Professor Broussais."

"Broussias? I've never heard of him—"

"Yes, yes, of course, Broussais, the prophet of physiological medicine," interrupted his colleague, reproaching the other's lack of information with a look. (In those years, the state of medical instruction in Cuba was precisely what was to be expected of a Spanish colony. Given the absence of large lecture halls and of the practice of dissecting cadavers, instruction was completely oral—it was dispensed by means of obsolete treatises and conferences imparted by four professors—and it was dominated by the ecclesiastical spirit of the Middle Ages. During the three-year period in which the liberals managed to reestablish the Constitution of 1812 for

423

Spain and it dominions, the Dominican Order lost control of the University of Havana, opening up opportunities for the initiation of reforms demanded by Romay and other doctors. But in 1823, upon the reinstatement of the absolutist monarchy in Madrid, with military assistance provided by the French throne, the old Order would return to governance. Nevertheless, at the time of my expulsion from Cuba, a young doctor by the name of Gutiérrez who was serving in the San Ambrosio military hospital took it into his head to introduce Broussais' concepts. I had the opportunity to read his *Catecismo de la Medicina Fisiológica*, an excellent translation of my teacher's work.)

The questions ended at noon and, returning to the house, I went looking for Maryse in order to tell her that I was sure I'd passed the exam.

"Doña Marisa and Don Julián left in the calash very early this morning. Just after you left, Master," Tomasa told me.

I guessed that they'd gone to visit a church. Lately, convinced that Robledo's affliction was incurable, Maryse had returned to religion in search of a miracle. But the clock struck one, then one-thirty and, after it struck two, I sat down to lunch at Tomasa's suggestion. As I began dessert, I heard a harsh knocking at the door. Hoping to get there before Segundo, the frail doorman, I left my seat and went down the stairs: it was the mail. There were two letters for me, both from Toulouse. One was from Françoise; the other bore the letterhead of Lebrun & Ducharme. I returned to the table to read them.

In very few lines, as was her custom, Françoise told me happily that things had been resolved, apparently definitively, between her and Pierre. Nevertheless, due to the poverty that had befallen the country, the money that she earned in her seamstress shop was scarcely enough for them to eat. Pierre had not run into trouble as a deserter, since he'd been able to offer testimony that he'd fled to the mountains out of his hatred for Napoleon's regime. Nevertheless, months later, accused of propagating anti-monarchist rumors, he'd had no choice but to sell his carriage and horses in order to pay the fine with which he'd been punished. "Little Pierre-Henri couldn't be better. His health is perfect and I, myself, have taught him to read. I often speak to him about you. He's learned to know you as 'Aunt Henriette.' She closed, saying that because Pierre's brother had paved the way to Spain, where liberal politics appeared to have triumphed, they had decided to relocate there as well. She would let me know as soon as she had an address to give me.

I approved of my friends' decision, wishing them the greatest success in their new destination. I drank a glass of wine to their health and opened the second, much bulkier, letter.

After a page of preambles, Ducharme—surely now married to Lebrun's daughter—regretted that he was unable to send my rent from Foix to Suazo and Martinez, my bankers in Havana. The children of the Viscount of La Muraille, the old owner of my properties, had reclaimed the property for themselves. According to them, Curchet had never been the owner. He had merely held it in usufruct for life and, as such, the clause in his will stipulating that the lands pass to Aunt Margot was not legally binding. The Viscount, one of the first *émigrés*, had died in Baden-Baden; his widow and children, who moved to Vienna, had washed their hands of the property, assuming the lands would never be returned to them, and not planning, in any case, to return to France. Now that they'd returned, however, they were not only claiming the land as theirs but were also demanding that I pay them the rents accumulated between Curchet's death in 1795 and the present time.

"Swine!" I shouted, pounding my fist on the table, causing the plates to jump. "To hell with them!"

"May it be so, Master," said an alarmed Tomasa, retreating with the custard dish.

Indignant, I continued reading. Of course, the arguments made by La Muraille's descendents were false. "In the elder Monsieur Lebrun's files, there is a title that shows Monsieur Curchet as sole proprietor of the estate." It was just that the lawyers for the other side were presenting a concocted document. "The matter could go to the courts, and shall, if this is your wish, although we must inform you that the possibility of attaining a just ruling is very remote. All of the information with regard to the case has mysteriously disappeared from the Land Register and we are under the impression that the courts are inclined to favor the descendents of a member of the nobility whose devotion to the King has been exemplary." It was precisely the sort of thing that was happening all over France. In summation, considering that La Muraille's children had agreed to withdraw their demand that I pay them the accumulated rents if I renounced any right I believed myself to have over the château and its lands, his recommendation was that I accede to the other party's wishes. In any case, the three small farms and vineyards with which my Uncle Curchet had augmented the original inheritance still belonged to me, though clearly, the rent from them didn't amount to much. Before signing off in weepy paragraphs and passing along Lebrun's sorrow and "eternal friendship," he allowed himself to remind me that, if I needed money, I could always sell my jewels or mortgage the house on Saint-Honoré. As a postscript, he had written: "Madame Renaud, your reply is most urgent."

Beside myself with rage, I went out into the street to walk off my foul mood. I walked to the Plaza de Armas, where I reread Ducharme's letter. Although I hadn't made a decision as to my answer, I returned to the house. It was the time of day when ladies in Havana went out in their *quitrines*, and I was sure that Maryse and Robledo would have already returned home. But they had not. Concerned about their tardiness, I sat down in the courtyard. Every so often, when I heard an approaching carriage, I went to the door. Shortly after the boom of the cannon by which the city marked nine o'clock, a pair of soldiers stopped in front of the house. One of them dismounted and walked toward me.

"Good evening, sir. Is this the home of Don Julián Robledo?"

"Has something happened?"

"I honestly don't know where to begin," said the man, a sergeant. "Well, sir, we've come to give Don Enrique Fabelo some sad news."

"Faber, you mean. I am that person," I said, my heart in my throat. "What has happened?"

"A terrible shame. Don Julián and his wife have died in an accident. Their postilion, a Negro named Francisco, told us that you were the only white person left in the house. We've come to inform you."

Mute with emotion, I invited the sergeant and his partner in with a faint gesture. I let them talk.

They served in the Chorrera Tower garrison, at the mouth of the Almendares River. Around three in the afternoon, Francisco had appeared before an officer of the guard saying that he feared for his masters' lives. Detained as a suspect, he had led a squadron on horseback to the place where he'd left Don Julián's calash. According to him, around ten in the morning they were riding along the

426

river when his master decided that he wanted to cool his feet in the water, something he was quite fond of doing. He and Doña Marisa got down from the calash in that very spot, following a footpath that led to the river. After two hours or so, Francisco had tied the calash to a tree and had set off down the path himself. As he didn't see either of his masters, he walked along the bank until he found Doña Marisa's fan lying next to a place in the river known to be dangerous for its depth. The grass along the banks was flattened and there were fresh tracks in the mud, indicating that someone had recently gone down to the river that way. Seeing that, the Negro had run frightened to the garrison.

"But then how do you know that they're dead?" I asked, impatient.

"They're dead, sir. Downriver, we found Doña Marisa's body first; her dress was hooked on the protruding roots of a tree. Then, a hundred steps further on, half-hidden by the huge leaves of a malanga, we saw Don Julián's body. We removed their cadavers from the water and took them in the calash to the garrison, where they were examined by our doctor. Neither of them showed any signs of violence and, when they were turned face down and their ribs compressed, water came out of their mouths and noses in torrents. There's no doubt that both of them drowned. According to the Negro's statement, Don Julián was a strong swimmer. He could not say if Doña Marisa was as well. Do you happen to know, sir?"

"I can attest that she did not know how to swim," I replied.

"He also told us that Don Julián has had something wrong with his head for a few months now," the other man put in. "Can you confirm his words?"

"It's true. Senile dementia. Maybe Don Julián allowed himself to be carried off by the current and Doña Marisa, trying to save him and not realizing how deep the river was there, threw herself into the water," I said sadly, imagining the scene.

"Nevertheless, the Negro swears he heard no cries for help," asserted the soldier. "He avows that he's not hard of hearing, and the calash was found near the deep spot."

"You know how Negroes are, sir," said the sergeant, turning to me, attempting to dispel the suspicion of a possible suicide. "They go along, so absorbed singing about this and that, they don't pay attention to what's going on around them. Maybe he fell asleep and didn't even realize it."

"He swears that he did not fall asleep."

"That one likes to read novels," said the sergeant in a mocking tone. "He's a romantic."

"What I'm saying is that it's not clear what really happened. It's my opinion," he protested, defending his point of view against that of his superior.

"It was obviously an accident! Control yourself or I'll put you on early-morning guard duty for a month!"

"When will the bodies arrive? I need to make arrangements," I said.

"Sometime around midnight," replied the sergeant. "We're at your service, Don Enrique. If you need any help at all. . . . "

I felt so dazed and weak that I asked them to accompany me to the best funeral home in the city so I could make arrangements for the wake.

⁂

How many times have I asked myself what really happened that day on the Almendares? Accident? Suicide?

Both things at once? Of course, Maryse wasn't one to declare defeat when faced with an obstacle. Then, imagining that Robledo had resolved to end his life, why hadn't she called for help instead of throwing herself into the river?

Tonight, however, when I'm feeling more tired and bored than usual; precisely tonight, when I feel sick of everything, the pain in my bones, the restlessness of insomnia, when not even Milly's abrupt confession has moved me ("Madame, help me, I don't know what to do, I've fallen in love with Daniel, Monsieur Petit's grandson, and he's eight years younger than me"); tonight, when I feel I have nothing left to delight in, not even having sufficient wisdom to be able to offer Milly a piece of advice ("Don't allow the moment to slip away; go to bed with him"); tonight, Maryse's presence floats within me like a stew, warm and thick with memories, Maryse, who I killed today in a simple and distant river alongside her mad prince; tonight, now, right now, when the reason for her death no longer interests me (what does it matter if it was suicide or accident when

428

the ultimate reason was love?); tonight, when my whole body tells me that I won't manage to finish writing down all that I've lived, that I should be thinking of how to plot a final ending, an ending sufficiently remote, sufficiently compact so that you, whose name I can't possibly guess, might not reproach me for having defrauded you and will instead linger lovingly inside my story; tonight, more than on any other night, when I feel the threat of death, when I ask myself why everything must remain incomplete, why nothing has a true conclusion, only an arbitrary ending, provisional, false teeth, a wooden leg, "and they lived happily ever after," or "the man's head disappeared beneath the waves," or "Robledo threw himself into the river and Maryse followed him out of love"; tonight, recently departed from my circle of mushrooms and yellow flowers, Fairy Godmother with her stiffened wings and her face a wrinkled raisin, telling me quickly that her final years are upon her, announcing her imminent disappearance, speaking of her slow resurrection in the juice of blackberries and wild strawberries, "time is God's measurement and all that is living upon the earth must die and be reborn forever and ever and ever"; tonight, when nothing and no one can give me the answer I seek. (Might the ink of my words be the juice of my resurrection? Because if that were true, I fear I only have strength left for a partial resuscitation. Forty years of my life would dry up in the inkwell. Oh, my God, so much to tell and my days grow short!) And yet, now a door has begun to open to me, the revelatory mouth of a snail's shell: my story is not these pages that you are reading but rather one my flesh has written in time, submerged writing, letters in water and lime, invisible ink that not even I can bring to light; tonight, oh, tonight, I've just glimpsed that vast generative power that locks away a second of anyone's life, orgasm or pistol-shot, a yes or a no, word or void, gesture or intention, and this is how true stories are constructed, rhizome stories, mangrove tales, where one who writes a silence or an action is always in the middle of things, here and there, inside and out, a lone informant from the net of stories, web of webs covering the body of God; tonight, at last, on this strange night that has raised Maryse in my memory, I tell you that I have made a mistake, that I believed I was reliving my hours through you, without understanding that I had already written them indelibly with my acts, second by second, minute by minute, and it is in that time, and not in yours, in which I am perpetually reborn, consequence and cause, daughter and mother, mother and daughter, because the words that attest to my existence don't run only between my parents' wedding in Lausanne and Milly and Daniel's love in New York, but rather spill out by the handful, stories that fate allows to fall, crashing and becoming confused with the other stories that came before and sinking into the paradox of the chicken and the egg, and after such grand words, who else but me can you blame for the opium I prescribed for myself?; it's not that I think what you are reading doesn't deserve to be read (what more could I want than to interest you in my life?), but the hours of proximity that now unite us grant me the right to be frank: what I am telling you, in my own way and to my own taste, is not my life, but merely its tiny glow.

ॐ

Since Robledo's cousin—his only living relative—lived in Trinidad, a city quite distant from Havana, I was left to take charge of the wake and burial, huge social events in accordance with local custom. After three truly nightmarish days, I threw myself on my cot and cried for Maryse. Once again I asked myself why those I loved the most always left my side. In my frustration, I evoked the forest clearing to tell my sorrows to Fairy Godmother. But for some reason my mind conjured nothing more than the outlines of the magic circle, only to have even these fade away. One week later, looking at myself in the mirror, I'd expected to be confronted with a face absolutely gnawed away by grief. I was mistaken. True, my eyelids were red, but I saw neither a single gray hair on my head nor any new wrinkles on my skin. With a sigh of resignation, my image withdrew from the mirror.

Robledo's cousin, Don Jaime Echevarría, did not resemble him in the slightest. He was short, with yellowish skin and narrow shoulders. He said he was delighted to make my acquaintance. But between his words of gratitude for my having taken charge of the "delicate situation," I could read that his real interest was to find out if "Doña Marisa had nearby relations." Incapable of carrying on a conversation about Maryse, I told him a bit brutally that I would testify that she had none so that he could take possession of his cousin's assets as soon as possible.

That same afternoon, I wrote to Ducharme, authorizing him to make arrangements with La Muraille's descendents. I was prepared to lose the château and its lands, but not the forest—how could I possibly hand over my clearing, Dunsinane's grave, and the little stone house in which he'd been born to those swine? In the event that they protested, he could give them the property with the farms and vineyards, but the forest was not negotiable and I wanted that made extremely clear. As for the house on Saint-Honoré, it should be mortgaged, the credit remitted to my bankers in Havana.

A few days later the letter from the Protomedicato arrived: "We, doctors Don Nicolás del Valle, honorary physician of the Chamber and Regent protomedico of the Protomedicato Tribunal of this ever loyal city of Havana and Island of Cuba, and Don Lorenzo Hernández, honorary consulting physician and second protomedico; members of the Patriotic Society of said city, judges, examiners, visitors, and lord mayors of all physicians, surgeons, apothecaries, phlebotomists, herniaists, algebraists, occultists, distillers, midwives, leprocists, and all else comprising the medical faculty, etc. In such capacity our Tribunal did grant audience to one Don Enrique Faber, a native of Switzerland, subject of the King of France, five feet and eight inches in height, color white, eyes blue, small mouth with good dentition, hair and eyebrows blond, beardless, twenty years of age and of the Catholic, Apostolic, and Roman religion, and he did relate to us having studied as surgeon under bona fide instructors for the time stipulated by law, of which he provided ample information, with authentic documents viewed by us in all our authority, and he did conclude with a petition that we admit him to be examined; and being in agreement, we did henceforth admit him, and we did examine him in theory and practice, in two successive hours, asking him many and various questions about the matter at hand and any other we deemed appropriate, to which he did respond well and thoroughly, and having made the customary oath to defend insofar as possible the Immaculate Conception of Our Lady the Virgin Mary, to use his faculties well and faithfully, to give alms to the poor through the course of his work, and in so doing to uphold the laws and proclamations of the honest and licit precepts of this Tribunal, renouncing all regicide and tyrannicide, we did approve and order that title and license be granted him so that he may and shall, in all cities, towns, and regions, practice any and all manner of treatment;

visiting the ill, training students, and practicing whatsoever approved and validated surgeons may and must practice, reserving for himself without exception, all the graces, benefits, and privileges, exemptions, immunities and prerogatives that are owed to him as a Romanist Surgeon. In virtue of which we issue the present document, signed by our hand, and countersigned by the undersigned notary, which shall henceforth be valid under condition that the law of *media annata* be satisfied, without which requirement this title shall be rendered null and void."

In addition, in a second document, written in rhetoric every bit as medieval as the first, I was named as an officer of the Protomedicato in the city of Baracoa, on the far eastern side of the island, charged with the responsibility of "examining candidates, issuing diplomas, inspecting hospitals, and overseeing the best possible development of the medical professions in said city and adjacent villages." Clearly, as a disciple of Broussais and Larrey, they wanted to send me as far away as possible—Baracoa was more than three hundred leagues from Havana. Nevertheless, fed up with Havana and with living in a house that didn't belong to me, I decided to accept the appointment.

After transferring my account to a banker in Santiago de Cuba, I set off with very few belongings and with no plans other than to earn a living.

25

STRETCHED SLEEPILY ALONG A NARROW peninsula, and isolated from the rest of Cuba by injurious roads and a raw and monumental natural world, Baracoa was its own little island. The humble homeland of sailors, fishermen, and smugglers, life there had revolved around the sea since time immemorial. More a village than a city, every imaginable item was peddled on its four paltry streets, especially on the one called Mercaderes. Anchored at its modest port, their flags prudently lowered, a Colombian pirate brig might sit alongside a Baltimore clipper, an ailing Haitian schooner and a trade ship from Jamaica or Martinique or Curaçao. They bought leather, honey, wax, precious woods, coffee, and tobacco, as well as cassava bread, dried coconut, salted fish, ham, and lard for the return journey; they sold fabric, ceramics, costume jewelry, iron objects, pins, books and paper, knives and hunting muskets, rum, wine and, from time to time, a handful of slaves. Although slave trafficking was prohibited by royal decree and severely punishable, almost everyone in the city was involved in it in one way or another. This state of affairs was made possible by the fact that both civil and ecclesiastical authorities looked the other way. There was no jail, properly speaking, and the clergy not only tolerated smuggling—a cause for excommunication in other eras—but also went so far as to permit the existence of a cult founded on the discovery, amid the wild foliage of the forest, of a few pieces of wood in the shape of a cross. Not to mention that they did nothing whatsoever to prevent the mixing of Christianity with the witchcraft and superstitions brought over by the blacks, which, to me, seemed to take matters a little too far. In any case, the European race was in the minority there. Of every ten inhabitants, three could call themselves white, another three were Negro, and the rest were slaves. As money was scarce, old and new coins of various nations exchanged hands; the same pocket might hold a napoleon and a louis d'or, a dollar and a Dutch florin, an old piece of eight, perhaps some infamous pirate's plunder alongside a Peruvian silver *macuquina* piece. As for copper coins, everything was accepted, no matter where it might have come from; Mexico or Portugal, it was all the same. Obviously, Spanish was spoken there, a singsong Spanish peppered with archaisms that would have delighted Christopher. But there was also a fair amount of French spoken, especially among the older people. Having fled the revolution in Saint-Domingue, thousands of settlers and their families had ended up in Baracoa. Some had continued on to Louisiana or Canada; others opted to stay in the area, and they'd established coffee plantations in the region's most protected valleys. Given how steep the landscape was, they grew so little in the way of sugarcane that three rickety mills were sufficient to grind what was produced. Some even spoke a bit of broken English, not only because it was conducive to business; certain shady individuals from Jamaica and Florida had landed there as well—fugitives from justice, deserters, hucksters, charlatans—living off the gambling dens and clandestine prostitutes they brought over from Haiti or Cartagena to work for a season. It was a mulatto from Savannah named Wilson, accused of seducing a white woman, who gave me my first lessons in English in exchange for my having removed two stones from his gall bladder.

I didn't make much money, what one might call hard cash, through my profession. And not because I lacked clients, but rather because of the general poverty of most of the population. Suffice to say that the public offices that were sold for thousands of reales in Havana could be gotten here at bargain prices—a position as a high constable in the capital cost more than three hundred thousand reales; in Baracoa, it could be had for five hundred. Not even the merchants, primarily Spaniards and foreigners, had carriages; what was more, since very few people could buy and maintain horses, it was not uncommon to see the local ladies, dressed in their finest ball gowns and shaded by parasols, parading by atop the very same oxen that had pulled the plows that morning. In any event, four months after I'd opened my practice in a little hut on the main street, I was already living comfortably on the outskirts of town. In exchange for a monthly rent of fifteen reales (or its equivalent in copper), I had at my disposal a wood and brick house with two little dirt-floored huts attached, like wings, on either side. Since I received most payments for my services in kind, I had already accumulated a noisy rooster, a sty with a dozen suckling pigs, a decent horse, two goats, each with her kid, and a black and growling mastiff to intimidate the wild dogs that sometimes came down from the mountains on moonless nights to raid whatever they could find. My pantry overflowed with fruit, coconuts and bananas, yams, pumpkins, cassava bread, and ears of corn. Twice a month, on the second and fourth Fridays, I opened my practice to the truly destitute. Not seeing any reason to leave, for the time being, a place where I felt so needed and welcomed, I had a frame made for my *Woman* and hired as servants a black woman named Felipa and her niece Norberta, who, in addition to seeing to the domestic chores, also took charge of the growing demands of my barnyard.

It was true what I'd been told when I first arrived: Baracoa had its own climate. While on the rest of the island the dry season prevailed, in Baracoa it was the rainy season, or, better put, the torrential downpour season. Since this was the most unhealthful of the seasons, my first months there were exhausting: dozens of cases of every possible kind of fever—including typhoid—filled the hospital and one of the huts attached to my house. As if that weren't enough, there were no leeches to be had there. "Maybe in Guantánamo," guessed Areces, the only apothecary I'd been able to find. Except it had been impossible to get to Guantánamo for weeks. Even in good weather, many found the barriers that nature had imposed in the region insurmountable. Suffice to say that not even the riders who delivered the mail attempted to make it to Baracoa, obliging anyone interested in sending a letter to do so by boat to Santiago de Cuba. That city was about seventy leagues from Baracoa, but traveling there by land was an undertaking worthy of La Condamine or Humbolt. I'll explain: as much as it rained, the rain fell only on the north slope of the high mountain range at the base of which the village, the corrals, the work yards, and the coffee plantations were situated. The low and heavy storm clouds that blew out of the northeast would explode in torrents of water upon crashing into the mountainside, permitting very few to cross over to the other side of the mountain. And so, anyone wishing to travel south (in the direction of Guantánamo, Santiago de Cuba, el Cobre, el Caney, los Tiguabos) had to first open a route through dense vegetation—the road would be washed out after just one week of rain—while scaling craggy heights of hundreds of meters; further on, negotiate the prickly, cramped pine forests, the deep ravines and dangerous mountain ridges, then descend through a vast desert-like terrain, defended by cacti and walls of spiky vegetation that sank into a basin of arid earth and suffocating air that gave out in the direction of Guantánamo, or continue westward through a long valley until coming upon a trail across a formidable mountain range, beyond which lay, at the foot of a sort of stone amphitheater, the city and port of Santiago de Cuba.

Not that this isolation was uncomfortable for me. I had decided to stay there until I knew, definitively, what arrangement my lawyers had come to with the descendants of the Viscount La Muraille. Despite my precise instructions, I was afraid of losing my forest, which was, for me, the most important thing I had left. Also, over the years, the people of Baracoa had learned to entertain themselves without any help from the rest of the island. Not only did they perform, in the old style, the Creole dances of Saint-Domingue, accompanied by drums and songs sung by "French" Negroes (as slaves from that island were called), but they had also introduced innovations to the local music. Adding to this the tunes the sailors continually brought from ports all over the Caribbean, including from *terra firma*, it becomes easy to image the huge variety of music and dances there were—so numerous that I've forgotten their bizarre names. Due to my position as protomedico and a certain affection I'd inspired among the locals, I received constant invitations to attend the jubilant parties with which they celebrated baptisms, birthdays, weddings, or the saint day of one Virgin or another believed to perform miracles. Music was made simply: plucking strings, blowing into earthenware jugs, shaking and scratching gourds and beating irons and goatskin drums. Nevertheless, as I felt a bit out of place amid these gatherings, my most favored pastime was exploring that picturesque region. Sometime I went to the west, to the abundant river that flowed beneath a gorgeous vault of intertwined foliage; at others I went east, descending half a dozen terraced headlands, all the way to the easternmost point of the entire island—a place called *Maisí*. It was there I first saw an iguana, a strange-looking lizard whose meat, which I never dared to sample, was highly coveted by the locals. Most frequently on my excursions I would wander through the cool and tangled jungle that began to creep up the mountainside just beyond my barnyard. The trees that Robledo had pointed out to me in Vuelta Abajo grew there, among many others; ferns and parasitic plants of all varieties abounded, among them the sumptuous orchid. There was ripe fruit within arm's reach, especially cherimoya, guava, and cashew, whose delicious nut was eaten roasted. Adhered to the trunks of palms and coconut trees, to the cedars and *guásimas*, were the most brightly colored snails imaginable, tiny toys painted with green, blue, red, black, and yellow stripes. Some Sundays, when I was able to set off early in the morning, I would make it quite far up the mountainside. There I found the caves that the primitive inhabitants of Cuba had used as homes. It was still possible to scrape the earth and find their bones and stone tools, which I quickly began collecting. Arriving home with some little idol or earthenware fragment, both Felipa and Norberta would make the sign of the cross over them and utter strange prayers. According to them, that part of the mountain was haunted, and it was not uncommon to see the spirits of the Indians moving amid the trees like tremulous blue flames.

I've related this, not because I fancy myself a naturalist or an explorer, but to illustrate that my time in that land of rugged solitude, where the only wealth that existed was that of the Natural Kingdom, was far from undesirable. In truth, I had found there, on the other side of the ocean, a silence and peace similar to what I had in my forest. For a time I was sincerely happy, and that state of placidity, conducive to remembering my dear Maryse, could have gone on for God only knows how long. Except that on one of my excursions, sitting under the dome of a ceiba tree eating wild guavas, I saw the slim figure of Fairy Godmother pass by, singing and crowned in orchids. It wasn't as it always had been, the product of my imagination; it was a Fairy Godmother of flesh and blood, walking in the real world, her step light, almost transparent, as though she were floating above the moss and ferns, with the same woman's body with which she'd appeared before me, a year ago, in my room in Havana. Perplexed, I found myself unable to immediately stand up and follow her. When I did manage to rise, I could no longer find her. I called out to her in vain until the sun went down.

You'll have noticed that I have a somewhat obsessive temperament. And so, like the fly fallen in a cup of milk, that vision upset my tranquility. Impatiently, I would tend to the last patients of the afternoon and, not even going into the house first, I would turn my horse toward the steep spot of ferns and orchids where she had crossed my path before vanishing into the thicket. On one occasion, dusk already falling, I heard her laugh amid the final twittering of the birds. Like a mad woman, parting the dense foliage of the creeping vines, I cast about looking for her. In deep darkness, I finally left the place, with my face and hands scratched by thorns and the fear that I'd fallen under some sort of bewitchment. Nevertheless, I kept looking for her, but the days went by and neither one nor the other Fairy Godmother, the imaginary or the real, answered my call.

Meanwhile, a ship from Santiago de Cuba delivered a remittance of seven thousand reales from the mortgage on my house in Paris, my order of laudanum and Peruvian powders, and news of the consecutive deaths of the Queen Consort Maria Isabel, the Queen Mother Maria Luisa, and the abdicated King Charles IV. Given the inconvenience of celebrating three separate funeral rites, the authorities decided to commemorate the departed royals in one grand event that would include eulogies and prayers by the local rector and two priests, a public procession of the Holy Cross of la Parra, and speeches delivered by the mayor and the constable from a platform hung with black silk serge, followed by a recitation of laudatory poems to be read by their actual authors. As an officer of the Protomedicato and the town council physician, I was invited to sit on the platform alongside the provincial officer of the Holy Brotherhood. It had been declared a day of mourning until six in the evening, and the plaza was surrounded by stands selling printed verses of remembrance and all manner of sweets and refreshments. The place, inundated with people, horses, and ox-carts, looked like a festival. Suddenly, surveying the scene once again from the platform, I saw, clear as day, the figure of Fairy Godmother standing out in sharp relief from the crowd. She was sitting atop a donkey, and an acquaintance of mine, a man named Chicoy, the youngest and poorest scribe in Baracoa, was holding the reins. She was wearing the crown of orchids she'd had on in the mountains. I jumped up from my stool and, slipping through the crowd without taking my eyes off her, I contrived to come up alongside her. As our eyes met, I realized that mine had played a bad trick on me. That thin fifteen-year-old girl, with her black eyes, ivory complexion, bare feet and mended dress, was not my fairy. To be sure, she did resemble her, so much so that, if my old friend had had a sister, it could well have been her.

"Doctor Faber!" Chicoy greeted me. "How wonderful it all looks! We are fortunate that it hasn't rained."

"Quite so," I responded.

"Allow me to give you some verses that I've composed for the occasion," he said, handing me a sheet. "They've been quite popular, though I find them a bit dithyrambic."

"Thank you."

Seeing my gaze return to the girl, he said: "Doña Juana de León, a distant cousin."

"At your service, sir. Call me Juanita; that's what everyone calls me," she said from atop the donkey. Her voice, low and murmuring, was nothing like Fairy Godmother's. Yet suddenly the expression in her eyes changed and I felt the damp and mysterious gaze of the mistress of the forest travel my body from head to toe. Confused and speechless, I extended my hand, inviting her to dismount. She took it and slid off the side of the donkey. Immediately, as though she'd known me for years, she took my arm and began walking and whispering: "How long I've waited for you! I've dreamed of you since I was a little girl. I dreamed that you looked just as you do and that you came from the other side of the sea. I've done nothing but think of you since I saw you in the mountains. I was about to return to the Castle of the Orchids to see if I could find you again. If I didn't do it, it was only so that we could be formally introduced, as good manners require. What would you have thought of me?"

Entranced by her words, I scarcely managed to stammer: "I've been looking for you in the mountains. Once I heard you laughing. I thought you were a fairy."

"It must have been an Indian spirit. Sometimes they come down to the place where we saw each other. There are no fairies in Baracoa. I don't think there are anywhere in Cuba. Here we have only the spirits of the dead, *lloronas*, water mothers, and *güijes*."

"Then how do you know about fairies?"

"My cousin Chicoy lends me books. He's almost as poor as I am, but he's a member of the poetry circle and he borrows them from his friends."

"What are water mothers and *güijes?*"

"You don't want to know."

Our conversation was taking place in an alley near the plaza where, the hours of mourning officially over, the garrison musicians had begun to play marches.

"I haven't seen you at the dances," I said.

"I don't go out much," she replied evasively. "I should go back now. My cousin will be worried."

"May I pay you a visit at your house?" I asked, hoping to initiate a relationship.

"No. Not at my house. We can meet in the mountains, in the place where the orchids are. I'll go there on Sunday, though I can't tell you what time."

And again I felt the gaze of Fairy Godmother. (Yes, I've already said it, Fairy Godmother is, and always has been, a product of my imagination. But both her form and her name come out of an illustrated edition of *Cinderella* that Françoise used to read to me in the clearing. For years I took her for a real being, although from a different world. She was my closest friend and, while the gardener's daughters gathered blackberries and mushrooms, I would stretch out on the grass and talk to her without moving my lips. It wasn't until my days of sorrow in Foix that I realized that she was the very frontier of my own self.)

When I took her hand, I found it hot.

"You have a fever."

"It's nothing," she said, her mouth forming a grimace.

"Do you feel ill?"

"It's nothing," she repeated, and left me at a run.

⁂

The day after the homage to the royals, my need to know more about her led me to visit Chicoy in the dilapidated hut that served as both his home and office.

"She's an orphan. Her mother died in childbirth and she lived in the mountains with her father until she was ten. A strange man. He never worked for anybody. He spent years and years searching for the Treasure of Monsiú."

"What is that?" I interrupted.

"A rich old man's treasure. A Frenchman. He came from the United States when I was a child, must have been twenty years ago now. He brought a barrel filled with silver spoons that were inventoried by the customs house. He started to build a coffee plantation in the mountains, but at that time there were Cimarron slaves in Toa, not far from here, and they killed him with machetes before he ever revealed the place where he'd buried the spoons. If you'll forgive the question, what is making you laugh, sir?"

"The many turns the world takes," I said, wishing that Maryse were alive to laugh with me.

"Many turns, so very true," said Chicoy, unaware that the name Monsiú was not unknown to me. "Well, my cousin Juanita suddenly found herself alone in the mountains. Fortunately, her great Aunt Asunción took her in. They live in the lower part of the city and are very poor, more so than me even, which is saying something. Obviously, I can't help them much. Sometimes I give them a bit of sugar, coffee, and cassava bread, also some fish or meat that I take from my own pantry. I feel sorry for them, especially Juanita. Occasionally on a Sunday I take her to the mountains on my donkey. She feels more at ease there than in the house. Sometimes she gathers flowers for her parents' graves."

"Her health is not good," I said. "Yesterday she had a fever."

"I've found her worse lately," agreed Chicoy. "Her father died of consumption. I've told her to go see you on the poor people's day. I'd even come with her. But she doesn't want to."

"You should continue to insist," I said, as though I weren't planning to go to see her on Sunday. "Bring her to my office as soon as possible. Don't worry. I won't charge you."

The day of our meeting arrived at last and, unable to contain myself, I saddled my horse at dawn. I waited for her all morning amid the orchids. I was too restless to keep still: I'd sit down on a rock, stand up, walk among the trees, and return to my horse all over again. I made up my mind that she wasn't coming, but when I checked the time I was surprised to see that it was just past midday. I would wait for her until sunset. I wanted nothing from her. I would be content just having her near me, listening to the low murmur of her voice, feeling her bewitching gaze spread over me. When I heard her singing off to my right, I went to meet her. As always, she was barefoot and, as I took her hands, I asked myself how she could walk on that rough terrain without hurting her feet.

"I can't stay," she whispered with her head lowered. "My cousin is waiting for me in the Palace of the Snails and I must get back right away. He says he has some papers to copy before tomorrow."

"The Palace of the Snails?"

"It's over there," she said, pointing in the direction she'd come. "If you look closely, you'll see that there are always snails stuck to the tree trunks. When I was a little girl, I named many places in the mountains. We lived near here. If I weren't in such a hurry, I'd take you to see what's left of my house. A hill of guano, that's what's left," she said, laughing. "Now let's pick some flowers. My cousin should see me return with some."

"Your hands are hot. Do you feel all right?"

"It's nothing," she said, disentangling her hands from mine.

"You should come to my office. I would like to examine you."

"I don't want you to see me as a sick person," she said, furrowing her brow.

"But you might be," I said, and I yanked the stem of an orchid and put it in the neckline of her dress. She looked at me and asked flirtatiously: "Am I pretty or ugly?"

"Beautiful. You are very beautiful. You look like a flower," I said, blushing.

"An orchid?"

"The most beautiful of all."

"Then here," she said, and, standing on her tiptoes, she kissed me.

I hugged her and held her against my body. We stayed like that for a while, in silence, and I could feel her in my nipples.

"I need to go now," she said suddenly, sliding out of my arms. Then she looked at me for a few seconds with that gaze of hers, and started off running toward the vine thicket without saying goodbye.

℘

There they were, she and Chicoy, waiting for me outside my door, along with half a dozen patients bearing chickens in cages. When I invited her in, she whispered: "I had to see you." I made her sit down and I took her pulse and her temperature; then, I pressed my ear against her warm back, which trembled at the contact. As soon as I head her breathe deeply and cough, I knew that she was the victim of consumption, or tuberculosis, the new name for that slow but inexorable ailment.

"You are ill," I told her, with Chicoy now present. "You need rest. Above all, a good diet."

"I can't do any of that. My aunt is very old and I do all the washing, ironing, sweeping, and whatever cooking there may be. She's in charge of sewing and mending the torn clothing that people bring to us. That's what we live on. What she earns is barely enough for us to eat like birds."

I looked at Chicoy in search of some solution, but he shrugged his shoulders, telling me with that gesture that there was nothing, or very little, that he could do.

The cries of pain from an old man that had been brought to me on a stretcher forced me to show them to the door of my tiny exam room.

"I'll see you tomorrow," I told them as we said goodbye.

That night I realized that I was in love—that strange unease that causes one to tremble inside and to feel weak, to remember the first kiss over and over again, every slightest detail of that meeting of lips, the small gestures, the inflection of the voice, the gaze. But how could we continue our romance without my reveling my true identity? If I was sure of anything, it was her sexual inclinations. Then, how to tell her that I was as much a woman as she? And not only that: even if my imposture didn't bother her and she were capable of loving me as a woman, what assurances would I have that she would remain silent, that she would hide my secret? Flustered by so much thinking and my failure to see any solution to the problems I posed to myself, I moved on to considering her state of health. There was no question that her illness would kill her. But it would do so little by little, and long periods of remission were not uncommon. Further, there were cases, when the body is assisted by the proper treatment, in which the pulmonary lesions cured themselves. But, clearly, in her case—her body's fragility, the physical labor, the poor diet—the end could be upon her in two or three years. I had more than enough food, so I could certainly offer her everything that she might want to eat. As for keeping her at rest, the best thing would be to invite her and her aunt to live in my house for a while. They could stay in one of the huts, and Felipa and Norberta could take charge of their chores. What was more, in my house she would enjoy the good mountain air.

She received my proposition with a shy smile, and Chicoy with a hug of gratitude. That very afternoon, however, an old woman burst into my office, ignoring everyone waiting outside my door. She was ancient, her face so furrowed with wrinkles that it looked like a crumpled up ball of paper. It was Doña Asunción, Juanita's aunt.

"I've come to clarify the situation between us," she said determinedly, as soon as she'd taken a seat. "I appreciate your good intentions, but you will understand that if we move into your house we will become the target of gossip for the entire town. They'll say terrible things about Juanita, and they'll accuse me of prostituting her. Our misery, which, heaven knows, is great, should not mislead you: we are poor but decent. We've never given any cause for foolishness or gossip."

"I don't doubt it. However—"

"And don't think we are ignorant, sir. I myself, with all the work I've always had, taught Juanita to read and write. I have educated her, sir. When I took her in, she was like a little mountain animal. Furthermore, and certainly you will have taken note of this already, we have not a drop of African blood. My great-great-grandfather was the grand-nephew of Don Pedro de León, second mayor of Baracoa and pacifier of the Indians. Surely you've heard of Chief Guamá?"

"I've heard a bit, but this is about your niece's health. About her life, even. Believe me that I don't exaggerate," I said, taken by surprise at the lack of rationality in her judgment.

"And what is death compared to honor? Nothing, sir. Absolutely nothing. People are born and they die, lives come and go, but the honor of noble blood endures in memory," she said, suffocating on the vehemence with which she uttered those words. "You are a foreigner and you are unfamiliar with our customs. Otherwise, you would know that no woman in our country with an ounce of self-respect would ever go to live in the home of a single man."

"There are other women in the house," I protested.

"Two black women, and one of them, Norberta, has quite a reputation. Her mother's mother came from Santa Marta to work a season, and she was lucky enough to take up with the Negro Miguel, a knife and scissors grinder who spent the few reales he earned on whiskey. Of course, Don Prudencio, the parish priest at the time, convinced them to marry. But Nievecita, Norberta's mother, is the fruit of concubinage. I'm saying this, and I've never slandered anyone."

Since the nonsense I was hearing showed no signs of abating and my office was full of children with diarrhea, I tried to put an end to the discussion with a new offer.

"As you wish, Doña Asunción. In any case, please know that I am committed to helping your niece get well. We doctors also have our honor and it would be a failure of the principles of my profession if, capable of saving her life, I allowed her to die without lifting a finger."

"What are you insinuating, sir? That you'll support Juanita and me? We'd die first! We support ourselves! Who do you think you are?" she shouted in my face, and stood up. "You are speaking with a person of illustrious lineage!"

I let her go, my mouth hanging open in surprise. She limped a little and, watching her through the window as she laboriously climbed the hill of my steep street, I felt sorry for her. It appeared that modern times had not yet arrived in Baracoa. But, in that case, what to do?

⁂

Determined to clear things up with Chicoy, I went to see him in his hut. I found him in shirtsleeves, composing verses.

"Forgive me for not receiving you in my jacket, Doctor Faber. Doña Asunción is mending it."

"It's precisely her that I've come to discuss," I said, and I related the retails of our conversation.

"Oh, Doctor!" he sighed, after hearing my complaints. "That's how life is in these mountains. I understand you perfectly. Thanks to my reading, I have some education, and I know that here we live as though it were still the times of the Crusades. What can I tell you? I also feel myself a victim of backwardness and poverty. My spirit is not lofty, but at least it flies above those of most people in this city. And yet, here you have me, with a donkey for a steed, copying documents for an ochavo a page, when I'm not writing letters for illiterates and rhymes for the love struck. To judge by the little

445

I earn, I will never be able to pay the four hundred reales it costs to become a public scribe," he lamented, chewing the end of his quill. "I can't think of any solution at the moment. Doña Asunción is stubborn. Neither I, nor anyone, could make her change her mind. I am sorry for my cousin Juanita, who is also a martyr, although without knowing it. Do you think she'll die soon?"

"In a year or two if things go on the way they are."

"What a pity! Isn't there some kind of medicine that could save her?"

"No. Only rest and a good diet."

"There are Negroes here who use herbs to make cures."

"Pure superstition. No herb will prolong her life."

"Then there's nothing to be done," he said, dipping his quill into the inkwell.

"I have an idea. I have a barnyard. I could make sure you get goat's milk, pork, chickens, anything she needs. And you could give these things to Doña Asunción as though they were gifts from you. What do you think? Naturally, I'd pay you for your services."

Chicoy picked up the quill and began to chew on it again.

"I could take a few things to them," he said. "Not a lot. They know I'm poor. But I'll be completely honest with you. My cousin has confessed to me that she's in love with you. She commissioned the very love sonnet I'm composing right now. If you wait a little, I'll finish it. I only have four verses left."

"For me?" I asked, moved.

"She thinks that her love might be returned. At least she harbors hope. Anyway, forgive me for butting in to your affairs, but, assuming that Juanita is correct in terms of your feelings, is there something standing in the way of your asking her hand in marriage? Don't answer me now, I beg of you. Think about it after you've read our sonnet. I say 'ours' because, while the meter and rhyme are mine, the ideas are hers. But I should warn you that, even were you to ask Doña Asunción for my cousin's hand, you cannot count on her consent. You are a foreigner, and French, which makes matters worse. Of course, I'll do whatever I can to ensure that the marriage occurs, but it won't be easy to convince Doña Asunción that you aren't in support of Napoleon Bonaparte's return, since here, he's considered one rung lower than the antichrist. Everyone knows that you served in his army."

While Chicoy finished his sonnet, I thought about his proposition. Certainly, it was the most logical way to unite two beings who loved one another, as long as they were a man and a woman. But why not a woman and a woman? I tried to imagine myself married to Juanita, the joy of seeing her every day of the week, of eating and drinking and sleeping together, of roaming the forest as she pointed her finger and named her palaces and castles. Seeing Chicoy blowing on the paper to dry the ink, I decided to bet everything I had. I would confess the truth to Juanita. If she accepted me as I was, I'd propose to her.

"Here you have it," said the scribe, and he extended his arm with a magnanimous gesture. "You'll note my admiration for the classics."

"Thank you, my friend," I said, taking the paper. "As for the idea of marriage, before I can give an answer, I must speak with Juanita alone. You'll understand that this is an important step and there are things we should discuss in private."

"I don't see any problem with that. I'll bring her to your office tomorrow."

"Not to my office," I said, out of professional prudence. "We'll meet on Sunday in the mountains. Where the orchids grow."

"As you wish. I am at your disposal."

26

EDUCATED WITHIN THE MATERIALIST AND prosaic medicine of the French schools of my era, and trained in the dissection room and on the battlefield, I've scarcely ever taken an interest in psychology, much less in hypnotism and phrenology. I feel I haven't missed out on much and I don't regret my lack of interest. That discipline has yet to produce a prophet, one who might offer a convincing explanation for depressive states, the cause of obsessions and irrational fear; one who might illuminate, with his science, the dark labyrinths in which crime and pleasure are born, dreams and hallucinations, desire and guilt and, above all, and most relevant to me, one who might decipher the riddle of love. Oh, how I would love to travel through time and listen to that teacher who will no doubt arrive; to have the opportunity to read his books so as to learn more about myself! Why have I been capable of loving other women without ceasing to be a woman myself and, without it preventing me from loving men with equal ardor and authenticity? The funny thing is, even supposing that such boundaryless love were the consequence of an abnormal psyche, I've never felt it as a misfortune, limitation, illness, or chronic aberration, nor even as a cause for concern. My desire has always taken shape in a completely natural way, as though it were a physiological function. For me, the genders seemed to disappear and, as occurs with friendship, I experienced feelings of love on a higher, more general plane, that is, as a *human being*. If I speak of this here, it is to make it very clear that I fell in love with Juanita not because I felt like a man or because I desired her as though she were one. I loved her woman to woman, as I loved

Nadezhda and Fauriel. And I loved her blindly, heedless of the consequences that our union could bring.

∞

Shall I reproduce here the proceedings from my trial, published in Cuban newspapers that portrayed me as an aberration, a bearded lady or spider woman or some other circus freak? I haven't yet decided. It would be easy enough to find, among my papers, the newspaper serial entitled *Enriqueta Faber. The Woman Doctor before the Court*, hugely popular in Havana in those days, and copy out the pages as I think best. Yet, I hesitate. And it's not that I put any stock in the words uttered by my judges, magistrates, prosecutors, and defenders. It's that what was, for me, a true Mount Calvary, can be quite boring to read—the same vague accusations, the same arbitrary interpretations of the law, even my lawyer's and my own justifications. Because, as the erudite Vidaurre, my defender in the appeals trial, would ask repeatedly: "Does any law exist that prohibits women from dressing as men, and that expressly punishes one who does so?" And, of course, there was no such law, and this void was filled instead with the prejudices of those who judged and condemned me.

While I have not forgotten the dates of my court appearances, it is impossible for me to pinpoint when I realized that Juanita, Chicoy, and Doña Asunción had set a trap for me. I can say only that, once married and installed as the woman of my house, Juanita transformed into another person. The passion she'd claimed to feel for me suddenly began to vanish, and the night came when she asked me to leave her alone, to go to sleep in a different room because my snoring kept her awake.

"Snoring? No one's ever told me that I snore," I replied.

"Well, you do. You can't hear yourself because you sleep like a stone. You snore so much that I'm awake all night. Just look at how weak I am. I can barely walk anymore."

When my desire would flare and, almost surreptitiously, I'd slip between the sheets of her bed—formerly my own—and begin to caress her, she'd stay motionless and mute as a statue or simply reject me out of hand.

"Leave me alone, Enriqueta. My head hurts. My cousin told

450

me yesterday that marriage has not been good for me. He thinks I'm paler and more drawn than ever."

"I think you're better than you were. You've gained a few pounds and you almost never have fevers anymore," I said idiotically. An idiot a thousand times over, since, despite all my education and everything I'd seen and lived through, it never occurred to me to think that those villagers might possess sufficient intelligence and cleverness to swindle me.

"What happens is that I get the fevers during the day, when you're in your office. It's a good thing that dear Chicoy comes to keep me company and read novels to me. If it weren't for that, I don't know what would become of me."

One day I realized that I felt jealous of Chicoy, although I should clarify that never in my wildest dreams did it occur to me that there was anything between him and Juanita other than the affection that exists between relatives. It simply annoyed me that she, my wife, who had married me knowing that I was a woman and who had pledged me her eternal love, now appeared to prefer his company to mine.

"Chicoy is like a brother to me," she would say, hearing my timid complaints. "I don't know why it should bother you that he comes to visit me. We've always been very close. If you don't believe me, ask my Aunt Asunción."

I would never have dreamed of asking Doña Asunción anything, removed as she now was from Juanita and our conjugal situation. But after changing my mind once or twice, thinking it beneath me, I asked my servants how frequently Chicoy visited the house.

"Two, even three times a week," said Filipa.

"Doña Juanita receives him in her room and they spend hours and hours in there," said Norberta, making it clear that she found the matter quite suspect.

One afternoon, jealousy eating away at my insides, I closed my office and returned to the house. Even before I'd arrived, when, from the street, I saw Chicoy's mule tied to one of my lemon trees, my heart began to pound in my chest. My hands trembled as I opened the door. Norberta came out from the kitchen to greet me or to ask me what I wanted for supper, but I signaled to her to stay quiet. I approached Juanita's door. I assumed she'd have the bolt latched and I threw myself against it with all my force. Over the noise and the broken boards and hinges, I saw what I had not wanted to see: a flustered Juanita looking at me over Chicoy's penis, still inside her mouth.

Naturally, she wouldn't declare any of this in the complaint she lodged before the court in Santiago de Cuba. In the wretched pages her lawyer composed—and now I do think I should share certain details of my trial—she affirmed that: "In the year 1819, an individual purporting to be named Enrique Faber, with a degree as a Doctor of Surgery and a native of Switzerland, solicited my hand in marriage. Given the circumstances of orphanhood and destitution in which I found myself, I succumbed to said person's wishes, without it having been possible for me to suspect that the intent of this abominable creature was to profane the sacraments and to mock my person in the most cruel and detestable manner possible, taking advantage of my good faith, my innocence, and the inexperience to which I was subject as a result of my great modesty. Certain details, which decency prevents me from mentioning, obliged me to spy on this individual's movements until once, believing me asleep, said individual became careless, and I was able to confirm her true condition. This discovery, which the monster was not expecting, obliged her to confess to me her incapacity for the conjugal state, and she humiliated herself to the extreme of telling me that she would allow me the freedom to take as lovers whatever men I so chose, since our separation was not convenient for her business. Finding these ideas unworthy of any person of even the most minimal morality, and incapable of consenting to her proposals, which were as disgraceful as they were scandalous, I rejected them outright. The false husband, having been made aware of my repulsion and of the indignation resulting from the hoax she had inflicted upon me, offered to absent herself immediately so that no one would ever discover her whereabouts and my misfortune would never become public. In effect, she left Baracoa before I could ascertain her plans and situation; but instead of going someplace far away to hide her defects, she settled in Tiguabos, where of late it is rumored that said doctor is a woman, just as I am. This rumor having reached my ears, and in consideration of the fact that the people who thought it to be true might be disposed to declaring it, I now find myself in the position of having to request nullification of my marriage and the punishment that such excesses merit, so that they might serve as a warning and so that, in the future, said individual might not sacrifice another unlucky woman such as myself, making a mockery of the most sacred institutions of our magnificent religion and of the social order; since, while out of modesty I have maintained my silence for four years, Divine Providence has demanded that the public become aware of these crimes so that they do not go unpunished, and so that my spurious spouse may not find new victims to humiliate."

Hearing the judge read that string of falsehoods, I thought it would be easy to refute them. As for the matter of my true sex, it was a case of her word against mine, and I enjoyed public esteem and held a position as an official of the Protomedicato. I should add that, while I had already been arrested and taken to jail, I was still dressed as a man. What follows is a transcription of the interrogations to which I was subjected, reproduced exactly as they appeared in publication:

JUDGE: State your name, nationality, age, marital status and profession.

ENRIQUETA: My name is Enrique Faber, native of Lausanne, Switzerland. I am thirty-two years of age; married in the city of Baracoa to Juana de León. I am a doctor by profession and hold the corresponding degree.

JUDGE: How long ago did you marry in Baracoa?

ENRIQUETA: Almost four years ago.

JUDGE: How long has it been since you absented yourself from Baracoa, what was the reason for this absence, and where have you resided subsequently?

ENRIQUETA: I left Baracoa three-and-a-half years ago. I stayed in Santiago de Cuba for a few days, awaiting the boat that makes the crossing to and from Havana. I wanted to speak personally with the regents of the Protomedicato. I wanted them to transfer me to a different place as officer of that institution. After being in Havana for three months, I was told that the only available village was San Anselmo de los Tiguabos, and I set off for my new destination. I arrived at the beginning of May, 1820, which I remember because of the celebrations commemorating the restoration of the constitutional regime. I practiced medicine in Tiguabos until I was arrested and sent to the jail in this city.

JUDGE: I should inform you that, before your arrest, this court heard the testimony of witnesses about the accusations that appear in Juana de León's statement, the content of which we have just heard. This said, I ask you: are you acquainted with a mulatto named Hipólito Wilson, and do you know if he has a house in the village of Tiguabos?

ENRIQUETA: Yes, sir, I know him from Baracoa, where he was a patient of mine. Lacking resources with which to pay me, he offered to teach me a bit of the English language. After a few months, he went to live in Tiguabos.

JUDGE: Do you know an individual named José Ramos?

ENRIQUETA: No.

JUDGE: Explain then a conversation that took place in the month of November, 1822, in the house of the aforementioned Ramos. He swears that you participated in said conversation in which Ramos wagered an ounce of gold that a certain thing he claimed insistently was indeed true.

ENRIQUETA: I had not remembered who Ramos was, but now, with respect to the incident to which Your Honor refers, I understand who he must be. What happened was that Hipólito Wilson told me that there was a young man who was betting all manner of things that I did not pertain to the masculine sex, and I told him that I would go to see him with my own money to wager the opposite. Indeed, accompanied by Hipólito Wilson, I went to his house, but Ramos did not want to affirm his statement, and this denial occurred in Wilson's presence.

JUDGE: And did you, as the offended party, make any sort of complaint to the Lord Mayor of the town?

ENRIQUETA: No, sir, I did not lodge a complaint, although I did make amicable mention of the incident to him.

JUDGE: Do you know a Biscayan gentleman named Don Juan Antonio Gausardía?

ENRIQUETA: Yes.

JUDGE: What has been the nature of your relationship with the aforementioned individual?

ENRIQUETA: As this individual is the owner of a tavern, I used to go there to eat, paying him the corresponding price. This is the only interaction I had with him.

JUDGE: Were you ever in his company in the town of Caney?

ENRIQUETA: One day during festival, when I went to visit that town, I came across Mister Gausardía and several other people in the road on the way there. We went to Caney as a group and ate together in a tavern.

JUDGE: Was Ramos among the persons in attendance that day in the aforementioned tavern in Caney?

ENRIQUETA: He was there out of pure coincidence.

JUDGE: What happened after the meal?

ENRIQUETA: We set out on the return journey to Tiguabos. Ramos, having joined with the group, repeated that he'd wager a gold coin that I was a woman.

JUDGE: Did you hear Ramos say these words?

ENRIQUETA: No. I was ahead of him, with Gausardía. Ramos was behind me with some other people, but I learned of his wager afterwards.

JUDGE: This proceeding is adjourned, to be continued should it be deemed necessary. I must inform you that you are to be formally held prisoner while your conduct is examined and that, in accordance with article 300 of the Constitution, you are informed that the reason for your incarceration is the lawsuit brought against you by your wife, Doña Juana de León, who accuses you of having seduced and deceived her, leading her through the marriage sacrament despite your being a woman just as she is, and being unable to fulfill the duties of the conjugal state, circumstances that are to be proven before me by means of a physical exam carried out by two physicians, the results of which are to be verified by this court's scribe.

ENRIQUETA: It will be a simple matter for me to defend myself and to prove my innocence. I would request that Your Honor attend to the matter of designating the physicians who are to examine my body as soon as possible so that this lamentable episode in which I find myself involved might be concluded once and for all.

I thought that this moment of audacity would convince the judge that I wasn't a woman. But I was wrong. The following morning, the court scribe and two doctors entered my cell. My pleas and bribes were all in vain. Even when I ended up confessing myself a woman, they forced me to undress. My humiliation was absolute. They took everything of value I possessed, including my watch and the gold chain that held Aunt Margot's portrait; they stripped me of my clothing and boots; they left me a tattered dress, a shawl that smelled of rancid sweat, and a crude pair of shoes.

❧

For over ten years my secret had never been made public. Neither Fauriel nor Maryse, Uncle Charles nor Madame Cavent, Christopher nor Robledo, Pierre nor Françoise had revealed it. But one can only take the bucket to the well so many times before it breaks. Not only had Juanita betrayed and made a fool of me; because of her I was now in jail, and all of the effort and sacrifices I'd made to hide my identity had been demolished in a single blow. Tomorrow or the day after, or whenever it was that the judge saw fit, I'd be summoned so that I might, under oath, confess to, or defend myself against the charges levied against me. Furious at first, little by little I fell into a lethargic dejection that made me forget about hunger and thirst. Lying on the filthy cot in my cell, I spent hours staring at the ceiling and, when night fell and the ceiling disappeared into the darkness, I stared into the nothingness, unable to think of anything beyond my misfortune. When daylight came in through the small window that looked out over the prison yard, I noticed a small, rolled-up piece of paper tied to the iron bars. I looked at it for a long time without much curiosity. When I realized that I was still staring it, I stood up, pushed the cot over to the window, climbed up on it and removed the paper. I read it then and there: it was a message from Wilson warning me that, as a means of public ridicule, I was to be paraded on a donkey down the city's main street, barefoot and wearing a penitent's nightdress; I thought of the story of Lady Godiva and smiled. I would not give my accusers or judges, much less the gawking public, that pleasure. On the floor was an earthenware jug filled with water. I smashed it against the wall and looked for the sharpest piece. It wouldn't be as effective as a knife, but with a little persistence, I could find a vein. I'd let blood from my arm, just like the thousands of lettings I'd done in my life, except this time, I wouldn't stop the bleeding. Determined, I picked up the shard, turned it sharp edge down, and brought it near my skin, but when I was about to make the incision, my hand began to tremble. I tried to cut myself four or five times, to no avail; my fingers had lost all their strength and I could scarcely use them. Suddenly, the door to my cell opened: "Let's go, *marimacho*, you're to return to the court so you can make your confession," said one of the jailors.

Taken before the same judge, a fellow named Rodríguez, who tried to hide his near baldness with a ridiculous hairdo, I swore to tell the truth, and nothing but the truth. After answering a few questions aimed at verifying further details of my life, the interrogation took a different turn.

> JUDGE: Do you remember the statement you issued in this same room on the seventh day of this month and, if not, do you wish for it to be read aloud?
>
> ENRIQUETA: It's of no use.
>
> JUDGE: You have declared that, on the way back to Tiguabos, Ramos wagered money that you were a woman, a bet you became aware of later.
>
> ENRIQUETA: Correct. While we were watering the horses in the river that runs alongside the road, an individual, whose name I do not know, approached me and touched my chest.
>
> JUDGE: Continue.
>
> ENRIQUETA: This individual said, in insultingly vulgar terms, that he couldn't be sure if I were a man or woman and, that being the case, he would not pay Ramos the ounce of gold he had wagered. Then Ramos suggested that they undress me, to which Mister Gausardía and others were opposed.
>
> JUDGE: Is it true that you paid Hipólito Wilson to kill Ramos?
>
> ENRIQUETA: It is not true. I merely told him that he should try to convince Ramos that I wasn't a woman.
>
> JUDGE: When the subject in question was arrested

for inebriation and disturbance of the peace in Mister Gausardía's tavern, he stated that you gave him one hundred and fifty pesos.

ENRIQUETA: It was less, I don't remember how much. He is very poor, and he's an acquaintance of mine.

JUDGE: Relate the conversation you had with Tomás Olivares, the mayor of Tiguabos, about your sex.

ENRIQUETA: Ramos would not stop saying that I was a woman and, knowing that there were others who would take him at his word, I went to see Don Tomás one evening. I managed to persuade him that I was a man.

JUDGE: You deceived him. Admit it. You deceived a civil authority.

ENRIQUETA: I was afraid of being discovered.

JUDGE: You also deceived the parish priest in Baracoa, who married you to Juana de León thinking you were a man.

ENRIQUETA: It's true that I committed a sacrilege and that I'm guilty in the eyes of the church, but I do not believe that I am guilty in the eyes of the law. In France, a woman is not jailed because she has dressed as a man. I have always lived in accordance with the law and have attempted to do good for others.

JUDGE: Explain what methods you employed to deceive Doña Juana de León and to obtain her consent for marriage.

ENRIQUETA: Juana de León married me knowing that I was a woman. I never deceived her.

JUDGE: The defendant will understand that it is her word against the plaintiff's.

ENRIQUETA: I'm telling the truth. I'm not accustomed to lying.

JUDGE: You have lied, not once, but many times. In addition to lying in your own country, as you yourself have confessed, you came to this loyal Island of Cuba under a false passport, deceived the eminent magistrates of the Protomedicato by pretending to be a man, and signed the marriage act with Doña Juana de León as Enrique Faber, making a mockery of one of the most sacred sacraments of the Holy Mother Church. I advise you to retract your words. You have sworn to tell the truth and perjury is a crime.

ENRIQUETA: I swear under oath that Juana de León knew that I was a woman before the wedding took place.

JUDGE: Are you insinuating that the plaintiff is a pervert?

ENRIQUETA: No. I'm only insinuating that she's a liar.

JUDGE: Supposing this were the case, which no one would believe since you've given ample proof of your lack of candor and honesty, what motives would she have had to marry sacrilegiously?

ENRIQUETA: When I met Juana de León she was living in the most dire poverty and was suffering from tuberculosis. Marriage to me offered her a better life— good food to eat, rest, and, above all, money to spend.

JUDGE: State your motives for seducing her and convincing her to marry you.

ENRIQUETA: I needed someone to keep me company and to love me. Although, I repeat, there was never any seduction or deception on my part.

JUDGE: What do you have to say about the immoral propositions that you made to the plaintiff?

ENRIQUETA: I do not know to what Your Honor refers.

JUDGE: That you suggested to her that she commit adultery.

ENRIQUETA: I did not suggest it to her. I told her that she could continue her relationship with the lover she already had, Mister Faustino Chicoy, or with any other. Allow me to describe what happened: one afternoon I surprised my wife with this individual. This caused a quarrel between us, after which I decided to move away from Baracoa. She responded to my decision by threatening that, were I to do so, she was prepared to make my true sex public. As this would have prevented me from continuing to practice as a doctor, I proposed that we remain formally married, but that she would be free to have as many lovers as she might want and that I would give her the seven thousand reales I kept in my chest of drawers.

JUDGE: Do you have any written document that would prove the existence of such a scandalous contract?

ENRIQUETA: No, it was a verbal agreement. Nevertheless,

I can prove its existence. Juana de León has waited almost four years to file her complaint. Why did she delay for so long? Because, during that time, she demanded five thousand reales on three separate occasions, and she would have gone on doing so, had the suspicion that I was a woman not arisen in Tiguabos. Were I to be discovered, she'd be exposed as having consented. So, she decided to nip the situation in the bud; that is, to denounce me before her silence could compromise her.

JUDGE: If what you say is true, surely you'll have the receipts, signed by Doña Juana, that correspond to these supposed payments; or, in the event of their absence, letters from the aforementioned person asking you for these sums.

ENRIQUETA: There were no such receipts or letters. On every occasion, I gave the money to her relative and lover, Faustino Chicoy, who came to Tiguabos to get it.

JUDGE: And you handed over these large sums of money to a third party without assuring that they would end up in Doña Juana's hands?

ENRIQUETA: Chicoy showed me letters that Juana de León had written to me, in which she always threatened to turn me in.

JUDGE: Do you have any of these letters?

ENRIQUETA: No. Chicoy kept them, just as was stipulated in the letters.

JUDGE: Do you consider yourself a victim of Juana de León?

ENRIQUETA: I've never thought of it like that. Although at the beginning of our relationship I proceeded in good faith, and she did not, in the end, we used one another mutually for our own purposes.

JUDGE: State Doña Juana de León's age when she married you.

ENRIQUETA: Fifteen.

JUDGE: Does it not seem strange to you that a fifteen-year-old, almost a girl, could have deceived you, a person more than twice her age and who has been a married woman, a widow, a medical student in Paris, a veteran of two wars and an impostor?

ENRIQUETA: I ask myself the same question.

JUDGE: I am tiring of your impudence, for which I must rebuke you. In any event, we will move on to the defense. Do you wish to defend yourself or would you prefer a public attorney to do so?

ENRIQUETA: I do not need anyone. In my defense, I say only that Juana de León's accusations are false and that I have never harmed anyone.

JUDGE: These proceeding are adjourned, under condition that they be reconvened at any time deemed suitable.

My sentence came down a week later. It was a different judge who read it, a man with enormous side whiskers and a loud voice. I copy the court's verdict as recorded in the brittle pages of *Enriqueta Faber*: "In the city of Santiago de Cuba, on this 19th day of June, 1823, Señor Don Eduardo María Ferrer, retired Lieutenant Colonel, constitutional Mayor, and Substitute Judge under this Jurisdiction, declared: that in view of the criminal proceeding brought against Doña Enriqueta Faber, native of Lausanne, Switzerland, initiated at the request of Doña Juana de León, native to and resident of the city of Baracoa, for the horrible crimes of having gone about disguised in men's clothing from the time of her arrival on this Island, being truly and completely a woman; of having contracted marriage, as described by León in a written statement visible on page 6, accompanied by the certificate issued by the priest Don Felipe Salamé certifying the marriage ceremony; in view of declarations 14 through 16 of the indictment, acknowledging the medical exam performed by physicians licensed in medicine and surgery, Doctors Don Bartolomé Segura and Don José Fernández, and by Attorney José de la Caridad Ibarra, in which it is sworn that Doña Enriqueta is a woman, being that under no circumstances could she be mistaken for the other sex; the statements of confession, in which she describes her detestable crimes, and recounts the story of her life from the age of sixteen, when she became the widow of a Hussar officer with the French army, named Don Juan Bautista Roberto Renaud, until she began to use the disguise; the accusation formulated by the Public Prosecutor, on page 52; the statement of evidence on the verso of page 55; the ratifications of the witnesses at the summary proceeding; the allegations put forth by the Minister of Justice in favor of the people's case; with all else having been taken into account, the Minister has proven the established accusation, despite Doña Enriqueta's having refuted it in her own defense. And in consequence, in consideration of the derisive and vile mockery that she has dared to inflict on Divinity in contracting matrimony with a person of her same sex, which horrifying and godless act sins against our august religion and the reverence due such a holy sacrament, without the least fear of incurring the gravest of sanctions, of both canonical and civil order, which condemn and punish such sinister dealings; in consequence as well of the insult and scandal that she has brought on the Republic, no less by means of said delinquencies than through her male disguise, condemned by all the laws of the universe, through the falsification of which she was able to obtain a license from the Protomedicato and the title of Officer in the city of Baracoa, with insult to and mockery of its respectable Tribunal, of his Excellence Señor Captain General of the Island, and of all other authorities and corporations constituted within it; the aforementioned Doña Enriqueta Faber is sentenced to imprisonment in the house of corrections established in the city of Havana, for ten years, under the special vigilance of the competent authorities, with the stipulation that, her sentence completed, she shall remain incarcerated until such a time as she may be remitted to any foreign land, with the absolute prohibition to return, under any pretext whatsoever, to any Spanish dominions, and is hereby warned that, should she be discovered in said dominions, her sentence shall be doubled along with any further penalties for which there be cause. This sentence shall be made public by means of the Government press, so that its publication shall produce the consequent effects on the businesses and people native to this Island. She is further ordered to pay all costs associated with these proceeding, reserving to Juana de León all rights against Doña Faber and her assets, so that she may deduct from them where and when she deems convenient."

JUDGE: Does the condemned have anything to say?
ENRIQUETA: I request that Your Honor send the pubic defender to my cell. I need him to instruct me with regard to requesting an appeal.

☙

Recovered from the paralyzing depression into which I'd fallen since being manhandled by the doctors, I was able to reflect upon my situation. What had I lost? What did I still have? What did I stand to gain? My economic situation was desperate. La Muraille's children had secured the estate at Foix as well as the surrounding properties that Curchet had acquired; after I'd paid off my legal expenses, Juanita would strip me of the rest of my savings and sell my furniture, including my *Woman;* confined to prison for ten years, I wouldn't even be able to fulfill the mortgage requirements on the house in Paris. My only possession was my forest, which, while of incomparable value to me, in terms of my pocketbook, meant very little. I had also lost the possibility of earning a living in Cuba and any Spanish-held land, although, all things considered, this didn't much matter: with Maryse dead, there was nothing tying me to that island, stricken by sugar and slavery. Eventually, I'd be expelled, but that would be more reward than punishment. Where I'd be sent couldn't have mattered less to me. From wherever it was I'd arrange to return to France, and at least there I'd have the little stone cottage to live in. And, suddenly, I remembered my jewels. Of course, Aunt Margot's jewels, thousands and thousands of francs. I would not die of hunger. And that was if I decided to live as a woman, otherwise—certainly the most likely scenario—I'd go back to being Henri Faber, a military surgeon retired for disability, and I'd open a practice in Paris or in Burgundy or Marseilles or any other city that wasn't in the Languedoc. Because, for my lawyers, Lebrun and Ducharme, for my old tenant D'Alencourt and the people of Foix and Toulouse who knew me, I would go on being Madame Henriette Renaud, née Faber-Cavent, a tireless traveler with libidinous tendencies—with no other proof than my word, no one had believed that Dunsi was the product of a legitimate marriage—whom they'd catch a glimpse of now and again, when nostalgia called her back to the forest on the banks of the Ariège. On top of all that I had my health and a knowledge of the world, not to mention that I still had my third marriage ahead of me. Of course, I shouldn't get my hopes up about my appeal. If it were accepted by the magistrates of the Provincial Court of Puerto Príncipe, it might be only in order to ratify my sentence. And so I passed the time in my cell, waiting for the ship that would take me to Havana as prisoner, trying to see my lamentable situation with some optimism, and telling myself that this entire Cuban adventure would only contribute to my life experience.

After ten days at sea with good weather, I saw once again the Castillo del Morro, the church towers, and the cheerful colors of the houses of Havana. My anxiety grew in tandem with our approach to the bay. I asked myself if there would be people waiting to hurl trash and insults at me, as had happened when I'd left Santiago. My question was answered immediately: more than a hundred wretched souls crowded on the dock. The details of my trial having been published by the official press, I was now the scapegoat who allowed every beggar and slave, cripple and cuckold, anyone who'd ever felt aggrieved, to enjoy a few moments of triumph at my expense. By the time I arrived at the women's prison, my clothes were stained with rotten eggs and tomatoes, and a well-aimed cabbage had left a lump on my right cheek. Not even in prison did I cease to suffer insults, but I stand to gain nothing by recounting them. I prefer to speak of Romay's lovely gesture: despite becoming the target for small-minded gossip, he came to visit me on two occasions. He treated me the same as always, and I remain grateful for his kindness in visiting me and for the fruit and candies that he brought me. And suddenly, to both my captors' and my surprise, a dispatch form the Provincial Court arrived, ordering my transfer "with all possible haste," to the city of Puerto Príncipe. The date set for my appeals trial was September 30th.

⚭

Since I felt, at the time, like an utter outlander, something like a *cassoulet* in a Cuban kitchen, I was pleased to learn that my defense attorney was not a native son of Puerto Príncipe, but rather a foreigner as well—Peruvian, in his case. I was even happier to learn that he was a well-known scholar, the author of several works of jurisprudence, whose interest in my case had led him to renounce his post as judge in the Royal Court of Puerto Príncipe in order to be able to defend me before his colleagues. His name was Manuel de Vidaurre.

Among the anonymous pages of *Enriqueta Faber*, I found the following description of Vidaurre: "He was pleasing in appearance. Thin, tall, and crowned in prematurely gray hair, he had very delicate and white skin, ennobled by the sweetest and most benevolent of gazes. His aquiline nose lent an air of distinction to his entire face, and his blue eyes were attractively pleasant." Not one bit of this is true. He was short and chubby, of fiery temperament and penetrating eyes. He did not attempt to hide his baldness. In any event, he came to visit me in jail as soon as he'd received word of my arrival and, while I answered his questions, he diligently filled several pages of his notebook.

Of the appeals trial, I'll limit myself to reproducing only Vidaurre's closing arguments. I do so because, in their time, they were as singular as the famous voice crying out in the desert; to make them known today is my small tribute to his ideas.

"Crime is produced by pleasure, and so it is understood that punishment must be based on pain. Nevertheless, to lead men and women to the gallows, to burn them at the stake, to multiply and refine means of torture, are remedies as facile as they are ineffective in preventing crime. To guide the spirit, to govern the heart, to channel passions toward good, to take advantage of sensitivity, to limit the other's desire for freedom, is the legislator's very own task. A crime is a deed that takes pleasure in the evil that causes it. Legislative bodies should see to it that the citizen enjoys this same deed, or another equal or similar, without causing harm. If this is not possible, they should impede the power to cause it. They should endeavor to distract the desire for that deed, which is based on evil. To this end, the first resort shall be the illustration of an understanding of philosophy and the direction of will by means of a moral code without prejudices. Enriqueta Faber is not a criminal. Society, from the moment it denied women civil and political rights, turning them into furniture, dolls for men's pleasure, is guiltier than she is. My client was correct to dress as a man, not only because the law does not forbid it, but also because, appearing as a man, she was able to study, work, and have the freedom of movement to carry out good deeds. What criminal is this, who follows her husband through the cannon fire of the great battles, who heals the wounded, who treats the poor and helpless free of charge, and who married only in order to bring serenity to an unfortunate, ill orphan? We men monopolize everything for ourselves. Who sells ribbons and pins in the shops? Men do. Who sews vests, pants, and shirts? Men do. Who cooks? The great chefs are men, as are the majority of mediocre ones. The day will come, if we continue in this way, when our sons, instead of taking up the plow to work the earth or the ax to fell the forests, will devote themselves to washing and ironing clothes and even cutting and adorning women's dresses. Here is the problem: after her husband's death, Enriqueta Faber felt the call of a vocation, that of becoming a doctor so as to confront death and to help her fellow human beings. Could the young widow, dressed as a woman, study medicine? No. Could any woman, dressed as a woman, study to be a lawyer or an engineer? No. Could she be a soldier? No. Would it be permissible for her to aspire to the priesthood? Of course not. Honorable gentlemen, because our laws, customs, and masculine egos have willed it to be so, women today are no different than minors. The social contract does not exist for them. As long as women do not take part in politics and in the making of laws, and do so in equal numbers to men, we will live in an unjust world. Let them marry, you'll say. But why marry if marriage does not protect them either, but rather reduces them to machines for producing children within the four walls of their homes? We must allow the more attractive half of the human species to aspire, at the very least, to the rights afforded to laborers. Open workshops and factories to women. Allow them to work so that they do not die like flowers in a vase, so that they might not be mired in the caverns of vice. It is that vicious judge from Santiago de Cuba who should be here on the stand instead of Enriqueta, he who insisted on witnessing my client's naked body by means of those doctors' cruel examination; a pointless and abusive examination, from the moment the defendant decided to confess her sex. Neither, honorable judges, may it be sustained, outside of pure prejudice, that Enriqueta has committed a sacrilege. It was never her intention to offend Divinity, because, to the contrary, through her marriage she was seeking tranquility of spirit and the sanctity of the hearth, requesting the blessings of the Catholic priests. The day will come when marriage will be for everyone. As for the public order, Enriqueta has not disturbed it, nor has she attempted to rebel against the political and civic institutions of the State; she has neither killed, nor wounded, nor stolen from anybody. We are the criminals, those of us who oppress women; the reprobates are the Governments that do not tolerate women sitting alongside you in order to pass judgment on men. My client does not need the world's sympathy, because, upon heroically accepting the arbitrary verdict of your justice, or ours, if you prefer, she has acceded to the status of martyr, a status worthy of the greatest respect and admiration. She has already given all the money and assets she had to Doña Juana de León, her so-called spouse. She has turned a nearly incurable tubercular girl into a robust and evidently healthy woman. She has turned a beggar into a well-off lady who will soon marry again. Your name, Enriqueta Faber, will be recorded in the history of Cuba and in the annals of medicine; you shall be recognized as the first woman surgeon to graduate from a University, as the first female military surgeon to serve on the battlefield, the first woman to practice her profession as a physician in Europe and America. Your glory and valor are assured for posterity. As for everyone else, if they condemn you now, all the worse for them; their names will be the target of mockery, for their incompetence as much as their cowardice. As for me, after having given it a great deal of thought, and having examined your conscience through the crucible of my own honorable conscience, I absolve you, Enriqueta, completely and without reservation."

Four days later, I was taken to the courtroom to hear the verdict: "In light of that presented by the Honorable Judge, Enriqueta Faber is hereby remanded to service at the Hospital de Paula, in the city of Havana, for four years, at the completion of which, she shall leave the Island under condition of perpetual banishment from all Spanish territories. She shall be stripped of her physician's title and residence card, both of which she obtained under the name Enrique Faber, and she shall be responsible for the procedural fees associated with each. His most Excellent Superior Political Commander-in-Chief, the Protomedicato, and the most senior Lord Judge shall be duly notified. Signed: Reboredo, Álvarez, Portilla, Gómez, Frías, Bernal, and Agramonte y Recio."

27

THE HOSPITAL DE PAULA, IN which I'd been sentenced to serve, was not unknown to me. It was (and surely still is) located on the far southern end of the Paseo de la Alameda, on a small promontory that protruded from the bay, protected by a parapet and sentry post. Many times Maryse and I, leaving the *quitrín* next to the staircase that led to the Paseo, had walked up to its doors and back, chatting about this and that, allowing our words and the breeze to guide us back toward the fanciful façade of the Teatro Principal. I also knew something about the medical services performed there, as well as the hospital's administration. It had always been under the directorship of the Bishop's diocese, which required that the hospital's directors and chaplains be clerics native to Havana. Romay had taken me on a tour of its wards, which were passably clean, though a bit crowded—in my day, the number of patients vacillated between one hundred and thirty and one hundred and forty. As in the Salpetrière, the patients were convicts from the House of Corrections, generally thieves and prostitutes, destitute old women and beggars, almost all of whom were afflicted with tuberculosis, tumorous masses, and venereal diseases. Almost all of them were black. Slave women were also treated there, provided their masters paid the corresponding fees. A chapel dedicated to Saint Francis of Paola had been erected alongside the building in which mass was held on Sundays and holy feast days.

The air was good there, and it was possible to entertain oneself watching the ships enter the harbor, drop and weigh anchor. But proximity to the thick and foul-smelling waters of the wharf was a cause of fevers, most particularly yellow fever. Perhaps because I'd breathed the air of so many nations both temperate and frigid, as well as the emanations from swamps and decomposing bodies, this scourge was, for me, an enemy held at bay.

My first disillusion with the place arose the very day of my arrival. In the midst of a dry and long-winded lecture on my duties and extremely limited rights, the administrator insisted that I was to be prohibited from practicing medicine. It did no good for me to show him the paper on which my sentence was recorded, which did not specify what my services to the hospital were to be. His response was: "For all intents and purposes you are no longer a doctor. Both your license and your post as officer of the Protomedicato have been revoked."

"Very well," I sighed. "Tell me, then, what are to be my tasks?"

"Cleaning the building. You will sweep, wash, and mop the floors. Except on Sundays, which goes without saying."

"The entire building?" I said in disbelief.

"You will share the work with two other women. Finally, you should know that, although this isn't a prison, you are forbidden to go out into the street. Do not forget this. Any attempt on your part to go beyond the front gates will be considered an attempt at escape. The consequence of this is an increase to your sentence, from one to three years, depending upon the circumstances. Is that understood?"

"Yes, sir."

"It's time for lunch. You may go to the dining hall. Turn right as you leave my office."

When I arrived at the dining hall, I took a seat at the far end of a bench; the two long tables were packed with inmates, servants, and young men in vests who I assumed were medical students. Seeing that no one paid me any mind, I stood and introduced myself. Hearing my name, everyone stopped eating and looked at me, or, better put, they examined me as though I were a griffin or had two heads, a reaction to which I'd already become accustomed. In order to break the spell, I asked who could give me instructions so that I could get started with the cleaning.

And so began my seclusion in the Hospital de Paula. The days passed slowly and monotonously, as though I were trapped in one of those interminable *Intendance* convoys. My hands soon became calloused from so much sweeping and mopping. Of course, I wasn't capable of ignoring the fact that I was a doctor, and while I cleaned the wards I took an interest in the patients. With time, it became the doctors' habit to consult with me about the administration of a drug or a surgical procedure. This made Romay laugh, when he visited me from time to time. "Just look at you, Enriqueta," he would say. "Your lawyer Vidaurre was right. Once a doctor, always a doctor, and it makes no difference whatsoever if one is dressed as a man or a woman."

In my meager luggage I'd brought a few books, all of them gifts from Vidaurre before he left Puerto Príncipe. I was allowed to keep them because they were the works of saints and pious sorts: Sor Juana Inés de la Cruz, Saint John of the Cross, Saint Teresa of Ávila, Friar Louis of Granada. When I read the work by the Mexican nun, whom I hadn't before known existed, I realized that my impassioned defender's ideas owed a great deal to hers. Another pastime of mine was watching the ships through my window, the figureheads on their prows bursting into my line of sight like some sort of unexpected illusionist. (What has become of you, Piet Vaalser, with your doves and boxes and handkerchiefs, and your magician's cape embroidered with half-moons and comets?) Quite often the ships dropped anchor right in the center of my view, on the other side of the bay, just at the foot of the battery of La Cabaña. There they would remain for a few days, surrounded by small launches unloading pieces of machinery, heavy crates, and passengers, only to disappear again beyond my window frame. Before setting sail, they would always take on new passengers, and it was these travelers I observed most closely, the colors of their dresses, their parasols, their white handkerchiefs waving goodbye to relatives and friends invisible to me, bidding them farewell for what might be months, or perhaps forever. I would follow them with my gaze until they entered the hull of the ship; I would count them one by one as they climbed the narrow staircase, watch as its frame was hoisted from the upper works while the sails were unfurled and the anchors weighed, and then the ocean, that vast and perilous waterway that led to Bristol, to Brest, to Boston, to Cádiz, or to Lisbon, and me, anchored in that godforsaken hospital, and thus passed the weeks and months and years.

I was always delighted to catch sight of the *Neptune*, the steamship that made the tiny crossing between Havana and Matanzas, and also the one that came in from New Orleans, both owned by the company in which the unfortunate Robledo had invested, not knowing that he was carving out his cousin's fortune rather than his own. The nights also provided entertainment: if there was an opera or a concert at the Teatro Principal, I could hear the music, and even the voices of the sopranos and tenors traveling with some humble Italian company that had sworn to great success at La Scala. My elbows on the windowsill, tracking the lights of the fishing boats and schooners heading out of the harbor, I would enjoy the muted sound of the violins, above which floated, like silver birds, the flute and clarinet. In truth, at least from my window here in New York, it wasn't so bad there. The war had been so much worse. But after three years of confinement, my nerves began to give way. I would awake in a foul mood, call the doctors useless and the students idiots, complain about the food, or forget to clean one of the privies.

One Sunday as I was ruminating over my bitterness, I saw a beautiful ship-of-the-line flying a French flag maneuver into the bay. It wasn't just another boat to me: its name, the polished bronze letters of which I was able to make out, was the *Languedoc*. I spent most of the morning observing the goings-on on board. When one of the dinghies was lowered, I made out the captain's plumed bicorn amid the oarsmen; when I saw him disappear to my left, I assumed he was headed to the marina's Command Headquarters in order to deliver some important military dispatch. After lunch I spent the afternoon watching the ship, every so often exchanging waves with the sailors gazing at the city from up in the rigging. The captain returned to his boat at dusk. Given my familiarity with the customs of the port, I knew that this meant the ship would set sail at dawn; when a ship was to remain at anchor for several days, its captain invariably preferred to stay in a hotel or as a guest of the frivolous local nobility which, made rich from sugar, had obtained Marquisates and Earldoms in exchange for sacks of money. This realization was all it took for an unstoppable urge to grip me. No matter how many times I told myself that I only had one year of my sentence left, that it wasn't worth the risk, my willpower had crumbled irreparably. I felt that I must escape at all costs. Night fell. Barefoot and lightly dressed, I waited for the sentry, a man named Moscote who generally worked the night watch, to fall asleep. He was an insufferable individual. On moonlit nights, when he could make out my shape in the window, he would blow kisses and make indecent hand gestures at me. In any case, I needed only to wait for the glow of his inevitable cigarette to go out to know that he'd be snoring within minutes. His sentry box gone dark, I slid from my window and moved along a cornice that ran between the building's two stories; I came to a place where a pine tree's branches touched the wall and from there it was easy to drop into the street. Diving into the water and swimming to the *Languedoc* was not a problem in and of itself, but I would need to wait for the lights from the fishing boats heading out of the bay to pass by. Sitting on the parapet, ready to jump, I waited and waited, twisted into a terrible knot of anxiety. But that night it seemed as though every fisherman in Havana had decided to try his luck. To kill time, I imagined myself swimming to the ship, making my final stroke before touching the anchor chain, taking hold of it to catch my breath, and then shouting: *Vive la France!* I'd be hoisted aboard and taken before a surprised duty officer, to whom I'd say: "I am Madame Faber-Cavent, a French traveler. I've been kidnapped by bandits and have managed to escape. I'd be grateful, from the bottom of my heart, if you'd take me on board." Since the ship would be leaving the port early in the morning, the captain wouldn't have time to make many inquiries. Possibly he'd served under Napoleon, perhaps in the blockade against England, in which case I'd speak to him of the time when, after accompanying my husband to the Russian campaign. . . . But my digressions were to be short-lived. A giant pair of hands grabbed me about the waist, lifted me in the air, and threw me like a sailor's rucksack over a strapping shoulder.

"From the hospital, eh?" bellowed Moscote. I tried to get free of his arm; begged him not to betray me. It was useless. "If I let you go, they'd punish me." And then he shouted all over again: "From the hospital, eh? The woman doctor has tried to escape!" Candlelight appeared in the windows. The outer gate opened.

I'd had fourteen months left to serve. They increased my sentence by three more years. It was as though I were arriving at the hospital for the very first time. To make matters worse, as part of my punishment, they shaved my head and forced me to wear a habit that had belonged to a nun who'd taken ill with yellow fever and been brought to the hospital to die.

෴

Nothing mattered to me anymore. I did my work in silence, impersonally. I could scarcely touch food and, more than merely sleeping, I'd throw myself on my cot to sink deliberately into a stupor as warm and merciful as that brought on by opium, my will to live evaporating drop by drop as the weeks wore on. I was certain that I would die before finishing my sentence, and I think it may have been true, had it not been for something on the order of a miracle, a word I always find difficult to employ. Seeing me so downtrodden, Romay had managed to secure Bishop Espada's intercession. I was to be expelled from Cuba immediately.

I was to board the schooner the *Collector* under the command of Capitan Plumet, which would set sail for New Orleans with the first breeze of dawn. I had been told nothing until the last minute. I had not a single coin to my name. By way of luggage, I carried a nightshirt, a pair of stockings, and a second nun's habit. I sat on the cot and waited for them to call me, the bundle of clothes on my knees. At five o'clock, the new administrator, an officious and hunchbacked priest, came for me. Instead of bidding me good morning, he said, almost in outrage: "Do not think that you are free. You are traveling under a convict's passport. You are to be remanded to the authorities in New Orleans." He would hand me over personally to the ship's captain. It was so early that the port was empty of onlookers. This time, at least, there would be no one to humiliate me.

We walked toward the dock in the light of a lantern carried by a slave. I thought of how I was leaving my *Woman in Battle Dress* behind. Where would it end up? But, above all, I was leaving Maryse behind, this time, forever, and with her, all of her affection, always without buts or conditions. I was broken and alone; no one to write to, no one to go visit. There, in the gloom, was the *Collector*, its outlines still blurred, nothing more than a gray mass beneath the cawing of invisible seagulls. It would take me to a new time whose calendar began with days of ash. While the priest handed my papers over to the captain, the first rays of sun began to dapple the ship's rigging, tingeing its flag red and blue. A barefoot sailor helped me up the planks of the gangway and, as I climbed, I determined not to look toward the city, whose towers and façades would be reemerging from the shadows. Like Lot, I was afraid that something would happen if I turned my head, forcing me to remain there forever.

To be sure, nothing good awaited me in New Orleans; perhaps jail again or, in the best of cases, seclusion in another hospital, or in a convent. And yet, as I set foot on deck, as I took my first step amid the colors of things, I knew that not all had been lost. I felt tired, very tired now, but on the boat, I'd have time to think.

∂

I've just recovered from the attack of melancholy brought on by my last page. I say "my last," because I know that I lack the strength to go on. True, I managed to compose some manner of ending, an incidental, provisional end, I might add, because I wasn't even able to speak of those strange nights of voodoo in New Orleans, or of my productive association with Marie Laveau, or of how I met my third husband, or of my clandestine return to Havana, or of my encounter with Christopher in London; lost to silence are the days in Ireland and Egypt, my friendship with Garibaldi, my last nights of love in the haunted house in Venice. How much I would give to be able to tell all of that! Two or three years would be enough, two or three years that I know I do not have. In the end, why go on? Even if it were possible for me to illuminate with my pen all that I have lived, I would be forced to conclude that my story would still end with a tentative, necessarily open-ended finale, and I'd still lament having written an unfinished book. And perhaps my life is nothing more than that; precisely that lack of something that I've always sensed, that leak in the roof or chink in the door that neither I nor anyone else has ever been able to fix; that incessant loss that every day leaves me suspended in the middle of things, small and hanging like a comma, but with the determination to carry ever onward. Who knows?

Author's Note

Henriette Faber was born in Lausanne, Switzerland in 1791, and married an officer in Napoleon Bonaparte's army. Shortly after she was widowed, she decided to dress as a man in order to study medicine at the University of Paris. She served as a military surgeon during the disastrous Russian campaign of 1812. Transferred to Spain, she fell prisoner to Wellington's troops at the battle of Vitoria, and served in that capacity as a physician in the Miranda de Ebro Hospital. After the peace accord of 1814, she decided to settle in the Caribbean, first in Guadeloupe and later in Cuba, where she practiced medicine in the town of Baracoa. There she married another woman, Juana de León, signing the marriage certificate with the name Enrique Faber. In 1823, her true sex was revealed, and she found herself embroiled in a sensational legal trial. After filing an appeal with the Court of Puerto Príncipe (today known as Camagüey), she was sentenced to serve four years in the women's hospital in Havana. Due to her attempts at escape, she was expelled to New Orleans and prohibited to ever again reside in Spain or any Spanish-held territory. It is not known for certain where she spent the remainder of her life.

Although, in *Woman in Battle Dress*, I have dramatized certain episodes of this singular woman's life, both my account as well as the majority of the characters and specific situations are fictitious.

The bibliography about Henriette (Enriqueta) Faber is scarce, given that her life story is practically unknown outside of Cuba. I consulted the following works:

Emilio Bacardí Moreau, *Crónicas de Santiago de Cuba*, 2nd edition, volume 2, Madrid, Breogán, 1972, pp. 218–219.

Francisco Calcagno, *Un casamiento misterioso*, 8th edition, Barcelona and Buenos Aires, Editorial Baucol, 1911.

—*Diccionario biográfico cubano*, New York, Imprenta N. Ponce de León, 1878, pp. 272–273.

María Julia de Laura, "Laura Martínez de Carvajal y del Camino (primera graduada de medicina en Cuba) en el septuagésimo quinto aniversario de su graduación (15 de julio de 1889)," *Cuad-*

ernos de Historia de la Salud Pública, number 28, Havana, Ministry of Public Health, 1964.

Leví Marrero, "La cirujana suiza que para ejercer como tal debió hacer creer que era hombre," *Cuba: economía y sociedad*, volume 11, Madrid, Editorial Playor, 1988.

Emilio Roig de Leuchsenring, *Médicos y medicina en Cuba: histories, biografía, costumbrismo*, Havana, Museo Histórico de la Ciencias Médicas Carlos J. Finlay, 1965.

Inciano D. Toirac Escasena, *Baracoa: vicissitudes y florecimiento*, 1988, pp. 91–111.

Andrés Clemente Vázquez, *Enriqueta Faber*, Havana, Imprenta La Universal, 1894.

Acknowledgments

As I was writing *Woman in Battle Dress* I received help from many people. Here I would like to name those who contributed most, both to the final editing of the manuscript as well as to the work's promotion. First, with much love and admiration, I thank my wife, Hilda Otaño Benítez, who suggested changes of crucial importance to both the structure of various passages, as well as to the characterization of the protagonists. Without her participation, my novel would have been less consistent. Doris Summer, Judith Thorn, and Cristina Court, as friends, women, and writers with a critical eye, read parts of the manuscript and made valuable suggestions that I nearly always accepted. César Alegre listened patiently as I argued with myself over the content of each chapter, offering his observations over the space of many months. I should also thank my colleague James Maraniss, who translated the manuscript into English with great originality and dedication[1]; to Ilán Stavans and Jesús Díaz, who solicited chapters for *Hopscotch* and *Encuentro*, the publications they direct, respectively; to Roberto González-Echevarría, Julio Ortega, Caryl Phillips, and Iván de la Nuez, for having helped gain visibility for the project; to Robert Rosbottom, Beatriz Peña, and the staff at the Robert Frost Library of Amherst College, for the bibliographic information with which they provided me; to Katharina von Schütz and Leandro Soto, who furnished materials and ideas for the graphic design; to Roberta Helinski, who copied and mailed off the manuscript. My most sincere gratitude goes out to all of them.

---

1 James Maraniss published two translated excerpts from the novel: "*Woman in Battle Dress: Henriette Faber on Board the Schooner Collector*" (*Hopscotch: A Cultural Review*: Vol. 2, No. 2, 2001); and "Excerpts from *Woman in Battle Dress*" (*Mandorla*: Issue 12, 2009, pp. 192–216). His translation of the complete novel has not been published.—JP

ANTONIO BENÍTEZ-ROJO (1931–2005) was a Cuban novelist, essayist, and short-story writer. He was widely regarded as the most significant Cuban author of his generation. His work has been translated into nine languages and collected in more than fifty anthologies. One of his most influential publications, *La Isla que se Repite*, was published in 1989 by Ediciones del Norte, and published in English as *The Repeating Island* by Duke University Press in 1997.

JESSICA POWELL has translated numerous Latin American authors, including works by César Vallejo, Jorge Luis Borges, Ernesto Cardenal, Maria Moreno, Ana Lidia Vega Serova, and Edmundo Paz Soldán. Her translation (with Suzanne Jill Levine) of Adolfo Bioy Casares and Silvina Ocampo's novel *Where There's Love, There's Hate*, was published by Melville House in 2013. She is the recipient of a 2011 National Endowment for the Arts Translation Fellowship in support of this translation of *Woman in Battle Dress*.